PENGUIN CLASSICS

AMERICAN NOTES

CHARLES DICKENS was born at Portsmouth on 7 February 1812, the second of eight children. Dickens's childhood experiences were similar to those depicted in *David Copperfield*. His father, who was a government clerk, was imprisoned for debt and Dickens was sent to work in a blacking factory at the age of twelve. He received little formal education, but he taught himself shorthand and became a reporter of parliamentary debates for the *Morning Chronicle*. He began to publish sketches in various periodicals, which were subsequently republished as *Sketches by Boz*. *The Pickwick Papers* was published in 1836–7 and after a slow start became a publishing phenomenon and Dickens's characters the centre of a popular cult. He began *Oliver Twist* in 1837, followed by *Nicholas Nickleby* (1838–9) and *The Old Curiosity Shop* (1840–41). After finishing *Barnaby Rudge* (1841) Dickens set off for America; he went full of enthusiasm for the young republic but, in spite of a triumphant reception, he returned disillusioned. His experiences are recorded in *American Notes* (1842). His first setback came when *Martin Chuzzlewit* (1843–4) did not repeat its predecessors' success but this was quickly redressed by the huge popularity of the *Christmas Books*, of which the first, *A Christmas Carol*, appeared in 1843. During 1844–6 Dickens travelled abroad and he began *Dombey and Son* while in Switzerland. This and his next novel, *David Copperfield*, were more serious in theme and more carefully planned than his early novels. In his later work his social criticism became more radical and his comedy more savage. In 1850 Dickens started the weekly periodical *Household Words*, succeeded in 1859 by *All the Year Round*; in these he published *Bleak House* (1852–3), *Hard Times* (1854), *Little Dorrit* (1855–7), *A Tale of Two Cities* (1859), *Great Expectations* (1860–61) and *Our Mutual Friend* (1864–5). Dickens's health was failing during the 1860s and the physical strain of the public readings which he began in 1858 speeded his decline and he collapsed during a farewell series in England. His last novel, *The Mystery of Edwin Drood*, was never completed and he died on 9 June 1870.

JOHN S. WHITLEY is Reader in American Studies and Chairman of American Studies at the University of Sussex. He was formerly Dean of the School of English and American Studies and taught for several years in the United States. He is the author of critical studies of William Golding and Scott

Fitzgerald and co-editor of an anthology of modern American short stories. He has written on Dashiell Hammett, Raymond Chandler, Mark Twain, detective fiction, and American fiction and drama. He is presently working on studies of William Dean Howells, and of aspects of the American cinema.

ARNOLD GOLDMAN is Honorary Professor of American Studies at the University of Kent at Canterbury, where he is Head of Curriculum Development Services. Formerly Deputy Chief Executive of the Council for National Academic Awards, he has taught English and American Studies at the Universities of Keele, Sussex and Manchester and in America. Author of two books on James Joyce, he has written about Yeats, Synge, Hawthorne, Melville, Poe, Faulkner, Fitzgerald and other modern authors.

CHARLES DICKENS

AMERICAN NOTES

FOR
GENERAL CIRCULATION

Edited and with an introduction
by John S. Whitley and
Arnold Goldman

PENGUIN BOOKS

PENGUIN BOOKS

Published by the Penguin Group
Penguin Books Ltd, 27 Wrights Lane, London W8 5TZ, England
Penguin Books USA Inc., 375 Hudson Street, New York, New York 10014, USA
Penguin Books Australia Ltd, Ringwood, Victoria, Australia
Penguin Books Canada Ltd, 10 Alcorn Avenue, Toronto, Ontario, Canada M4V 3B2
Penguin Books (NZ) Ltd, 182–190 Wairau Road, Auckland 10, New Zealand

Penguin Books Ltd, Registered Offices: Harmondsworth, Middlesex, England

First published 1842
Published in the Penguin English Library 1972
Reprinted in Penguin Classics 1985
7 9 10 8

Introduction and Notes copyright © John S. Whitley and Arnold Goldman 1972
Charles Dickens Note copyright © Angus Calder, 1985
All rights reserved

Printed in England by Clays Ltd, St Ives plc
Set in Monotype Fournier

CONTENTS

CHARLES DICKENS

A NOTE BY ANGUS CALDER

CHARLES DICKENS was born at Portsmouth on 7 February 1812. He was the second of the eight children of John Dickens, a clerk in the Naval Pay Office, whose mother had been in service to Lord Crewe. Although John Dickens was hard-working, he was rarely able to live within his income, and this brought a series of crises upon his family, which lived under the shadow of menacing social insecurity.

John Dickens's work took him from place to place, so that Charles spent his early childhood in Portsmouth, London, and Chatham. He was happiest at Chatham, where he attended a school run by a young Baptist minister, who recognized his abilities and paid him special attention. In 1823 the family moved to London, faced with financial disaster, and, to help out, a relative of Mrs Dickens offered Charles work in a blacking business which he managed. Two days before his twelfth birthday the boy began work at a factory at Hungerford Stairs, labelling bottles for six shillings a week.

Shortly before this John Dickens had been arrested for debt, and soon the whole family, except for Charles who was found lodgings, joined him in the Marshalsea Debtors' Prison. The double blow – his menial job and the family shame – gave Charles a shock which transformed him. In later years he told only his wife and his closest friend, John Forster, of these experiences, which haunted him till his death.

After three months in prison, John Dickens was released by process of having himself declared an Insolvent Debtor, but it was not until weeks later that he withdrew Charles from work and sent him to school, where he did well. At fifteen, Charles began work in the office of a firm of Gray's Inn attorneys. Sensing a vocation elsewhere, he taught himself shorthand, and eighteen months later began to work as a freelance reporter in the court of Doctors' Commons.

In 1829 or 1830 he fell passionately in love with Maria Beadnell, the daughter of a banker. Their affair staggered fruitlessly on until the summer of 1833. Meanwhile, he began to report parliamentary debates, and won himself a high reputation for speed and accuracy. His first *Sketches by Boz* appeared in magazines soon after he was twenty-one. In 1834 he joined the reporting staff of the *Morning Chronicle*. A well-received volume of his *Sketches* appeared on his twenty-fourth birthday.

His growing reputation secured him a commission from the publishers, Chapman and Hall, to provide the text to appear in monthly instalments beside sporting plates by a popular artist, Seymour. He 'thought of Mr Pickwick'. Two days after the first number appeared he married Catherine Hogarth, the daughter of a fellow-journalist, on the prospect. Although early sales were disappointing, *Pickwick Papers* (1836–7) soon became a publishing phenomenon, and Dickens's characters the centre of a popular cult. Part of the secret was the method of cheap serial publication, which Dickens used for all his subsequent novels (some, in fact, being serialized in weekly magazines edited by himself), and which was copied by other writers.

While *Pickwick* was still running, Dickens began *Oliver Twist* (1837). *Nicholas Nickleby* (1838–9) provided him with a third success, and sales of *The Old Curiosity Shop* (1840–41) reached 100,000. After finishing *Barnaby Rudge* (1841), Dickens set off with his wife for the United States. He went full of enthusiasm for the young republic, but returned heartily disillusioned, in spite of a triumphant reception. His experiences are recorded in *American Notes* (1842).

His first setback came when *Martin Chuzzlewit* (1843–4) did not repeat the extraordinary success of its predecessors, though he promptly inaugurated his triumphant series of *Christmas Books* with *A Christmas Carol* (1843). He now travelled abroad, first to Italy (1844–5) and then to Switzerland and Paris (1846). During a brief interlude in England he projected, not another novel, but a paper, the *Daily News*. This first appeared in January 1846, but Dickens resigned after only seventeen days as editor.

His next novel, *Dombey and Son* (1846–8), was more wholly serious and more carefully planned than his early work. In *David Copperfield* (1849–50), he explored his own childhood and youth, thinly disguised. In the 1850s he increased his already intense interest in public affairs. He founded *Household Words*, a weekly magazine which combined entertainment with social purpose; it was succeeded in 1859 by *All the Year Round*, which sold as many as 300,000 copies. *Bleak House* (1852–3) and *Hard Times* (1854) have strong social themes, and *Little Dorrit* (1855–7) continues Dickens's bitter public denunciation of the whole framework of government and administration which had mismanaged the Crimean War.

In 1858 he separated from his wife. Although Kate, a shadowy, slow person, had given him ten children, she had never suited his exuberant temperament very well. He befriended a young actress, Ellen Ternan, who may have become his mistress. He was now living mainly in Kent, at Gad's Hill, near his boyhood home of Chatham. *A Tale of Two Cities* (1859), *Great Expectations* (1860–61), and *Our Mutual Friend* (1864–5) completed his life's main work of fourteen major novels. By the mid 1860s his health was failing, partly under the strain of his successful but exhausting public readings from his own work, which had begun in 1858. An immensely profitable but physically shattering series of readings in America (1867–8) speeded his decline, and he collapsed during a 'farewell' series in England. His last novel, *Edwin Drood* (1870), was never completed; he suffered a stroke at Gad's Hill on 8 June 1870 and died the following day. Lamentation was demonstrative and universal, and he was buried in the Poets' Corner of Westminster Abbey.

Dickens's extreme energy was not exhausted by his unique success as a novelist. His weekly journalism made heavy demands on his time after 1850, and he constantly turned to the stage, first, in many amateur theatricals, given privately or for charity, where he produced and took leading roles with great brilliance, and, later, in his public readings. His concern with social reform in his novels and journalism was matched by an active personal interest in several charitable projects.

Furthermore, as Lionel Trilling puts it, 'the mere record of his conviviality is exhausting'. His typical relaxation was a long walk at great speed, and he was dedicated to any and every sort of game or jollification. In the early days of his success, observers were sometimes displeased by his flamboyant dress and a hint of vulgarity in his manners, but he had powerful, magnetizing eyes and overwhelming charm. Beneath his high spirits, friends could detect a permanent emotional insecurity and restlessness, which flavours the tragi-comic world of his novels.

Two biographies stand out among many: John Forster's *Life* (1872–4, many times reprinted); and Edgar Johnson's *Charles Dickens, His Tragedy and Triumph* (London: Gollancz, 1953), which embodies material neglected or suppressed by Forster. Readers interested in Dickens's methods as a novelist will be enlightened by John Butt's and Kathleen Tillotson's *Dickens at Work* (London: Methuen, 1957). There are innumerable specialized studies of his work, life, and views. A magazine exclusively devoted to this subject, *The Dickensian*, is published three times a year by the Dickens Fellowship.

INTRODUCTION

IF Charles Dickens was the most famous Englishman to visit the United States in the nineteenth century and if *American Notes* is arguably the best-known account of an Englishman's travels across the Atlantic, it is important to remember that many others made the same trip and wrote about it: during the period 1815–60 there were over 200 such books and they were very popular. When Dickens departed from England in 1842 he had read most of the important travel books and his own work should be seen as a part of Anglo-American relations during the period between the end of the War of 1812 and the commencement of the American Civil War.

During these years, despite such 'incidents' as the Canadian border question, the tensions surrounding control of the Panama Canal and the British refusal to surrender the slaves from the 'Creole' to Secretary of State Webster, political and social relations progressed with a reasonable amount of harmony. This was partly due to skilled diplomats on both sides; Castlereagh and Bagot for the British and, among the Americans, Adams and Rush; and partly due to the forging of strong links through the constant flow of men, goods and ideas between the two countries. Cotton and wheat came into Britain and iron, textiles and hardware flowed across the Atlantic in the opposite direction, causing great developments in Sheffield, Birmingham, the Lancashire mill towns, Boston, Philadelphia, Chicago and St Louis; a rich, powerful world with enormous potential and an axis running between the great ports of New York and Liverpool. According to Brebner, '. . . much of what happened in Great Britain was almost as important in the lives of North Americans as what happened at home,'[1] and this is borne out by seeing how closely connected chronologically were the trade depressions in both countries, occurring in both in 1815, 1825 and 1837. Britain invested heavily in the new land and both countries worked hard to improve sea communications.

Another cargo of great importance was human beings. Despite

1. John Bartlett Brebner, *North Atlantic Triangle* (New Haven and London, 1945), p. 109.

the frequently appalling steerage conditions on most ships (see Dickens's treatment of this in *Martin Chuzzlewit*) immigrants flocked over from Great Britain; Lancastrian mill-workers, Irish labourers, miners, journeyman potters; what the British Parliament was to call 'this ruinous drain of the most useful part of the population of the United Kingdom'.[2] 1,600,000 went over between 1815 and 1850 and between 1820 and 1849 well over half the immigrants arriving in the United States were English-speaking. Radical newspapers such as *The True Sun*, the *Morning Chronicle* and *The Poor Man's Guardian* chanted the glories of the New World, listing its careful economy, the right of every man to the ballot, the absence of bribery and corruption at election time and the possibility that as many as two-thirds of all adults were proprietors. Tory magazines countered that the separation of church and state was conducive to nothing but immorality, that violence ruined any pretence to law, that elections were 'rigged' with the same regularity as in Britain since threats were as potent as bribes; but sheer weight of opinion brought results. Travellers and critics could scorn, as did Augustus Foster, the American claim to greatness based on the infinite possibilities of the future,[3] but to the masses of Europe such a claim was all that was needed. The American destiny offered the chance to assert *individual* rights, the inalienable right of a man to everything he made and earned.

Ideas crossed the Atlantic as readily as goods. Augustus Foster's views on many European immigrants seem rather outrageous: 'A German who has just arrived fresh and set free from serving barons or counts is like a great carthorse turned loose upon a plain, kicking and snorting in all directions. They revel in their new state and appear to be delighted with rolling about in the mire of democracy,'[4] but there is little doubt that, during this period, the English-speaking immigrants were more concerned than others with working at the new democracy, giving their allegiance to what Frank Thistlethwaite has called 'a rational experiment in human government'.[5]

2. Quoted in J. B. McMaster, *History of the People of the United States*, vol. 4, (New York, 1885–1920), p. 389.

3. A. Foster, *Jeffersonian America*, ed. R. B. Davis (San Marino, 1954).

4. ibid., p. 274.

5. F. Thistlethwaite, *The Anglo-American Connection in the Early Nineteenth Century* (Philadelphia, 1959), p. 72.

Utopians, such as Birkbeck, Flower and Robert Owen, pursued communitarian ideals in various parts of the country and Owen greatly influenced America's progress in labour relations. Activists such as Robert Dale and Frances Wright pioneered trade unions and British immigrants were instrumental in editing radical papers such as the *New Harmony Gazette* and *The Radical Reformer* and in relaying information to British publications like *The Westminster Review* and *The Northern Star*. Through such agencies a common climate of belief in democratic ideals was established.

In the field of humanitarianism there was close cooperation and rapport between the two countries over peace, anti-slavery and temperance movements. The British Anti-Slavery Society influenced Tappan, Leavitt and Wright to form the American Anti-Slavery Society in 1833. Lloyd Garrison began publication of the *Liberator* and fanatical anti-slavery lecturers such as George Thompson and Charles Stuart were imported from Great Britain. Dickens felt obliged to include a full chapter on slavery in *American Notes*, and one useful guide to transatlantic opinion on this subject was *Uncle Tom's Cabin* (a best-seller in the United States when *Moby Dick* was virtually ignored), the American book with the largest immediate sale in Britain during the nineteenth century – over a million copies in 1852.

Ideas of reform were exchanged on the subjects of education and public institutions. In the 1840s it was discovered that the British government spent less on its schools than the city of Boston, and by 1870 the teaching of religious instruction on a non-denominational basis had been allowed in British schools and London University had been founded on an American (i.e. non-sectarian) model. Dickens and other travellers gave much of their time in America to visiting and describing prisons, asylums and hospitals and these descriptions promoted changes in comparable British institutions.

There existed, however, a darker side to Anglo-American relations during this period and Dickens's work must be seen as part of this, too, in order to explain, among other things, why he left so much out of *American Notes*. This darker side, venomous and petty, is largely to be explained in terms of the quest for a national culture in America, the many travel books written by Britons and the use made of reviews of these books in a paper war which has come to be known as 'The Battle of the Quarterlies'.

Following the War of Revolution the Americans sought to turn their backs on European traditions and create a distinctly American culture. Graduating in the Bowdoin College class of 1825, Longfellow stridently proclaimed the greatness awaiting American writers: '. . . palms are to be won by our native writers! – by those, that have been nursed and brought up . . . in the civil and religious freedom of our country.'[6] Noah Webster wrote in the preface to his famous spelling book that 'America must be as independent in literature as she is in politics.'[7] This led to an absurd over-praising of American writers on the grounds of their 'Americanness'. As early as 1794 'John Whittler' was writing in *The United States Magazine*: 'The writings of a Trumbull, a Dwight, a Barlow, and an Humphries, are as highly esteemed even by foreigners, as those of a Butler, a Milton, a Pope, or an Addison.'[8]

The British journals naturally greeted this kind of estimation with malevolent glee. Sidney Smith's calculated attack in the *Edinburgh Review* in 1820 is more famous than most but may be taken as typical:

'In the four quarters of the globe, who reads an American book? or goes to an American play? or looks at an American picture or statue?'[9] There was impatience and envy on the part of the Americans and affronted spite from the British.

This situation was not helped by the vexed question of international copyright. Throughout the period Americans could and did publish vast numbers of English novels and other works without paying the authors any royalties. In 1838 a bill was proposed in England which provided for reciprocal international copyright but the Congress of the United States failed to respond and, despite tireless work by right-minded people on both sides throughout the century, such an agreement did not come into effect until 1891. Of course, piracy was rampant in both countries with unscrupulous publishers prepared to edit, cut or even rewrite in order to be first on the market and closest to popular taste. Dickens took up cudgels with characteristic energy on behalf of this cause. Just before his

6. Quoted in J. L. Davis, J. T. Frederick, F. L. Mott, *American Literature: An Anthology and Critical Survey* (New York, 1948), vol. 1, p. 355.

7. Quoted in R. Nye, *The Cultural Life of the New Nation 1776–1830* (New York, 1963), p. 239.

8. ibid., p. 241.

9. *Edinburgh Review*, vol. 33, January 1820, p. 79.

1842 trip he read J. G. Lockhart's life of Scott and was very moved by the description of that novelist, sick and miserable, spending his days in poverty when he should have been living in comfort from the returns on the huge sale of his books in the United States. Dickens's concern was also bolstered by first-hand discoveries of how much money he himself was losing.[10] Like other Englishmen who drew this wholesale theft to the attention of the American public, he was roundly berated for his pains. During this period the international copyright issue possibly did more harm to Anglo-American relations than any other single factor.

Other reasons for the two-way vituperative criticism are not hard to find. Many British travellers found their dreams of a new Paradise shattered and could not hide the bitterness from their books. A major reason for the acidity of Frances Trollope's *Domestic Manners of the Americans* must simply be the failure of her commercial enterprises in Cincinnati and her fall into abject poverty during the last few months of her stay in America. Alternatively, many travellers went to America with Tory prejudices and pre-possessed notions of a rough wilderness inhabited by brutes and consequently saw what they wished to see. Captain Marryat candidly acknowledged that the great object of his *Diary in America* (1839) was 'to do serious injury to the cause of democracy'.[11] In either case the magazine reviewer had to rely on their reports and was only too pleased to find so many venomous criticisms. Too often a Tory bias in the book was increased by the reviewer's own right-wing sentiments. Sometimes the magazine articles about America influenced travellers before they made their journey. The constant flow of emigrants worried the British government and even Cobden spoke out strongly against the loss of so many skilled workers. It is therefore not unnatural that such a diehard Tory magazine as the *Quarterly Review* should be willing to assist the government's efforts to curb the slide by underplaying American virtues when the books in question might dwell on them.

Just as American periodicals cried for genuine American writers whilst pirating as much British material as they could get; just as American writers sneered at European traditions yet relied heavily

10. E. F. Payne, *Dickens' Days in Boston* (New York, 1927).

11. Quoted by G. D. Lillibridge, *Beacon of Freedom* (Philadelphia, 1955), p. xiv.

upon them (Charles Brockden Brown is a case in point); so America both defied and needed European recognition. Michelet once remarked of the United States: 'Elle est jeune, et elle brûle d'être en rapport avec le globe,'[12] and this tended to make the nation peculiarly sensitive to foreign criticism. Mrs Trollope reported that 'Other nations have been called thin-skinned, but the citizens of the Union have, apparently, no skins at all; they wince if a breeze blows over them, unless it be tempered with adulation.'[13] In *Pickwick Papers* Mr Weller outlined a plan to Sam for smuggling Pickwick out of the Fleet in a disembowelled piano:

'Have a passage ready taken for 'Merriker. The 'Merriken gov'ment will never give him up, when they find as he's got money to spend, Sammy. Let the gov'ner stop there till Mrs Bardell's dead . . . and then let him come back and write a book about the 'Merrikens as'll pay all his expenses and more, if he blows 'em up enough.' [Ch. 45]

Finding that a relatively innocuous work like *American Notes* could cause an outrage, Dickens made Hannibal Chollop in *Martin Chuzzlewit* an absurd epitome of American touchiness:

'We are the intellect of virtue of the airth, the cream of human natur', and the flower of moral force. Our backs is easy ris. We must be cracked-up, or they rises, and we snarls. We show our teeth, I tell you, fierce. You'd better crack us up, you had.' [Ch. 33]

As early as 1810 the *Edinburgh Review* was setting down the line of abuse in a mischievous résumé of Ashe's books: 'Their inhabitants, it seems, are all abominably vicious; but in degrees very nicely distinguished; – the middle states being bad – the northern very bad – and the southern execrable:'[14] and in America *Niles's Weekly Register* had conducted a series of attacks on England in 1812. But the battle was really joined in January 1814 when the *Quarterly Review* published 'Inchiquin's Favorable View of the United States', a slashing assault on all facets of American life. The tone of the article was set by the following passage: 'In America the "man of the people" is one who frequents the grog-shops,

12. Quoted by H. T. Tuckerman, *America and her Commentators* (New York, 1864), p. 265.

13. Frances Trollope, *Domestic Manners of the Americans*, ed. D. Smalley (New York, 1949), p. 355.

14. *Edinburgh Review*, vol. 15, January 1810, p. 442.

smokes his segar and harangues the populace with violent and inflamatory abuse of the hostile faction.'[15] According to the article, the quarter sessions were run by party politics and the judges had no real power; there was too much violence, and religious fanaticism served to cloak sexual promiscuity; the famed classless society was 'all belly',[16] devoid of manners, 'a vulgarity of vice and hostility to all the graces of life';[17] there was a widespread hatred of England and her institutions, and the people of England were cautioned that if they wanted peace with America they must trust little to kindness 'and nothing at all to kin'.[18]

The criticisms received serious replies from Timothy Dwight in his *Remarks on the Review of Inchiquin's Letters* and from J. K. Paulding in his *The United States and England*. Paulding attacked the British government for paying travellers to give a deliberately false impression of life in America, and both he and Dwight sifted through the chronicles of English history to find parallel instances of loose living and chaotic government. Dwight also made the point (much repeated, with justification, by American journals) that British travellers deliberately averted their eyes from all the magnificent sights of a new land being opened up and he placed great emphasis on canal and railroad construction, for: 'Never within historic times had any other people presented so interesting a spectacle to observers. Yet all these phases of life were passed over in silence, or if mentioned were mentioned as fit subjects for ridicule and contempt.'[19]

Using reviews of travel books as springboards for their attacks, the British periodicals frequently tried to disguise the blows by abusing the authors first; the *Athenaeum* describing Mrs Trollope as a 'sarcastic tattler';[20] the *Quarterly* attributing 'the simplicity of a sucking child'[21] to Henry Fearon and the *Edinburgh* dismissing Marryat with 'a life at sea is a sorry preparation for judging of life ashore';[22] but they were always careful, no matter what their

15. *Quarterly Review*, vol. 10, January 1814, p. 501.
16. ibid., p. 512.
17. ibid., p. 514.
18. ibid., p. 539.
19. McMaster, op. cit., vol. 5, pp. 311–12.
20. *Athenaeum*, 1832, p. 219.
21. *Quarterly Review*, vol. 21, January 1819, p. 128.
22. *Edinburgh Review*, vol. 70, October 1839, p. 125.

blanket judgements of the books might be, to choose quotations guaranteed to incense the Americans, such as this from J. Bristed's *Resources of the United States* (1818): '. . . a horrible perversion of justice corrupts the whole body of the commonwealth'.[23]

Most attempts at conciliation were soon undercut by the reviewer's desire to patronize. In two issues of the *Edinburgh* in 1820 Sidney Smith tried to ease the friction by admitting the existence of a party in England embittered towards America, but stressing that many more held her in high esteem and watched her actions with great regard. However, he ruined the effect by continually adding patronizing overtones, trying to persuade 'Brother Jonathan' that he '. . . must not . . . be dazzled by the galaxy of epithets by which his orators and newspaper scribblers endeavour to persuade their supporters that they are the greatest . . . and the most moral people on earth. The effect of this is unspeakably ludicrous on this side of the Atlantic.'[24] The exchange of scurrilities continued well into the 1840s and as late as 1874 Ruskin was attacking Americans in the *Dublin Review*: 'What thoughts they have not learned from England are foolish thoughts; what words they have not learned from England, unseemly words; the vile among them not being able to be humorous parrots, but only obscene mockingbirds.'[25]

H. C. Allen has pointed out that during the period when the *Quarterly Review* and its partners were abusing the United States, many British magazines were most sympathetic to American aims and ambitions, among them the *Eclectic Review*, the *Gentleman's Magazine*, the *London Magazine* and, most important of all, the radical *Westminster Review* which saw 'our Transatlantic brethren'[26] going on speedily 'in the march of improvement',[27] and underlined the effete snob-gentility of most British travellers by quoting Ouseley: '. . . when I exclaim "This is a noble, an extraordinary country!" I am answered in Abigail phrase – "But, shocking, the people eat with their knives." '[28]

23. *Quarterly Review*, vol. 21, January 1819, p. 4.

24. *Edinburgh Review*, vol. 33, January 1820, pp. 78–9.

25. *Dublin Review*, vol. 23, July 1874. Quoted in C. Gohdes, *American Literature in Nineteenth-Century England* (London, 1944). p. 132.

26. *Westminster Review*, vol. 12, October 1829, p. 447. See also H. C. Allen, *Great Britain and the United States* (London, 1954), pp. 129–53.

27. *Westminster Review*, loc. cit.   28. ibid.

It is ironical that the American magazines which defended their country stoutly were often replicas of their British counterparts in layout, style and copy, and the *New York Mirror* said in 1827: 'The magazines of the United States are generally modeled after those of the mother country.'[29] But such indications of entente did little to curb the quarrelsome nature of so many of the travel books. The majority American opinion of these works and their authors was summed up by Tom Hood in his 'Boz in America':

Numerous have been the writers on the land of the stars and stripes – a host of travelled ladies and gentlemen, liberals and illiberals, utilitarians and inutilitarians – human bowls of every bias have trundled over the United States without hitting, or in the opinion of the natives, even coming near the jack.[30]

Hood went on to hope that 'Boz', on his first trip, would prove to be more perceptive and less jingoistic than his predecessors.

Professor Allen Nevins once divided these transatlantic visits into two periods. In the first period (1789–1825) the travellers were, he insisted, '. . . representatives of a period of practical investigation of America'[31] because 'the predominant motive of the British traveller in coming to this country was utilitarian inquiry'.[32] The second period (1825–45) he termed that of 'Tory condescension'[33] because the type of traveller had changed, coming now from the upper and professional classes instead of the middle and working classes, and because 'the eagerness of conservative or reactionary men to rush to the defence of Old English institutions'[34] was intensified by the bitter jibes of the British quarterlies which of necessity affected 'the judgement of even the fairest and most liberal of the travellers in America'.[35]

This distinction seems very arbitrary. Accusations of prejudice were just as common during the first period as the second and

29. Quoted in F. L. Mott, *A History of American Magazines* (New York, 1930), p. 393.

30. Quoted in *The Dickensian*, March 1942, p. 84.

31. A. Nevins, *American Social History as recorded by British Travellers* (New York, 1934), p. 9.

32. ibid., p. 10.

33. ibid., p. 111.

34. ibid., p. 112.

35. ibid.

travellers of the third and fourth decades of the century were hardly more Tory than their predecessors (they were, after all, further removed from the War of Independence). When Professor Nevins decided that another pronounced influence upon the growth of Tory condescension was 'the activity of the great reviews'[36] he seemed to forget that their most savage storm of abuse came during the years 1810–25, that is, during the latter half of his first period. There is a considerable diversity of opinion among the travellers on certain topics, particularly education and government, but there are many striking similarities between travellers widely separated in time, for instance those between Dickens and Augustus Foster, who was in America more than thirty years before the novelist. There is a definite continuity in the outlook of the visitors, the phenomena which caught their attention and their reactions.

The predominating motive behind these visits to the United States was curiosity; the desire to discover just how far the settlers had progressed in the creation of a democratic state, and just how successful their experiments in government, economics, law and agriculture were proving to be. Often, however, the traveller was guided by his own particular interests. Thus Birkbeck and Flower discuss agricultural conditions, as does William Cobbett; Lieutenant De Roos is keenly interested in the organization of American dockyards and the state of her naval power; Melish in economic conditions and the possibilities of trade; Harriet Martineau in government, economics and slavery and Silk Buckingham in moral reform and the temperance movement. Some wished simply to serve their own personal needs. Thomas Cooper went '. . . to determine whether America and what part of it was eligible for a person like myself with a small fortune and a large family to settle in'.[37] Others gave information and tips to those contemplating the move. One traveller, Henry Fearon, made the journey at the request of thirty-nine English families: 'to ascertain whether any, and what part of the United States would be suitable for their residence',[38] and Joseph Pickering entitled his book, *Inquiries of an Emigrant*.

36. ibid., p. 111.

37. T. Cooper, *Some Information Respecting America* (London, 1794), p iii.

38. Quoted in Jane Mesick, *The English Traveller in America 1785–183.* (New York, 1923), p. 4.

being a narrative of an English farmer from the year 1824–1830.
Emigrants received advice on how to endure a steerage crossing
and ward off seasickness; to make the journey in early spring to
avoid the intense heat; to beware of the excessive drinking of
spirits and to be very careful from whom they obtained their land.
Fraudulent dealings in real estate were very common at this time.
A brief discussion of the Cairo Company is included in Ch. 12,
note 8 (p. 352), and it is no accident that in *Martin Chuzzlewit*
Dickens made the crooked land agent, Scadder, the literal epitome
of a Janus-faced nation:

Two grey eyes lurked deep within this agent's head, but one of them
had no sight in it, and stood stock-still. With that side of his face he
seemed to listen to what the other side was doing. Thus each profile had
a distinct expression, and when the movable side was most in action,
the rigid one was in its coldest state of watchfulness. [Ch. 21]

Many accounts stressed the hardships settlers might have to face;
Fearon and Mrs Trollope dramatizing the solitude of backwoods
settlers and Parkinson outlining the horrors of Indian atrocities.

New England, and the land north of the Ohio, west of Pittsburgh
and the Alleghanies; these were the areas highly recommended for
settlement. Virginia and the Carolinas were to be avoided, as was
the 'wet grave' of New Orleans. The southern states were repeatedly
condemned, not merely by the presence of slavery, but also because
of scenes of appalling violence which, the travellers claimed, were
commonplace in the region. Thomas Ashe[39] was not alone in
describing the 'gouging' matches in the South where the object was
to fix the thumbs in the eyes of an opponent and, with one quick
thrust, remove both at once from the sockets.

There were many beautiful places to see, but getting there was a
problem. Most travellers found stage-coaches unpalatable, especially
when going over 'corduroy' roads (see Ch. 14, note 4, p. 354).
Dickens likened the movement of the coach over those to riding up
a steep flight of stairs in an omnibus. Graceful steamboats frequently
impressed, but there were continual dangers beneath the apparently
calm waters and the captains often pushed their vessels so hard that
collisions, fires and explosions were uncomfortably frequent. That
notoriously bad traveller, Basil Hall, fumed: 'Oh, the misery of a

39. T. Ashe, *Travels in America Performed in 1806* (London, 1808).

long night on board of a crowded steamboat! In the middle of the cabin blazed and smoked a red-hot stove, the ferruginous vapours of which were mixed with such a steaming and breathing of brandy, gin and tobacco as, for my sins, I have seldom encountered before.'[40] Many travellers besides Dickens found steamboats and stage-coaches full of Americans spitting tobacco juice. H. T. Tuckerman said that the habit was rare by 1864,[41] but in the first years of this century Rupert Brooke dubbed America 'El Cuspidorado'.[42] Mrs Trollope, as one might expect, had something to say on this: 'I am inclined to think this most vile and universal habit of chewing tobacco is the cause of a remarkable peculiarity in the male physiognomy of Americans; their lips are almost uniformly thin and compressed.'[43]

American drinking habits, posture, social laxity, unattractive women and, especially, table-manners, are dwelt on inordinately. Dickens had much to say about the last item both in his letters and in *American Notes*, and it is useful to compare his description in the present work (p. 203) with the obscene ritual at Pawkinses lodging-house in *Martin Chuzzlewit*:

All the knives and forks were working away at a rate that was quite alarming; very few words were spoken; and everybody seemed to eat his utmost in self-defence, as if a famine were expected ... and it had become high time to assert the first law of nature.

Great heaps of indigestible matter melted away as ice before the sun. Dyspeptic individuals bolted their food in wedges; feeding, not themselves, but broods of nightmares, who were continually standing at livery within them. [Ch. 16]

The Americans continually castigated British travellers for seeing only the surface of American life, but in *Martin Chuzzlewit* Dickens describes the Americans as only surface, and that is the moral point. They exist as a catalogue of puppets with no inner life, quite unable to relate meaningfully to anyone else. Dickens turned his limitation as a traveller into novelist's gold.

Travellers discussed in detail American curiosity, vanity, sensitivity to criticism and the rampant urge to acquire wealth and property.

40. B. Hall, *Travels in North America in the Years 1827–1828* (Edinburgh 1930), vol. 2, p. 382.

41. Tuckerman, op. cit., p. 254.

42. Quoted in Allen, op. cit., p. 156.

43. Trollope, op. cit., p. 234.

Dickens made greed the watchword of *his* American nation in *Martin Chuzzlewit* and Silk Buckingham, the reformer, saw it as a main contributory factor in the increase of crime. Many saw this love of wealth as responsible for the wholesale piracy of English books and hence for the lack of a flourishing American literature.

Contradictions abound in these books. Travellers point out the immorality prevalent in the United States, then point with awe at remarkable church attendance records, then abandon their admiration of this to point to its effect in inculcating an alarming prudery. Captain Marryat shocked a young lady by mentioning the word 'leg'.[44] In *Martin Chuzzlewit* Dickens makes the figure of Mrs Hominy – grim, canting, bound tightly in a rigid show of prudery – yet another epitome of American shallowness, an outward pantomime of squeamish propriety to hide a lack of moral principle. Many travellers, especially Mrs Trollope, felt that the lack of an established church led to unseemly jealousy and disunion among the large number of religious sects.

One reason for the lack of an American literature was given as a slavish addiction to reading newspapers. At this time the United States possessed a notorious 'yellow' press, headed by such figures as James Gordon Bennett, committed to gossip and malicious slander, especially in its comments on England. According to Augustus Foster, the quickest way to make a fortune was to edit a newspaper constantly making such disparaging remarks. Boardman, however, liked the American press and insisted that 'no namby-pamby trash of fashionable movements, routs, and dinners find their way into its columns',[45] and the travellers had to admit that throughout the Union the commonest people were surprisingly well-informed on political matters through poring over every paper which came their way. The periodicals were generally of a low standard, though notable exceptions were said to be *The Portfolio*, the *Knickerbocker Magazine*, and, finest of all, the *North American Review*. Architecture seemed plagiaristic and the wooden houses were often pathetically inadequate; though there was no lack of skill in design and construction and buildings in New York, Philadelphia, Baltimore and Washington were often described as 'magnificent'. A great deal of original talent was exhibited by

44. Nevins, op. cit., pp. 245–6.
45. J. Boardman, *America and the Americans* (London, 1833), p. 78.

American painters, of whom West, Trumbull and Allston were the most famous; but the general public was barren of taste and enthusiastic practice was severely limited through lack of support. Theatres, while far too reliant on British companies and plays, were always entertaining, if somewhat rowdy.

Much mirth was caused by the American language. Noah Webster had early insisted that Americans already had a distinct language ready for use even in the highest forms of literature and the *North American Review* asserted that 'on the whole, the English language is better spoken here than in England'.[46] To English travellers American pronunciation seemed very droll. Marryat paid great attention to transatlantic differences of phraseology and grammar, such as the American love of compound substantives and adjectives, and the differences in meaning with such words as 'clever' and 'smart'.[47] Dickens was highly amused by that jack-of-all-trades word 'fix', and might well have agreed with Marryat that 'it is remarkable how very debased the language has become in a short period in America'.[48] Of course, most of these comments show a limited awareness of the American language, but as we saw with the descriptions of eating habits, Dickens was prepared to use his limited awareness to describe a limited and curiously artificial world in *Martin Chuzzlewit*. The use of such forms as 'toe' (for 'to'), the interrogative 'yes', the weakening of the final syllable ('Natur') and the replacement of the adverb by the adjective ('alarming' for 'alarmingly') make up a catalogue of cant as impressive as that created by Jonson in, say, *The Alchemist*. At one point Dickens uses the adjective instead of the adverb brilliantly to expose the two-facedness of Kettle and Choke. Kettle, relating to Mark the delights of Eden, remarks: ' "It is an awful lovely place, sure-ly. And frightful wholesome, like-wise." ' The adverbial sense works in one way, the adjectival in quite another.

Fun is often poked in this period at the excessive hyperbole and overloading of American rhetoric: language which seemed to have little to do with anything except language. Carl Bode sees it as a healthy sign that the Americans loved rhetoric,[49] while Constance

46. *North American Review*, July 1821, p. 30.
47. Nevins, op. cit., p. 40.   48. ibid.
49. C. Bode, *The Anatomy of American Popular Culture 1840–1861* (Berkeley and Los Angeles, 1959), pp. 159–60.

Rourke insisted that this style was part of a comic mythology, a love of 'putting on' British travellers,[50] but J. Hillis Miller attests to Dickens's accuracy: 'As is shown by authentic examples of the kind of language Dickens was parodying, metaphor or personification cut loose from any tradition of substantial analogy was the habitual trope of even the most distinguished American orators of the middle nineteenth century.'[51] Whatever the historical truth, Dickens wrote *Martin Chuzzlewit* in a climate which felt American oratory to be notably absurd and he makes an integral and brilliant use of this in the novel. The sheer nullity behind the façade, the absolute impossibility of the travellers establishing any line of communication or contact with the American characters, stems from these characters existing only as long-playing records of complete gibberish. One of the Literary Ladies greets Pogram with: 'Mind and matter glide swift into the vortex of immensity. Howls the sublime, and softly sleeps the calm Ideal, in the whispering chambers of Imagination.' As in the plays of Ben Jonson, particularized lingo creates characters who are pure externals, units in a world where values have become completely upturned.

Schools, universities, hospitals, asylums and prisons were often praised by travellers. There seemed to be few beggars, though a good deal of drunkenness. Law courts were cheap and speedy, but also slovenly, ill-mannered, lacking in dignity, and not infrequently ignorant, biased and corrupt. Trade was described at length and the manual versatility of settlers admired. The American scenery took the breath away, as did American food: later in the century Thackeray remembered that, having eaten an American oyster, he felt as if he had swallowed a baby.[52] There were few mills, but the one at Lowell, where a great many young ladies worked, was a model one, to be contrasted with the poverty and misery current in England. However, there were few descriptions of American home and family life, a facet which many natives felt to be influential in the nation's progress and well-being. Interiors in general, whether of tavern, church or private home, were noticeably absent from these books. Politics, economics and religion were rarely

50. C. Rourke, *American Humour* (New York, 1953), p. 60.

51. J. Hillis Miller, *Charles Dickens: The World of His Novels* (London, 1958), p. 130.

52. Nevins, op. cit., p. 4.

discussed at the level of principle (Harriet Martineau being a notable exception). Detailed pictures of the countryside were rare and there was little feeling for environment. Of course, what really caught the attention were the new sights and experiences to which the nineteenth-century Englishman was not accustomed. Storms, sunsets, animals, forests, canyons; all were liberally sprinkled across the pages of these books. In some sense the making of a nation did emerge, but no book gave a true idea of the opening-up of a continent; of the lives of the human beings who were making history. There were reiterated glows of promise for the future but little evidence of how that promise was to be fulfilled.

According to Jane Mesick: 'English travellers seem to have depended little on one another . . . if the average traveller took his information from the fellow-countrymen who preceded him, the fact is not apparent.'[53] But though not readily apparent, it seems likely that travellers were so influenced. Having decided to cross to the New World it seems illogical to suppose that they would not read current travel-books and so, when they came face to face with experiences previously described in these works, echoes would appear in their own pages. One might compare Dickens's description of Philadelphia:

It is a handsome city but distractingly regular. After walking about it for an hour or two, I felt that I would have given the world for a crooked street,

with Mrs Trollope's:

The city is built with extreme and almost wearisome regularity . . . all is even, straight, uniform, and uninteresting:[54]

or Basil Hall's quoting of a chauvinistic Boston high-school boy:

'Gratitude! Gratitude to England! What does America owe to her? Such gratitude as the young lion owes to its dam, which brings it forth on the desert wilds, and leaves it to perish there. No! We owe her nothing! For eighteen hundred years the world has slumbered in ignorance of liberty, and of the true rights of freedom. At length America arose in all her glory, to give the world the long-desired lesson'[55]

53. Mesick, op. cit., pp. 342–3.
54. Trollope, op. cit., p. 260.
55. Hall, op. cit., vol. 2, p. 168.

with the speech of the 'glowing young Columbian' at the meeting of the Watertoast Sympathisers in *Martin Chuzzlewit*.

The preceding comments should make clear how important it is to see Dickens as one of many travellers to America in this period. He saw the places they saw; he made much, like them, of public institutions; his comments on the blacker aspects of American manners, such as spitting, boasting, sharp practice, and on steamboats, stage-coaches, slavery and American culture are in close rapport with many of the works published prior to his visit. Of course, his position as the most famous English novelist of the day meant that he had less privacy than most of the others. Rather absurdly he wanted both to be lionized and left to his own devices, and his lack of freedom deeply affected the writing of *American Notes*. An article in the *Memphis Morning Bulletin* in 1859 had this to say: 'During his visit to this country, Dickens had but little opportunity of seeing the real "people" through the crevices in the crowd of toadies and flunkies around the celebrity.'[56] He was flattered, cajoled and bullied by the people he met. Too often his opinions of the American people are polarized between the riff-raff who wouldn't leave him alone and the literary aristocrats of the Eastern seaboard (such as Longfellow and Felton) who exerted perhaps too great an influence on the novelist's opinions of the New World. From this mixture of his personal circumstances and the general circumstances of Anglo-American relations of that time emerges a work which is both extremely disappointing in its omissions and pervasive flatness and fascinating as a record of the ways in which the foremost creative writer of his day responded to the most exciting social and political experiment of his time.

*

A knowledge of the cultural circumstances of Dickens's trip to America is deeply helpful in understanding the development of *American Notes*. As they stand, Dickens's gradual revulsion from the American scene may seem to lack an 'objective correlative'. The decision to leave out of his account that which, as it seemed to him, occurred to him specifically and only because he was 'Boz', was taken in the supposed interests of presenting a journey and a

56. Quoted by J. D. Rust, 'Dickens and the Americans: An Unnoticed Letter', *Nineteenth-Century Fiction*, June 1956, p. 70.

response less idiosyncratic and more applicable to most Englishmen. The result was a curious compromise which in many ways, though it has been deplored, gives the book its unique flavour: a gradual increase in feeling throughout, based on no necessitating circumstances, which imparts a dream-like quality at considerable and meaningful variance with the common-sense traveller's notes.

In fact, Dickens's journey to America was traumatic, literally. Begun in the clear light of day:

... the air was so clear, the houses were so bright and gay; the sign-boards were painted in such gaudy colours; the gilded letters were so very golden; the bricks were so very red, the stone was so very white, the blinds and area railings were so very green, the knobs and plates upon the street doors so marvellously bright and twinkling ...,

it proceeded to dream and nightmare vision:

At length, upon the morning of the third day, we arrived at a spot so much more desolate than any we had yet beheld, that the forlornest places we had passed were, in comparison with it, full of interest. At the junction of the two rivers, on ground so flat and low and marshy, that at certain seasons of the year it is inundated to the house-tops, lies a breeding-place of fever, ague, and death; vaunted in England as a mine of Golden Hope, and speculated in, on the faith of monstrous representations, to many people's ruin. A dismal swamp, on which the half-built houses rot away: cleared here and there for the space of a few yards; and teeming, then, with rank unwholesome vegetation, in whose baleful shade the wretched wanderers who are tempted hither droop, and die, and lay their bones; the hateful Mississippi circling and eddying before it, and turning off upon its southern course a slimy monster hideous to behold; a hotbed of disease, an ugly sepulchre, a grave un-cheered by any gleam of promise: a place without one single quality, in earth or air or water, to commend it: such is this dismal Cairo.

Though Dickens begins *American Notes* with a eupeptic and common-sense cheerfulness, there are hints of his apprehensions even from the start. The comedy is exorcism. Just as he will eventually characterize America generally as a land of duplicity and chicanery, so at the outset he laments the deception practised by the advertisements which assured him of the commodiousness of his transatlantic ship. He notes that he colluded in his deception, picturing his 'state-room' as 'that small snug chamber of the imagination'. Disabused, he begins to see it as a 'box', then a

'hearse', a 'coffin' and a 'trap', and the clever way the accommodation is arranged to serve multiple purposes takes on an ominous –
though still comic – aspect: 'every nook and corner and individual
piece of furniture was something else besides what it pretended to
be, and was a mere trap and deception and place of secret stowage,
whose ostensible purpose was its least useful one'. Amiable enough
here, though with some edge to it, this imagery would later be
extended more grimly to American prisons and to the natural
environment.

The dislocations of the sea-journey itself are handled with comic
extravagance. 'The state-room is standing on its head', he reports,
and relates the hilarious scene where the ship's rocking and rolling
renders him unable to succour his womenfolk with the conventional
brandy and water (p. 67). That the voyage produced serious
insights as well is, however, stressed when, 'alone and thoughtful',
Dickens meditates on its effects upon perception:

At first, too, and even when the hour, and all the objects it exalts,
have come to be familiar, it is difficult, alone and thoughtful, to hold
them to their proper shapes and forms. They change with the wandering
fancy; assume the semblance of things left far away; put on the well-
remembered aspect of favourite places dearly loved; and even people
them with shadows. Streets, houses, rooms; figures so like their usual
occupants, that they have startled me by their reality, which far exceeded, as it seemed to me, all power of mine to conjure up the absent; have,
many and many a time, at such an hour, grown suddenly out of objects
with whose real look, and use, and purpose, I was as well acquainted as
with my own two hands.

These effects are a foretaste of later and deeper dislocations and
'culture-shock'.

First, however, Dickens lands at Halifax, Nova Scotia, a portion
of the New World still British. He presents Halifax as a false
America, a transatlantic community more than manageable for the
traveller, one wholly unchanged from its British origins and
requiring no adaptation, no adjustment. Of Halifax's 'Legislative
Council and General Assembly' he comments, 'it was like looking
at Westminster through the wrong end of a telescope', and 'in
short, everything went on, and promised to go on, just as it does at
home upon the like occasions'. This idyll, the traveller's vision of
travel *sans peine* is soon to be shattered, and *American* America is

defined by its distance from Halifax's miniature presentment of a neat-and-tidy England-in-America.

Dickens begins his 'American' notes with a survey of 'institutions' in two related senses of the word: abstractly, in terms of the form and system of governance, and concretely, in terms of particular establishments, as schools, hospitals, prisons. The former had already become a standard British jest, the American boasting of his country's 'insti-too-tions' – trebly foolish by way of mispronunciation, conscious stressing of what better societies left unsaid (and were the better *for* leaving unsaid), and misuse of language, as mere improvised arrangements not a century old could hardly deserve such a flattering term. Dickens, like Harriet Martineau before him, had a sociological interest in the institutional,[57] and *American Notes* attempts to relate the American system and its concrete establishments to the style and manners of the people, the tone and quality of life. Dickens's effort to articulate and focus connections between the abstract forms of life, the demeanour of the people and even the landscape are a striking imaginative triumph in the book.

At first his eye is on the institutional establishments from which England may learn:

Whatever the defects of American universities may be, they disseminate no prejudices; rear no bigots; dig up the buried ashes of no old superstitions; never interpose between the people and their improvement; exclude no man because of his religious opinions; above all, in their whole course of study and instruction, recognize a world, and a broad one too, lying beyond the college walls.

Soon he progresses to more complex examples. In the inordinate space given to the education of deaf-and-dumb Laura Bridgman we are shown a full-dress instance of what the positive democratic philosophy of America can do. Where others would abandon their natural outcasts, their maimed and deformed, the American commitment to optimism, effort, reform, perfectibility and equality conditions it to rescue even its very least. From being a wild animal, Laura Bridgman learns humanity and is helped to take a place in

57. See S. M. Lipset, 'Harriet Martineau's America', in Harriet Martineau, *Society in America*, ed. S. M. Lipset (New York, 1962, and Gloucester, Mass. 1968), pp. 5 ff.

society. It would be difficult to underestimate the significance – even to *religious* significance – Dickens saw in the process.

Dickens admired those American 'institutions' which treated their inmates as *human beings*, whether they were blind, mad, indigent, orphaned, delinquent or criminal. He has a few reservations about too-liberal prisons, but great praise for the American 'cell block' system, which gives prisoners an earnest of social being, and nothing but condemnation for the methods of 'solitary confinement' which he also saw being developed. Just as he examines the health of the country[58] in terms of its climate, its manners – even to the unhygienic practice of spitting – and its politics – 'A hundred times in every week, some new most paltry exhibition of that narrow-minded and injurious Party Spirit which is the Simoom of America, sickening and blighting everything of wholesome life within its reach ...' – so his primary criticism of the system of solitary confinement in prisons is its effect upon the health of the prisoner, physical, mental and spiritual. He conjures up a nightmare vision of total breakdown (see pp. 153–6).[59]

58. The imagery gives interesting connections with Tobias Smollett's *Travels through France and Italy* (1766), and *The Expedition of Humphrey Clinker* (1770).

59. In May, 1844, Henry James, Sr, suffered a breakdown which he later described as follows:

'One day, however, towards the close of May, having eaten a comfortable dinner, I remained sitting at the table after the family had dispersed, idly gazing at the embers in the grate, thinking of nothing, and feeling only the exhilaration incident to a good digestion, when suddenly – in a lightning-flash as it were – "fear came upon me, and trembling, which made all my bones to shake." To all appearance it was a perfectly insane and abject terror, without ostensible cause, and only to be accounted for, to my perplexed imagination, by some damned shape squatting invisible to me within the precincts of the room, and raying out from his fetid personality influences fatal to life. The thing had not lasted ten seconds before I felt myself a wreck; that is, reduced from a state of firm, vigorous, joyful manhood to one of almost helpless infancy.' Henry James, Sr, *Society the Redeemed Form of Man* (1879), quoted from F. O. Matthiessen, ed., *The James Family* (New York, 1961), p. 161.

The episode occurred when James, as he later saw, was refusing to admit even to himself that his deepest views of religion and life had altered.

The nature of the apparition as a projection of suppressed self and James's reflections on panic fear bear interestingly on Dickens's description of the solitary prisoner's 'phantom in the corner'. Was Dickens sublimating an apprehension about American life and what it was doing to him which he was not ready to acknowledge directly?

Dickens discovered to his satisfaction that the institution of slavery had an adverse effect upon the land:

The tract of country through which it takes its course was once productive; but the soil has been exhausted by the system of employing a great amount of slave labour in forcing crops, without strengthening the land: and it is now little better than a sandy desert overgrown with trees. Dreary and uninteresting as its aspect is, I was glad to the heart to find anything on which one of the curses of this horrible institution has fallen; and had greater pleasure in contemplating the withered ground, than the richest and most thriving cultivation in the same place could possibly have afforded me.

In this district, as in all others where slavery sits brooding (I have frequently heard this admitted, even by those who are its warmest advocates:) there is an air of ruin and decay abroad, which is inseparable from the system. The barns and outhouses are mouldering away; the sheds are patched and half roofless; the log cabins (built in Virginia with external chimneys made of clay or wood) are squalid in the last degree. There is no look of decent comfort anywhere. The miserable stations by the railway side; the great wild woodyards, whence the engine is supplied with fuel; the negro children rolling on the ground before the cabin doors, with dogs and pigs; the biped beasts of burden slinking past: gloom and dejection are upon them all.

From this point in the *Notes* there is a shift of focus from the institutional to the land itself, and while he is physically moving inland, it is tempting to see his picture of the American 'West' (as it then was) as symbolic of his sense of the inner meaning of the more settled areas. At the least it may reflect a mapping, intentional or unintentional, of his feelings about the institutions and manners he has been experiencing on to the landscape of the interior.

An amount of decay had been hinted at on his trip to inspect the factories of Lowell, Mass. (see pp. 112–13). It becomes progressively emphasized and is the keynote of the latter half of the book. The very trees and vegetation of the wilderness are in a state of perpetual decomposition. Far from an Eden, we are in a land where an effort at civilization has been made and is failing:

Then there were new settlements and detached log-cabins and frame-houses, full of interest for strangers from an old country: cabins with simple ovens, outside, made of clay; and lodgings for the pigs, nearly as good as many of the human quarters; broken windows, patched with worn-out hats, old clothes, old boards, fragments of blankets and paper;

and home-made dressers standing in the open air without the door, whereon was ranged the household store, not hard to count, of earthen jars and pots. The eye was pained to see the stumps of great trees thickly strewn in every field of wheat, and seldom to lose the eternal swamp and dull morass, with hundreds of rotten trunks and twisted branches steeped in its unwholesome water. It was quite sad and oppressive, to come upon great tracts where settlers had been burning down the trees, and where their wounded bodies lay about, like those of murdered creatures, while here and there some charred and blackened giant reared aloft two withered arms, and seemed to call down curses on his foes. . . .

At lengthened intervals a log cabin, with its little space of cleared land about it, nestles under a rising ground, and sends its thread of blue smoke curling up into the sky. It stands in the corner of the poor field of wheat, which is full of great unsightly stumps, like earthy butchers'-blocks. Sometimes the ground is only just now cleared: the felled trees lying yet upon the soil: and the log-house only this morning begun. As we pass this clearing, the settler leans upon his axe or hammer, and looks wistfully at the people from the world. The children creep out of the temporary hut, which is like a gypsy tent upon the ground, and clap their hands and shout. The dog only glances round at us, and then looks up into his master's face again, as if he were rendered uneasy by any suspension of the common business, and had nothing more to do with pleasurers. And still there is the same, eternal foreground. The river has washed away its banks, and stately trees have fallen down into the stream. Some have been there so long, that they are mere dry, grizzly skeletons. Some have just toppled over, and, having earth yet about their roots, are bathing their green heads in the river, and putting forth new shoots and branches. Some are almost sliding down, as you look at them. And some were drowned so long ago, that their bleached arms start out from the middle of the current, and seem to try to grasp the boat, and drag it under water.

Dickens's imagery of decay and dissolution is immensely striking. He interweaves it at all levels of his analysis of American life. Cumulatively it takes on a life of its own, as a symbol of the inner reality of America, a nightmarish and horrific vision. The cynosure of his symbol is undoubtedly his picture of the confluence of the Mississippi and Ohio Rivers, the master-image of the swampy grave:

Nor was the scenery, as we approached the junction of the Ohio and Mississippi Rivers, at all inspiriting in its influence. The trees were stunted in their growth; the banks were low and flat; the settlements and log cabins fewer in number: their inhabitants more wan and wretched than any we had encountered yet. No songs of birds were in the air, no pleasant scents, no moving lights and shadows from swift passing clouds. Hour after hour, the changeless glare of the hot, unwinking sky, shone upon the same monotonous objects. Hour after hour, the river rolled along as wearily and slowly as the time itself . . . .

But what words shall describe the Mississippi, great father of rivers, who (praise be to Heaven) has no young children like him! An enormous ditch, sometimes two or three miles wide, running liquid mud, six miles an hour: its strong and frothy current choked and obstructed everywhere by huge logs and whole forest trees: now twining themselves together in great rafts, from the interstices of which a sedgy, lazy foam works up, to float upon the water's top: now rolling past like monstrous bodies, their tangled roots showing like matted hair; now glancing singly by like giant leeches; and now writhing round and round in the vortex of some small whirlpool, like wounded snakes. The banks low, the trees dwarfish, the marshes swarming with frogs, the wretched cabins few and far apart, their inmates hollow-cheeked and pale, the weather very hot, mosquitoes penetrating into every crack and crevice of the boat, mud and slime on everything: nothing pleasant in its aspect, but the harmless lightning which flickers every night upon the dark horizon.

It is impossible to shake off the feeling that the episodes which follow are successive attempts to encapsulate the nature of his experience in America, and if a progressive loss of ability to explain in a common-sense and analytical manner is involved, if Dickens is retreating in a significant sense from the task he originally set himself, it is also true that he is falling back on – and developing – techniques of communication present in his major fiction. Dickens the novelist and Dickens the mythicist are the spirits brooding over the latter events of his American journey.

The disappointing flatness of the Looking-Glass prairie summarizes Dickens's sense of the sameness and dullness of American life, which has previously been a running theme in the book. After an attempt to cheer himself up by a side-trip to Canada, where he hopes desperately to discover a 'British' civilization somewhere in the New World,[60] he returns for a last glimpse of America in a

60 . How else explain the extent to which he is appalled by the rudeness and obscenities in the guest book on the British side of Niagara (pp. 244–5)?

Shaker village. Whatever qualities the Shakers possessed for others – and it is now thought that their art and handicraft were a considerable influence on modern design – Dickens sees in them a moribund community, America *in extremis*, and the picture of their zombie-like, posthumous existence forms a fitting conclusion to his first experience of America.

*

The significance of Dickens's American journey in his career is quite possibly greater than is commonly thought. He left England as one kind of reformer and he returned another. This movement 'right-ward' he had seen in other, earlier travellers, and had thought himself armed against it. His experience did not turn him into a Tory – though he wrote Forster that it might do to many (see p. 306) – but it drew a line beyond which he would not trespass. 'Democracy' could go too far, he found, in that side of life in America where privacy and personal liberties were largely eroded. He seems to have come to feel, though he does not state it directly, that the absence of these qualities was the other face of what he admired, that interest in others and that equal treatment symbolized in the treatment of patients in certain mental hospitals, of factory girls in Lowell, of prisoners in cell blocks.

The trip appears also to have given Dickens further insight into the nature of evil. Depths of hypocrisy, malice, duplicity appear to have been unveiled to him and he embodied them in the book to which he addressed himself upon completion of the *Notes*, *Martin Chuzzlewit*. A third of the way through the novel, Dickens sent his titular hero to America, to sample a caricature version of his own experience, but even before he transferred his novel to American soil he had already projected the characters of British villains (Pecksniff, Tigg, Jonas), whose malignancy and depravity touch upon chords not before sounded by him.

It may be that Dickens underwent a form of psychic collapse in America – though to the public eye he fulfilled his outward obligations. A sense of spiritual strain and chaotic feeling, of an upheaval of personality, is difficult to suppress. He strove for a kind of balance, even in the act of crystallizing this discontent, through his letters home during the trip, a selection of which is included in this volume (pp. 301–328), embodying manageable if disturbing visions of America there and in the composition of *American Notes* itself. He regained his balance partly by this professional involvement in turning many of his impressions to account and partly by the suppression of a range of feelings. That he was in specifiable ways a different man, as an emotional and political being, after his first American trip, seems certain.

SELECTED FURTHER READING

A. O. J. COCKSHUT *The Imagination of Charles Dickens* (London, 1961).

PHILIP COLLINS *Dickens and Education* (London, 1965).

R. J. CRUIKSHANK *Charles Dickens and Early Victorian England* (London, 1949).

G. H. FORD *Dickens and His Readers* (Princeton, 1955).

W. E. HOUGHTON *The Victorian Frame of Mind 1830–1870* (New Haven, 1957).

HUMPHREY HOUSE *The Dickens World* (London, 1941).

EDGAR JOHNSON *Charles Dickens: His Tragedy and Triumph*, 2 vols. (London, 1953).

STEVEN MARCUS *Dickens From Pickwick to Dombey* (London, 1965).

J. HILLIS MILLER *Charles Dickens: The World of His Novels* (London, 1958).

GEORGE ORWELL 'Charles Dickens', *Critical Essays* (London, 1946).

ANGUS WILSON *The World of Charles Dickens* (London, 1970).

EDMUND WILSON 'Dickens: The Two Scrooges', *The Wound and the Bow* (London, 1942).

ACKNOWLEDGEMENTS

THE editors wish to thank the following people for their help and advice: Peter Burke, Howell Daniels, A. G. S. Enser (Borough Librarian of Eastbourne), Beynon John, Stuart Morgan, Angus Ross, T. J. Sheppard (Public Relations Manager, Canadian Pacific).

ACKNOWLEDGMENTS

A NOTE ON THE TEXT

THE text of *American Notes for General Circulation* has been established by comparing copies of the following editions, all published by Chapman and Hall, London: 1842 (the first edition), 1842 (the second edition), 1850 (the Cheap Edition), 1859 (the Library Edition), 1867, 1868 (the Charles Dickens Edition) and the Gadshill Edition edited by Andrew Lang (n.d.).

Copy has been set from the Gadshill Edition, corrected in cases of substantive difference to the first edition (except where differences are establishable as errors); deletions and alterations after the first edition are noted. Additions made subsequent to the first edition have, however, been left in the text, surrounded by square brackets, and the editions of their introduction likewise noted (see Textual Notes).

Dickens retained the greatest part of his punctuation throughout all editions to which he attended (1842, 1850 and 1868). The punctuation of the Gadshill Edition is followed in general, but in a few cases where the first edition offers a superior alternative, either in respect of clarity of sense, artistic point or Dickens's more usual practice, the original punctuation (or spelling) has been silently restored.

*Facsimile of the title page
of the first edition*

AMERICAN NOTES

FOR

GENERAL CIRCULATION.

———◆———

BY CHARLES DICKENS.

IN TWO VOLUMES.

VOL. I.

LONDON:
CHAPMAN AND HALL, 186, STRAND.
MDCCCXLII.

I DEDICATE

THIS BOOK

TO THOSE FRIENDS OF MINE

IN AMERICA

WHO,

GIVING ME A WELCOME

I MUST EVER GRATEFULLY

AND PROUDLY REMEMBER,

LEFT MY JUDGMENT

FREE;

AND WHO,

LOVING THEIR COUNTRY,

CAN BEAR THE TRUTH,

WHEN IT IS TOLD

GOOD HUMOUREDLY,

AND IN A KIND SPIRIT.

Dedication deleted in 1859

PREFACE TO
THE CHEAP EDITION*

It is nearly eight years since this book was first published. I present it, unaltered, in the Cheap Edition; and such of my opinions as it expresses, are quite unaltered too.

My readers have opportunities of judging for themselves whether the influences and tendencies which I distrust in America, have any existence not in my imagination. They can examine for themselves whether there has been anything in the public career of that country during these past eight years, or whether there is anything in its present position, at home or abroad, which suggests that those influences and tendencies really do exist. As they find the fact, they will judge me. If they discern any evidence of wrong-going in any direction that I have indicated, they will acknowledge that I had reason in what I wrote. If they discern no such thing, they will consider me altogether mistaken.

Prejudiced, I never have been otherwise than in favour of the United States. No visitor can ever have set foot on those shores, with a stronger faith in the Republic than I had, when I landed in America.

I purposely abstain from extending these observations to any length. I have nothing to defend, or to explain away. The truth is the truth; and neither childish absurdities, nor unscrupulous contradictions, can make it otherwise. The earth would still move round the sun, though the whole Catholic Church said No.

I have many friends in America, and feel a grateful interest in the country. To represent me as viewing it with ill-nature, animosity, or partisanship, is merely to do a very foolish thing, which is always a very easy one: and which I have disregarded for eight years, and could disregard for eighty more.

London, *June 22, 1850.*

---

*Preface added in 1850. [Ed.]

PREFACE*

MY readers have opportunities of judging for themselves whether the influences and tendencies which I distrusted in America, had, at that time, any existence but in my imagination. They can examine for themselves whether there has been anything in the public career of that country since, at home or abroad, which suggests that those influences and tendencies really did exist. As they find the fact, they will judge me. If they discern any evidences of wrong-going, in any direction that I have indicated, they will acknowledge that I had reason in what I wrote. If they discern no such indications, they will consider me altogether mistaken – but not wilfully.

Prejudiced, I am not, and never have been, otherwise than in favour of the United States. I have many friends in America, I feel a grateful interest in the country, I hope and believe it will success-fully work out a problem of the highest importance to the whole human race. To represent me as viewing AMERICA with ill-nature, coldness, or animosity, is merely to do a very foolish thing: which is always a very easy one.

---

* This Preface, mostly a shortened version of the Preface of 1850, first appeared in the Library Edition (1859) and was reprinted in the Charles Dickens Edition (1868). [Ed.]

CONTENTS

AMERICAN NOTES
FOR GENERAL CIRCULATION

CHAPTER I

Going Away

I SHALL never forget the one-fourth serious and three-fourths comical astonishment, with which, on the morning of the third of January eighteen-hundred-and-forty-two, I opened the door of, and put my head into, a 'state-room' on board the Britannia steam-packet, twelve hundred tons burden per register, bound for Halifax and Boston, and carrying Her Majesty's mails.

That this state-room had been specially engaged for 'Charles Dickens, Esquire, and Lady,' was rendered sufficiently clear even to my scared intellect by a very small manuscript, announcing the fact, which was pinned on a very flat quilt, covering a very thin mattress, spread like a surgical plaster on a most inaccessible shelf. But that this was the state-room concerning which Charles Dickens, Esquire, and Lady, had held daily and nightly conferences for at least four months preceding: that this could by any possibility be that small snug chamber of the imagination, which Charles Dickens, Esquire, with the spirit of prophecy strong upon him, had always foretold would contain at least one little sofa, and which his lady, with a modest yet most magnificent sense of its limited dimensions, had from the first opined would not hold more than two enormous portmanteaus in some odd corner out of sight (portmanteaus which could now no more be got in at the door, not to say stowed away, than a giraffe could be persuaded or forced into a flower-pot): that this utterly impracticable, thoroughly hopeless, and profoundly preposterous box, had the remotest reference to, or connection with, those chaste and pretty, not to say gorgeous little bowers, sketched by a masterly hand, in the highly varnished lithographic plan hanging up in the agent's counting-house in the city of London: that this room of state, in short, could be anything but a pleasant fiction and cheerful jest of the captain's, invented and put in practice for the better relish and enjoyment of the real state-room presently to be disclosed: – these were truths which I really could not, for the moment, bring my mind at all to bear upon or comprehend. And I sat down upon a kind of horsehair slab, or perch, of which there were two within; and looked, without any expression of countenance whatever, at some friends who had come on board with us, and who were crushing their faces into all manner of shapes by endeavouring to squeeze them through the small doorway.

We had experienced a pretty smart shock before coming below, which, but that we were the most sanguine people living, might have prepared us for the worst. The imaginative artist to whom I have already made allusion, has depicted in the same great work, a chamber of almost interminable perspective, furnished, as Mr Robins [1] would say, in a style of more than Eastern splendour, and filled (but not inconveniently so) with groups of ladies and gentlemen, in the very highest state of enjoyment and vivacity. Before descending into the bowels of the ship, we had passed from the deck into a long narrow apartment, not unlike a gigantic hearse with windows in the sides; having at the upper end a melancholy stove, at which three or four chilly stewards were warming their hands; while on either side, extending down its whole dreary length, was a long, long table, over each of which a rack, fixed to the low roof, and stuck full of drinking-glasses and cruet-stands, hinted dismally at rolling seas and heavy weather. I had not at that time seen the ideal presentment of this chamber which has since gratified me so much, but I observed that one of our friends [2] who had made the arrangements for our voyage, turned pale on entering, retreated on the friend behind him, smote his forehead involuntarily, and said, below his breath, 'Impossible! it cannot be!' or words to that effect. He recovered himself however by a great effort, and after a preparatory cough or two, cried, with a ghastly smile which is still before me, looking at the same time round the walls, 'Ha! the breakfast-room, steward – eh?' We all foresaw what the answer must be: we knew the agony he suffered. He had often spoken of *the saloon*; had taken in and lived upon the pictorial idea; had usually given us to understand, at home, that to form a just conception of it, it would be necessary to multiply the size and furniture of an ordinary drawing-room by seven, and then fall short of the reality. When the man in reply avowed the truth; the blunt, remorseless, naked truth; 'This is the saloon, sir' – he actually reeled beneath the blow.

In persons who were so soon to part, and interpose between their else daily communication the formidable barrier of many thousand miles of stormy space, and who were for that reason anxious to cast no other cloud, not even the passing shadow of a moment's disappointment or discomfiture, upon the short interval of happy companionship that yet remained to them – in persons so situated, the natural transition from these first surprises was obviously into peals of hearty laughter; and I can report that I, for one, being still seated upon the slab or perch before mentioned, roared outright until the vessel rang again. Thus, in less than two minutes after coming upon it for the first time, we all by common consent agreed that this state-room was the pleasantest and most facetious and capital contrivance possible; and that to have had it one inch larger, would have been quite a disagreeable and deplorable state of things. And with this; and with showing how, – by very nearly closing the door, and twining in and out like serpents, and by counting the little washing-slab as standing-room, – we could manage to insinuate four people into it, all at one time; and entreating each other to observe how very airy it was (in dock), and how there was a beautiful port-hole which could be kept open all day (weather permitting), and how there was quite a large bull's-eye just over the looking-glass which would render shaving a perfectly easy and delightful process (when the ship didn't roll too much); we arrived, at last, at the unanimous conclusion that it was rather spacious than otherwise: though I do verily believe that, deducting the two berths, one above the other, than which nothing smaller for sleeping in was ever made except coffins, it was no bigger than one of those hackney cabriolets which have the door behind, and shoot their fares out, like sacks of coals, upon the pavement.

Having settled this point to the perfect satisfaction of all parties, concerned and unconcerned, we sat down round the fire in the ladies' cabin – just to try the effect. It was rather dark, certainly; but somebody said, 'of course it would be light, at sea,' a proposition to which we all assented; echoing 'of course, of course;' though it would be exceedingly difficult to say why we thought so. I remember, too, when we had discovered and exhausted another topic of consolation in the circumstance of this ladies' cabin adjoining our state-room, and the consequently immense feasibility of sitting there at all times and seasons, and had fallen into a momentary silence, leaning our faces on our hands and looking at the fire, one of our party said, with the solemn air of a man who had made a discovery, 'What a relish mulled claret will have down here!' which appeared to strike us all most forcibly; as though there were something spicy and high-flavoured in cabins, which essentially improved that composition, and rendered it quite incapable of perfection anywhere else.

There was a stewardess, too, actively engaged in producing clean sheets and tablecloths from the very entrails of the sofas, and from unexpected lockers, of such artful mechanism, that it made one's head ache to see them opened one after another, and rendered it quite a distracting circumstance to follow her proceedings, and to find that every nook and corner and individual piece of furniture was something else besides what it pretended to be, and was a mere trap and deception and place of secret stowage, whose ostensible purpose was its least useful one.

God bless that stewardess for her piously fraudulent account of January voyages! God bless her for her clear recollection of the companion passage of last year, when nobody was ill, and everybody danced from morning to night, and it was 'a run' of twelve days, and a piece of the purest frolic, and delight, and jollity! All happiness be with her for her bright face and her pleasant Scotch tongue, which had sounds of old Home in it for my fellow traveller; and for her predictions of fair winds and fine weather (all wrong, or I shouldn't be half so fond of her); and for the ten thousand small fragments of genuine womanly tact, by which, without piecing them elaborately together, and patching them up into shape and form and case and pointed application, she nevertheless did plainly show that all young mothers on one side of the Atlantic were near and close at hand to their little children left upon the other; and that what seemed to the uninitiated a serious journey, was, to those who were in the secret, a mere frolic, to be sung about and whistled at! Light be her heart, and gay her merry eyes, for years!

The state-room had grown pretty fast; but by this time it had expanded into something quite bulky, and almost boasted a bay-window to view the sea from. So we went upon deck again in high spirits; and there, everything was in such a state of bustle and active preparation, that the blood quickened its pace, and whirled through one's veins on that clear frosty morning with involuntary mirthfulness. For every gallant ship was riding slowly up and down, and every little boat was plashing noisily in the water; and knots of people stood upon the wharf, gazing with a kind of 'dread delight' on the far-famed fast American steamer; and one party of men were 'taking in the milk,' or, in other words, getting the cow on board; and another were filling the icehouses to the very throat with fresh provisions; with butchers'-meat and garden-stuff, pale suckingpigs, calves' heads in scores, beef, veal, and pork, and poultry out of all proportion; and others were coiling ropes, and busy with oakum yarns; and others were lowering heavy packages into the hold; and the purser's head was barely visible as it loomed in a state of exquisite perplexity from the midst of a vast pile of passengers' luggage; and there seemed to be nothing going on anywhere, or uppermost in the mind of anybody, but preparations for this mighty voyage. This, with the bright cold sun, the bracing air, the crisply-curling water, the thin white crust of morning ice upon the decks which crackled with a sharp and cheerful sound beneath the lightest tread, was irresistible. And when, again upon the shore, we turned and saw from the vessel's mast her name signalled in flags of joyous colours, and fluttering by their side the beautiful American banner with its stars and stripes, – the long three thousand miles and more, and, longer still, the six whole months of absence, so dwindled and faded, that the ship had gone out and come home again, and it was broad spring already in the Coburg Dock at Liverpool.

I have not inquired among my medical acquaintance, whether Turtle, and cold Punch, with Hock, Champagne, and Claret, and all the slight et cetera usually included in an unlimited order for a good dinner – especially when it is left to the liberal construction of my faultless friend, Mr Radley, of the Adelphi Hotel[3] – are peculiarly calculated to suffer a sea-change; or whether a plain mutton-chop, and a glass or two of sherry, would be less likely of conversion into foreign and disconcerting material. My own opinion is, that whether one is discreet or indiscreet in these particulars, on the eve of a sea-voyage, is a matter of little consequence; and that, to use a common phrase, 'it comes to very much the same thing in the end.' Be this as it may, I know that the dinner of that day was undeniably perfect; that it comprehended all these items, and a great many more; and that we all did ample justice to it. And I know too, that, bating a certain tacit avoidance of any allusion to to-morrow; such as may be supposed to prevail between delicate-minded turnkeys, and a sensitive prisoner who is to be hanged next morning; we got on very well, and, all things considered, were merry enough.

When the morning – *the* morning – came, and we met at breakfast, it was curious to see how eager we all were to prevent a moment's pause in the conversation, and how astoundingly gay everybody was: the forced spirits of each member of the little party having as much likeness to his natural mirth, as hot-house peas at five guineas the quart, resemble in flavour the growth of the dews, and air, and rain of Heaven. But as one o'clock, the hour for going aboard, drew near, this volubility dwindled away by little and little, despite the most persevering efforts to the contrary, until at last, the matter being now quite desperate, we threw off all disguise; openly speculated upon where we should be this time to-morrow, this time next day, and so forth; and entrusted a vast number of messages to those who intended returning to town that night, which were to be delivered at home and elsewhere without fail, within the very shortest possible space of time after the arrival of the railway train at Euston Square. And commissions and remembrances do so crowd upon one at such a time, that we were still busied with this employment when we found ourselves fused, as it were, into a dense conglomeration of passengers and passengers' friends and passengers' luggage, all jumbled together on the deck of a small steamboat, and panting and snorting off to the packet, which had worked out of dock yesterday afternoon and was now lying at her moorings in the river.

And there she is! all eyes are turned to where she lies, dimly discernible through the gathering fog of the early winter afternoon; every finger is pointed in the same direction; and murmurs of interest and admiration – as 'How beautiful she looks!' 'How trim she is!' – are heard on every side. Even the lazy gentleman with his hat on one side and his hands in his pockets, who has dispensed so much consolation by inquiring with a yawn of another gentleman whether he is 'going across' – as if it were a ferry – even he condescends to look that way, and nod his head, as who should say, 'No mistake about *that:*' and not even the sage Lord Burleigh in his nod,[4] included half so much as this lazy gentleman of might who has made the passage (as everybody on board has found out already; it's impossible to say how) thirteen times without a single accident! There is another passenger very much wrapped-up, who has been frowned down by the rest, and morally trampled upon and crushed, for presuming to inquire with a timid interest how long it is since the poor President went down.[5] He is standing close to the lazy gentleman, and says with a faint smile that he believes She is a very strong Ship; to which the lazy gentleman, looking first in his questioner's eye and then very hard in the wind's, answers unexpectedly and ominously, that She need be. Upon this the lazy gentleman instantly falls very low in the popular estimation, and the passengers, with looks of defiance, whisper to each other that he is an ass, and an impostor, and clearly don't know anything at all about it.

But we are made fast alongside the packet, whose huge red funnel is smoking bravely, giving rich promise of serious intentions. Packing-cases, portmanteaus, carpet-bags, and boxes, are already passed from hand to hand, and hauled on board with breathless rapidity. The officers, smartly dressed, are at the gangway handing the passengers up the side, and hurrying the men. In five minutes' time, the little steamer is utterly deserted, and the packet is beset and over-run by its late freight, who instantly pervade the whole ship, and are to be met with by a dozen in every nook and corner: swarming down below with their own baggage, and stumbling over other people's; disposing themselves comfortably in wrong cabins, and creating a most horrible confusion by having to turn out again; madly bent upon opening locked doors, and on forcing a passage into all kinds of out-of-the-way places where there is no thoroughfare; sending wild stewards, with elfin hair, to and fro upon the breezy decks on unintelligible errands, impossible of execution: and in short, creating the most extraordinary and bewildering tumult. In the midst of all this, the lazy gentleman, who seems to have no luggage of any kind—not so much as a friend, even – lounges up and down the hurricane-deck, coolly puffing a cigar; and, as this unconcerned demeanour again exalts him in the opinion of those who have leisure to observe his proceedings, every time he looks up at the masts, or down at the decks, or over the side, they look there too, as wondering whether he sees anything wrong anywhere, and hoping that, in case he should, he will have the goodness to mention it.

What have we here? The captain's boat! and yonder the captain himself. Now, by all our hopes and wishes, the very man he ought to be![6] A well-made, tight-built, dapper little fellow; with a ruddy face, which is a letter of invitation to shake him by both hands at once; and with a clear blue honest eye, that it does one good to see one's sparkling image in. 'Ring the bell!' 'Ding, ding, ding!' the very bell is in a hurry. 'Now for the shore – who's for the shore?' – 'These gentlemen, I am sorry to say.' They are away, and never said, Good b'ye. Ah! now they wave it from the little boat. 'Good b'ye! Good b'ye!' Three cheers from them; three more from us; three more from them: and they are gone.

To and fro, to and fro, to and fro again a hundred times! This waiting for the latest mail-bags is worse than all. If we could have gone off in the midst of that last burst, we should have started triumphantly: but to lie here, two hours and more, in the damp fog, neither staying at home nor going abroad, is letting one gradually down into the very depths of dulness and low spirits. A speck in the mist, at last! That's something. It is the boat we wait for! That's more to the purpose. The captain appears on the paddle-box with his speaking trumpet; the officers take their stations; all hands are on the alert; the flagging hopes of the passengers revive; the cooks pause in their savoury work, and look out with faces full of interest. The boat comes alongside; the bags are dragged in anyhow, and flung down for the moment anywhere. Three cheers more: and as the first one rings upon our ears, the vessel throbs like a strong giant that has just received the breath of life; the two great wheels turn fiercely round for the first time; and the noble ship, with wind and tide astern, breaks proudly through the lashed and foaming water.

CHAPTER 2

The Passage Out

WE all dined together that day; and a rather formidable party we were: no fewer than eighty-six strong. The vessel being pretty deep in the water, with all her coals on board and so many passengers, and the weather being calm and quiet, there was but little motion; so that before the dinner was half over, even those passengers who were most distrustful of themselves plucked up amazingly; and those who in the morning had returned to the universal question, 'Are you a good sailor?' a very decided negative, now either parried the inquiry with the evasive reply, 'Oh! I suppose I'm no worse than anybody else;' or, reckless of all moral obligations, answered boldly 'Yes:' and with some irritation too, as though they would add, 'I should like to know what you see in *me*, sir, particularly, to justify suspicion!'

Notwithstanding this high tone of courage and confidence, I could not but observe that very few remained long over their wine; and that everybody had an unusual love of the open air; and that the favourite and most coveted seats were invariably those nearest to the door. The tea-table, too, was by no means as well attended as the dinner-table; and there was less whist-playing than might have been expected. Still, with the exception of one lady, who had retired with some precipitation at dinner-time, immediately after being assisted to the finest cut of a very yellow boiled leg of mutton with very green capers, there were no invalids as yet; and walking, and smoking, and drinking of brandy-and-water (but always in the open air), went on with unabated spirit, until eleven o'clock or thereabouts, when 'turning in' – no sailor of seven hours' experience talks of going to bed – became the order of the night. The perpetual tramp of boot-heels on the decks gave place to a heavy silence, and the whole human freight was stowed away below, excepting a very few stragglers, like myself, who were probably, like me, afraid to go there.

To one unaccustomed to such scenes, this is a very striking time on shipboard. Afterwards, and when its novelty had long worn off, it never ceased to have a peculiar interest and charm for me. The gloom through which the great black mass holds its direct and certain course; the rushing water, plainly heard, but dimly seen; the broad, white, glistening track, that follows in the vessel's wake; the men on the look-out forward, who would be scarcely visible against the dark sky, but for their blotting out some score of glistening stars; the helmsman at the wheel, with the illuminated card before him, shining, a speck of light amidst the darkness, like something sentient and of Divine intelligence; the melancholy sighing of the wind through block, and rope, and chain; the gleaming forth of light from every crevice, nook, and tiny piece of glass about the decks, as though the ship were filled with fire in hiding, ready to burst through any outlet, wild with its resistless power of death and ruin. At first, too, and even when the hour, and all the objects it exalts, have come to be familiar, it is difficult, alone and thoughtful, to hold them to their proper shapes and forms. They change with the wandering fancy; assume the semblance of things left far away; put on the well-remembered aspect of favourite places dearly loved; and even people them with shadows. Streets, houses, rooms; figures so like their usual occupants, that they have startled me by their reality, which far exceeded, as it seemed to me, all power of mine to conjure up the absent; have, many and many a time, at such an hour, grown suddenly out of objects with whose real look, and use, and purpose, I was as well acquainted as with my own two hands.

My own two hands, and feet likewise, being very cold, however, on this particular occasion, I crept below at midnight. It was not exactly comfortable below. It was decidedly close; and it was impossible to be unconscious of the presence of that extraordinary compound of strange smells, which is to be found nowhere but on board ship, and which is such a subtle perfume that it seems to enter at every pore of the skin, and whisper of the hold. Two passengers' wives (one of them my own) lay already in silent agonies on the sofa; and one lady's maid (*my* lady's) was a mere bundle on the floor, execrating her destiny, and pounding her curl-papers among the stray boxes. Everything sloped the wrong way: which in itself was an aggravation scarcely to be borne. I had left the door open, a moment before, in the bosom of a gentle declivity, and, when I turned to shut it, it was on the summit of a lofty eminence. Now every plank and timber creaked, as if the ship were made of wicker-work; and now crackled, like an enormous fire of the driest possible twigs. There was nothing for it but bed; so I went to bed.

It was pretty much the same for the next two days, with a tolerably fair wind and dry weather. I read in bed (but to this hour I don't know what) a good deal; and reeled on deck a little; drank cold brandy-and-water with an unspeakable disgust, and ate hard biscuit perseveringly: not ill, but going to be.

It is the third morning. I am awakened out of my sleep by a dismal shriek from my wife, who demands to know whether there's any danger. I rouse myself, and look out of bed. The water-jug is plunging and leaping like a lively dolphin; all the smaller articles are afloat, except my shoes, which are stranded on a carpet-bag, high and dry, like a couple of coal-barges. Suddenly I see them spring into the air, and behold the looking-glass, which is nailed to the wall, sticking fast upon the ceiling. At the same time the door entirely disappears, and a new one is opened in the floor. Then I begin to comprehend that the state-room is standing on its head.

Before it is possible to make any arrangement at all compatible with this novel state of things, the ship rights. Before one can say 'Thank Heaven!' she wrongs again. Before one can cry she *is* wrong, she seems to have started forward, and to be a creature actually running of its own accord, with broken knees and failing legs, through every variety of hole and pitfall, and stumbling constantly. Before one can so much as wonder, she takes a high leap into the air. Before she has well done that, she takes a deep dive into the water. Before she has gained the surface, she throws a summerset.[1] The instant she is on her legs, she rushes backward. And so she goes on staggering, heaving, wrestling, leaping, diving, jumping, pitching, throbbing, rolling, and rocking: and going through all these movements, sometimes by turns, and sometimes all together: until one feels disposed to roar for mercy.

A steward passes. 'Steward!' 'Sir?' 'What *is* the matter? what *do* you call this?' 'Rather a heavy sea on, sir, and a head-wind.'

A head-wind! Imagine a human face upon the vessel's prow, with fifteen thousand Samsons in one bent upon driving her back, and hitting her exactly between the eyes whenever she attempts to advance an inch. Imagine the ship herself, with every pulse and artery of her huge body swoln and bursting under this mal-treatment, sworn to go on or die. Imagine the wind howling, the sea roaring, the rain beating: all in furious array against her. Picture the sky both dark and wild, and the clouds, in fearful sympathy with the waves, making another ocean in the air. Add to all this, the clattering on deck and down below; the tread of hurried feet; the loud hoarse shouts of seamen; the gurgling in and out of water through the scuppers; with, every now and then, the striking of a heavy sea upon the planks above, with the deep, dead, heavy sound of thunder heard within a vault; – and there is the head-wind of that January morning.

I say nothing of what may be called the domestic noises of the ship: such as the breaking of glass and crockery, the tumbling down of stewards, the gambols, overhead, of loose casks and truant dozens of bottled porter, and the very remarkable and far from exhilarating sounds raised in their various state-rooms by the seventy passengers who were too ill to get up to breakfast. I say nothing of them: for although I lay listening to this concert for three or four days, I don't think I heard it for more than a quarter of a minute, at the expiration of which term, I lay down again, excessively sea-sick.

Not sea-sick, be it understood, in the ordinary acceptation of the term: I wish I had been: but in a form which I have never seen or heard described, though I have no doubt it is very common. I lay there, all the day long, quite coolly and contentedly; with no sense of weariness, with no desire to get up, or get better, or take the air; with no curiosity, or care, or regret, of any sort or degree, saving that I think I can remember, in this universal indifference, having a kind of lazy joy – of fiendish delight, if anything so lethargic can be dignified with the title – in the fact of my wife being too ill to talk to me. If I may be allowed to illustrate my state of mind by such an example, I should say that I was exactly in the condition of the elder Mr Willet, after the incursion of the rioters into his bar at Chigwell.[2] Nothing would have surprised me. If, in the momentary illumination of any ray of intelligence that may have come upon me in the way of thoughts of Home, a goblin postman, with a scarlet coat and bell, had come into that little kennel before me, broad awake in broad day, and, apologising for being damp through walking in the sea, had handed me a letter directed to myself, in familiar characters, I am certain I should not have felt one atom of astonishment: I should have been perfectly satisfied. If Neptune himself had walked in, with a toasted shark on his trident, I should have looked upon the event as one of the very commonest everyday occurrences.

Once – once – I found myself on deck. I don't know how I got there, or what possessed me to go there, but there I was; and completely dressed too, with a huge pea-coat on, and a pair of boots such as no weak man in his senses could ever have got into. I found myself standing, when a gleam of consciousness came upon me, holding on to something. I don't know what. I think it was the boatswain: or it may have been the pump: or possibly the cow. I can't say how long I had been there; whether a day or a minute. I recollect trying to think about something (about anything in the whole wide world, I was not particular) without the smallest effect. I could not even make out which was the sea, and which the sky, for the horizon seemed drunk, and was flying wildly about, in all directions. Even in that incapable state, however, I recognised the lazy gentleman standing before me: nautically clad in a suit of shaggy blue, with an oilskin hat. But I was too imbecile, although I knew it to be he, to separate him from his dress; and tried to call him, I remember, *Pilot*. After another interval of total unconsciousness, I found he had gone, and recognised another figure in its place. It seemed to wave and fluctuate before me as though I saw it reflected in an unsteady looking-glass; but I knew it for the captain; and such was the cheerful influence of his face, that I tried to smile: yes, even then I tried to smile. I saw by his gestures that he addressed me; but it was a long time before I could make out that he remonstrated against my standing up to my knees in water – as I was; of course I don't know why. I tried to thank him, but couldn't. I could only point to my boots – or wherever I supposed my boots to be – and say in a plaintive voice, 'Cork soles:' at the same time endeavouring, I am told, to sit down in the pool. Finding that I was quite insensible, and for the time a maniac, he humanely conducted me below.

There I remained until I got better: suffering, whenever I was recommended to eat anything, an amount of anguish only second to that which is said to be endured by the apparently drowned, in the process of restoration to life. One gentleman on board had a letter of introduction to me from a mutual friend in London. He sent it below with his card, on the morning of the head-wind; and I was long troubled with the idea that he might be up, and well, and a hundred times a day expecting me to call upon him in the saloon. I imagined him one of those cast-iron images – I will not call them men – who ask, with red faces, and lusty voices, what sea-sickness means, and whether it really is as bad as it is represented to be. This was very torturing indeed; and I don't think I ever felt such perfect gratification and gratitude of heart, as I did when I heard from the ship's doctor that he had been obliged to put a large mustard poultice on this very gentleman's stomach. I date my recovery from the receipt of that intelligence.

It was materially assisted though, I have no doubt, by a heavy gale of wind, which came slowly up at sunset, when we were about ten days out, and raged with gradually increasing fury until morning, saving that it lulled for an hour a little before midnight. There was something in the unnatural repose of that hour, and in the after gathering of the storm, so inconceivably awful and tremendous, that its bursting into full violence was almost a relief.

The labouring of the ship in the troubled sea on this night I shall never forget. 'Will it ever be worse than this?' was a question I had often heard asked, when everything was sliding and bumping about, and when it certainly did seem difficult to comprehend the possibility of anything afloat being more disturbed, without toppling over and going down. But what the agitation of a steam-vessel is, on a bad winter's night in the wild Atlantic, it is impossible for the most vivid imagination to conceive. To say that she is flung down on her side in the waves, with her masts dipping into them, and that, springing up again, she rolls over on the other side, until a heavy sea strikes her with the noise of a hundred great guns, and hurls her back – that she stops, and staggers, and shivers, as though stunned, and then, with a violent throbbing at her heart, darts onward like a monster goaded into madness, to be beaten down, and battered, and crushed, and leaped on by the angry sea – that thunder, lightning, hail, and rain, and wind, are all in fierce contention for the mastery – that every plank has its groan, every nail its shriek, and every drop of water in the great ocean its howling voice – is nothing. To say that all is grand, and all appalling and horrible in the last degree, is nothing. Words cannot express it. Thoughts cannot convey it. Only a dream can call it up again, in all its fury, rage, and passion.

And yet, in the very midst of these terrors, I was placed in a situation so exquisitely ridiculous, that even then I had as strong a sense of its absurdity as I have now, and could no more help laughing than I can at any other comical incident, happening under circumstances the most favourable to its enjoyment. About midnight we shipped a sea, which forced its way through the skylights, burst open the doors above, and came raging and roaring down into the ladies' cabin, to the unspeakable consternation of my wife and a little Scotch lady – who, by the way, had previously sent a message to the captain by the stewardess, requesting him, with her compliments, to have a steel conductor immediately attached to the top of every mast, and to the chimney, in order that the ship might not be struck by lightning. They, and the handmaid before mentioned, being in such ecstasies of fear that I scarcely knew what to do with them, I naturally bethought myself of some restorative or comfortable cordial; and nothing better occurring to me, at the moment, than hot brandy-and-water, I procured a tumbler-full without delay. It being impossible to stand or sit without holding on, they were all heaped together in one corner of a long sofa – a fixture extending entirely across the cabin – where they clung to each other in momentary expectation of being drowned. When I approached this place with my specific, and was about to administer it, with many consolatory expressions, to the nearest sufferer, what was my dismay to see them all roll slowly down to the other end! And when I staggered to that end, and held out the glass once more, how immensely baffled were my good intentions by the ship giving another lurch, and their all rolling back again! I suppose I dodged them up and down this sofa, for at least a quarter of an hour, without reaching them once; and by the time I did catch them, the brandy-and-water was diminished, by constant spilling, to a teaspoonful. To complete the group, it is necessary to recognise in this disconcerted dodger, a very pale individual, who had shaved his beard and brushed his hair, last, at Liverpool: and whose only articles of dress (linen not included) were a pair of dreadnought trousers; a blue jacket, formerly admired upon the Thames at Richmond; no stockings; and one slipper.

Of the outrageous antics performed by that ship next morning; which made bed a practical joke, and getting up, by any process short of falling out, an impossibility; I say nothing. But anything like the utter dreariness and desolation that met my eyes when I, literally, 'tumbled up' on deck at noon, I never saw. Ocean and sky were all of one dull, heavy, uniform, lead colour. There was no extent of prospect even over the dreary waste that lay around us, for the sea ran high, and the horizon encompassed us like a large black hoop. Viewed from the air, or some tall bluff on shore, it would have been imposing and stupendous no doubt; but seen from the wet and rolling decks, it only impressed one giddily and painfully. In the gale of last night the life-boat had been crushed by one blow of the sea like a walnut-shell; and there it hung dangling in the air: a mere faggot of crazy boards. The planking of the paddle-boxes had been torn sheer away. The wheels were exposed and bare; and they whirled and dashed their spray about the decks at random. Chimney, white with crusted salt; topmasts struck; stormsails set; rigging all knotted, tangled, wet, and drooping: a gloomier picture it would be hard to look upon.

I was now comfortably established by courtesy in the ladies' cabin, where, besides ourselves, there were only four other passengers. First, the little Scotch lady before mentioned, on her way to join her husband at New York, who had settled there three years before. Secondly and thirdly, an honest young Yorkshireman, connected with some American house; domiciled in that same city, and carrying thither his beautiful young wife to whom he had been married but a fortnight, and who was the fairest specimen of a comely English country girl I have ever seen. Fourthly, fifthly, and lastly, another couple: newly married too, if one might judge from the endearments they frequently interchanged: of whom I know no more than that they were rather a mysterious, run-away kind of couple; that the lady had great personal attractions also; and that the gentleman carried more guns with him than Robinson Crusoe, wore a shooting-coat, and had two great dogs on board. On further consideration, I remember that he tried hot roast pig and bottled ale as a cure for sea-sickness; and that he took these remedies (usually in bed) day after day, with astonishing perseverance. I may add, for the information of the curious, that they decidedly failed.

The weather continuing obstinately and almost unprecedentedly bad, we usually straggled into this cabin, more or less faint and miserable, about an hour before noon, and lay down on the sofas to recover; during which interval, the captain would look in to communicate the state of the wind, the moral certainty of its changing to-morrow (the weather is always going to improve to-morrow, at sea), the vessel's rate of sailing, and so forth. Observations there were none to tell us of, for there was no sun to take them by. But a description of one day will serve for all the rest. Here it is.

The captain being gone, we compose ourselves to read, if the place be light enough; and if not, we doze and talk alternately. At one, a bell rings, and the stewardess comes down with a steaming dish of baked potatoes, and another of roasted apples; and plates of pig's face, cold ham, salt beef; or perhaps a smoking mess of rare hot collops. We fall to upon these dainties; eat as much as we can (we have great appetites now); and are as long as possible about it. If the fire will burn (it *will* sometimes) we are pretty cheerful. If it won't, we all remark to each other that it's very cold, rub our hands, cover ourselves with coats and cloaks, and lie down again to doze, talk, and read (provided as aforesaid), until dinner-time. At five, another bell rings, and the stewardess reappears with another dish of potatoes – boiled, this time – and store of hot meat of various kinds: not forgetting the roast pig, to be taken medicinally. We sit down at table again (rather more cheerfully than before); prolong the meal with a rather mouldy dessert of apples, grapes, and oranges; and drink our wine and brandy-and-water. The bottles and glasses are still upon the table, and the oranges and so forth are rolling about according to their fancy and the ship's way, when the doctor comes down, by special nightly invitation, to join our evening rubber: immediately on whose arrival we make a party at whist, and as it is a rough night and the cards will not lie on the cloth, we put the tricks in our pockets as we take them. At whist we remain with exemplary gravity (deducting a short time for tea and toast) until eleven o'clock, or thereabouts; when the captain comes down again, in a sou'-wester hat tied under his chin, and a pilot-coat: making the ground wet where he stands. By this time the card-playing is over, and the bottles and glasses are again upon the table; and after an hour's pleasant conversation about the ship, the passengers, and things in general, the captain (who never goes to bed, and is never out of humour) turns up his collar for the deck again; shakes hands all round; and goes laughing out into the weather as merrily as to a birthday party.

As to daily news, there is no dearth of that commodity. This passenger is reported to have lost fourteen pounds at Vingt-et-un[3] in the saloon yesterday; and that passenger drinks his bottle of champagne every day, and how he does it (being only a clerk), nobody knows. The head engineer has distinctly said that there never was such times – meaning weather – and four good hands are ill, and have given in, dead beat. Several berths are full of water, and all the cabins are leaky.[4] The ship's cook, secretly swigging damaged whiskey, has been found drunk; and has been played upon by the fire-engine until quite sober. All the stewards have fallen down-stairs at various dinner-times, and go about with plasters in various places. The baker is ill, and so is the pastry-cook. A new man, horribly indisposed, has been required to fill the place of the latter officer; and has been propped and jammed up with empty casks in a little house upon deck, and commanded to roll out pie-crust, which he protests (being highly bilious) it is death to him to look at. News! A dozen murders on shore would lack the interest of these slight incidents at sea.

Divided between our rubber and such topics as these, we were running (as we thought) into Halifax Harbour, on the fifteenth night, with little wind and a bright moon – indeed, we had made the Light at its outer entrance, and put the pilot in charge – when suddenly the ship struck upon a bank of mud. An immediate rush on deck took place of course; the sides were crowded in an instant; and for a few minutes we were in as lively a state of confusion as the greatest lover of disorder would desire to see. The passengers, and guns, and water-casks, and other heavy matters, being all huddled together aft, however, to lighten her in the head, she was soon got off; and after some driving on towards an uncomfortable line of objects (whose vicinity had been announced very early in the disaster by a loud cry of 'Breakers a-head!') and much backing of paddles, and heaving of the lead into a constantly decreasing depth of water, we dropped anchor in a strange outlandish-looking nook which nobody on board could recognise, although there was land all about us, and so close that we could plainly see the waving branches of the trees.

It was strange enough, in the silence of midnight, and the dead stillness that seemed to be created by the sudden and unexpected stoppage of the engine which had been clanking and blasting in our ears incessantly for so many days, to watch the look of blank astonishment expressed in every face: beginning with the officers, tracing it through all the passengers, and descending to the very stokers and furnace-men, who emerged from below, one by one, and clustered together in a smoky group about the hatchway of the engine-room, comparing notes in whispers. After throwing up a few rockets and firing signal-guns in the hope of being hailed from the land, or at least of seeing a light – but without any other sight or sound presenting itself – it was determined to send a boat on shore. It was amusing to observe how very kind some of the passengers were, in volunteering to go ashore in this same boat: for the general good, of course: not by any means because they thought the ship in an unsafe position, or contemplated the possibility of her heeling over in case the tide were running out. Nor was it less amusing to remark how desperately unpopular the poor pilot became in one short minute. He had had his passage out from Liverpool, and during the whole voyage had been quite a notorious character, as a teller of anecdotes and cracker of jokes. Yet here were the very men who had laughed the loudest at his jests, now flourishing their fists in his face, loading him with imprecations, and defying him to his teeth as a villain!

The boat soon shoved off, with a lantern and sundry blue lights on board; and in less than an hour returned; the officer in command bringing with him a tolerably tall young tree, which he had plucked up by the roots, to satisfy certain distrustful passengers whose minds misgave them that they were to be imposed upon and ship-wrecked, and who would on no other terms believe that he had been ashore, or had done anything but fraudulently row a little way into the mist, specially to deceive them, and compass their deaths. Our captain had foreseen from the first that we must be in a place called the Eastern Passage; and so we were. It was about the last place in the world in which we had any business or reason to be, but a sudden fog, and some error on the pilot's part, were the cause.[5] We were surrounded by banks, and rocks, and shoals of all kinds, but had happily drifted, it seemed, upon the only safe speck that was to be found thereabouts. Eased by this report, and by the assurance that the tide was past the ebb, we turned in at three o'clock in the morning.

I was dressing about half-past nine next day, when the noise above hurried me on deck. When I had left it overnight, it was dark, foggy, and damp, and there were bleak hills all round us. Now, we were gliding down a smooth, broad stream, at the rate of eleven miles an hour: our colours flying gaily; our crew rigged out in their smartest clothes; our officers in uniform again; the sun shining as on a brilliant April day in England; the land stretched out on either side, streaked with light patches of snow; white wooden houses; people at their doors; telegraphs working; flags hoisted; wharfs appearing; ships; quays crowded with people; distant noises; shouts; men and boys running down steep places towards the pier: all more bright and gay and fresh to our unused eyes than words can paint them. We came to a wharf, paved with uplifted faces; got alongside, and were made fast, after some shouting and straining of cables; darted, a score of us, along the gangway, almost as soon as it was thrust out to meet us, and before it had reached the ship – and leaped upon the firm glad earth again!

I suppose this Halifax would have appeared an Elysium,[6] though it had been a curiosity of ugly dulness. But I carried away with me a most pleasant impression of the town and its inhabitants, and have preserved it to this hour. Nor was it without regret that I came home, without having found an opportunity of returning thither, and once more shaking hands with the friends I made that day.

It happened to be the opening of the Legislative Council and General Assembly, at which ceremonial the forms observed on the commencement of a new Session of Parliament in England were so closely copied, and so gravely presented on a small scale, that it was like looking at Westminster through the wrong end of a telescope. The governor,[7] as her Majesty's representative, delivered what may be called the Speech from the Throne. He said what he had to say manfully and well. The military band outside the building struck up 'God save the Queen' with great vigour before his Excellency had quite finished; the people shouted; the in's rubbed their hands; the out's shook their heads; the Government party said there never was such a good speech; the Opposition declared there never was such a bad one; the Speaker and members of the House of Assembly withdrew from the bar to say a great deal among themselves and do a little: and, in short, everything went on, and promised to go on, just as it does at home upon the like occasions.

The town is built on the side of a hill, the highest point being commanded by a strong fortress, not yet quite finished. Several streets of good breadth and appearance extend from its summit to the water-side, and are intersected by cross streets running parallel with the river. The houses are chiefly of wood. The market is abundantly supplied; and provisions are exceedingly cheap. The weather being unusually mild at that time for the season of the year, there was no sleighing: but there were plenty of those vehicles in yards and by-places, and some of them, from the gorgeous quality of their decorations, might have 'gone on' without alteration as triumphal cars in a melodrama at Astley's.[8] The day was uncommonly fine; the air bracing and healthful; the whole aspect of the town cheerful, thriving, and industrious.

We lay there seven hours, to deliver and exchange the mails. At length, having collected all our bags and all our passengers (including two or three choice spirits, who, having indulged too freely in oysters and champagne, were found lying insensible on their backs in unfrequented streets), the engines were again put in motion, and we stood off for Boston.

Encountering squally weather again in the Bay of Fundy, we tumbled and rolled about as usual all that night and all next day. On the next afternoon, that is to say, on Saturday, the twenty-second of January, an American pilot-boat came alongside, and soon afterwards the Britannia steam-packet, from Liverpool, eighteen days out, was telegraphed at Boston.[9]

The indescribable interest with which I strained my eyes, as the first patches of American soil peeped like molehills from the green sea, and followed them, as they swelled, by slow and almost imperceptible degrees, into a continuous line of coast, can hardly be exaggerated. A sharp keen wind blew dead against us; a hard frost prevailed on shore; and the cold was most severe. Yet the air was so intensely clear, and dry, and bright, that the temperature was not only endurable, but delicious.

How I remained on deck, staring about me, until we came alongside the dock, and how, though I had had as many eyes as Argus, I should have had them all wide open, and all employed on new objects – are topics which I will not prolong this chapter to discuss. Neither will I more than hint at my foreigner-like mistake, in supposing that a party of most active persons, who scrambled on board at the peril of their lives as we approached the wharf, were newsmen,[10] answering to that industrious class at home; whereas, despite the leathern wallets of news slung about the necks of some, and the broad sheets in the hands of all, they were Editors,[11] who boarded ships in person (as one gentleman in a worsted comforter informed me), 'because they liked the excitement of it.' Suffice it in this place to say, that one of these invaders, with a ready courtesy for which I thank him here most gratefully, went on before to order rooms at the hotel; and that when I followed, as I soon did, I found myself rolling through the long passages with an involuntary imitation of the gait of Mr T. P. Cooke,[12] in a new nautical melodrama.

'Dinner, if you please,' said I to the waiter.

'When?' said the waiter.

'As quick as possible,' said I.

'Right away?'[13] said the waiter.

After a moment's hesitation, I answered 'No,' at hazard.

'*Not* right away?' cried the waiter, with an amount of surprise that made me start.

I looked at him doubtfully, and returned, 'No; I would rather have it in this private room. I like it very much.'

At this, I really thought the waiter must have gone out of his mind: as I believe he would have done, but for the interposition of another man, who whispered in his ear, 'Directly.'

'Well! and that's a fact!' said the waiter, looking helplessly at me: 'Right away.'

I saw now that 'Right away' and 'Directly' were one and the same thing. So I reversed my previous answer, and sat down to dinner in ten minutes afterwards; and a capital dinner it was.

The hotel (a very excellent one) is called the Tremont House.[14] It has more galleries, colonnades, piazzas, and passages than I can remember, or the reader would believe; and is some trifle smaller than Bedford Square.

CHAPTER 3

Boston

IN all the public establishments of America, the utmost courtesy prevails. Most of our Departments are susceptible of considerable improvement in this respect, but the Custom-house above all others would do well to take example from the United States and render itself somewhat less odious and offensive to foreigners. The servile rapacity of the French officials is sufficiently contemptible; but there is a surly boorish incivility about our men, alike disgusting to all persons who fall into their hands, and discreditable to the nation that keeps such ill-conditioned curs snarling about its gates.

When I landed in America, I could not help being strongly impressed with the contrast their Custom-house presented, and the attention, politeness and good humour with which its officers discharged their duty.

As we did not land at Boston, in consequence of some detention at the wharf, until after dark, I received my first impressions of the city in walking down to the Custom-house on the morning after our arrival, which was Sunday. I am afraid to say, by the way, how many offers of pews and seats in church for that morning were made to us, by formal note of invitation, before we had half finished our first dinner in America, but if I may be allowed to make a moderate guess, without going into nicer calculation, I should say that at least as many sittings were proffered us, as would have accommodated a score or two of grown-up families. The number of creeds and forms of religion to which the pleasure of our company was requested, was in very fair proportion.

Not being able, in the absence of any change of clothes, to go to church that day, we were compelled to decline these kindnesses, one and all; and I was reluctantly obliged to forego the delight of hearing Dr Channing,[1] who happened to preach that morning for the first time in a very long interval. I mention the name of this distinguished and accomplished man (with whom I soon afterwards had the pleasure of becoming personally acquainted), that I may have the gratification of recording my humble tribute of admiration and respect for his high abilities and character; and for the bold philanthropy with which he has ever opposed himself to that most hideous blot and foul disgrace – Slavery.

To return to Boston. When I got into the streets upon this Sunday morning, the air was so clear, the houses were so bright and gay; the signboards were painted in such gaudy colours; the gilded letters were so very golden; the bricks were so very red, the stone was so very white, the blinds and area railings were so very green, the knobs and plates upon the street doors so marvellously bright and twinkling; and all so slight and unsubstantial in appearance – that every thoroughfare in the city looked exactly like a scene in a pantomime. It rarely happens in the business streets that a tradesman, if I may venture to call anybody a tradesman, where everybody is a merchant, resides above his store; so that many occupations are often carried on in one house, and the whole front is covered with boards and inscriptions. As I walked along, I kept glancing up at these boards, confidently expecting to see a few of them change into something; and I never turned a corner suddenly without looking out for the clown and pantaloon, who, I had no doubt, were hiding in a doorway or behind some pillar close at hand. As to Harlequin and Columbine,[2] I discovered immediately that they lodged (they are always looking after lodgings in a pantomime) at a very small clockmaker's one story high, near the hotel; which, in addition to various symbols and devices, almost covering the whole front, had a great dial hanging out – to be jumped through, of course.

The suburbs are, if possible, even more unsubstantial-looking than the city. The white wooden houses (so white that it makes one wink to look at them), with their green jalousie blinds, are so sprinkled and dropped about in all directions, without seeming to have any root at all in the ground; and the small churches and chapels are so prim, and bright, and highly varnished; that I almost believed the whole affair could be taken up piecemeal like a child's toy, and crammed into a little box.

The city is a beautiful one, and cannot fail, I should imagine, to impress all strangers very favourably. The private dwelling-houses are, for the most part, large and elegant; the shops extremely good; and the public buildings handsome. The State House is built upon the summit of a hill, which rises gradually at first, and afterwards by a steep ascent, almost from the water's edge. In front is a green enclosure, called the Common. The site is beautiful: and from the top there is a charming panoramic view of the whole town and neighbourhood. In addition to a variety of commodious offices, it contains two handsome chambers; in one the House of Representatives of the State hold their meetings: in the other, the Senate. Such proceedings as I saw here, were conducted with perfect gravity and decorum; and were certainly calculated to inspire attention and respect.

There is no doubt that much of the intellectual refinement and superiority of Boston, is referable to the quiet influence of the University of Cambridge,[3] which is within three or four miles of the city. The resident professors at that university are gentlemen of learning and varied attainments; and are, without one exception that I can call to mind, men who would shed a grace upon, and do honour to, any society in the civilised world. Many of the resident gentry in Boston and its neighbourhood, and I think I am not mistaken in adding, a large majority of those who are attached to the liberal professions there, have been educated at this same school. Whatever the defects of American universities may be, they disseminate no prejudices; rear no bigots; dig up the buried ashes of no old superstitions; never interpose between the people and their improvement; exclude no man because of his religious opinions; above all, in their whole course of study and instruction, recognise a world, and a broad one too, lying beyond the college walls.

It was a source of inexpressible pleasure to me to observe the almost imperceptible, but not less certain effect, wrought by this institution among the small community of Boston; and to note at every turn the humanising tastes and desires it has engendered; the affectionate friendships to which it has given rise; the amount of vanity and prejudice it has dispelled. The golden calf they worship at Boston is a pigmy compared with the giant effigies set up in other parts of that vast counting-house which lies beyond the Atlantic; and the almighty dollar sinks into something comparatively insignificant, amidst a whole Pantheon of better gods.

Above all, I sincerely believe that the public institutions and charities of this capital of Massachusetts are as nearly perfect, as the most considerate wisdom, benevolence, and humanity, can make them. I never in my life was more affected by the contemplation of happiness, under circumstances of privation and bereavement, than in my visits to these establishments.

It is a great and pleasant feature of all such institutions in America, that they are either supported by the State or assisted by the State; or (in the event of their not needing its helping hand) that they act in concert with it, and are emphatically the people's. I cannot but think, with a view to the principle and its tendency to elevate or depress the character of the industrious classes, that a Public Charity is immeasurably better than a Private Foundation, no matter how munificently the latter may be endowed. In our own country, where it has not, until within these later days, been a very popular fashion with governments to display any extraordinary regard for the great mass of the people or to recognise their existence as improvable creatures, private charities, unexampled in the history of the earth, have arisen, to do an incalculable amount of good among the destitute and afflicted. But the government of the country, having neither act nor part in them, is not in the receipt of any portion of the gratitude they inspire; and, offering very little shelter or relief beyond that which is to be found in the workhouse and the jail, has come, not unnaturally, to be looked upon by the poor rather as a stern master, quick to correct and punish, than a kind protector, merciful and vigilant in their hour of need.

The maxim that out of evil cometh good, is strongly illustrated by these establishments at home; as the records of the Prerogative Office in Doctors' Commons[4] can abundantly prove. Some immensely rich old gentleman or lady, surrounded by needy relatives, makes, upon a low average, a will a-week. The old gentleman or lady, never very remarkable in the best of times for good temper, is full of aches and pains from head to foot; full of fancies and caprices; full of spleen, distrust, suspicion, and dislike. To cancel old wills, and invent new ones, is at last the sole business of such a testator's existence; and relations and friends (some of whom have been bred up distinctly to inherit a large share of the property, and have been, from their cradles, specially disqualified from devoting themselves to any useful pursuit, on that account) are so often and so unexpectedly and summarily cut off, and re-instated, and cut off again, that the whole family, down to the remotest cousin, is kept in a perpetual fever. At length it becomes plain that the old lady or gentleman has not long to live; and the plainer this becomes, the more clearly the old lady or gentleman perceives that everybody is in a conspiracy against their poor old dying relative; wherefore the old lady or gentleman makes another last will – positively the last this time – conceals the same in a china teapot, and expires next day. Then it turns out, that the whole of the real and personal estate is divided between half-a-dozen charities; and that the dead and gone testator has in pure spite helped to do a great deal of good, at the cost of an immense amount of evil passion and misery.

The Perkins Institution and Massachusetts Asylum for the Blind, at Boston, is superintended by a body of trustees who make an annual report to the corporation.[5] The indigent blind of that state are admitted gratuitously. Those from the adjoining state of Connecticut, or from the states of Maine, Vermont, or New Hampshire, are admitted by a warrant from the state to which they respectively belong; or, failing that, must find security among their friends, for the payment of about twenty pounds English for their first year's board and instruction, and ten for the second. 'After the first year,' say the trustees, 'an account current will be opened with each pupil; he will be charged with the actual cost of his board, which will not exceed two dollars per week;' a trifle more than eight shillings English; 'and he will be credited with the amount paid for him by the state, or by his friends; also with his earnings over and above the cost of the stock which he uses; so that all his earnings over one dollar per week will be his own. By the third year it will be known whether his earnings will more than pay the actual cost of his board; if they should, he will have it at his option to remain and receive his earnings, or not. Those who prove unable to earn their own livelihood will not be retained; as it is not desirable to convert the establishment into an almshouse, or to retain any but working bees in the hive. Those who by physical or mental imbecility are disqualified from work, are thereby disqualified from being members of an industrious community; and they can be better provided for in establishments fitted for the infirm.'

I went to see this place one very fine winter morning: an Italian sky above, and the air so clear and bright on every side, that even my eyes, which are none of the best, could follow the minute lines and scraps of tracery in distant buildings. Like most other public institutions in America, of the same class, it stands a mile or two without the town, in a cheerful healthy spot; and is an airy, spacious, handsome edifice. It is built upon a height, commanding the harbour. When I paused for a moment at the door, and marked how fresh and free the whole scene was – what sparkling bubbles glanced upon the waves, and welled up every moment to the surface, as though the world below, like that above, were radiant with the bright day, and gushing over in its fulness of light: when I gazed from sail to sail away upon a ship at sea, a tiny speck of shining white, the only cloud upon the still, deep, distant blue – and, turning, saw a blind boy with his sightless face addressed that way, as though he too had some sense within him of the glorious distance: I felt a kind of sorrow that the place should be so very light, and a strange wish that for his sake it were darker. It was but momentary, of course, and a mere fancy, but I felt it keenly for all that.

The children were at their daily tasks in different rooms, except a few who were already dismissed, and were at play. Here, as in many institutions, no uniform is worn; and I was very glad of it, for two reasons. Firstly, because I am sure that nothing but senseless custom and want of thought would reconcile us to the liveries and badges we are so fond of at home. Secondly, because the absence of these things presents each child to the visitor in his or her own proper character, with its individuality unimpaired; not lost in a dull, ugly, monotonous repetition of the same unmeaning garb: which is really an important consideration. The wisdom of encouraging a little harmless pride in personal appearance even among the blind, or the whimsical absurdity of considering charity and leather breeches inseparable companions, as we do, requires no comment.

Good order, cleanliness, and comfort, pervaded every corner of the building. The various classes, who were gathered round their teachers, answered the questions put to them with readiness and intelligence, and in a spirit of cheerful contest for precedence which pleased me very much. Those who were at play, were gleesome and noisy as other children. More spiritual and affectionate friendships appeared to exist among them, than would be found among other young persons suffering under no deprivation; but this I expected and was prepared to find. It is a part of the great scheme of Heaven's merciful consideration for the afflicted.

In a portion of the building, set apart for that purpose, are workshops for blind persons whose education is finished, and who have acquired a trade, but who cannot pursue it in an ordinary manufactory because of their deprivation. Several people were at work here; making brushes, mattresses, and so forth; and the cheerfulness, industry, and good order discernible in every other part of the building, extended to this department also.

On the ringing of a bell, the pupils all repaired, without any guide or leader, to a spacious music-hall, where they took their seats in an orchestra erected for that purpose, and listened with manifest delight to a voluntary on the organ, played by one of themselves. At its conclusion, the performer, a boy of nineteen or twenty, gave place to a girl; and to her accompaniment they all sang a hymn, and afterwards a sort of chorus. It was very sad to look upon and hear them, happy though their condition unquestionably was; and I saw that one blind girl, who (being for the time deprived of the use of her limbs, by illness) sat close beside me with her face towards them, wept silently the while she listened.

It is strange to watch the faces of the blind, and see how free they are from all concealment of what is passing in their thoughts; observing which, a man with eyes may blush to contemplate the mask he wears. Allowing for one shade of anxious expression which is never absent from their countenances, and the like of which we may readily detect in our own faces if we try to feel our way in the dark, every idea, as it rises within them, is expressed with the lightning's speed and nature's truth. If the company at a rout, or drawing-room at court, could only for one time be as unconscious of the eyes upon them as blind men and women are, what secrets would come out, and what a worker of hypocrisy this sight, the loss of which we so much pity, would appear to be!

The thought occurred to me as I sat down in another room, before a girl, blind, deaf, and dumb; destitute of smell; and nearly so, of taste: before a fair young creature with every human faculty, and hope, and power of goodness and affection, inclosed within her delicate frame, and but one outward sense – the sense of touch.[6] There she was, before me; built up, as it were, in a marble cell, impervious to any ray of light, or particle of sound; with her poor white hand peeping through a chink in the wall, beckoning to some good man for help, that an Immortal soul might be awakened.

Long before I looked upon her, the help had come. Her face was radiant with intelligence and pleasure. Her hair, braided by her own hands, was bound about a head, whose intellectual capacity and development were beautifully expressed in its graceful outline, and its broad open brow; her dress, arranged by herself, was a pattern of neatness and simplicity; the work she had knitted, lay beside her; her writing-book was on the desk she leaned upon. – From the mournful ruin of such bereavement, there had slowly risen up this gentle, tender, guileless, grateful-hearted being.

Like other inmates of that house, she had a green ribbon bound round her eyelids. A doll she had dressed lay near upon the ground. I took it up, and saw that she had made a green fillet such as she wore herself, and fastened it about its mimic eyes.

She was seated in a little enclosure, made by school-desks and forms, writing her daily journal. But soon finishing this pursuit, she engaged in an animated communication with a teacher who sat beside her. This was a favourite mistress with the poor pupil. If she could see the face of her fair instructress, she would not love her less, I am sure.

I have extracted a few disjointed fragments of her history, from an account, written by that one man [7] who has made her what she is. It is a very beautiful and touching narrative; and I wish I could present it entire.

Her name is Laura Bridgman. 'She was born in Hanover, New Hampshire, on the twenty-first of December, 1829. She is described as having been a very sprightly and pretty infant, with bright blue eyes. She was, however, so puny and feeble until she was a year and a half old, that her parents hardly hoped to rear her. She was subject to severe fits, which seemed to rack her frame almost beyond her power of endurance: and life was held by the feeblest tenure: but when a year and a half old, she seemed to rally; the dangerous symptoms subsided; and at twenty months old, she was perfectly well.

'Then her mental powers, hitherto stinted in their growth, rapidly developed themselves; and during the four months of health which she enjoyed, she appears (making due allowance for a fond mother's account) to have displayed a considerable degree of intelligence.

'But suddenly she sickened again; her disease raged with great violence during five weeks, when her eyes and ears were inflamed, suppurated, and their contents were discharged. But though sight and hearing were gone for ever, the poor child's sufferings were not ended. The fever raged during seven weeks; for five months she was kept in bed in a darkened room; it was a year before she could walk unsupported, and two years before she could sit up all day. It was now observed that her sense of smell was almost entirely destroyed; and, consequently, that her taste was much blunted.

'It was not until four years of age that the poor child's bodily health seemed restored, and she was able to enter upon her apprenticeship of life and the world.

'But what a situation was hers! The darkness and the silence of the tomb were around her: no mother's smile called forth her answering smile, no father's voice taught her to imitate his sounds: – they, brothers and sisters, were but forms of matter which resisted her touch, but which differed not from the furniture of the house, save in warmth, and in the power of locomotion; and not even in these respects from the dog and the cat.

'But the immortal spirit which had been implanted within her could not die, nor be maimed nor mutilated; and though most of its avenues of communication with the world were cut off, it began to manifest itself through the others. As soon as she could walk, she began to explore the room, and then the house; she became familiar with the form, density, weight, and heat, of every article she could lay her hands upon. She followed her mother, and felt her hands and arms, as she was occupied about the house; and her disposition to imitate, led her to repeat everything herself. She even learned to sew a little, and to knit.'

The reader will scarcely need to be told, however, that the opportunities of communicating with her, were very, very limited; and that the moral effects of her wretched state soon began to appear. Those who cannot be enlightened by reason, can only be controlled by force; and this, coupled with her great privations, must soon have reduced her to a worse condition than that of the beasts that perish, but for timely and unhoped-for aid.

'At this time, I was so fortunate as to hear of the child, and immediately hastened to Hanover to see her. I found her with a well-formed figure; a strongly-marked, nervous-sanguine temperament; a large and beautifully-shaped head; and the whole system in healthy action. The parents were easily induced to consent to her coming to Boston, and on the 4th of October, 1837, they brought her to the Institution.

'For a while, she was much bewildered; and after waiting about two weeks, until she became acquainted with her new locality, and somewhat familiar with the inmates, the attempt was made to give her knowledge of arbitrary signs, by which she could interchange thoughts with others.

'There was one of two ways to be adopted: either to go on to build up a language of signs on the basis of the natural language which she had already commenced herself, or to teach her the purely arbitrary language in common use: that is, to give her a sign for every individual thing, or to give her a knowledge of letters by combination of which she might express her idea of the existence, and the mode and condition of existence, of any thing. The former would have been easy, but very ineffectual; the latter seemed very difficult, but, if accomplished, very effectual. I determined therefore to try the latter.

'The first experiments were made by taking articles in common use, such as knives, forks, spoons, keys, &c., and pasting upon them labels with their names printed in raised letters. These she felt very carefully, and soon, of course, distinguished that the crooked lines *spoon*, differed as much from the crooked lines *key*, as the spoon differed from the key in form.

'Then small detached labels, with the same words printed upon them, were put into her hands; and she soon observed that they were similar to the ones pasted on the articles. She showed her perception of this similarity by laying the label *key* upon the key, and the label *spoon* upon the spoon. She was encouraged here by the natural sign of approbation, patting on the head.

'The same process was then repeated with all the articles which she could handle; and she very easily learned to place the proper labels upon them. It was evident, however, that the only intellectual exercise was that of imitation and memory. She recollected that the label *book* was placed upon a book, and she repeated the process first from imitation, next from memory, with only the motive of love of approbation, but apparently without the intellectual perception of any relation between the things.

'After a while, instead of labels, the individual letters were given to her on detached bits of paper: they were arranged side by side so as to spell *book*, *key*, &c.; then they were mixed up in a heap and a sign was made for her to arrange them herself so as to express the words *book*, *key*, &c.; and she did so.

'Hitherto, the process had been mechanical, and the success about as great as teaching a very knowing dog a variety of tricks. The poor child had sat in mute amazement, and patiently imitated everything her teacher did; but now the truth began to flash upon her: her intellect began to work: she perceived that here was a way by which she could herself make up a sign of anything that was in her own mind, and show it to another mind; and at once her countenance lighted up with a human expression: it was no longer a dog, or parrot: it was an immortal spirit, eagerly seizing upon a new link of union with other spirits! I could almost fix upon the moment when this truth dawned upon her mind, and spread its light to her countenance; I saw that the great obstacle was over-come; and that henceforward nothing but patient and persevering, but plain and straightforward, efforts were to be used.

'The result thus far, is quickly related, and easily conceived; but not so was the process; for many weeks of apparently unprofitable labour were passed before it was effected.

'When it was said above, that a sign was made, it was intended to say, that the action was performed by her teacher, she feeling his hands, and then imitating the motion.

'The next step was to procure a set of metal types, with the different letters of the alphabet cast upon their ends; also a board, in which were square holes, into which holes she could set the types; so that the letters on their ends could alone be felt above the surface.

'Then, on any article being handed to her, for instance, a pencil, or a watch, she would select the component letters, and arrange them on her board, and read them with apparent pleasure.

'She was exercised for several weeks in this way, until her vocabulary became extensive; and then the important step was taken of teaching her how to represent the different letters by the position of her fingers, instead of the cumbrous apparatus of the board and types. She accomplished this speedily and easily, for her intellect had begun to work in aid of her teacher, and her progress was rapid.

'This was the period, about three months after she had com-menced, that the first report of her case was made, in which it was stated that "she has just learned the manual alphabet, as used by the deaf mutes, and it is a subject of delight and wonder to see how rapidly, correctly, and eagerly, she goes on with her labours. Her teacher gives her a new object, for instance, a pencil, first lets her examine it, and get an idea of its use, then teaches her how to spell it by making the signs for the letters with her own fingers: the child grasps her hand, and feels her fingers, as the different letters are formed; she turns her head a little on one side like a person listening closely; her lips are apart; she seems scarcely to breathe; and her countenance, at first anxious, gradually changes to a smile, as she comprehends the lesson. She then holds up her tiny fingers, and spells the word in the manual alphabet; next, she takes her types and arranges her letters; and last, to make sure that she is right, she takes the whole of the types composing the word, and places them upon or in contact with the pencil, or whatever the object may be."

'The whole of the succeeding year was passed in gratifying her eager inquiries for the names of every object which she could possibly handle; in exercising her in the use of the manual alphabet; in extending in every possible way her knowledge of the physical relations of things; and in proper care of her health.

'At the end of the year a report of her case was made, from which the following is an extract.

' "It has been ascertained beyond the possibility of doubt, that she cannot see a ray of light, cannot hear the least sound, and never exercises her sense of smell, if she have any. Thus her mind dwells in darkness and stillness, as profound as that of a closed tomb at midnight. Of beautiful sights, and sweet sounds, and pleasant odours, she has no conception; nevertheless, she seems as happy and playful as a bird or a lamb; and the employment of her intellectual faculties, or the acquirement of a new idea, gives her a vivid pleasure, which is plainly marked in her expressive features. She never seems to repine, but has all the buoyancy and gaiety of childhood. She is fond of fun and frolic, and when playing with the rest of the children, her shrill laugh sounds loudest of the group.

' "When left alone, she seems very happy if she have her knitting or sewing, and will busy herself for hours; if she have no occupation, she evidently amuses herself by imaginary dialogues, or by recalling past impressions; she counts with her fingers, or spells out names of things which she has recently learned, in the manual alphabet of the deaf mutes. In this lonely self-communion she seems to reason, reflect, and argue; if she spell a word wrong with the fingers of her right hand, she instantly strikes it with her left, as her teacher does, in sign of disapprobation; if right, then she pats herself upon the head, and looks pleased. She sometimes purposely spells a word wrong with the left hand, looks roguish for a moment and laughs, and then with the right hand strikes the left, as if to correct it.

' "During the year she has attained great dexterity in the use of the manual alphabet of the deaf mutes; and she spells out the words and sentences which she knows, so fast and so deftly, that only those accustomed to this language can follow with the eye the rapid motions of her fingers.

' "But wonderful as is the rapidity with which she writes her thoughts upon the air, still more so is the ease and accuracy with which she reads the words thus written by another; grasping their hands in hers, and following every movement of their fingers, as letter after letter conveys their meaning to her mind. It is in this way that she converses with her blind playmates, and nothing can more forcibly show the power of mind in forcing matter to its purpose than a meeting between them. For if great talent and skill are necessary for two pantomimes to paint their thoughts and feelings by the movements of the body, and the expression of the countenance, how much greater the difficulty when darkness shrouds them both, and the one can hear no sound!

' "When Laura is walking through a passage-way, with her hands spread before her, she knows instantly every one she meets, and passes them with a sign of recognition: but if it be a girl of her own age, and especially if it be one of her favourites, there is instantly a bright smile of recognition, and a twining of arms, a grasping of hands, and a swift telegraphing upon the tiny fingers; whose rapid evolutions convey the thoughts and feelings from the outposts of one mind to those of the other. There are questions and answers, exchanges of joy or sorrow, there are kissings and part-ings, just as between little children with all their senses."

'During this year, and six months after she had left home, her mother came to visit her, and the scene of their meeting was an interesting one.

'The mother stood some time, gazing with overflowing eyes upon her unfortunate child, who, all unconscious of her presence, was playing about the room. Presently Laura ran against her, and at once began feeling her hands, examining her dress, and trying to find out if she knew her; but not succeeding in this, she turned away as from a stranger, and the poor woman could not conceal the pang she felt, at finding that her beloved child did not know her.

'She then gave Laura a string of beads which she used to wear at home, which were recognised by the child at once, who, with much joy, put them around her neck, and sought me eagerly to say she understood the string was from her home.

'The mother now sought to caress her, but poor Laura repelled her, preferring to be with her acquaintances.

'Another article from home was now given her, and she began to look much interested; she examined the stranger much closer, and gave me to understand that she knew she came from Hanover; she even endured her caresses, but would leave her with indifference at the slightest signal. The distress of the mother was now painful to behold; for, although she had feared that she should not be recognised, the painful reality of being treated with cold indifference by a darling child, was too much for woman's nature to bear.

'After a while, on the mother taking hold of her again, a vague idea seemed to flit across Laura's mind, that this could not be a stranger; she therefore felt her hands very eagerly, while her countenance assumed an expression of intense interest; she became very pale; and then suddenly red; hope seemed struggling with doubt and anxiety, and never were contending emotions more strongly painted upon the human face: at this moment of painful uncertainty, the mother drew her close to her side, and kissed her fondly, when at once the truth flashed upon the child, and all mistrust and anxiety disappeared from her face, as with an expression of exceeding joy she eagerly nestled to the bosom of her parent, and yielded herself to her fond embraces.

'After this, the beads were all unheeded; the playthings which were offered to her were utterly disregarded; her playmates, for whom but a moment before she gladly left the stranger, now vainly strove to pull her from her mother; and though she yielded her usual instantaneous obedience to my signal to follow me, it was evidently with painful reluctance. She clung close to me, as if bewildered and fearful; and when, after a moment, I took her to her mother, she sprang to her arms, and clung to her with eager joy.

'The subsequent parting between them, showed alike the affection, the intelligence, and the resolution of the child.

'Laura accompanied her mother to the door, clinging close to her all the way, until they arrived at the threshold, where she paused, and felt around, to ascertain who was near her. Perceiving the matron, of whom she is very fond, she grasped her with one hand, holding on convulsively to her mother with the other; and thus she stood for a moment; then she dropped her mother's hand; put her handkerchief to her eyes; and turning round, clung sobbing to the matron; while her mother departed, with emotions as deep as those of her child.

*   *   *

'It has been remarked in former reports, that she can distinguish different degrees of intellect in others, and that she soon regarded, almost with contempt, a new-comer, when, after a few days, she discovered her weakness of mind. This unamiable part of her character has been more strongly developed during the past year.

'She chooses for her friends and companions, those children who are intelligent, and can talk best with her; and she evidently dislikes to be with those who are deficient in intellect, unless, indeed, she can make them serve her purposes, which she is evidently inclined to do. She takes advantage of them, and makes them wait upon her, in a manner that she knows she could not exact of others; and in various ways she shows her Saxon blood.

'She is fond of having other children noticed and caressed by the teachers, and those whom she respects; but this must not be carried too far, or she becomes jealous. She wants to have her share, which, if not the lion's, is the greater part; and if she does not get it, she says, "*My mother will love me.*"

'Her tendency to imitation is so strong, that it leads her to actions which must be entirely incomprehensible to her, and which can give her no other pleasure than the gratification of an internal faculty. She has been known to sit for half an hour, holding a book before her sightless eyes, and moving her lips, as she has observed seeing people do when reading.

'She one day pretended that her doll was sick; and went through all the motions of tending it, and giving it medicine; she then put it carefully to bed, and placed a bottle of hot water to its feet, laughing all the time most heartily. When I came home, she insisted upon my going to see it, and feel its pulse; and when I told her to put a blister on its back, she seemed to enjoy it amazingly, and almost screamed with delight.

'Her social feelings, and her affections, are very strong; and when she is sitting at work, or at her studies, by the side of one of her little friends, she will break off from her task every few moments, to hug and kiss them with an earnestness and warmth that is touching to behold.

'When left alone, she occupies and apparently amuses herself, and seems quite contented; and so strong seems to be the natural tendency of thought to put on the garb of language, that she often soliloquizes in the *finger language*, slow and tedious as it is. But it is only when alone, that she is quiet: for if she becomes sensible of the presence of any one near her, she is restless until she can sit close beside them, hold their hand, and converse with them by signs.

'In her intellectual character it is pleasing to observe an insatiable thirst for knowledge, and a quick perception of the relations of things. In her moral character, it is beautiful to behold her continual gladness, her keen enjoyment of existence, her expansive love, her unhesitating confidence, her sympathy with suffering, her conscientiousness, truthfulness, and hopefulness.'

Such are a few fragments from the simple but most interesting and instructive history of Laura Bridgman. The name of her great benefactor and friend, who writes it, is Dr Howe. There are not many persons, I hope and believe, who, after reading these passages, can ever hear that name with indifference.

A further account has been published by Dr Howe, since the report from which I have just quoted. It describes her rapid mental growth and improvement during twelve months more, and brings her little history down to the end of last year. It is very remarkable, that as we dream in words, and carry on imaginary conversations, in which we speak both for ourselves and for the shadows who appear to us in those visions of the night, so she, having no words, uses her finger alphabet in her sleep. And it has been ascertained that when her slumber is broken, and is much disturbed by dreams, she expresses her thoughts in an irregular and confused manner on her fingers: just as we should murmur and mutter them indistinctly, in the like circumstances.

I turned over the leaves of her Diary, and found it written in a fair legible square hand, and expressed in terms which were quite intelligible without any explanation. On my saying that I should like to see her write again, the teacher who sat beside her, bade her, in their language, sign her name upon a slip of paper, twice or thrice. In doing so, I observed that she kept her left hand always touching, and following up, her right, in which, of course, she held the pen. No line was indicated by any contrivance, but she wrote straight and freely.

She had, until now, been quite unconscious of the presence of visitors; but, having her hand placed in that of the gentleman who accompanied me, she immediately expressed his name upon her teacher's palm. Indeed her sense of touch is now so exquisite, that having been acquainted with a person once, she can recognise him or her after almost any interval. This gentleman had been in her company, I believe, but very seldom, and certainly had not seen her for many months. My hand she rejected at once, as she does that of any man who is a stranger to her. But she retained my wife's with evident pleasure, kissed her, and examined her dress with a girl's curiosity and interest.

She was merry and cheerful, and showed much innocent playfulness in her intercourse with her teacher. Her delight on recognising a favourite playfellow and companion – herself a blind girl – who silently, and with an equal enjoyment of the coming surprise, took a seat beside her, was beautiful to witness. It elicited from her at first, as other slight circumstances did twice or thrice during my visit, an uncouth noise which was rather painful to hear. But on her teacher touching her lips, she immediately desisted, and embraced her laughingly and affectionately.

I had previously been into another chamber, where a number of blind boys were swinging, and climbing, and engaged in various sports. They all clamoured, as we entered, to the assistant-master, who accompanied us, 'Look at me, Mr Hart! Please, Mr Hart, look at me!' evincing, I thought, even in this, an anxiety peculiar to their condition, that their little feats of agility should be *seen*. Among them was a small laughing fellow, who stood aloof, entertaining himself with a gymnastic exercise for bringing the arms and chest into play; which he enjoyed mightily; especially when, in thrusting out his right arm, he brought it into contact with another boy. Like Laura Bridgman, this young child was deaf, and dumb, and blind.

Dr Howe's account of this pupil's first instruction is so very striking, and so intimately connected with Laura herself, that I cannot refrain from a short extract. I may premise that the poor boy's name is Oliver Caswell; that he is thirteen years of age; and that he was in full possession of all his faculties, until three years and four months old. He was then attacked by scarlet fever; in four weeks became deaf; in a few weeks more, blind; in six months, dumb. He showed his anxious sense of this last deprivation, by often feeling the lips of other persons when they were talking, and then putting his hand upon his own, as if to assure himself that he had them in the right position.

'His thirst for knowledge,' says Dr Howe, 'proclaimed itself as soon as he entered the house, by his eager examination of everything he could feel or smell in his new location. For instance, treading upon the register of a furnace, he instantly stooped down, and began to feel it, and soon discovered the way in which the upper plate moved upon the lower one; but this was not enough for him, so lying down upon his face, he applied his tongue first to one, then to the other, and seemed to discover that they were of different kinds of metal.

'His signs were expressive: and the strictly natural language, laughing, crying, sighing, kissing, embracing, &c., was perfect.

'Some of the analogical signs which (guided by his faculty of imitation) he had contrived, were comprehensible; such as the waving motion of his hand for the motion of a boat, the circular one for a wheel, &c.

'The first object was to break up the use of these signs and to substitute for them the use of purely arbitrary ones.

'Profiting by the experience I had gained in the other cases, I omitted several steps of the process before employed, and commenced at once with the finger language. Taking, therefore, several articles having short names, such as key, cup, mug, &c., and with Laura for an auxiliary, I sat down, and taking his hand, placed it upon one of them, and then with my own, made the letters *key*. He felt my hands eagerly with both of his, and on my repeating the process, he evidently tried to imitate the motions of my fingers. In a few minutes he contrived to feel the motions of my fingers with one hand, and holding out the other he tried to imitate them, laughing most heartily when he succeeded. Laura was by, interested even to agitation; and the two presented a singular sight: her face was flushed and anxious, and her fingers twined in among ours so closely as to follow every motion, but so lightly as not to embarrass them; while Oliver stood attentive, his head a little aside, his face turned up, his left hand grasping mine, and his right held out: at every motion of my fingers his countenance betokened keen attention; there was an expression of anxiety as he tried to imitate the motions; then a smile came stealing out as he thought he could do so, and spread into a joyous laugh the moment he succeeded, and felt me pat his head, and Laura clap him heartily upon the back, and jump up and down in her joy.

'He learned more than a half-dozen letters in half an hour, and seemed delighted with his success, at least in gaining approbation. His attention then began to flag, and I commenced playing with him. It was evident that in all this he had merely been imitating the motions of my fingers, and placing his hand upon the key, cup, &c., as part of the process, without any perception of the relation between the sign and the object.

'When he was tired with play I took him back to the table, and he was quite ready to begin again his process of imitation. He soon learned to make the letters for *key*, *pen*, *pin*; and by having the object repeatedly placed in his hand, he at last perceived the relation I wished to establish between them. This was evident, because, when I made the letters *pin*, or *pen*, or *cup*, he would select the article.

'The perception of this relation was not accompanied by that radiant flash of intelligence, and that glow of joy, which marked the delightful moment when Laura first perceived it. I then placed all the articles on the table, and going away a little distance with the children, placed Oliver's fingers in the positions to spell *key*, on which Laura went and brought the article: the little fellow seemed much amused by this, and looked very attentive and smiling. I then caused him to make the letters *bread*, and in an instant Laura went and brought him a piece: he smelled at it; put it to his lips; cocked up his head with a most knowing look; seemed to reflect a moment; and then laughed outright, as much as to say, "Aha! I understand now how something may be made out of this."

'It was now clear that he had the capacity and inclination to learn, that he was a proper subject for instruction, and needed only persevering attention. I therefore put him in the hands of an intelligent teacher, nothing doubting of his rapid progress.'

Well may this gentleman call that a delightful moment, in which some distant promise of her present state first gleamed upon the darkened mind of Laura Bridgman. Throughout his life, the recollection of that moment will be to him a source of pure, unfading happiness; nor will it shine less brightly on the evening of his days of Noble Usefulness.

The affection that exists between these two – the master and the pupil – is as far removed from all ordinary care and regard, as the circumstances in which it has had its growth, are apart from the common occurrences of life. He is occupied now, in devising means of imparting to her, higher knowledge; and of conveying to her some adequate idea of the Great Creator of that universe in which, dark and silent and scentless though it be to her, she has such deep delight and glad enjoyment.

Ye who have eyes and see not, and have ears and hear not; ye who are as the hypocrites of sad countenances, and disfigure your faces that ye may seem unto men to fast; learn healthy cheerfulness, and mild contentment, from the deaf, and dumb, and blind! Self-elected saints with gloomy brows, this sightless, earless, voiceless child may teach you lessons you will do well to follow. Let that poor hand of hers lie gently on your hearts; for there may be something in its healing touch akin to that of the Great Master whose precepts you misconstrue, whose lessons you pervert, of whose charity and sympathy with all the world, not one among you in his daily practice knows as much as many of the worst among those fallen sinners, to whom you are liberal in nothing but the preachment of perdition!

As I rose to quit the room, a pretty little child of one of the attendants came running in to greet its father. For the moment, a child with eyes, among the sightless crowd, impressed me almost as painfully as the blind boy in the porch had done, two hours ago. Ah! how much brighter and more deeply blue, glowing and rich though it had been before, was the scene without, contrasting with the darkness of so many youthful lives within!

At SOUTH BOSTON, as it is called, in a situation excellently adapted for the purpose, several charitable institutions are clustered together. One of these, is the State Hospital for the insane; admirably conducted on those enlightened principles of conciliation and kindness, which twenty years ago would have been worse than heretical, and which have been acted upon with so much success in our own pauper asylum at Hanwell.[8] 'Evince a desire to show some confidence, and repose some trust, even in mad people,' said the resident physician, as we walked along the galleries, his patients flocking round us unrestrained. Of those who deny or doubt the wisdom of this maxim after witnessing its effects, if there be such people still alive, I can only say that I hope I may never be summoned as a Juryman on a Commission of Lunacy whereof they are the subjects; for I should certainly find them out of their senses, on such evidence alone.

Each ward in this institution is shaped like a long gallery or hall, with the dormitories of the patients opening from it on either hand. Here they work, read, play at skittles, and other games; and when the weather does not admit of their taking exercise out of doors, pass the day together. In one of these rooms, seated, calmly, and quite as a matter of course, among a throng of madwomen, black and white, were the physician's wife and another lady, with a couple of children. These ladies were graceful and handsome; and it was not difficult to perceive at a glance that even their presence there, had a highly beneficial influence on the patients who were grouped about them.

Leaning her head against the chimney-piece, with a great assumption of dignity and refinement of manner, sat an elderly female, in as many scraps of finery as Madge Wildfire herself.[9] Her head in particular was so strewn with scraps of gauze and cotton and bits of paper, and had so many queer odds and ends stuck all about it, that it looked like a bird's-nest. She was radiant with imaginary jewels; wore a rich pair of undoubted gold spectacles; and gracefully dropped upon her lap, as we approached, a very old greasy newspaper, in which I dare say she had been reading an account of her own presentation at some Foreign Court.

I have been thus particular in describing her, because she will serve to exemplify the physician's manner of acquiring and retaining the confidence of his patients.

'This,' he said aloud, taking me by the hand, and advancing to the fantastic figure with great politeness – not raising her suspicions by the slightest look or whisper, or any kind of aside, to me: 'This lady is the hostess of this mansion, sir. It belongs to her. Nobody else has anything whatever to do with it. It is a large establishment, as you see, and requires a great number of attendants. She lives, you observe, in the very first style. She is kind enough to receive my visits, and to permit my wife and family to reside here; for which, it is hardly necessary to say, we are much indebted to her. She is exceedingly courteous, you perceive,' on this hint she bowed, condescendingly, 'and will permit me to have the pleasure of introducing you: a gentleman from England, Ma'am: newly arrived from England, after a very tempestuous passage: Mr Dickens, – the lady of the house!'

We exchanged the most dignified salutations with profound gravity and respect, and so went on. The rest of the madwomen seemed to understand the joke perfectly (not only in this case, but in all the others, except their own), and to be highly amused by it. The nature of their several kinds of insanity was made known to me in the same way, and we left each of them in high good humour. Not only is a thorough confidence established, by these means, between [the] physician and patient, in respect of the nature and extent of their hallucinations, but it is easy to understand that opportunities are afforded for seizing any moment of reason, to startle them by placing their own delusion before them in its most incongruous and ridiculous light.

Every patient in this asylum sits down to dinner every day with a knife and fork; and in the midst of them sits the gentleman, whose manner of dealing with his charges, I have just described. At every meal, moral influence alone restrains the more violent among them from cutting the throats of the rest; but the effect of that influence is reduced to an absolute certainty, and is found, even as a means of restraint, to say nothing of it as a means of cure, a hundred times more efficacious than all the strait-waistcoats, fetters, and handcuffs, that ignorance, prejudice, and cruelty have manufactured since the creation of the world.

In the labour department, every patient is as freely trusted with the tools of his trade as if he were a sane man. In the garden, and on the farm, they work with spades, rakes, and hoes. For amusement, they walk, run, fish, paint, read, and ride out to take the air in carriages provided for the purpose. They have among themselves a sewing society to make clothes for the poor, which holds meetings, passes resolutions, never comes to fisty-cuffs or bowie-knives as sane assemblies have been known to do elsewhere; and conducts all its proceedings with the greatest decorum. The irritability, which would otherwise be expended on their own flesh, clothes, and furniture, is dissipated in these pursuits. They are cheerful, tranquil, and healthy.

Once a week they have a ball, in which the Doctor and his family, with all the nurses and attendants, take an active part. Dances and marches are performed alternately, to the enlivening strains of a piano; and now and then some gentleman or lady (whose proficiency has been previously ascertained) obliges the company with a song: nor does it ever degenerate, at a tender crisis, into a screech or howl; wherein, I must confess, I should have thought the danger lay. At an early hour they all meet together for these festive purposes; at eight o'clock refreshments are served; and at nine they separate.

Immense politeness and good breeding are observed throughout. They all take their tone from the Doctor; and he moves a very Chesterfield[10] among the company. Like other assemblies, these entertainments afford a fruitful topic of conversation among the ladies for some days; and the gentlemen are so anxious to shine on these occasions, that they have been sometimes found 'practising their steps' in private, to cut a more distinguished figure in the dance.

It is obvious that one great feature of this system, is the inculcation and encouragement, even among such unhappy persons, of a decent self-respect. Something of the same spirit pervades all the Institutions at South Boston.

There is the House of Industry. In that branch of it, which is devoted to the reception of old or otherwise helpless paupers, these words are painted on the walls: 'WORTHY OF NOTICE. SELF-GOVERNMENT, QUIETUDE, AND PEACE, ARE BLESSINGS.' It is not assumed and taken for granted that being there they must be evil-disposed and wicked people, before whose vicious eyes it is necessary to flourish threats and harsh restraints. They are met at the very threshold with this mild appeal. All within-doors is very plain and simple, as it ought to be, but arranged with a view to peace and comfort. It costs no more than any other plan of arrangement, but it speaks an amount of consideration for those who are reduced to seek a shelter there, which puts them at once upon their gratitude and good behaviour. Instead of being parcelled out in great, long, rambling wards, where a certain amount of weazen life may mope, and pine, and shiver, all day long, the building is divided into separate rooms, each with its share of light and air. In these, the better kind of paupers live. They have a motive for exertion and becoming pride, in the desire to make these little chambers comfortable and decent. I do not remember one but it was clean and neat, and had its plant or two upon the window-sill, or row of crockery upon the shelf, or small display of coloured prints upon the whitewashed wall, or, perhaps, its wooden clock behind the door.

The orphans and young children are in an adjoining building; separate from this, but a part of the same Institution. Some are such little creatures, that the stairs are of Lilliputian measurement, fitted to their tiny strides. The same consideration for their years and weakness is expressed in their very seats, which are perfect curiosities, and look like articles of furniture for a pauper doll's-house. I can imagine the glee of our Poor Law Commissioners[11] at the notion of these seats having arms and backs; but small spines being of older date than their occupation of the Board-room at Somerset House, I thought even this provision very merciful and kind.

Here again, I was greatly pleased with the inscriptions on the wall, which were scraps of plain morality, easily remembered and understood: such as 'Love one another' – 'God remembers the smallest creature in his creation:' and straight-forward advice of that nature. The books and tasks of these smallest of scholars, were adapted, in the same judicious manner, to their childish powers. When we had examined these lessons, four morsels of girls (of whom one was blind) sang a little song, about the merry month of May, which I thought (being extremely dismal) would have suited an English November better. That done, we went to see their sleeping-rooms on the floor above, in which the arrangements were no less excellent and gentle than those we had seen below. And after observing that the teachers were of a class and character well suited to the spirit of the place, I took leave of the infants with a lighter heart than ever I have taken leave of pauper infants yet.

Connected with the House of Industry, there is also an Hospital, which was in the best order, and had, I am glad to say, many beds unoccupied. It had one fault, however, which is common to all American interiors: the presence of the eternal, accursed, suffocating, red-hot demon of a stove, whose breath would blight the purest air under Heaven.[12]

There are two establishments for boys in this same neighbourhood. One is called the Boylston school, and is an asylum for neglected and indigent boys who have committed no crime, but who in the ordinary course of things would very soon be purged of that distinction if they were not taken from the hungry streets and sent here. The other is a House of Reformation for Juvenile Offenders. They are both under the same roof, but the two classes of boys never come in contact.

The Boylston boys, as may be readily supposed, have very much the advantage of the others in point of personal appearance. They were in their school-room when I came upon them, and answered correctly, without book, such questions as where was England; how far was it; what was its population; its capital city; its form of government; and so forth. They sang a song too, about a farmer sowing his seed: with corresponding action at such parts as ''tis thus he sows,' 'he turns him round,' 'he claps his hands;' which gave it greater interest for them, and accustomed them to act together, in an orderly manner. They appeared exceedingly well-taught, and not better taught than fed; for a more chubby-looking full-waistcoated set of boys, I never saw.

The juvenile offenders had not such pleasant faces by a great deal, and in this establishment there were many boys of colour. I saw them first at their work (basket-making, and the manufacture of palm-leaf hats), afterwards in their school, where they sang a chorus in praise of Liberty: an odd, and, one would think, rather aggravating, theme for prisoners. These boys are divided into four classes, each denoted by a numeral, worn on a badge upon the arm. On the arrival of a new-comer, he is put into the fourth or lowest class, and left, by good behaviour, to work his way up into the first. The design and object of this Institution is to reclaim the youthful criminal by firm but kind and judicious treatment; to make his prison a place of purification and improvement, not of demoralisation and corruption; to impress upon him that there is but one path, and that one sober industry, which can ever lead him to happiness; to teach him how it may be trodden, if his footsteps have never yet been led that way; and to lure him back to it if they have strayed: in a word, to snatch him from destruction, and restore him to society a penitent and useful member. The importance of such an establishment, in every point of view, and with reference to every consideration of humanity and social policy, requires no comment.

One other establishment closes the catalogue. It is the House of Correction for the State, in which silence is strictly maintained, but where the prisoners have the comfort and mental relief of seeing each other, and of working together. This is the improved system of Prison Discipline which we have imported into England, and which has been in successful operation among us for some years past.

America, as a new and not over-populated country, has, in all her prisons, the one great advantage, of being enabled to find useful and profitable work for the inmates; whereas, with us, the prejudice against prison labour is naturally very strong, and almost insurmountable, when honest men who have not offended against the laws are frequently doomed to seek employment in vain. Even in the United States, the principle of bringing convict labour and free labour into a competition which must obviously be to the disadvantage of the latter, has already found many opponents, whose number is not likely to diminish with access of years.

For this very reason though, our best prisons would seem at the first glance to be better conducted than those of America. The treadmill is conducted with little or no noise; five hundred men may pick oakum in the same room, without a sound; and both kinds of labour admit of such keen and vigilant superintendence, as will render even a word of personal communication among the prisoners almost impossible. On the other hand, the noise of the loom, the forge, the carpenter's hammer, or the stonemason's saw, greatly favour those opportunities of intercourse – hurried and brief no doubt, but opportunities still – which these several kinds of work, by rendering it necessary for men to be employed very near to each other, and often side by side, without any barrier or partition between them, in their very nature present. A visitor, too, requires to reason and reflect a little, before the sight of a number of men engaged in ordinary labour, such as he is accustomed to out of doors, will impress him half as strongly as the contemplation of the same persons in the same place and garb would, if they were occupied in some task, marked and degraded everywhere as belonging only to felons in jails. In an American state prison or house of correction, I found it difficult at first to persuade myself that I was really in a jail: a place of ignominious punishment and endurance. And to this hour I very much question whether the humane boast that it is not like one, has its root in the true wisdom or philosophy of the matter.

I hope I may not be misunderstood on this subject, for it is one in which I take a strong and deep interest. I incline as little to the sickly feeling which makes every canting lie or maudlin speech of a notorious criminal a subject of newspaper report and general sympathy, as I do to those good old customs of the good old times which made England, even so recently as in the reign of the Third King George, in respect of her criminal code and her prison regulations, one of the most bloody-minded and barbarous countries on the earth. If I thought it would do any good to the rising generation, I would cheerfully give my consent to the disinterment of the bones of any genteel highwayman (the more genteel, the more cheerfully), and to their exposure, piece-meal, on any sign-post, gate, or gibbet, that might be deemed a good elevation for the purpose. My reason is as well convinced that these gentry were as utterly worthless and debauched villains, as it is that the laws and jails hardened them in their evil courses, or that their wonderful escapes were effected by the prison-turnkeys who, in those admirable days, had always been felons themselves, and were, to the last, their bosom-friends and pot-companions. At the same time I know, as all men do or should, that the subject of Prison Discipline is one of the highest importance to any community; and that in her sweeping reform and bright example to other countries on this head, America has shown great wisdom, great benevolence, and exalted policy. In constrasting her system with that which we have modelled upon it, I merely seek to show that with all its drawbacks, ours has some advantages of its own.*

* Apart from the profit made by the useful labour of prisoners, which we can never hope to realize to any great extent, and which it is perhaps not expedient for us to try to gain, there are two prisons in London, in all respects equal, and in some decidedly superior, to any I saw or have ever heard or read of in America. One is the Tothill Fields Bridewell, conducted by Lieutenant A. F. Tracey, R.N.; the other the Middlesex House of Correction, superintended by Mr Chesterton. This gentleman also holds an appointment in the

The House of Correction which has led to these remarks, is not walled, like other prisons, but is palisaded round about with tall rough stakes, something after the manner of an enclosure for keeping elephants in, as we see it represented in Eastern prints and pictures. The prisoners wear a parti-coloured dress; and those who are sentenced to hard labour, work at nail-making, or stone-cutting. When I was there, the latter class of labourers were employed upon the stone for a new custom-house in course of erection at Boston. They appeared to shape it skilfully and with expedition, though there were very few among them (if any) who had not acquired the art within the prison gates.

The women, all in one large room, were employed in making light clothing, for New Orleans and the Southern States. They did their work in silence, like the men; and like them, were overlooked by the person contracting for their labour, or by some agent of his appointment. In addition to this, they are every moment liable to be visited by the prison officers appointed for that purpose.

The arrangements for cooking, washing of clothes, and so forth, are much upon the plan of those I have seen at home. Their mode of bestowing the prisoners at night (which is of general adoption) differs from ours, and is both simple and effective. In the centre of a lofty area, lighted by windows in the four walls, are five tiers of cells, one above the other; each tier having before it a light iron gallery, attainable by stairs of the same construction and material: excepting the lower one, which is on the ground. Behind these, back to back with them and facing the opposite wall, are five corresponding rows of cells, accessible by similar means: so that supposing the prisoners locked up in their cells, an officer stationed on the ground, with his back to the wall, has half their number under his eye at once; the remaining half being equally under the observation of another officer on the opposite side; and all in one great apartment. Unless this watch be corrupted or sleeping on his post, it is impossible for a man to escape; for even in the event of his forcing the iron door of his cell without noise (which is exceedingly

---

Public Service. Both are enlightened and superior men: and it would be as difficult to find persons better qualified for the functions they discharge with firmness, zeal, intelligence, and humanity, as it would be to exceed the perfect order and arrangement of the institutions they govern.

improbable), the moment he appears outside, and steps into that one of the five galleries on which it is situated, he must be plainly and fully visible to the officer below. Each of these cells holds a small truckle-bed, in which one prisoner sleeps; never more. It is small, of course; and the door being not solid, but grated, and without blind or curtain, the prisoner within is at all times exposed to the observation and inspection of any guard who may pass along that tier at any hour or minute of the night. Every day, the prisoners receive their dinner, singly, through a trap in the kitchen wall; and each man carries his to his sleeping cell to eat it, where he is locked up, alone, for that purpose, one hour. The whole of this arrangement struck me as being admirable; and I hope that the next new prison we erect in England may be built on this plan.

I was given to understand that in this prison no swords or fire-arms, or even cudgels, are kept; nor is it probable that, so long as its present excellent management continues, any weapon, offensive or defensive, will ever be required within its bounds.

Such are the Institutions at South Boston! In all of them, the unfortunate or degenerate citizens of the State are carefully instructed in their duties both to God and man; are surrounded by all reasonable means of comfort and happiness that their condition will admit of; are appealed to, as members of the great human family, however afflicted, indigent, or fallen; are ruled by the strong Heart, and not by the strong (though immeasurably weaker) Hand. I have described them at some length: firstly, because their worth demanded it; and secondly, because I mean to take them for a model, and to content myself with saying of others we may come to, whose design and purpose are the same, that in this or that respect they practically fail, or differ.

I wish by this account of them, imperfect in its execution, but in its just intention, honest, I could hope to convey to my readers one-hundredth part of the gratification, the sights I have described, afforded me.

To an Englishman, accustomed to the paraphernalia of Westminster Hall, an American Court of Law is as odd a sight as, I suppose, an English Court of Law would be to an American. Except in the Supreme Court at Washington (where the judges wear a plain black robe), there is no such thing as a wig or gown connected with the administration of justice. The gentlemen of the bar being barristers and attorneys too (for there is no division of those functions as in England) are no more removed from their clients than attorneys in our Court for the Relief of Insolvent Debtors are, from theirs. The jury are quite at home, and make themselves as comfortable as circumstances will permit. The witness is so little elevated above, or put aloof from, the crowd in the court, that a stranger entering during a pause in the proceedings would find it difficult to pick him out from the rest. And if it chanced to be a criminal trial, his eyes, in nine cases out of ten, would wander to the dock in search of the prisoner, in vain; for that gentleman would most likely be lounging among the most distinguished ornaments of the legal profession, whispering suggestions in his counsel's ear, or making a toothpick out of an old quill with his penknife.

I could not but notice these differences, when I visited the courts at Boston. I was much surprised at first, too, to observe that the counsel who interrogated the witness under examination at the time, did so *sitting*. But seeing that he was also occupied in writing down the answers, and remembering that he was alone and had no 'junior,' I quickly consoled myself with the reflection that law was not quite so expensive an article here, as at home; and that the absence of sundry formalities which we regard as indispensable, had doubtless a very favourable influence upon the bill of costs.

In every Court, ample and commodious provision is made for the accommodation of the citizens. This is the case all through America. In every Public Institution, the right of the people to attend, and to have an interest in the proceedings, is most fully and distinctly recognised. There are no grim door-keepers to dole out their tardy civility by the sixpenny-worth; nor is there, I sincerely believe, any insolence of office of any kind. Nothing national is exhibited for money; and no public officer is a showman. We have begun of late years to imitate this good example. I hope we shall continue to do so; and that in the fulness of time, even deans and chapters may be converted.

In the civil court an action was trying, for damages sustained in some accident upon a railway. The witnesses had been examined, and counsel was addressing the jury. The learned gentleman (like a few of his English brethren) was desperately long-winded, and had a remarkable capacity of saying the same thing over and over again. His great theme was 'Warren the ĕn*gine* driver,' whom he pressed into the service of every sentence he uttered. I listened to him for about a quarter of an hour; and, coming out of court at the expiration of that time, without the faintest ray of enlightenment as to the merits of the case, felt as if I were at home again.

In the prisoners' cell, waiting to be examined by the magistrate on a charge of theft, was a boy. This lad, instead of being committed to a common jail, would be sent to the asylum at South Boston, and there taught a trade; and in the course of time he would be bound apprentice to some respectable master. Thus, his detection in this offence, instead of being the prelude to a life of infamy and a miserable death, would lead, there was a reasonable hope, to his being reclaimed from vice, and becoming a worthy member of society.

I am by no means a wholesale admirer of our legal solemnities, many of which impress me as being exceedingly ludicrous. Strange as it may seem too, there is undoubtedly a degree of protection in the wig and gown – a dismissal of individual responsibility in dressing for the part – which encourages that insolent bearing and language, and that gross perversion of the office of a pleader for The Truth, so frequent in our courts of law. Still, I cannot help doubting whether America, in her desire to shake off the absurdities and abuses of the old system, may not have gone too far into the opposite extreme; and whether it is not desirable, especially in the small community of a city like this, where each man knows the other, to surround the administration of justice with some artificial barriers against the 'Hail fellow, well met' deportment of everyday life. All the aid it can have in the very high character and ability of the Bench, not only here but elsewhere, it has, and well deserves to have; but it may need something more: not to impress the thoughtful and the well-informed, but the ignorant and heedless; a class which includes some prisoners and many witnesses. These institutions were established, no doubt, upon the principle that those who had so large a share in making the laws, would certainly respect them. But experience has proved this hope to be fallacious; for no men know better than the Judges of America, that on the occasion of any great popular excitement the law is powerless, and cannot, for the time, assert its own supremacy.

The tone of society in Boston is one of perfect politeness,

courtesy, and good breeding. The ladies are unquestionably very beautiful – in face: but there I am compelled to stop. Their education is much as with us; neither better nor worse. I had heard some very marvellous stories in this respect; but not believing them, was not disappointed. Blue ladies[13] there are, in Boston; but like philosophers of that colour and sex in most other latitudes, they rather desire to be thought superior than to be so. Evangelical ladies there are, likewise, whose attachment to the forms of religion, and horror of theatrical entertainments, are most exemplary. Ladies who have a passion for attending lectures are to be found among all classes and all conditions. In the kind of provincial life which prevails in cities such as this, the Pulpit has great influence. The peculiar province of the Pulpit in New England (always excepting the Unitarian Ministry) would appear to be the denouncement of all innocent and rational amusements. The church, the chapel, and the lecture-room, are the only means of excitement excepted; and to the church, the chapel, and the lecture-room, the ladies resort in crowds.

Wherever religion is resorted to, as a strong drink, and as an escape from the dull monotonous round of home, those of its ministers who pepper the highest will be the surest to please. They who strew the Eternal Path with the greatest amount of brimstone, and who most ruthlessly tread down the flowers and leaves that grow by the wayside, will be voted the most righteous; and they who enlarge with the greatest pertinacity on the difficulty of getting into heaven, will be considered by all true believers certain of going there: though it would be hard to say by what process of reasoning this conclusion is arrived at. It is so at home, and it is so abroad. With regard to the other means of excitement, the Lecture, it has at least the merit of being always new. One lecture treads so quickly on the heels of another, that none are remembered; and the course of this month may be safely repeated next, with its charm of novelty unbroken, and its interest unabated.

The fruits of the earth have their growth in corruption. Out of the rottenness of these things, there has sprung up in Boston a sect of philosophers known as Transcendentalists.[14] On inquiring what this appellation might be supposed to signify, I was given to understand that whatever was unintelligible would be certainly transcendental. Not deriving much comfort from this elucidation, I pursued the inquiry still further, and found that the Transcendentalists are followers of my friend Mr Carlyle,[15] or should I rather say, of a follower of his, Mr Ralph Waldo Emerson.[16] This gentleman has written a volume of Essays, in which, among much that is dreamy and fanciful (if he will pardon me for saying so), there is much more that is true and manly, honest and bold. Transcendentalism has its occasional vagaries (what school has not?), but it has good healthful qualities in spite of them; not least among the number a hearty disgust of Cant, and an aptitude to detect her in all the million varieties of her everlasting wardrobe. And therefore if I were a Bostonian, I think I would be a Transcendentalist.

The only preacher I heard in Boston was Mr Taylor,[17] who addresses himself peculiarly to seamen, and who was once a mariner himself. I found his chapel down among the shipping, in one of the narrow, old, water-side streets, with a gay blue flag waving freely from its roof. In the gallery opposite to the pulpit were a little choir of male and female singers, a violoncello, and a violin. The preacher already sat in the pulpit, which was raised on pillars, and ornamented behind him with painted drapery of a lively and somewhat theatrical appearance. He looked a weather-beaten hard-featured man, of about six or eight and fifty; with deep lines graven as it were into his face, dark hair, and a stern, keen eye. Yet the general character of his countenance was pleasant and agreeable.

The service commenced with a hymn, to which succeeded an extemporary prayer. It had the fault of frequent repetition, incidental to all such prayers; but it was plain and comprehensive in its doctrines, and breathed a tone of general sympathy and charity, which is not so commonly a characteristic of this form of address to the Deity as it might be. That done he opened his discourse, taking for his text a passage from the Song of Solomon, laid upon the desk before the commencement of the service by some unknown member of the congregation: 'Who is this coming up from the wilderness, leaning on the arm of her Beloved!'

He handled this text in all kinds of ways, and twisted it into all manner of shapes; but always ingeniously, and with a rude eloquence, well adapted to the comprehension of his hearers. Indeed if I be not mistaken, he studied their sympathies and understandings much more than the display of his own powers. His imagery was all drawn from the sea, and from the incidents of a seaman's life; and was often remarkably good. He spoke to them of 'that glorious man, Lord Nelson,' and of Collingwood;[18] and drew nothing in, as the saying is, by the head and shoulders, but brought it to bear upon his purpose, naturally, and with a sharp mind to its effect. Sometimes, when much excited with his subject, he had an odd way – compounded of John Bunyan, and Balfour of Burley[19] – of taking his great quarto bible under his arm and pacing up and down the pulpit with it; looking steadily down, meantime, into the midst of the congregation. Thus, when he applied his text to the first assemblage of his hearers, and pictured the wonder of the church at their presumption in forming a congregation among themselves, he stopped short with his bible under his arm in the manner I have described, and pursued his discourse after this manner:

'Who are these – who are they – who are these fellows? where do they come from? Where are they going to? – Come from! What's the answer?' – leaning out of the pulpit, and pointing downward with his right hand: 'From below!' – starting back again, and looking at the sailors before him: 'From below, my brethren. From under the hatches of sin, battened down above you by the evil one. That's where you came from!' – a walk up and down the pulpit: 'and where are you going' – stopping abruptly: 'where are you going? Aloft!' – very softly, and pointing upward: 'Aloft!' – louder: 'aloft!' – louder still: 'That's where you are going – with a fair wind, – all taut and trim, steering direct for Heaven in its glory, where there are no storms or foul weather, and where the wicked cease from troubling, and the weary are at rest.' – Another walk: 'That's where you're going to, my friends. That's it. That's the place. That's the port. That's the haven. It's a blessed harbour – still water there, in all changes of the winds and tides; no driving ashore upon the rocks, or slipping your cables and running out to sea, there: Peace – Peace – Peace – all peace!' – Another walk, and patting the bible under his left arm: 'What! These fellows are coming from the wilderness, are they? Yes. From the dreary, blighted wilderness of Iniquity, whose only crop is Death. But do they lean upon anything – do they lean upon nothing, these poor seamen?' – Three raps upon the bible: 'Oh yes. – Yes. – They lean upon the arm of their Beloved' – three more raps: 'upon the arm of their Beloved' – three more, and a walk: 'Pilot, guiding-star, and compass, all in one, to all hands – here it is' – three more: 'Here it is.

They can do their seamån's duty manfully, and be easy in their minds in the utmost peril and danger, with this' – two more: 'They can come, even these poor fellows can come, from the wilderness leaning on the arm of their Beloved, and go up – up – up!' – raising his hand higher, and higher, at every repetition of the word, so that he stood with it at last stretched above his head, regarding them in a strange, rapt manner, and pressing the book triumphantly to his breast, until he gradually subsided into some other portion of his discourse.

I have cited this, rather as an instance of the preacher's eccentricities than his merits, though taken in connection with his look and manner, and the character of his audience, even this was striking. It is possible, however, that my favourable impression of him may have been greatly influenced and strengthened, firstly, by his impressing upon his hearers that the true observance of religion was not inconsistent with a cheerful deportment and an exact discharge of the duties of their station, which, indeed, it scrupulously required of them; and secondly, by his cautioning them not to set up any monopoly in Paradise and its mercies. I never heard these two points so wisely touched (if indeed I have ever heard them touched at all), by any preacher of that kind before.

Having passed the time I spent in Boston, in making myself acquainted with these things, in settling the course I should take in my future travels, and in mixing constantly with its society, I am not aware that I have any occasion to prolong this chapter. Such of its social customs as I have not mentioned, however, may be told in a very few words.

The usual dinner-hour is two o'clock. A dinner party takes place at five; and at an evening party, they seldom sup later than eleven; so that it goes hard but one gets home, even from a rout, by midnight. I never could find out any difference between a party at Boston and a party in London, saving that at the former place all assemblies are held at more rational hours; that the conversation may possibly be a little louder and more cheerful; that a guest is usually expected to ascend to the very top of the house to take his cloak off; that he is certain to see, at every dinner, an unusual amount of poultry on the table; and at every supper, at least two mighty bowls of hot stewed oysters, in any one of which a half-grown Duke of Clarence might be smothered easily.[20]

There are two theatres in Boston,[21] of good size and construction, but sadly in want of patronage. The few ladies who resort to them, sit, as of right, in the front rows of the boxes.

The bar is a large room with a stone floor, and there people stand and smoke, and lounge about, all the evening: dropping in and out as the humour takes them. There too the stranger is initiated into the mysteries of Gin-sling, Cocktail, Sangaree, Mint Julep, Sherry-cobbler, Timber Doodle, and other rare drinks.[22] The House is full of boarders, both married and single, many of whom sleep upon the premises, and contract by the week for their board and lodging: the charge for which diminishes as they go nearer the sky to roost. A public table is laid in a very handsome hall for breakfast, and for dinner, and for supper. The party sitting down together to these meals will vary in number from one to two hundred: sometimes more. The advent of each of these epochs in the day is proclaimed by an awful gong, which shakes the very window-frames as it reverberates through the house, and horribly disturbs nervous foreigners. There is an ordinary for ladies, and an ordinary for gentlemen.

In our private room the cloth could not, for any earthly consideration, have been laid for dinner without a huge glass dish of cranberries in the middle of the table; and breakfast would have been no breakfast unless the principal dish were a deformed beef-steak with a great flat bone in the centre, swimming in hot butter, and sprinkled with the very blackest of all possible pepper. Our bedroom was spacious and airy, but (like every bedroom on this side of the Atlantic) very bare of furniture, having no curtains to the French bedstead or to the window. It had one unusual luxury, however, in the shape of a wardrobe of painted wood, something smaller than an English watch-box; or if this comparison should be insufficient to convey a just idea of its dimensions, they may be estimated from the fact of my having lived for fourteen days and nights in the firm belief that it was a shower-bath.

CHAPTER 4

An American Railroad. Lowell and its Factory System

BEFORE leaving Boston, I devoted one day to an excursion to Lowell.[1] I assign a separate chapter to this visit; not because I am about to describe it at any great length, but because I remember it as a thing by itself, and am desirous that my readers should do the same.

I made acquaintance with an American railroad, on this occasion, for the first time. As these works are pretty much alike all through the States, their general characteristics are easily described.

There are no first and second class carriages as with us; but there is a gentlemen's car and a ladies' car: the main distinction between which is that in the first, everybody smokes; and in the second, nobody does. As a black man never travels with a white one, there is also a negro car; which is a great, blundering, clumsy chest, such as Gulliver put to sea in, from the kingdom of Brobdingnag.[2] There is a great deal of jolting, a great deal of noise, a great deal of wall, not much window, a locomotive engine, a shriek, and a bell.

The cars are like shabby omnibuses, but larger: holding thirty, forty, fifty, people. The seats, instead of stretching from end to end, are placed crosswise. Each seat holds two persons. There is a long row of them on each side of the caravan, a narrow passage up the middle, and a door at both ends. In the centre of the carriage there is usually a stove, fed with charcoal or anthracite coal; which is for the most part red-hot. It is insufferably close; and you see the hot air fluttering between yourself and any other object you may happen to look at, like the ghost of smoke.

In the ladies' car, there are a great many gentlemen who have ladies with them. There are also a great many ladies who have nobody with them: for any lady may travel alone, from one end of the United States to the other, and be certain of the most courteous and considerate treatment everywhere. The conductor or check-taker, or guard, or whatever he may be, wears no uniform. He walks up and down the car, and in and out of it, as his fancy dictates; leans against the door with his hands in his pockets and stares at you, if you chance to be a stranger; or enters into conversation with the passengers about him. A great many newspapers are pulled out, and a few of them are read. Everybody talks to you, or to anybody else who hits his fancy. If you are an Englishman, he expects that that railroad is pretty much like an English railroad. If you say 'No,' he says 'Yes?' (interrogatively), and asks in what respect they differ. You enumerate the heads of difference, one by one, and he says 'Yes?' (still interrogatively) to each. Then he guesses that you don't travel faster in England; and on your replying that you do, says, 'Yes?' again (still interrogatively), and, it is quite evident, don't believe it. After a long pause he remarks, partly to you, and partly to the knob on the top of his stick, that 'Yankees are reckoned to be considerable of a go-ahead people too;' upon which *you* say 'Yes,' and then *he* says 'Yes' again (affirmatively this time); and upon your looking out of window, tells you that behind that hill, and some three miles from the next station, there is a clever town in a smart lo-ca-tion, where he expects you have con-cluded to stop. Your answer in the negative naturally leads to more questions in reference to your intended route (always pronounced rout); and wherever you are going, you invariably learn that you can't get there without immense difficulty and danger, and that all the great sights are somewhere else.

If a lady take a fancy to any male passenger's seat, the gentleman who accompanies her gives him notice of the fact, and he immediately vacates it with great politeness. Politics are much discussed, so are banks, so is cotton. Quiet people avoid the question of the Presidency, for there will be a new election in three years and a half, and party feeling runs very high: the great constitutional feature of this institution being, that directly the acrimony of the last election is over, the acrimony of the next one begins; which is an unspeakable comfort to all strong politicians and true lovers of their country: that is to say, to ninety-nine men and boys out of every ninety-nine and a quarter.

Except when a branch road joins the main one, there is seldom more than one track of rails; so that the road is very narrow, and the view, where there is a deep cutting, by no means extensive. When there is not, the character of the scenery is always the same. Mile after mile of stunted trees: some hewn down by the axe, some blown down by the wind, some half fallen and resting on their neighbours, many mere logs half hidden in the swamp, others mouldered away to spongy chips. The very soil of the earth is made up of minute fragments such as these; each pool of stagnant water has its crust of vegetable rottenness; on every side there are the boughs, and trunks, and stumps of trees, in every possible stage of decay, decomposition, and neglect. Now you emerge for a few brief minutes on an open country, glittering with some bright lake or pool, broad as many an English river, but so small here that it scarcely has a name; now catch hasty glimpses of a distant town, with its clean white houses and their cool piazzas, its prim New England church and schoolhouse; when whir-r-r-r! almost before you have seen them, comes the same dark screen: the stunted trees, the stumps, the logs, the stagnant water – all so like the last that you seem to have been transported back again by magic.

The train calls at stations in the woods, where the wild impossibility of anybody having the smallest reason to get out, is only to be equalled by the apparently desperate hopelessness of there being anybody to get in. It rushes across the turnpike road, where there is no gate, no policeman, no signal: nothing but a rough wooden arch, on which is painted 'WHEN THE BELL RINGS, LOOK OUT FOR THE LOCOMOTIVE.' On it whirls headlong, dives through the woods again, emerges in the light, clatters over frail arches, rumbles upon the heavy ground, shoots beneath a wooden bridge which intercepts the light for a second like a wink, suddenly awakens all the slumbering echoes in the main street of a large town, and dashes on haphazard, pell-mell, neck-or-nothing, down the middle of the road. There – with mechanics working at their trades, and people leaning from their doors and windows, and boys flying kites and playing marbles, and men smoking, and women talking, and children crawling, and pigs burrowing, and unaccustomed horses plunging and rearing, close to the very rails – there – on, on, on – tears the mad dragon of an engine with its train of cars; scattering in all directions a shower of burning sparks from its wood fire; screeching, hissing, yelling, panting; until at last the thirsty monster stops beneath a covered way to drink, the people cluster round, and you have time to breathe again.

I was met at the station at Lowell by a gentleman intimately connected with the management of the factories there; and gladly putting myself under his guidance, drove off at once to that quarter of the town in which the works, the object of my visit, were situated. Although only just of age – for if my recollection serve me, it has been a manufacturing town barely one-and-twenty years – Lowell is a large, populous, thriving place.[3] Those indications of its youth which first attract the eye, give it a quaintness and oddity of character which, to a visitor from the old country, is amusing enough. It was a very dirty winter's day, and nothing in the whole town looked old to me, except the mud, which in some parts was almost knee-deep, and might have been deposited there, on the subsiding of the waters after the Deluge. In one place, there was a new wooden church, which, having no steeple, and being yet un-painted, looked like an enormous packing-case without any direc-tion upon it. In another there was a large hotel, whose walls and colonnades were so crisp, and thin, and slight, that it had exactly the appearance of being built with cards. I was careful not to draw my breath as we passed, and trembled when I saw a workman come out upon the roof, lest with one thoughtless stamp of his foot he should crush the structure beneath him, and bring it rattling down. The very river that moves the machinery in the mills (for they are all worked by water power), seems to acquire a new character from the fresh buildings of bright red brick and painted wood among which it takes its course; and to be as light-headed, thoughtless, and brisk a young river, in its murmurings and tumblings, as one would desire to see. One would swear that every 'Bakery,' 'Grocery,' and 'Bookbindery,' and other kind of store, took its shutters down for the first time, and started in business yesterday. The golden pestles and mortars fixed as signs upon the sun-blind frames outside the Druggists', appear to have been just turned out of the United States' Mint; and when I saw a baby of some week or ten days old in a woman's arms at a street corner, I found myself unconsciously wondering where it came from: never supposing for an instant that it could have been born in such a young town as that.

There are several factories in Lowell, each of which belongs to what we should term a Company of Proprietors, but what they call in America a Corporation. I went over several of these; such as a woollen factory, a carpet factory, and a cotton factory: examined them in every part; and saw them in their ordinary working aspect, with no preparation of any kind, or departure from their ordinary everyday proceedings. I may add that I am well acquainted with our manufacturing towns in England, and have visited many mills in Manchester and elsewhere in the same manner.

I happened to arrive at the first factory just as the dinner hour was over, and the girls were returning to their work; indeed the stairs of the mill were thronged with them as I ascended. They were all well dressed, but not to my thinking above their condition; for I like to see the humbler classes of society careful of their dress and appearance, and even, if they please, decorated with such little trinkets as come within the compass of their means. Supposing it confined within reasonable limits, I would always encourage this kind of pride, as a worthy element of self-respect, in any person I employed; and should no more be deterred from doing so, because some wretched female referred her fall to a love of dress, than I would allow my construction of the real intent and meaning of the Sabbath to be influenced by any warning to the well-disposed, founded on his backslidings on that particular day, which might emanate from the rather doubtful authority of a murderer in Newgate.

These girls, as I have said, were all well dressed: and that phrase necessarily includes extreme cleanliness. They had serviceable bonnets, good warm cloaks, and shawls; and were not above clogs and pattens. Moreover, there were places in the mill in which they could deposit these things without injury; and there were conveniences for washing. They were healthy in appearance, many of them remarkably so, and had the manners and deportment of young women: not of degraded brutes of burden. If I had seen in one of those mills (but I did not, though I looked for something of this kind with a sharp eye), the most lisping, mincing, affected, and ridiculous young creature that my imagination could suggest, I should have thought of the careless, moping, slatternly, degraded, dull reverse (I *have* seen that), and should have been still well pleased to look upon her.

The rooms in which they worked, were as well ordered as themselves. In the windows of some, there were green plants, which were trained to shade the glass; in all, there was as much fresh air, cleanliness, and comfort, as the nature of the occupation would possibly admit of. Out of so large a number of females, many of whom were only then just verging upon womanhood, it may be reasonably supposed that some were delicate and fragile in appearance: no doubt there were. But I solemnly declare, that from all the crowd I saw in the different factories that day, I cannot recall or separate one young face that gave me a painful impression; not one young girl whom, assuming it to be matter of necessity that she should gain her daily bread by the labour of her hands, I would have removed from those works if I had had the power.

They reside in various boarding-houses near at hand. The owners of the mills are particularly careful to allow no persons to enter upon the possession of these houses, whose characters have not undergone the most searching and thorough inquiry. Any complaint that is made against them, by the boarders, or by any one else, is fully investigated; and if good ground of complaint be shown to exist against them, they are removed, and their occupation is handed over to some more deserving person. There are a few children employed in these factories, but not many. The laws of the State forbid their working more than nine months in the year, and require that they be educated during the other three. For this purpose there are schools in Lowell; and there are churches and chapels of various persuasions, in which the young women may observe that form of Worship in which they have been educated.

At some distance from the factories, and on the highest and pleasantest ground in the neighbourhood, stands their hospital, or boarding-house for the sick: it is the best house in those parts, and was built by an eminent merchant for his own residence. Like that institution at Boston, which I have before described, it is not parcelled out into wards, but is divided into convenient chambers, each of which has all the comforts of a very comfortable home. The principal medical attendant resides under the same roof; and were the patients members of his own family, they could not be better cared for, or attended with greater gentleness and consideration. The weekly charge in this establishment for each female patient is three dollars, or twelve shillings English; but no girl employed by any of the corporations is ever excluded for want of the means of payment. That they do not very often want the means, may be gathered from the fact, that in July, 1841, no fewer than nine hundred and seventy-eight of these girls were depositors in the Lowell Savings Bank: the amount of whose joint savings was estimated at one hundred thousand dollars, or twenty thousand English pounds.

I am now going to state three facts, which will startle a large class of readers on this side of the Atlantic, very much.

Firstly, there is a joint-stock piano in a great many of the boarding-houses. Secondly, nearly all these young ladies subscribe to circulating libraries. Thirdly, they have got up among themselves a periodical called THE LOWELL OFFERING, 'A repository of original articles, written exclusively by females actively employed in the mills,' – which is duly printed, published, and sold; and whereof I brought away from Lowell four hundred good solid pages, which I have read from beginning to end.[4]

The large class of readers, startled by these facts, will exclaim, with one voice, 'How very preposterous!' On my deferentially inquiring why, they will answer, 'These things are above their station.' In reply to that objection, I would beg to ask what their station is.

It is their station to work. And they *do* work. They labour in these mills, upon an average, twelve hours a day, which is unquestionably work, and pretty tight work too. Perhaps it is above their station to indulge in such amusements, on any terms. Are we quite sure that we in England have not formed our ideas of the 'station' of working people, from accustoming ourselves to the contemplation of that class as they are, and not as they might be? I think if we examine our own feelings, we shall find that the pianos, and the circulating libraries, and even the Lowell Offering, startle us by their novelty, and not by their bearing upon any abstract question of right or wrong.

For myself, I know no station in which, the occupation of to-day cheerfully done and the occupation of to-morrow cheerfully looked to, any one of these pursuits is not most humanising and laudable. I know no station which is rendered more endurable to the person in it, or more safe to the person out of it, by having ignorance for its associate. I know no station which has a right to monopolise the means of mutual instruction, improvement, and rational entertainment; or which has ever continued to be a station very long, after seeking to do so.

Of the merits of the Lowell Offering as a literary production, I will only observe, putting entirely out of sight the fact of the articles having been written by these girls after the arduous labours of the day, that it will compare advantageously with a great many English Annuals. It is pleasant to find that many of its Tales are of the Mills and of those who work in them; that they inculcate habits of self-denial and contentment, and teach good doctrines of enlarged benevolence. A strong feeling for the beauties of nature, as displayed in the solitudes the writers have left at home, breathes through its pages like wholesome village air; and though a circulating library is a favourable school for the study of such topics, it has very scant allusion to fine clothes, fine marriages, fine houses, or fine life. Some persons might object to the papers being signed occasionally with rather fine names, but this is an American fashion. One of the provinces of the state legislature of Massachusetts is to alter ugly names into pretty ones, as the children improve upon the tastes of their parents. These changes costing little or nothing, scores of Mary Annes are solemnly converted into Bevelinas [5] every session.

It is said that on the occasion of a visit from General Jackson [6] or General Harrison [7] to this town (I forget which, but it is not to the purpose), he walked through three miles and a half of these young ladies all dressed out with parasols and silk stockings. But as I am not aware that any worse consequence ensued, than a sudden looking-up of all the parasols and silk stockings in the market; and perhaps the bankruptcy of some speculative New Englander who bought them all up at any price, in expectation of a demand that never came; I set no great store by the circumstance.

In this brief account of Lowell, and inadequate expression of the gratification it yielded me, and cannot fail to afford to any foreigner to whom the condition of such people at home is a subject of interest and anxious speculation, I have carefully abstained from drawing a comparison between these factories and those of our own land. Many of the circumstances whose strong influence has been at work for years in our manufacturing towns have not arisen here; and there is no manufacturing population in Lowell, so to speak: for these girls (often the daughters of small farmers) come from other States, remain a few years in the mills, and then go home for good.

The contrast would be a strong one, for it would be between the Good and Evil, the living light and deepest shadow. I abstain from it, because I deem it just to do so. But I only the more earnestly adjure all those whose eyes may rest on these pages, to pause and reflect upon the difference between this town and those great haunts of desperate misery: to call to mind, if they can in the midst of party strife and squabble, the efforts that must be made to purge them of their suffering and danger: and last, and foremost, to remember how the precious Time is rushing by.

I returned at night by the same railroad and in the same kind of car. One of the passengers being exceedingly anxious to expound at great length to my companion (not to me, of course) the true principles on which books of travel in America should be written by Englishmen, I feigned to fall asleep. But glancing all the way out at window from the corners of my eyes, I found abundance of entertainment for the rest of the ride in watching the effects of the wood fire, which had been invisible in the morning but were now brought out in full relief by the darkness: for we were travelling in a whirlwind of bright sparks, which showered about us like a storm of fiery snow.[8]

CHAPTER 5

Worcester. The Connecticut River. Hartford. New Haven. To New York

LEAVING Boston on the afternoon of Saturday the fifth of February, we proceeded by another railroad to Worcester: a pretty New England town, where we had arranged to remain under the hospitable roof of the Governor of the State, until Monday morning.

These towns and cities of New England (many of which would be villages in Old England), are as favourable specimens of rural America, as their people are of rural Americans. The well-trimmed lawns and green meadows of home are not there; and the grass, compared with our ornamental plots and pastures, is rank, and rough, and wild: but delicate slopes of land, gently-swelling hills, wooded valleys, and slender streams, abound. Every little colony of houses has its church and school-house peeping from among the white roofs and shady trees; every house is the whitest of the white; every Venetian blind the greenest of the green; every fine day's sky the bluest of the blue. A sharp dry wind and a slight frost had so hardened the roads when we alighted at Worcester, that their furrowed tracks were like ridges of granite. There was the usual aspect of newness on every object, of course. All the buildings looked as if they had been built and painted that morning, and could be taken down on Monday with very little trouble. In the keen evening air, every sharp outline looked a hundred times sharper than ever. The clean cardboard colonnades had no more perspective than a Chinese bridge on a tea-cup, and appeared equally well calculated for use. The razor-like edges of the detached cottages seemed to cut the very wind as it whistled against them, and to send it smarting on its way with a shriller cry than before. Those slightly-built wooden dwellings behind which the sun was setting with a brilliant lustre, could be so looked through and through, that the idea of any inhabitant being able to hide himself from the public gaze, or to have any secrets from the public eye, was not entertainable for a moment. Even where a blazing fire shone through the uncurtained windows of some distant house, it had the air of being newly-lighted, and of lacking warmth; and instead of awakening thoughts of a snug chamber, bright with faces that first saw the light round that same hearth, and ruddy with warm hangings, it came upon one suggestive of the smell of new mortar and damp walls.

So I thought, at least, that evening. Next morning when the sun was shining brightly, and the clear church bells were ringing, and sedate people in their best clothes enlivened the pathway near at hand and dotted the distant thread of road, there was a pleasant Sabbath peacefulness on everything, which it was good to feel. It would have been the better for an old church; better still for some old graves; but as it was, a wholesome repose and tranquillity pervaded the scene, which after the restless ocean and the hurried city, had a doubly grateful influence on the spirits.

We went on next morning, still by railroad, to Springfield. From that place to Hartford, whither we were bound, is a distance of only five-and-twenty miles, but at that time of the year the roads were so bad that the journey would probably have occupied ten or twelve hours. Fortunately, however, the winter having been unusually mild, the Connecticut River was 'open,' or, in other words, not frozen. The captain of a small steamboat was going to make his first trip for the season that day (the second February trip, I believe, within the memory of man), and only waited for us to go on board. Accordingly, we went on board, with as little delay as might be. He was as good as his word, and started directly.

It certainly was not called a small steamboat without reason. I omitted to ask the question, but I should think it must have been of about half a pony power. Mr Paap, the celebrated Dwarf,[1] might have lived and died happily in the cabin, which was fitted with common sash-windows like an ordinary dwelling-house. These windows had bright-red curtains, too, hung on slack strings across the lower panes; so that it looked like the parlour of a Lilliputian public-house, which had got afloat in a flood or some other water accident, and was drifting nobody knew where. But even in this chamber there was a rocking-chair. It would be impossible to get on anywhere, in America, without a rocking-chair.

I am afraid to tell how many feet short this vessel was, or how many feet narrow: to apply the words length and width to such measurement would be a contradiction in terms. But I may state that we all kept the middle of the deck, lest the boat should unexpectedly tip over; and that the machinery, by some surprising process of condensation, worked between it and the keel: the whole forming a warm sandwich, about three feet thick.

It rained all day as I once thought it never did rain anywhere, but in the Highlands of Scotland. The river was full of floating blocks of ice, which were constantly crunching and cracking under us; and the depth of water, in the course we took to avoid the larger masses, carried down the middle of the river by the current, did not exceed a few inches. Nevertheless, we moved onward, dexterously; and being well wrapped up, bade defiance to the weather, and enjoyed the journey. The Connecticut River is a fine stream; and the banks in summer-time are, I have no doubt, beautiful: at all events, I was told so by a young lady in the cabin; and she should be a judge of beauty, if the possession of a quality include the appreciation of it, for a more beautiful creature I never looked upon.

After two hours and a half of this odd travelling (including a stoppage at a small town, where we were saluted by a gun considerably bigger than our own chimney), we reached Hartford, and straightway repaired to an extremely comfortable hotel: except, as usual, in the article of bedrooms, which, in almost every place we visited, were very conducive to early rising.

We tarried here, four days. The town is beautifully situated in a basin of green hills; the soil is rich, well-wooded, and carefully improved. It is the seat of the local legislature of Connecticut, which sage body enacted, in bygone times, the renowned code of 'Blue

Laws,'² in virtue whereof, among other enlightened provisions, any citizen who could be proved to have kissed his wife on Sunday, was punishable, I believe, with the stocks. Too much of the old Puritan spirit exists in these parts to the present hour; but its influence has not tended, that I know, to make the people less hard in their bargains, or more equal in their dealings. As I never heard of its working that effect anywhere else, I infer that it never will, here. Indeed, I am accustomed, with reference to great professions and severe faces, to judge of the goods of the other world pretty much as I judge of the goods of this; and whenever I see a dealer in such commodities with too great a display of them in his window, I doubt the quality of the article within.

In Hartford stands the famous oak in which the charter of King Charles³ was hidden. It is now inclosed in a gentleman's garden. In the State House is the charter itself. I found the courts of law here, just the same as at Boston; the public Institutions almost as good. The Insane Asylum is admirably conducted, and so is the Institution for the Deaf and Dumb.

I very much questioned within myself, as I walked through the Insane Asylum, whether I should have known the attendants from the patients, but for the few words which passed between the former, and the Doctor, in reference to the persons under their charge. Of course I limit this remark merely to their looks; for the conversation of the mad people was mad enough.

There was one little prim old lady, of very smiling and good-humoured appearance, who came sidling up to me from the end of a long passage, and with a curtsey of inexpressible condescension, propounded this unaccountable inquiry:

'Does Pontefract still flourish, sir, upon the soil of England?'

'He does, ma'am,' I rejoined.

'When you last saw him, sir, he was —'

'Well, ma'am,' said I, 'extremely well. He begged me to present his compliments. I never saw him looking better.'

At this, the old lady was very much delighted. After glancing at me for a moment, as if to be quite sure that I was serious in my respectful air, she sidled back some paces; sidled forward again; made a sudden skip (at which I precipitately retreated a step or two); and said:

'*I* am an antediluvian, sir.'

I thought the best thing to say was, that I had suspected as much from the first. Therefore I said so.

'It is an extremely proud and pleasant thing, sir, to be an ante-diluvian,' said the old lady.

'I should think it was, ma'am,' I rejoined.

The old lady kissed her hand, gave another skip, smirked and sidled down the gallery in a most extraordinary manner, and ambled gracefully into her own bed-chamber.

In another part of the building, there was a male patient in bed; very much flushed and heated.

'Well,' said he, starting up, and pulling off his night-cap: 'It's all settled at last. I have arranged it with Queen Victoria.'

'Arranged what?' asked the Doctor.

'Why, that business,' passing his hand wearily across his fore-head, 'about the siege of New York.'

'Oh!' said I, like a man suddenly enlightened. For he looked at me for an answer.

'Yes. Every house without a signal will be fired upon by the British troops. No harm will be done to the others. No harm at all. Those that want to be safe, must hoist flags. That's all they'll have to do. They must hoist flags.'

Even while he was speaking, he seemed, I thought, to have some faint idea that his talk was incoherent. Directly he had said these words, he lay down again; gave a kind of a groan; and covered his hot head with the blankets.

There was another: a young man, whose madness was love and music. After playing on the accordion a march he had composed, he was very anxious that I should walk into his chamber, which I immediately did.

By way of being very knowing, and humouring him to the top of his bent, I went to the window, which commanded a beautiful prospect, and remarked, with an address upon which I greatly plumed myself:

'What a delicious country you have about these lodgings of yours!'

'Poh!' said he, moving his fingers carelessly over the notes of his instrument: '*Well enough for such an Institution as this!*'

I don't think I was ever so taken aback in all my life.

'I come here just for a whim,' he said coolly. 'That's all.'

'Oh! That's all!' said I.

'Yes. That's all. The Doctor's a smart man. He quite enters into it. It's a joke of mine. I like it for a time. You needn't mention it, but I think I shall go out next Tuesday!'

I assured him that I would consider our interview perfectly confidential; and rejoined the Doctor. As we were passing through a gallery on our way out, a well-dressed lady, of quiet and composed manners, came up, and proffering a slip of paper and a pen, begged that I would oblige her with an autograph. I complied, and we parted.

'I think I remember having had a few interviews like that, with ladies out of doors. I hope *she* is not mad?'

'Yes.'

'On what subject? Autographs?'

'No. She hears voices in the air.'

'Well!' thought I, 'it would be well if we could shut up a few false prophets of these later times, who have professed to do the same; and I should like to try the experiment on a Mormonist[4] or two to begin with.'

In this place, there is the best Jail for untried offenders in the world. There is also a very well-ordered State prison, arranged upon the same plan as that at Boston, except that here, there is always a sentry on the wall with a loaded gun. It contained at that time about two hundred prisoners. A spot was shown me in the sleeping ward, where a watchman was murdered some years since in the dead of night, in a desperate attempt to escape, made by a prisoner who had broken from his cell. A woman, too, was pointed out to me, who, for the murder of her husband, had been a close prisoner for sixteen years.

'Do you think,' I asked of my conductor, 'that after so very long an imprisonment, she has any thought or hope of ever regaining her liberty?'

'Oh dear yes,' he answered. 'To be sure she has.'

'She has no chance of obtaining it, I suppose?'

'Well, I don't know:' which, by-the-bye, is a national answer. 'Her friends mistrust her.'

'What have *they* to do with it?' I naturally inquired.

'Well, they won't petition.'

'But if they did, they couldn't get her out, I suppose?'

'Well, not the first time, perhaps, nor yet the second, but tiring and wearying for a few years might do it.'

'Does that ever do it?'

'Why yes, that'll do it sometimes. Political friends'll do it sometimes. It's pretty often done, one way or another.'

I shall always entertain a very pleasant and grateful recollection of Hartford. It is a lovely place, and I had many friends there, whom I can never remember with indifference. We left it with no little regret on the evening of Friday the 11th, and travelled that night by railroad to New Haven. Upon the way, the guard and I were formally introduced to each other (as we usually were on such occasions), and exchanged a variety of small-talk. We reached New Haven at about eight o'clock, after a journey of three hours, and put up for the night at the best inn.

New Haven, known also as the City of Elms, is a fine town. Many of its streets (as its *alias* sufficiently imports) are planted with rows of grand old elm-trees; and the same natural ornaments surround Yale College, an establishment of considerable eminence and reputation. The various departments of this Institution are erected in a kind of park or common in the middle of the town, where they are dimly visible among the shadowing trees. The effect is very like that of an old cathedral yard in England; and when their branches are in full leaf, must be extremely picturesque. Even in the winter time, these groups of well-grown trees, clustering among the busy streets and houses of a thriving city, have a very quaint appearance: seeming to bring about a kind of compromise between town and country; as if each had met the other half-way, and shaken hands upon it; which is at once novel and pleasant.

After a night's rest, we rose early, and in good time went down to the wharf, and on board the packet New York, *for* New York. This was the first American steamboat of any size that I had seen; and certainly to an English eye it was infinitely less like a steamboat than a huge floating bath. I could hardly persuade myself, indeed, but that the bathing establishment off Westminster Bridge, which I left a baby, had suddenly grown to an enormous size; run away from home; and set up in foreign parts as a steamer. Being in America, too, which our vagabonds do so particularly favour, it seemed the more probable.

The great difference in appearance between these packets and ours, is, that there is so much of them out of the water: the main-deck being enclosed on all sides, and filled with casks and goods, like any second or third floor in a stack of warehouses; and the promenade or hurricane-deck being a-top of that again. A part of the machinery is always above this deck; where the connecting-rod, in a strong and lofty frame, is seen working away like an iron top-sawyer. There is seldom any mast or tackle: nothing aloft but two tall black chimneys. The man at the helm is shut up in a little house in the fore part of the boat (the wheel being connected with the rudder by iron chains, working the whole length of the deck); and the passengers, unless the weather be very fine indeed, usually congregate below. Directly you have left the wharf, all the life, and stir, and bustle of a packet cease. You wonder for a long time how she goes on, for there seems to be nobody in charge of her; and when another of these dull machines comes splashing by, you feel quite indignant with it, as a sullen, cumbrous, ungraceful, unship-like leviathan: quite forgetting that the vessel you are on board of, is its very counterpart.

There is always a clerk's office on the lower deck, where you pay your fare; a ladies' cabin; baggage and stowage rooms; engineer's room; and in short a great variety of perplexities which render the discovery of the gentlemen's cabin, a matter of some difficulty. It often occupies the whole length of the boat (as it did in this case), and has three or four tiers of berths on each side. When I first descended into the cabin of the New York, it looked, in my unaccustomed eyes, about as long as the Burlington Arcade.[5]

The Sound which has to be crossed on this passage, is not always a very safe or pleasant navigation, and has been the scene of some unfortunate accidents. It was a wet morning, and very misty, and we soon lost sight of land. The day was calm, however, and brightened towards noon. After exhausting (with good help from a friend) the larder, and the stock of bottled beer, I lay down to sleep: being very much tired with the fatigues of yesterday. But I awoke from my nap in time to hurry up, and see Hell Gate, the Hog's Back, the Frying Pan, and other notorious localities, attractive to all readers of famous Diedrich Knickerbocker's History.[6] We were now in a narrow channel, with sloping banks on either side, be-sprinkled with pleasant villas, and made refreshing to the sight by turf and trees. Soon we shot in quick succession, past a lighthouse;

a madhouse (how the lunatics flung up their caps and roared in sympathy with the headlong engine and the driving tide!); a jail; and other buildings: and so emerged into a noble bay, whose waters sparkled in the now cloudless sunshine like Nature's eyes turned up to Heaven.

Then there lay stretched out before us, to the right, confused heaps of buildings, with here and there a spire or steeple, looking down upon the herd below; and here and there, again, a cloud of lazy smoke; and in the foreground a forest of ships' masts, cheery with flapping sails and waving flags. Crossing from among them to the opposite shore, were steam ferry-boats laden with people, coaches, horses, waggons, baskets, boxes: crossed and recrossed by other ferry-boats: all travelling to and fro: and never idle. Stately among these restless Insects, were two or three large ships, moving with slow majestic pace, as creatures of a prouder kind, disdainful of their puny journeys, and making for the broad sea. Beyond, were shining heights, and islands in the glancing river, and a distance scarcely less blue and bright than the sky it seemed to meet. The city's hum and buzz, the clinking of capstans, the ringing of bells, the barking of dogs, the clattering of wheels, tingled in the listening ear. All of which life and stir, coming across the stirring water, caught new life and animation from its free companionship; and, sympathising with its buoyant spirits, glistened as it seemed in sport upon its surface, and hemmed the vessel round, and plashed the water high about her sides, and, floating her gallantly into the dock, flew off again to welcome other comers, and speed before them to the busy port.

CHAPTER 6

New York

THE beautiful metropolis of America is by no means so clean a city as Boston, but many of its streets have the same characteristics; except that the houses are not quite so fresh-coloured, the signboards are not quite so gaudy, the gilded letters not quite so golden, the bricks not quite so red, the stone not quite so white, the blinds and area railings not quite so green, the knobs and plates upon the street doors not quite so bright and twinkling. There are many by-streets, almost as neutral in clean colours, and positive in dirty ones, as by-streets in London; and there is one quarter, commonly called the Five Points,[1] which, in respect of filth and wretchedness, may be safely backed against Seven Dials,[2] or any other part of famed St Giles's.

The great promenade and thoroughfare, as most people know, is Broadway; a wide and bustling street, which, from the Battery Gardens to its opposite termination in a country road, may be four miles long. Shall we sit down in an upper floor of the Carlton House Hotel (situated in the best part of this main artery of New York), and when we are tired of looking down upon the life below, sally forth arm-in-arm, and mingle with the stream?

Warm weather! The sun strikes upon our heads at this open window, as though its rays were concentrated through a burning-glass; but the day is in its zenith, and the season an unusual one. Was there ever such a sunny street as this Broadway! The pavement stones are polished with the tread of feet until they shine again; the red bricks of the houses might be yet in the dry, hot kilns; and the roofs of those omnibuses look as though, if water were poured on them, they would hiss and smoke, and smell like half-quenched fires. No stint of omnibuses here! Half-a-dozen have gone by within as many minutes. Plenty of hackney cabs and coaches too; gigs,[3] phaetons,[4] large-wheeled tilburies,[5] and private carriages – rather of a clumsy make, and not very different from the public vehicles, but built for the heavy roads beyond the city pavement. Negro coachmen and white; in straw hats, black hats, white hats, glazed caps, fur caps; in coats of drab,[6] black, brown, green, blue, nankeen,[7] striped jean and linen; and there, in that one instance (look while it passes, or it will be too late), in suits of livery. Some southern republican that, who puts his blacks in uniform, and swells with Sultan pomp and power. Yonder, where that phaeton with the well-clipped pair of grays has stopped – standing at their heads now – is a Yorkshire groom, who has not been very long in these parts, and looks sorrowfully round for a companion pair of top-boots, which he may traverse the city half a year without meeting. Heaven save the ladies, how they dress! We have seen more colours in these ten minutes, than we should have seen elsewhere, in as many days. What various parasols! what rainbow silks and satins! what pinking of thin stockings, and pinching of thin shoes, and fluttering of ribbons and silk tassels, and display of rich cloaks with gaudy hoods and linings! The young gentlemen are fond, you see, of turning down their shirt-collars and cultivating their whiskers, especially under the chin; but they cannot approach the ladies in their dress or bearing, being, to say the truth, humanity of quite another sort. Byrons of the desk and counter, pass on, and let us see what kind of men those are behind ye: those two labourers in holiday clothes, of whom one carries in his hand a crumpled scrap of paper from which he tries to spell out a hard name, while the other looks about for it on all the doors and windows.

Irishmen both! You might know them, if they were masked, by their long-tailed blue coats and bright buttons, and their drab trousers, which they wear like men well used to working dresses, who are easy in no others. It would be hard to keep your model republics going, without the countrymen and countrywomen of those two labourers. For who else would dig, and delve, and drudge, and do domestic work, and make canals and roads, and execute great lines of Internal Improvement! Irishmen both, and sorely puzzled too, to find out what they seek. Let us go down, and help them, for the love of home, and that spirit of liberty which admits of honest service to honest men, and honest work for honest bread, no matter what it be.

That's well! We have got at the right address at last, though it is written in strange characters truly, and might have been scrawled with the blunt handle of the spade the writer better knows the use of, than a pen. Their way lies yonder, but what business takes them there? They carry savings: to hoard up? No. They are brothers, those men. One crossed the sea alone, and working very hard for one half year, and living harder, saved funds enough to bring the other out. That done, they worked together, side by side, contentedly sharing hard labour and hard living for another term, and then their sisters came, and then another brother, and lastly, their old mother. And what now? Why, the poor old crone is restless in a strange land, and yearns to lay her bones, she says, among her people in the old graveyard at home: and so they go to pay her passage back: and God help her and them, and every simple heart, and all who turn to the Jerusalem of their younger days, and have an altar-fire upon the cold hearth of their fathers.

This narrow thoroughfare, baking and blistering in the sun, is Wall Street: the Stock Exchange and Lombard Street[8] of New York. Many a rapid fortune has been made in this street, and many a no less rapid ruin. Some of these very merchants whom you see hanging about here now, have locked up Money in their strong-boxes, like the man in the Arabian Nights, and opening them again, have found but withered leaves.[9] Below, here by the water-side, where the bowsprits of ships stretch across the footway, and almost thrust themselves into the windows, lie the noble American vessels which have made their Packet Service[10] the finest in the world. They have brought hither the foreigners who abound in all the streets: not, perhaps, that there are more here, than in other commercial cities; but elsewhere, they have particular haunts, and you must find them out; here, they pervade the town.

We cross Broadway again; gaining some refreshment from the heat, in the sight of the great blocks of clean ice which are being carried into shops and bar-rooms; and the pine-apples and water-melons profusely displayed for sale. Fine streets of spacious houses here, you see! – Wall Street has furnished and dismantled many of them very often – and here a deep green leafy square. Be sure that is a hospitable house with inmates to be affectionately remembered always, where they have the open door and pretty show of plants within, and where the child with laughing eyes is peeping out of window at the little dog below. You wonder what may be the use of this tall flagstaff in the by-street, with something like Liberty's head-dress on its top: so do I. But there is a passion for tall flag-staffs hereabout, and you may see its twin brother in five minutes, if you have a mind.

Again across Broadway, and so – passing from the many-coloured crowd and glittering shops – into another long main street, the Bowery. A railroad yonder, see, where two stout horses trot along, drawing a score or two of people and a great wooden ark, with ease. The stores are poorer here; the passengers less gay. Clothes ready-made, and meat ready-cooked, are to be bought in these parts; and the lively whirl of carriages is exchanged for the deep rumble of carts and waggons. These signs which are so plentiful, in shape like river buoys, or small balloons, hoisted by cords to poles, and dangling there, announce, as you may see by looking up, 'OYSTERS IN EVERY STYLE.' They tempt the hungry most at night, for then dull candles glimmering inside, illuminate these dainty words, and make the mouths of idlers water, as they read and linger.

What is this dismal-fronted pile of bastard Egyptian, like an enchanter's palace in a melodrama! – a famous prison, called The Tombs.[11] Shall we go in?

So. A long, narrow, lofty building, stove-heated as usual, with four galleries, one above the other, going round it, and communicating by stairs. Between the two sides of each gallery, and in its centre, a bridge, for the greater convenience of crossing. On each of these bridges sits a man: dozing or reading, or talking to an idle companion. On each tier, are two opposite rows of small iron doors. They look like furnace-doors, but are cold and black, as though the fires within had all gone out. Some two or three are open, and women, with drooping heads bent down, are talking to the inmates. The whole is lighted by a skylight, but it is fast closed; and from the roof there dangle, limp and drooping, two useless windsails.

A man with keys appears, to show us round. A good-looking fellow, and, in his way, civil and obliging.

'Are those black doors the cells?'

'Yes.'

'Are they all full?'

'Well, they're pretty nigh full, and that's a fact, and no two ways about it.'

'Those at the bottom are unwholesome, surely?'

'Why, we *do* only put coloured people in 'em. That's the truth.'

'When do the prisoners take exercise?'

'Well, they do without it pretty much.'

'Do they never walk in the yard?'

'Considerable seldom.'

'Sometimes, I suppose?'

'Well, it's rare they do. They keep pretty bright without it.'

'But suppose a man were here for a twelvemonth. I know this is only a prison for criminals who are charged with grave offences, while they are awaiting their trial, or are under remand, but the law here affords criminals many means of delay. What with motions for new trial, and in arrest of judgment, and what not, a prisoner might be here for twelve months, I take it, might he not?'

'Well, I guess he might.'

'Do you mean to say that in all that time he would never come out at that little iron door, for exercise?'

'He might walk some, perhaps – not much.'

'Will you open one of the doors?'

'All, if you like.'

The fastenings jar and rattle, and one of the doors turns slowly on its hinges. Let us look in. A small bare cell, into which the light enters through a high chink in the wall. There is a rude means of washing, a table, and a bedstead. Upon the latter, sits a man of sixty; reading. He looks up for a moment; gives an impatient dogged shake; and fixes his eyes upon his book again. As we withdraw our heads, the door closes on him, and is fastened as before. This man has murdered his wife, and will probably be hanged.

'How long has he been here?'

'A month.'

'When will he be tried?'

'Next term.'

'What is that?'

'Next month.'

'In England, if a man be under sentence of death, even, he has air and exercise at certain periods of the day.'

'Possible?'

With what stupendous and untranslatable coolness he says this, and how loungingly he leads on to the women's side: making, as he goes, a kind of iron castanet of the key and the stair-rail!

Each cell door on this side has a square aperture in it. Some of the women peep anxiously through it at the sound of footsteps; others shrink away in shame. – For what offence can that lonely child, of ten or twelve years old, be shut up here? Oh! that boy? He is the son of the prisoner we saw just now; is a witness against his father; and is detained here for safe keeping, until the trial; that's all.

But it is a dreadful place for the child to pass the long days and nights in. This is rather hard treatment for a young witness, is it not? – What says our conductor?

'Well, it an't a very rowdy life, and *that's* a fact!'

Again he clinks his metal castanet, and leads us leisurely away. I have a question to ask him as we go.

'Pray, why do they call this place The Tombs?'

'Well, it's the cant name.'

'I know it is. Why?'

'Some suicides happened here, when it was first built. I expect it come about from that.'

'I saw just now, that that man's clothes were scattered about the floor of his cell. Don't you oblige the prisoners to be orderly, and put such things away?'

'Where should they put 'em?'

'Not on the ground surely. What do you say to hanging them up?'

He stops, and looks round to emphasise his answer:

'Why, I say that's just it. When they had hooks they *would* hang themselves, so they're taken out of every cell, and there's only the marks left where they used to be!'

The prison-yard in which he pauses now, has been the scene of terrible performances. Into this narrow, grave-like place, men are brought out to die. The wretched creature stands beneath the gibbet on the ground; the rope about his neck; and when the sign is given, a weight at its other end comes running down, and swings him up into the air – a corpse.

The law requires that there be present at this dismal spectacle, the judge, the jury, and citizens to the amount of twenty-five. From the community it is hidden. To the dissolute and bad, the thing remains a frightful mystery. Between the criminal and them, the prison-wall is interposed as a thick gloomy veil. It is the curtain to his bed of death, his winding-sheet, and grave. From him it shuts out life, and all the motives to unrepenting hardihood in that last hour, which its mere sight and presence is often all-sufficient to sustain. There are no bold eyes to make him bold; no ruffians to uphold a ruffian's name before. All beyond the pitiless stone wall, is unknown space.

Let us go forth again into the cheerful streets.

Once more in Broadway! Here are the same ladies in bright colours, walking to and fro, in pairs and singly; yonder the very same light blue parasol which passed and repassed the hotel-window twenty times while we were sitting there. We are going to cross here. Take care of the pigs. Two portly sows are trotting up behind this carriage, and a select party of half-a-dozen gentlemen-hogs have just now turned the corner.

Here is a solitary swine, lounging homeward by himself. He has only one ear; having parted with the other to vagrant-dogs in the course of his city rambles. But he gets on very well without it; and leads a roving, gentlemanly, vagabond kind of life, somewhat answering to that of our club-men at home. He leaves his lodgings every morning at a certain hour, throws himself upon the town, gets through his day in some manner quite satisfactory to himself, and regularly appears at the door of his own house again at night, like the mysterious master of Gil Blas.[12] He is a free-and-easy, careless, indifferent kind of pig, having a very large acquaintance among other pigs of the same character, whom he rather knows by sight than conversation, as he seldom troubles himself to stop and exchange civilities, but goes grunting down the kennel, turning up the news and small-talk of the city, in the shape of cabbage-stalks and offal, and bearing no tails but his own: which is a very short one, for his old enemies, the dogs, have been at that too, and have left him hardly enough to swear by. He is in every respect a republican pig, going wherever he pleases, and mingling with the best society, on an equal, if not superior footing, for every one makes way when he appears, and the haughtiest give him the wall, if he prefer it. He is a great philosopher, and seldom moved, unless by the dogs before mentioned. Sometimes, indeed, you may see his small eye twinkling on a slaughtered friend, whose carcase garnishes a butcher's door-post, but he grunts out 'Such is life: all flesh is pork!' buries his nose in the mire again, and waddles down the gutter: comforting himself with the reflection that there is one snout the less to anticipate stray cabbage-stalks, at any rate.

They are the city scavengers, these pigs. Ugly brutes they are; having, for the most part, scanty brown backs, like the lids of old horsehair trunks: spotted with unwholesome black blotches. They have long, gaunt legs, too, and such peaked snouts, that if one of them could be persuaded to sit for his profile, nobody would recognise it for a pig's likeness. They are never attended upon, or fed, or driven, or caught, but are thrown upon their own resources in early life, and become preternaturally knowing in consequence. Every pig knows where he lives, much better than anybody could tell him. At this hour, just as evening is closing in, you will see them roaming towards bed by scores, eating their way to the last. Occasionally, some youth among them who has over-eaten himself, or has been much worried by dogs, trots shrinkingly homeward, like a prodigal son: but this is a rare case: perfect self-possession and self-reliance, and immovable composure, being their foremost attributes.

The streets and shops are lighted now; and as the eye travels down the long thoroughfare, dotted with bright jets of gas, it is reminded of Oxford Street or Piccadilly. Here and there a flight of broad stone cellar-steps appears, and a painted lamp directs you to the Bowling Saloon, or Ten-Pin alley; Ten-Pins being a game of mingled chance and skill, invented when the legislature passed an act forbidding Nine-Pins.[13] At other downward flights of steps, are other lamps, marking the whereabouts of oyster-cellars – pleasant retreats, say I: not only by reason of their wonderful cookery of oysters, pretty nigh as large as cheese-plates (or for thy dear sake, heartiest of Greek Professors!),[14] but because of all kinds of eaters of fish, or flesh, or fowl, in these latitudes, the swallowers of oysters alone are not gregarious; but subduing themselves, as it were, to the nature of what they work in, and copying the coyness of the thing they eat, do sit apart in curtained boxes, and consort by twos, not by two hundreds.

But how quiet the streets are! Are there no itinerant bands; no wind or stringed instruments? No, not one. By day, are there no Punches, Fantoccinis,[15] Dancing-dogs, Jugglers, Conjurers, Orchestrinas,[16] or even Barrel-organs? No, not one. Yes, I remember one. One barrel-organ and a dancing-monkey – sportive by nature, but fast fading into a dull, lumpish monkey, of the Utilitarian school.[17] Beyond that, nothing lively; no, not so much as a white mouse in a twirling cage.

Are there no amusements? Yes. There is a lecture-room across the way, from which that glare of light proceeds, and there may be evening service for the ladies thrice a week, or oftener. For the young gentlemen, there is the counting-house, the store, the bar-room: the latter, as you may see through these windows, pretty full. Hark! to the clinking sound of hammers breaking lumps of ice, and to the cool gurgling of the pounded bits, as, in the process of mixing, they are poured from glass to glass! No amusements? What are these suckers of cigars and swallowers of strong drinks, whose hats and legs we see in every possible variety of twist, doing, but amusing themselves? What are the fifty newspapers, which those precocious urchins are bawling down the street, and which are kept filed within, what are they but amusements? Not vapid, waterish amusements, but good strong stuff; dealing in round abuse and blackguard names; pulling off the roofs of private houses, as the Halting Devil did in Spain;[18] pimping and pandering for all degrees of vicious taste, and gorging with coined lies the most voracious maw; imputing to every man in public life the coarsest and the vilest motives; scaring away from the stabbed and prostrate body-politic, every Samaritan of clear conscience and good deeds; and setting on, with yell and whistle and the clapping of foul hands, the vilest vermin and worst birds of prey. – No amusements!

Let us go on again; and passing this wilderness of an hotel with stores about its base, like some Continental theatre, or the London Opera House shorn of its colonnade, plunge into the Five Points. But it is needful, first, that we take as our escort these two heads of the police, whom you would know for sharp and well-trained officers if you met them in the Great Desert.[19] So true it is, that certain pursuits, wherever carried on, will stamp men with the same character. These two might have been begotten, born, and bred, in Bow Street.

We have seen no beggars in the streets by night or day; but of other kinds of strollers, plenty. Poverty, wretchedness, and vice, are rife enough where we are going now.

This is the place: these narrow ways, diverging to the right and left, and reeking everywhere with dirt and filth. Such lives as are led here, bear the same fruits here as elsewhere. The coarse and bloated faces at the doors, have counterparts at home, and all the wide world over. Debauchery has made the very houses prematurely old. See how the rotten beams are tumbling down, and how the patched and broken windows seem to scowl dimly, like eyes that have been hurt in drunken frays. Many of those pigs live here. Do they ever wonder why their masters walk upright in lieu of going on all-fours? and why they talk instead of grunting?

So far, nearly every house is a low tavern; and on the bar-room walls, are coloured prints of Washington, and Queen Victoria of England, and the American Eagle. Among the pigeon-holes that hold the bottles, are pieces of plate-glass and coloured paper, for there is, in some sort, a taste for decoration, even here. And as sea-men frequent these haunts, there are maritime pictures by the dozen: of partings between sailors and their lady-loves, portraits of William, of the ballad, and his Black-Eyed Susan;[20] of Will Watch, the Bold

Smuggler;[21] of Paul Jones the Pirate,[22] and the like: on which the painted eyes of Queen Victoria, and of Washington to boot, rest in as strange companionship, as on most of the scenes that are enacted in their wondering presence.

What place is this, to which the squalid street conducts us? A kind of square of leprous houses, some of which are attainable only by crazy wooden stairs without. What lies beyond this tottering flight of steps, that creak beneath our tread? – a miserable room, lighted by one dim candle, and destitute of all comfort, save that which may be hidden in a wretched bed. Beside it, sits a man: his elbows on his knees: his forehead hidden in his hands. 'What ails that man?' asks the foremost officer. 'Fever,' he sullenly replies, without looking up. Conceive the fancies of a fevered brain, in such a place as this!

Ascend these pitch-dark stairs, heedful of a false footing on the trembling boards, and grope your way with me into this wolfish den, where neither ray of light nor breath of air, appears to come. A negro lad, startled from his sleep by the officer's voice – he knows it well – but comforted by his assurance that he has not come on business, officiously bestirs himself to light a candle. The match flickers for a moment, and shows great mounds of dusty rags upon the ground; then dies away and leaves a denser darkness than before, if there can be degrees in such extremes. He stumbles down the stairs and presently comes back, shading a flaring taper with his hand. Then the mounds of rags are seen to be astir, and rise slowly up, and the floor is covered with heaps of negro women, waking from their sleep: their white teeth chattering, and their bright eyes glistening and winking on all sides with surprise and fear, like the countless repetition of one astonished African face in some strange mirror.

Mount up these other stairs with no less caution (there are traps and pitfalls here, for those who are not so well escorted as ourselves) into the housetop; where the bare beams and rafters meet overhead, and calm night looks down through the crevices in the roof. Open the door of one of these cramped hutches full of sleeping negroes. Pah! They have a charcoal fire within; there is a smell of singeing clothes, or flesh, so close they gather round the brazier; and vapours issue forth that blind and suffocate. From every corner, as you glance about you in these dark retreats, some figure crawls half-awakened, as if the judgment-hour were near at hand, and every obscene grave were giving up its dead. Where dogs would howl to lie, women, and men, and boys slink off to sleep, forcing the dislodged rats to move away in quest of better lodgings.

Here too are lanes and alleys, paved with mud knee-deep, underground chambers, where they dance and game; the walls bedecked with rough designs of ships, and forts, and flags, and American Eagles out of number: ruined houses, open to the street, whence, through wide gaps in the walls, other ruins loom upon the eye, as though the world of vice and misery had nothing else to show: hideous tenements which take their name from robbery and murder: all that is loathsome, drooping, and decayed is here.

Our leader has his hand upon the latch of 'Almack's,' and calls to us from the bottom of the steps; for the assembly-room of the Five Point fashionables is approached by a descent.[23] Shall we go in? It is but a moment.

Heyday! the landlady of Almack's thrives! A buxom fat mulatto woman, with sparkling eyes, whose head is daintily ornamented with a handkerchief of many colours. Nor is the landlord much behind her in his finery, being attired in a smart blue jacket, like a ship's steward, with a thick gold ring upon his little finger, and round his neck a gleaming golden watch-guard. How glad he is to see us! What will we please to call for? A dance? It shall be done directly, sir: 'a regular break-down.'

The corpulent black fiddler, and his friend who plays the tambourine, stamp upon the boarding of the small raised orchestra in which they sit, and play a lively measure. Five or six couple come upon the floor, marshalled by a lively young negro, who is the wit of the assembly, and the greatest dancer known.[24] He never leaves off making queer faces, and is the delight of all the rest, who grin from ear to ear incessantly. Among the dancers are two young mulatto girls, with large, black, drooping eyes, and head-gear after the fashion of the hostess, who are as shy, or feign to be, as though they never danced before, and so look down before the visitors, that their partners can see nothing but the long fringed lashes.

But the dance commences. Every gentleman sets as long as he likes to the opposite lady, and the opposite lady to him, and all are so long about it that the sport begins to languish, when suddenly the lively hero dashes in to the rescue. Instantly the fiddler grins, and goes at it tooth and nail; there is new energy in the tambourine; new laughter in the dancers; new smiles in the landlady; new confidence in the landlord; new brightness in the very candles. Single shuffle, double shuffle, cut and cross-cut; snapping his fingers, rolling his eyes, turning in his knees, presenting the backs of his legs in front, spinning about on his toes and heels like nothing but the man's fingers on the tambourine; dancing with two left legs, two right legs, two wooden legs, two wire legs, two spring legs – all sorts of legs and no legs – what is this to him? And in what walk of life, or dance of life, does man ever get such stimulating applause as thunders about him, when, having danced his partner off her feet, and himself too, he finishes by leaping gloriously on the bar-counter, and calling for something to drink, with the chuckle of a million of counterfeit Jim Crows,[25] in one inimitable sound!

The air, even in these distempered parts, is fresh after the stifling atmosphere of the houses; and now, as we emerge into a broader street, it blows upon us with a purer breath, and the stars look bright again. Here are The Tombs once more. The city watch-house is a part of the building. It follows naturally on the sights we have just left. Let us see that, and then to bed.

What! do you thrust your common offenders against the police discipline of the town, into such holes as these? Do men and women, against whom no crime is proved, lie here all night in perfect dark-ness, surrounded by the noisome vapours which encircle that flagging lamp you light us with, and breathing this filthy and offensive stench! Why, such indecent and disgusting dungeons as these cells, would bring disgrace upon the most despotic empire in the world! Look at them, man – you, who see them every night, and keep the keys. Do you see what they are? Do you know how drains are made below the streets, and wherein these human sewers differ, except in being always stagnant?

Well, he don't know. He has had five-and-twenty young women locked up in this very cell at one time, and you'd hardly realise what handsome faces there were among 'em.

In God's name! shut the door upon the wretched creature who is in it now, and put its screen before a place, quite unsurpassed in all the vice, neglect, and devilry, of the worst old town in Europe.

Are people really left all night, untried, in those black sties? – Every night. The watch is set at seven in the evening. The magistrate opens his court at five in the morning. That is the earliest hour at which the first prisoner can be released; and if an officer appear against him, he is not taken out till nine o'clock or ten. – But if any one among them die in the interval, as one man did, not long ago? Then he is half-eaten by the rats in an hour's time; as that man was; and there an end.

What is this intolerable tolling of great bells, and crashing of wheels, and shouting in the distance? A fire. And what that deep red light in the opposite direction? Another fire. And what these charred and blackened walls we stand before? A dwelling where a fire has been. It was more than hinted, in an official report, not long ago, that some of these conflagrations were not wholly accidental, and that speculation and enterprise found a field of exertion, even in flames: but be this as it may, there was a fire last night, there are two to-night, and you may lay an even wager there will be at least one, to-morrow. So, carrying that with us for our comfort, let us say, Good night, and climb up-stairs to bed.

One day, during my stay in New York, I paid a visit to the different public institutions on Long Island [, or Rhode Island: I forget which]. One of them is a Lunatic Asylum. The building is handsome; and is remarkable for a spacious and elegant staircase. The whole structure is not yet finished, but it is already one of considerable size and extent, and is capable of accommodating a very large number of patients.

I cannot say that I derived much comfort from the inspection of this charity. The different wards might have been cleaner and better ordered; I saw nothing of that salutary system which had impressed me so favourably elsewhere; and everything had a lounging, listless, madhouse air, which was very painful. The moping idiot, cowering down with long dishevelled hair; the gibbering maniac, with his hideous laugh and pointed finger; the vacant eye, the fierce wild face, the gloomy picking of the hands and lips, and munching of the nails: there they were all, without disguise, in naked ugliness and horror. In the dining-room, a bare, dull, dreary place, with nothing for the eye to rest on but the empty walls, a woman was locked up alone. She was bent, they told me, on committing suicide. If any-thing could have strengthened her in her resolution, it would certainly have been the insupportable monotony of such an existence.

The terrible crowd with which these halls and galleries were filled, so shocked me, that I abridged my stay within the shortest limits, and declined to see that portion of the building in which the refractory and violent were under closer restraint. I have no doubt that the gentleman who presided over this establishment at the time I write of, was competent to manage it, and had done all in his power to promote its usefulness: but will it be believed that the miserable strife of Party feeling is carried even into this sad refuge of afflicted and degraded humanity? Will it be believed that the eyes which are to watch over and controul the wanderings of minds on which the most dreadful visitation to which our nature is exposed has fallen, must wear the glasses of some wretched side in Politics? Will it be believed that the governor of such a house as this, is appointed, and deposed, and changed perpetually, as Parties fluctuate and vary, and as their despicable weathercocks are blown this way or that? A hundred times in every week, some new most paltry exhibition of that narrow-minded and injurious Party Spirit, which is the Simoom [26] of America, sickening and blighting everything of wholesome life within its reach, was forced upon my notice; but I never turned my back upon it with feelings of such deep disgust and measureless contempt, as when I crossed the threshold of this madhouse on Long Island.

At a short distance from this building is another called the Alms House, that is to say, the workhouse of New York. This is a large Institution also: lodging, I believe, when I was there, nearly a thousand poor. It was badly ventilated, and badly lighted; was not too clean; and impressed me, on the whole, very uncomfortably. But it must be remembered that New York, as a great emporium of commerce, and as a place of general resort, not only from all parts of the States, but from most parts of the world, has always a large pauper population to provide for; and labours, therefore, under peculiar difficulties in this respect. Nor must it be forgotten that New York is a large town, and that in all large towns a vast amount of good and evil is intermixed and jumbled up together.

In the same neighbourhood is the Long Island Farm, where young orphans are nursed and bred. I did not see it, but I believe it is well conducted; and I can the more easily credit it, from knowing how mindful they usually are, in America, of that beautiful passage in the Litany which remembers all sick persons and young children. [27]

I was taken to these Institutions by water, in a boat belonging to the Long Island Jail, and rowed by a crew of prisoners, who were dressed in a striped uniform of black and buff, in which they looked like faded tigers. They took me, by the same conveyance, to the Jail itself.

It is an old prison, and quite a pioneer establishment, on the plan I have already described. I was glad to hear this, for it is unquestionably a very indifferent one. The most is made, however, of the means it possesses, and it is as well regulated as such a place can be.

The women work in covered sheds, erected for that purpose. If I remember right, there are no shops for the men, but be that as it may, the greater part of them labour in certain stone-quarries near at hand. The day being very wet indeed, this labour was suspended, and the prisoners were in their cells. Imagine these cells, some two or three hundred in number, and in every one a man, locked up; this one at his door for air, with his hands thrust through the grate; this one in bed (in the middle of the day, remember); and this one flung down in a heap upon the ground, with his head against the bars, like a wild beast. Make the rain pour down, outside, in torrents. Put the everlasting stove in the midst; hot, and suffocating, and vaporous, as a witch's cauldron. Add a collection of gentle odours, such as would arise from a thousand mildewed umbrellas, wet through, and a thousand buck-baskets, full of half-washed linen – and there is the prison, as it was that day.

The prison for the State at Sing Sing,[28] is, on the other hand, a model jail. That, and Mount Auburn,[29] are [, I believe,] the largest and best examples of the silent system.

In another part of the city, is the Refuge for the Destitute: an Institution whose object is to reclaim youthful offenders, male and female, black and white, without distinction; to teach them useful trades, apprentice them to respectable masters, and make them worthy members of society. Its design, it will be seen, is similar to that at Boston; and it is a no less meritorious and admirable establishment. A suspicion crossed my mind during my inspection of this noble charity, whether the superintendent had quite sufficient knowledge of the world and worldly characters; and whether he did not commit a great mistake in treating some young girls, who were to all intents and purposes, by their years and their past lives, women, as though they were little children; which certainly had a ludicrous effect in my eyes, and, or I am much mistaken, in theirs also. As the Institution, however, is always under a vigilant examination of a body of gentlemen of great intelligence and experience, it cannot fail to be well conducted; and whether I am right or wrong in this slight particular, is unimportant to its deserts and character, which it would be difficult to estimate too highly.

In addition to these establishments, there are, in New York, excellent hospitals and schools, literary institutions and libraries; an admirable fire department (as indeed it should be, having constant practice), and charities of every sort and kind. In the suburbs there is a spacious cemetery: unfinished yet, but every day improving. The saddest tomb I saw there was 'The Strangers' Grave. Dedicated to the different hotels in this city.'

There are three principal theatres. Two of them, the Park and the Bowery, are large, elegant, and handsome buildings, and are, I grieve to write it, generally deserted. The third, the Olympic, is a tiny show-box for vaudevilles and burlesques. It is singularly well conducted by Mr Mitchell,[30] a comic actor of great quiet humour and originality, who is well remembered and esteemed by London playgoers. I am happy to report of this deserving gentleman, that his benches are usually well filled, and that his theatre rings with merriment every night. I had almost forgotten a small summer theatre, called Niblo's,[31] with gardens and open air amusements attached; but I believe it is not exempt from the general depression under which Theatrical Property, or what is humorously called by that name, unfortunately labours.

The country round New York is surpassingly and exquisitely picturesque. The climate, as I have already intimated, is somewhat of the warmest. What it would be, without the sea breezes which come from its beautiful Bay in the evening time, I will not throw myself or my readers into a fever by inquiring.

The tone of the best society in this city, is like that of Boston; here and there, it may be, with a greater infusion of the mercantile spirit, but generally polished and refined, and always most hospitable. The houses and tables are elegant; the hours later and more rakish; and there is, perhaps, a greater spirit of contention in reference to appearances, and the display of wealth and costly living. The ladies are singularly beautiful.

Before I left New York I made arrangements for securing a

passage home in the George Washington packet ship, which was advertised to sail in June: that being the month in which I had determined, if prevented by no accident in the course of my ramblings, to leave America.

I never thought that going back to England, returning to all who are dear to me, and to pursuits that have insensibly grown to be a part of my nature, I could have felt so much sorrow as I endured, when I parted at last, on board this ship, with the friends who had accompanied me from this city. I never thought the name of any place, so far away and so lately known, could ever associate itself in my mind with the crowd of affectionate remembrances that now cluster about it. There are those in this city who would brighten, to me, the darkest winter-day that ever glimmered and went out in Lapland; and before whose presence even Home grew dim, when they and I exchanged that painful word which mingles with our every thought and deed; which haunts our cradle-heads in infancy, and closes up the vista of our lives in age.

CHAPTER 7

Philadelphia, and its Solitary Prison

THE journey from New York to Philadelphia, is made by railroad, and two ferries; and usually occupies between five and six hours. It was a fine evening when we were passengers in the train: and watching the bright sunset from a little window near the door by which we sat, my attention was attracted to a remarkable appearance issuing from the windows of the gentlemen's car immediately in front of us, which I supposed for some time was occasioned by a number of industrious persons inside, ripping open feather-beds, and giving the feathers to the wind. At length it occurred to me that they were only spitting, which was indeed the case; though how any number of passengers which it was possible for that car to contain, could have maintained such a playful and incessant shower of expectoration, I am still at a loss to understand: notwithstanding the experience in all salivatory phenomena which I afterwards acquired.

I made acquaintance, on this journey, with a mild and modest young quaker, who opened the discourse by informing me, in a grave whisper, that his grandfather was the inventor of cold-drawn castor oil. I mention the circumstance here, thinking it probable that this is the first occasion on which the valuable medicine in question was ever used as a conversational aperient.

We reached the city, late that night. Looking out of my chamber-window, before going to bed, I saw, on the opposite side of the way, a handsome building of white marble, which had a mournful ghost-like aspect, dreary to behold. I attributed this to the sombre influence of the night, and on rising in the morning looked out again, expecting to see its steps and portico thronged with groups of people passing in and out. The door was still tight shut, however; the same cold cheerless air prevailed; and the building looked as if the marble statue of Don Guzman could alone have any business to transact within its gloomy walls.[1] I hastened to inquire its name and purpose, and then my surprise vanished. It was the Tomb of many fortunes; the Great Catacomb of investment; the memorable United States Bank.

The stoppage of this bank, with all its ruinous consequences, had cast (as I was told on every side) a gloom on Philadelphia, under the depressing effect of which it yet laboured. It certainly did seem rather dull and out of spirits.

It is a handsome city, but distractingly regular. After walking about it for an hour or two, I felt that I would have given the world for a crooked street. The collar of my coat appeared to stiffen, and the brim of my hat to expand, beneath its quakerly influence. My hair shrunk into a sleek short crop, my hands folded themselves upon my breast of their own calm accord, and thoughts of taking lodgings in Mark Lane[2] over against the Market Place, and of making a large fortune by speculations in corn, came over me involuntarily.

Philadelphia is most bountifully provided with fresh water, which is showered and jerked about, and turned on, and poured off, everywhere. The Waterworks, which are on a height near the city, are no less ornamental than useful, being tastefully laid out as a public garden, and kept in the best and neatest order. The river is dammed at this point, and forced by its own power into certain high tanks or reservoirs, whence the whole city, to the top stories of the houses, is supplied at a very trifling expense.

There are various public institutions. Among them a most excellent Hospital – a quaker establishment, but not sectarian in the great benefits it confers; a quiet, quaint old Library, named after Franklin;[3] a handsome Exchange and Post Office; and so forth. In connection with the quaker Hospital, there is a picture by West,[4] which is exhibited for the benefit of the funds of the institution. The subject is, our Saviour healing the sick, and it is, perhaps, as favourable a specimen of the master as can be seen anywhere. Whether this be high or low praise, depends upon the reader's taste.

In the same room, there is a very characteristic and life-like portrait by Mr Sully,[5] a distinguished American artist.

My stay in Philadelphia was very short, but what I saw of its society, I greatly liked. Treating of its general characteristics, I should be disposed to say that it is more provincial than Boston or New York, and that there is, afloat in the fair city, an assumption of taste and criticism, savouring rather of those genteel discussions upon the same themes, in connection with Shakspeare and the Musical Glasses, of which we read in the Vicar of Wakefield.[6] Near the city, is a most splendid unfinished marble structure for the Girard College, founded by a deceased gentleman of that name and of enormous wealth, which, if completed according to the original design, will be perhaps the richest edifice of modern times. But the bequest is involved in legal disputes, and pending them the work has stopped; so that like many other great undertakings in America, even this is rather going to be done one of these days, than doing now.[7]

In the outskirts, stands a great prison, called the Eastern Penitentiary: conducted on a plan peculiar to the state of Pennsylvania. The system here, is rigid, strict, and hopeless solitary confinement. I believe it, in its effects, to be cruel and wrong.

In its intention, I am well convinced that it is kind, humane, and meant for reformation; but I am persuaded that those who devised this system of Prison Discipline, and those benevolent gentlemen who carry it into execution, do not know what it is that they are doing. I believe that very few men are capable of estimating the immense amount of torture and agony which this dreadful punishment, prolonged for years, inflicts upon the sufferers; and in guessing at it myself, and in reasoning from what I have seen written upon their faces, and what to my certain knowledge they feel within, I am only the more convinced that there is a depth of terrible endurance in it which none but the sufferers themselves can fathom, and which no man has a right to inflict upon his fellow-creature. I hold this slow and daily tampering with the mysteries of the brain, to be immeasurably worse than any torture of the body: and because its ghastly signs and tokens are not so palpable to the eye and sense of touch as scars upon the flesh; because its wounds are not upon the surface, and it extorts few cries that human ears can hear; therefore I the more denounce it, as a secret punishment which slumbering humanity is not roused up to stay. I hesitated once, debating with myself, whether, if I had the power of saying 'Yes' or 'No,' I would allow it to be tried in certain cases, where the terms of imprisonment were short; but now, I solemnly declare, that with no rewards or honours could I walk a happy man beneath the open sky by day, or lie me down upon my bed at night, with the consciousness that one human creature, for any length of time, no matter what, lay suffering this unknown punishment in his silent cell, and I the cause, or I consenting to it in the least degree.

I was accompanied to this prison by two gentlemen officially connected with its management, and passed the day in going from cell to cell, and talking with the inmates. Every facility was afforded me, that the utmost courtesy could suggest. Nothing was concealed or hidden from my view, and every piece of information that I sought, was openly and frankly given. The perfect order of the building cannot be praised too highly, and of the excellent motives of all who are immediately concerned in the administration of the system, there can be no kind of question.

Between the body of the prison and the outer wall, there is a spacious garden. Entering it, by a wicket in the massive gate, we pursued the path before us to its other termination, and passed into a large chamber, from which seven long passages radiate. On either side of each, is a long, long row of low cell doors, with a certain number over every one. Above, a gallery of cells like those below, except that they have no narrow yard attached (as those in the ground tier have), and are somewhat smaller. The possession of two of these, is supposed to compensate for the absence of so much air and exercise as can be had in the dull strip attached to each of the others, in an hour's time every day; and therefore every prisoner in this upper story has two cells, adjoining and communicating with, each other.

Standing at the central point, and looking down these dreary passages, the dull repose and quiet that prevails, is awful. Occasionally, there is a drowsy sound from some lone weaver's shuttle, or shoemaker's last, but it is stifled by the thick walls and heavy dungeon-door, and only serves to make the general stillness more profound. Over the head and face of every prisoner who comes into this melancholy house, a black hood is drawn; and in this dark shroud, an emblem of the curtain dropped between him and the living world, he is led to the cell from which he never again comes forth, until his whole term of imprisonment has expired. He never hears of wife or children; home or friends; the life or death of any single creature. He sees the prison-officers, but with that exception he never looks upon a human countenance, or hears a human voice. He is a man buried alive; to be dug out in the slow round of years; and in the mean time dead to everything but torturing anxieties and horrible despair.[8]

His name, and crime, and term of suffering, are unknown, even to the officer who delivers him his daily food. There is a number over his cell-door, and in a book of which the governor of the prison has one copy, and the moral instructor another: this is the index to his history. Beyond these pages the prison has no record of his existence: and though he live to be in the same cell ten weary years, he has no means of knowing, down to the very last hour, in what part of the building it is situated; what kind of men there are about him; whether in the long winter nights there are living people near, or he is in some lonely corner of the great jail, with walls, and passages, and iron doors between him and the nearest sharer in its solitary horrors.

Every cell has double doors: the outer one of sturdy oak, the other of grated iron, wherein there is a trap through which his food is handed. He has a Bible, and a slate and pencil, and, under certain restrictions, has sometimes other books, provided for the purpose, and pen and ink and paper. His razor, plate, and can, and basin, hang upon the wall, or shine upon the little shelf. Fresh water is laid on in every cell, and he can draw it at his pleasure. During the day, his bedstead turns up against the wall, and leaves more space for him to work in. His loom, or bench, or wheel, is there; and there he labours, sleeps and wakes, and counts the seasons as they change, and grows old.

The first man I saw, was seated at his loom, at work. He had been there six years, and was to remain, I think, three more. He had been convicted as a receiver of stolen goods, but even after this long imprisonment, denied his guilt, and said he had been hardly dealt by. It was his second offence.

He stopped his work when we went in, took off his spectacles, and answered freely to everything that was said to him, but always with a strange kind of pause first, and in a low, thoughtful voice. He wore a paper hat of his own making, and was pleased to have it noticed and commended. He had very ingeniously manufactured a sort of Dutch clock from some disregarded odds and ends; and his vinegar-bottle served for the pendulum. Seeing me interested in this contrivance, he looked up at it with a great deal of pride, and said that he had been thinking of improving it, and that he hoped the hammer and a little piece of broken glass beside it 'would play music before long.' He had extracted some colours from the yarn with which he worked, and painted a few poor figures on the wall. One, of a female, over the door, he called 'The Lady of the Lake.'[9]

He smiled as I looked at these contrivances to while away the time; but when I looked from them to him, I saw that his lip trembled, and could have counted the beating of his heart. I forget how it came about, but some allusion was made to his having a wife. He shook his head at the word, turned aside, and covered his face with his hands.

'But you are resigned now!' said one of the gentlemen after a short pause, during which he had resumed his former manner. He answered with a sigh that seemed quite reckless in its hopelessness, 'Oh yes, oh yes! I am resigned to it.' 'And are a better man, you think?' 'Well, I hope so: I'm sure I hope I may be.' 'And time goes pretty quickly?' 'Time is very long, gentlemen, within these four walls!'

He gazed about him – Heaven only knows how wearily! – as he said these words; and in the act of doing so, fell into a strange stare as if he had forgotten something. A moment afterwards he sighed heavily, put on his spectacles, and went about his work again.

In another cell, there was a German, sentenced to five years' imprisonment for larceny, two of which had just expired. With colours procured in the same manner, he had painted every inch of the walls and ceiling quite beautifully. He had laid out the few feet of ground, behind, with exquisite neatness, and had made a little bed in the centre, that looked by-the-by like a grave. The taste and ingenuity he had displayed in everything were most extraordinary; and yet a more dejected, heart-broken,wretched creature, it would be difficult to imagine. I never saw such a picture of forlorn affliction and distress of mind. My heart bled for him; and when the tears ran down his cheeks, and he took one of the visitors aside, to ask, with his trembling hands nervously clutching at his coat to detain him, whether there was no hope of his dismal sentence being commuted, the spectacle was really too painful to witness. I never saw or heard of any kind of misery that impressed me more than the wretchedness of this man.

In a third cell, was a tall, strong black, a burglar, working at his proper trade of making screws and the like. His time was nearly out. He was not only a very dexterous thief, but was notorious for his boldness and hardihood, and for the number of his previous convictions. He entertained us with a long account of his achievements, which he narrated with such infinite relish, that he actually seemed to lick his lips as he told us racy anecdotes of stolen plate, and of old ladies whom he had watched as they sat at windows in silver spectacles (he had plainly had an eye to their metal even from the other side of the street) and had afterwards robbed. This fellow, upon the slightest encouragement, would have mingled with his professional recollections the most detestable cant; but I am very much mistaken if he could have surpassed the unmitigated hypocrisy with which he declared that he blessed the day on which he came into that prison, and that he never would commit another robbery as long as he lived.

There was one man who was allowed, as an indulgence, to keep rabbits. His room having rather a close smell in consequence, they called to him at the door to come out into the passage. He complied of course, and stood shading his haggard face in the unwonted sunlight of the great window, looking as wan and unearthly as if he had been summoned from the grave. He had a white rabbit in his breast; and when the little creature, getting down upon the ground, stole back into the cell, and he, being dismissed, crept timidly after it, I thought it would have been very hard to say in what respect the man was the nobler animal of the two.

There was an English thief, who had been there but a few days out of seven years: a villainous, low-browed, thin-lipped fellow, with a white face; who had as yet no relish for visitors, and who, but for the additional penalty, would have gladly stabbed me with his shoemaker's knife. There was another German who had entered the jail but yesterday, and who started from his bed when we looked in, and pleaded, in his broken English, very hard for work. There was a poet, who after doing two days' work in every four-and-twenty hours, one for himself and one for the prison, wrote verses about ships (he was by trade a mariner), and 'the maddening wine-cup,' and his friends at home. There were very many of them. Some reddened at the sight of visitors, and some turned very pale. Some two or three had prisoner nurses with them, for they were very sick; and one, a fat old negro whose leg had been taken off within the jail, had for his attendant a classical scholar and an accomplished surgeon, himself a prisoner likewise. Sitting upon the stairs, engaged in some slight work, was a pretty coloured boy. 'Is there no refuge for young criminals in Philadelphia, then?' said I. 'Yes, but only for white children.' Noble aristocracy in crime!

There was a sailor who had been there upwards of eleven years, and who in a few months' time would be free. Eleven years of solitary confinement!

'I am very glad to hear your time is nearly out.' What does he say? Nothing. Why does he stare at his hands, and pick the flesh upon his fingers, and raise his eyes for an instant, every now and then, to those bare walls which have seen his head turn grey? It is a way he has sometimes.

Does he never look men in the face, and does he always pluck at those hands of his, as though he were bent on parting skin and bone? It is his humour: nothing more.

It is his humour too, to say that he does not look forward to going out; that he is not glad the time is drawing near; that he did look forward to it once, but that was very long ago; that he has lost all care for everything. It is his humour to be a helpless, crushed, and broken man. And, Heaven be his witness that he has his humour thoroughly gratified!

There were three young women in adjoining cells, all convicted at the same time of a conspiracy to rob their prosecutor. In the silence and solitude of their lives they had grown to be quite beautiful. Their looks were very sad, and might have moved the sternest visitor to tears, but not to that kind of sorrow which the contemplation of the men awakens. One was a young girl; not twenty, as I recollect; whose snow-white room was hung with the work of some former prisoner, and upon whose downcast face the sun in all its splendour shone down through the high chink in the wall, where one narrow strip of bright blue sky was visible. She was very penitent and quiet; had come to be resigned, she said (and I believe her); and had a mind at peace. 'In a word, you are happy here?' said one of my companions. She struggled – she did struggle very hard – to answer, Yes; but raising her eyes, and meeting that glimpse of freedom overhead, she burst into tears, and said, 'She tried to be; she uttered no complaint; but it was natural that she should sometimes long to go out of that one cell: she could not help *that*,' she sobbed, poor thing!

I went from cell to cell that day; and every face I saw, or word I heard, or incident I noted, is present to my mind in all its painfulness. But let me pass them by, for one, more pleasant, glance of a prison on the same plan which I afterwards saw at Pittsburg.

When I had gone over that, in the same manner, I asked the governor if he had any person in his charge who was shortly going out. He had one, he said, whose time was up next day; but he had only been a prisoner two years.

Two years! I looked back through two years of my own life – out of jail, prosperous, happy, surrounded by blessings, comforts, and good fortune – and thought how wide a gap it was, and how long those two years passed in solitary captivity would have been. I have the face of this man, who was going to be released next day, before me now. It is almost more memorable in its happiness than the other faces in their misery. How easy and how natural it was for him to say that the system was a good one; and that the time went 'pretty quick – considering;' and that when a man once felt that he had offended the law, and must satisfy it, 'he got along, somehow:' and so forth!

'What did he call you back to say to you, in that strange flutter?'

I asked of my conductor, when he had locked the door and joined me in the passage.

'Oh! That he was afraid the soles of his boots were not fit for walking, as they were a good deal worn when he came in; and that he would thank me very much to have them mended, ready.'

Those boots had been taken off his feet, and put away with the rest of his clothes, two years before!

I took that opportunity of inquiring how they conducted themselves immediately before going out; adding that I presumed they trembled very much.

'Well, it's not so much a trembling,' was the answer – 'though they do quiver – as a complete derangement of the nervous system. They can't sign their names to the book; sometimes can't even hold the pen; look about 'em without appearing to know why, or where they are; and sometimes get up and sit down again, twenty times in a minute. This is when they're in the office, where they are taken with the hood on, as they were brought in. When they get outside the gate, they stop, and look first one way and then the other; not knowing which to take. Sometimes they stagger as if they were drunk, and sometimes are forced to lean against the fence, they're so bad: – but they clear off in course of time.'

As I walked among these solitary cells, and looked at the faces of the men within them, I tried to picture to myself the thoughts and feelings natural to their condition. I imagined the hood just taken off, and the scene of their captivity disclosed to them in all its dismal monotony.

At first, the man is stunned. His confinement is a hideous vision; and his old life a reality. He throws himself upon his bed, and lies there abandoned to despair. By degrees the insupportable solitude and barrenness of the place rouses him from this stupor, and when the trap in his grated door is opened, he humbly begs and prays for work. 'Give me some work to do, or I shall go raving mad!'

He has it; and by fits and starts applies himself to labour; but every now and then there comes upon him a burning sense of the years that must be wasted in that stone coffin, and an agony so piercing in the recollection of those who are hidden from his view and knowledge, that he starts from his seat, and striding up and down the narrow room with both hands clasped on his uplifted head, hears spirits tempting him to beat his brains out on the wall.

Again he falls upon his bed, and lies there, moaning. Suddenly he starts up, wondering whether any other man is near; whether there is another cell like that on either side of him: and listens keenly.

There is no sound, but other prisoners may be near for all that. He remembers to have heard once, when he little thought of coming here himself, that the cells were so constructed that the prisoners could not hear each other, though the officers could hear them. Where is the nearest man – upon the right, or on the left? or is there one in both directions? Where is he sitting now – with his face to the light? or is he walking to and fro? How is he dressed? Has he been here long? Is he much worn away? Is he very white and spectre-like? Does *he* think of his neighbour too?

Scarcely venturing to breathe, and listening while he thinks, he conjures up a figure with its back towards him, and imagines it moving about in this next cell. He has no idea of the face, but he is certain of the dark form of a stooping man. In the cell upon the other side, he puts another figure, whose face is hidden from him also. Day after day, and often when he wakes up in the middle of the night, he thinks of these two men, until he is almost distracted. He never changes them. There they are always as he first imagined them – an old man on the right; a younger man upon the left – whose hidden features torture him to death, and have a mystery that makes him tremble.

The weary days pass on with solemn pace, like mourners at a funeral; and slowly he begins to feel that the white walls of the cell have something dreadful in them: that their colour is horrible: that their smooth surface chills his blood: that there is one hateful corner which torments him. Every morning when he wakes, he hides his head beneath the coverlet, and shudders to see the ghastly ceiling looking down upon him. The blessed light of day itself peeps in, an ugly phantom face, through the unchangeable crevice which is his prison window.

By slow but sure degrees, the terrors of that hateful corner swell until they beset him at all times; invade his rest, make his dreams hideous, and his nights dreadful. At first, he took a strange dislike to it; feeling as though it gave birth in his brain to something of corresponding shape, which ought not to be there, and racked his head with pains. Then he began to fear it, then to dream of it, and of men whispering its name and pointing to it. Then he could not bear to look at it, nor yet to turn his back upon it. Now, it is every night the lurking-place of a ghost: a shadow: – a silent something, horrible to see, but whether bird, or beast, or muffled human shape, he cannot tell.

When he is in his cell by day, he fears the little yard without. When he is in the yard, he dreads to re-enter the cell. When night comes, there stands the phantom in the corner. If he have the courage to stand in its place, and drive it out (he had once: being desperate), it broods upon his bed. In the twilight, and always at the same hour, a voice calls to him by name; as the darkness thickens, his Loom begins to live; and even that, his comfort, is a hideous figure, watching him till daybreak.

Again, by slow degrees, these horrible fancies depart from him one by one: returning sometimes, unexpectedly, but at longer intervals, and in less alarming shapes. He has talked upon religious matters with the gentleman who visits him, and has read his Bible, and has written a prayer upon his slate, and hung it up as a kind of protection, and an assurance of Heavenly companionship. He dreams now, sometimes, of his children or his wife, but is sure that they are dead or have deserted him. He is easily moved to tears; is gentle, submissive, and broken-spirited. Occasionally, the old agony comes back: a very little thing will revive it; even a familiar sound, or the scent of summer flowers in the air; but it does not last long, now: for the world without, has come to be the vision, and this solitary life, the sad reality.

If his term of imprisonment be short – I mean comparatively, for short it cannot be – the last half year is almost worse than all; for then he thinks the prison will take fire and he be burnt in the ruins, or that he is doomed to die within the walls, or that he will be detained on some false charge and sentenced for another term: or that something, no matter what, must happen to prevent his going at large. And this is natural, and impossible to be reasoned against, because, after his long separation from human life, and his great suffering, any event will appear to him more probable in the contemplation, than the being restored to liberty and his fellow-creatures.

If his period of confinement have been very long, the prospect of release bewilders and confuses him. His broken heart may flutter for a moment, when he thinks of the world outside, and what it might have been to him in all those lonely years, but that is all. The cell-door has been closed too long on all its hopes and cares. Better to have hanged him in the beginning than bring him to this pass, and send him forth to mingle with his kind, who are his kind no more.

On the haggard face of every man among these prisoners, the same expression sat. I know not what to liken it to. It had something of that strained attention which we see upon the faces of the blind and deaf, mingled with a kind of horror, as though they had all been secretly terrified. In every little chamber that I entered, and at every grate through which I looked, I seemed to see the same appalling countenance. It lives in my memory, with the fascination of a remarkable picture. Parade before my eyes, a hundred men, with one among them newly released from this solitary suffering, and I would point him out.

The faces of the women, as I have said, it humanises and refines. Whether this be because of their better nature, which is elicited in solitude, or because of their being gentler creatures, of greater patience and longer suffering, I do not know; but so it is. That the punishment is nevertheless, to my thinking, fully as cruel and as wrong in their case, as in that of the men, I need scarcely add.

My firm conviction is that, independent of the mental anguish it occasions – an anguish so acute and so tremendous, that all imagination of it must fall far short of the reality – it wears the mind into a morbid state, which renders it unfit for the rough contact and busy action of the world. It is my fixed opinion that those who have undergone this punishment, MUST pass into society again morally unhealthy and diseased. There are many instances on record, of men who have chosen, or have been condemned, to lives of perfect solitude, but I scarcely remember one, even among sages of strong and vigorous intellect, where its effect has not become apparent, in some disordered train of thought, or some gloomy hallucination. What monstrous phantoms, bred of despondency and doubt, and born and reared in solitude, have stalked upon the earth, making creation ugly, and darkening the face of Heaven!

Suicides are rare among these prisoners: are almost, indeed, unknown. But no argument in favour of the system, can reasonably be deduced from this circumstance, although it is very often urged. All men who have made diseases of the mind their study, know perfectly well that such extreme depression and despair as will change the whole character, and beat down all its powers of elasticity and self-resistance, may be at work within a man, and yet stop short of self-destruction. This is a common case.

That it makes the senses dull, and by degrees impairs the bodily faculties, I am quite sure. I remarked to those who were with me in this very establishment at Philadelphia, that the criminals who had been there long, were deaf. They, who were in the habit of seeing these men constantly, were perfectly amazed at the idea, which they regarded as groundless and fanciful. And yet the very first prisoner to whom they appealed – one of their own selection – confirmed my impression (which was unknown to him) instantly, and said, with a genuine air it was impossible to doubt, that he couldn't think how it happened, but he *was* growing very dull of hearing.

That it is a singularly unequal punishment, and affects the worst man least, there is no doubt. In its superior efficiency as a means of reformation, compared with that other code of regulations which allows the prisoners to work in company without communicating together, I have not the smallest faith. All the instances of reformation that were mentioned to me, were of a kind that might have been – and I have no doubt whatever, in my own mind, would have been – equally well brought about by the Silent System. With regard to such men as the negro burglar and the English thief, even the most enthusiastic have scarcely any hope of their conversion.

It seems to me that the objection that nothing wholesome or good has ever had its growth in such unnatural solitude, and that even a dog or any of the more intelligent among beasts, would pine, and mope, and rust away, beneath its influence, would be in itself a sufficient argument against this system. But when we recollect, in addition, how very cruel and severe it is, and that a solitary life is always liable to peculiar and distinct objections of a most deplorable nature, which have arisen here, and call to mind, moreover, that the choice is not between this system, and a bad or ill-considered one, but between it and another which has worked well, and is, in its whole design and practice, excellent; there is surely more than sufficient reason for abandoning a mode of punishment attended by so little hope or promise, and fraught, beyond dispute, with such a host of evils.

As a relief to its contemplation, I will close this chapter with a curious story arising out of the same theme, which was related to me, on the occasion of this visit, by some of the gentlemen concerned.

At one of the periodical meetings of the inspectors of this prison, a working man of Philadelphia presented himself before the Board, and earnestly requested to be placed in solitary confinement. On being asked what motive could possibly prompt him to make this strange demand, he answered that he had an irresistible propensity to get drunk; that he was constantly indulging it, to his great misery and ruin; that he had no power of resistance; that he wished to be put beyond the reach of temptation; and that he could think of no better way than this. It was pointed out to him, in reply, that the prison was for criminals who had been tried and sentenced by the law, and could not be made available for any such fanciful purposes; he was exhorted to abstain from intoxicating drinks, as he surely might if he would; and received other very good advice, with which he retired, exceedingly dissatisfied with the result of his application.

He came again, and again, and again, and was so very earnest and importunate, that at last they took counsel together, and said, 'He will certainly qualify himself for admission, if we reject him any more. Let us shut him up. He will soon be glad to go away, and then we shall get rid of him.' So they made him sign a statement which would prevent his ever sustaining an action for false imprisonment, to the effect that his incarceration was voluntary, and of his own seeking; they requested him to take notice that the officer in attendance had orders to release him at any hour of the day or night, when he might knock upon his door for that purpose; but desired him to understand, that once going out, he would not be admitted any more. These conditions agreed upon, and he still remaining in the same mind, he was conducted to the prison, and shut up in one of the cells.

In this cell, the man, who had not the firmness to leave a glass of liquor standing untasted on a table before him – in this cell, in solitary confinement, and working every day at his trade of shoe-making, this man remained nearly two years. His health beginning to fail at the expiration of that time, the surgeon recommended that he should work occasionally in the garden; and as he liked the notion very much, he went about this new occupation with great cheerfulness.

He was digging here, one summer day, very industriously, when the wicket in the outer gate chanced to be left open: showing, beyond, the well-remembered dusty road and sun-burnt fields. The way was as free to him as to any man living, but he no sooner raised his head and caught sight of it, all shining in the light, than, with the involuntary instinct of a prisoner, he cast away his spade, scampered off as fast as his legs would carry him, and never once looked back.

CHAPTER 8

Washington. The Legislature. and the President's House

WE left Philadelphia by steamboat, at six o'clock one very cold morning, and turned our faces towards Washington.

In the course of this day's journey, as on subsequent occasions, we encountered some Englishmen (small farmers, perhaps, or country publicans at home) who were settled in America, and were travelling on their own affairs. Of all grades and kinds of men that jostle one in the public conveyances of the States, these are often the most intolerable and most insufferable companions. United to every disagreeable characteristic that the worst kind of American travellers possess, these countrymen of ours display an amount of insolent conceit and cool assumption of superiority, quite monstrous to behold. In the coarse familiarity of their approach, and the effrontery of their inquisitiveness (which they are in great haste to assert, as if they panted to revenge themselves upon the decent old restraints of home), they surpass any native specimens that came within my range of observation: and I often grew so patriotic when I saw and heard them, that I would cheerfully have submitted to a reasonable fine, if I could have given any other country in the whole world, the honour of claiming them for its children.

As Washington may be called the head-quarters of tobacco-tinctured saliva, the time is come when I must confess, without any disguise, that the prevalence of those two odious practices of chewing and expectorating began about this time to be anything but agreeable, and soon became most offensive and sickening. In all the public places of America, this filthy custom is recognised. In the courts of law, the judge has his spittoon, the crier his, the witness his, and the prisoner his; while the jurymen and spectators are provided for, as so many men who in the course of nature must desire to spit incessantly. In the hospitals, the students of medicine are requested, by notices upon the wall, to eject their tobacco juice into the boxes provided for that purpose, and not to discolour the stairs. In public buildings, visitors are implored, through the same agency, to squirt the essence of their quids, or 'plugs,' as I have heard them called by gentlemen learned in this kind of sweetmeat, into the national spittoons, and not about the bases of the marble columns. But in some parts, this custom is inseparably mixed up with every meal and morning call, and with all the transactions of social life. The stranger, who follows in the track I took myself, will find it in its full bloom and glory, luxuriant in all its alarming recklessness, at Washington. And let him not persuade himself (as I once did, to my shame) that previous tourists have exaggerated its extent. The thing itself is an exaggeration of nastiness, which cannot be outdone.

On board this steamboat, there were two young gentlemen, with shirt-collars reversed as usual, and armed with very big walking-sticks; who planted two seats in the middle of the deck, at a distance of some four paces apart; took out their tobacco-boxes; and sat down opposite each other, to chew. In less than a quarter of an hour's time, these hopeful youths had shed about them on the clean boards, a copious shower of yellow rain; clearing, by that means, a kind of magic circle, within whose limits no intruders dared to come, and which they never failed to refresh and re-refresh before a spot was dry. This being before breakfast, rather disposed me, I confess, to nausea; but looking attentively at one of the expectorators, I plainly saw that he was young in chewing, and felt inwardly uneasy, himself. A glow of delight came over me at this discovery; and as I marked his face turn paler and paler, and saw the ball of tobacco in his left cheek, quiver with his suppressed agony, while yet he spat, and chewed, and spat again, in emulation of his older friend, I could have fallen on his neck and implored him to go on for hours.

We all sat down to a comfortable breakfast in the cabin below, where there was no more hurry or confusion than at such a meal in England, and where there was certainly greater politeness exhibited than at most of our stage-coach banquets. At about nine o'clock we arrived at the railroad station, and went on by the cars. At noon we turned out again, to cross a wide river in another steamboat; landed at a continuation of the railroad on the opposite shore; and went on by other cars; in which, in the course of the next hour or so, we crossed by wooden bridges, each a mile in length, two creeks, called respectively Great and Little Gunpowder. The water in both was blackened with flights of canvas-backed ducks,[1] which are most delicious eating, and abound hereabouts at that season of the year.

These bridges are of wood, have no parapet, and are only just wide enough for the passage of the trains; which, in the event of the smallest accident, would inevitably be plunged into the river. They are startling contrivances, and are most agreeable when passed.

We stopped to dine at Baltimore, and being now in Maryland, were waited on, for the first time, by slaves. The sensation of exacting any service from human creatures who are bought and sold, and being, for the time, a party as it were to their condition, is not an enviable one. The institution exists, perhaps, in its least repulsive and most mitigated form in such a town as this; but it *is* slavery; and though I was, with respect to it, an innocent man, its presence filled me with a sense of shame and self-reproach.

After dinner, we went down to the railroad again, and took our seats in the cars for Washington. Being rather early, those men and boys who happened to have nothing particular to do, and were curious in foreigners, came (according to custom) round the carriage in which I sat; let down all the windows; thrust in their heads and shoulders; hooked themselves on conveniently, by their elbows; and fell to comparing notes on the subject of my personal appearance, with as much indifference as if I were a stuffed figure. I never gained so much uncompromising information with reference to my own nose and eyes, the various impressions wrought by my mouth and chin on different minds, and how my head looks when it is viewed from behind, as on these occasions. Some gentlemen were only satisfied by exercising their sense of touch; and the boys (who are surprisingly precocious in America) were seldom satisfied, even by that, but would return to the charge over and over again. Many a budding president has walked into my room with his cap on his head and his hands in his pockets, and stared at me for two whole hours: occasionally refreshing himself with a tweak of his nose, or a draught from the water-jug; or by walking to the windows and inviting other boys in the street below, to come up and do likewise: crying, 'Here he is!' 'Come on!' 'Bring all your brothers!' with other hospitable entreaties of that nature.

We reached Washington at about half-past six that evening, and had upon the way a beautiful view of the Capitol, which is a fine building of the Corinthian order,[2] placed upon a noble and commanding eminence. Arrived at the hotel; I saw no more of the place that night; being very tired, and glad to get to bed.

Breakfast over next morning, I walk about the streets for an hour or two, and, coming home, throw up the window in the front and back, and look out. Here is Washington, fresh in my mind and under my eye.

Take the worst parts of the City Road and Pentonville, [or the straggling outskirts of Paris, where the houses are smallest,] preserving all their oddities, but especially the small shops and dwellings, occupied there (but not in Washington) by furniture-brokers, keepers of poor eating-houses, and fanciers of birds. Burn the whole down; build it up again in wood and plaster; widen it a little; throw in part of St John's Wood; put green blinds outside all the private houses, with a red curtain and a white one in every window; plough up all the roads; plant a great deal of coarse turf in every place where it ought *not* to be; erect three handsome buildings in stone and marble, anywhere, but the more entirely out of everybody's way the better: call one the Post Office, one the Patent Office, and one the Treasury; make it scorching hot in the morning, and freezing cold in the afternoon, with an occasional tornado of wind and dust; leave a brick-field without the bricks, in all central places where a street may naturally be expected: and that's Washington.

The hotel in which we live, is a long row of small houses fronting on the street, and opening at the back upon a common yard, in which hangs a great triangle. Whenever a servant is wanted, somebody beats on this triangle from one stroke up to seven, according to the number of the house in which his presence is required; and as all the servants are always being wanted, and none of them ever come, this enlivening engine is in full performance the whole day through. Clothes are drying in the same yard; female slaves, with cotton handkerchiefs twisted round their heads, are running to and fro on the hotel business; black waiters cross and recross with dishes in their hands; two great dogs are playing upon a mound of loose bricks in the centre of the little square; a pig is turning up his stomach to the sun, and grunting 'that's comfortable!'; and neither the men, nor the women, not the dogs, nor the pig, nor any created creature, takes the smallest notice of the triangle, which is tingling madly all the time.

I walk to the front window, and look across the road upon a long, straggling row of houses, one story high, terminating, nearly opposite, but a little to the left, in a melancholy piece of waste ground with frowzy grass, which looks like a small piece of country that has taken to drinking, and has quite lost itself. Standing anyhow and all wrong, upon this open space, like something meteoric that has fallen down from the moon, is an odd, lop-sided, one-eyed kind of wooden building, that looks like a church, with a flag-staff as long as itself sticking out of a steeple something larger than a tea-chest. Under the window is a small stand of coaches, whose slave-drivers are sunning themselves on the steps of our door, and talking idly together. The three most obtrusive houses near at hand are the three meanest. On one – a shop, which never has anything in the window, and never has the door open – is painted in large characters, 'THE CITY LUNCH.' At another, which looks like a backway to somewhere else, but is an independent building in itself, oysters are procurable in every style. At the third, which is a very, very little tailor's shop, pants are fixed to order; or in other words, pantaloons are made to measure. And that is our street in Washington.

It is sometimes called the City of Magnificent Distances, but it might with greater propriety be termed the City of Magnificent Intentions; for it is only on taking a bird's-eye view of it from the top of the Capitol, that one can at all comprehend the vast designs of its projector, an aspiring Frenchman.[3] Spacious avenues, that begin in nothing, and lead nowhere; streets, mile-long, that only want houses, roads and inhabitants; public buildings that need but a public to be complete; and ornaments of great thoroughfares, which only lack great thoroughfares to ornament – are its leading features. One might fancy the season over, and most of the houses gone out of town for ever with their masters. To the admirers of cities it is a Barmecide Feast;[4] a pleasant field for the imagination to rove in; a monument raised to a deceased project, with not even a legible inscription to record its departed greatness.

Such as it is, it is likely to remain. It was originally chosen for the seat of Government, as a means of averting the conflicting jealousies and interests of the different States; and very probably, too, as being remote from mobs: a consideration not to be slighted, even in America. It has no trade or commerce of its own: having little or no population beyond the President and his establishment; the members of the legislature who reside there during the session; the Government clerks and officers employed in the various departments; the keepers of the hotels and boarding-houses; and the tradesmen who supply their tables. It is very unhealthy. Few people would live in Washington, I take it, who were not obliged to reside there; and the tides of emigration and speculation, those rapid and regardless currents, are little likely to flow at any time towards such dull and sluggish water.

The principal features of the Capitol, are, of course, the two houses of Assembly. But there is, besides, in the centre of the building, a fine rotunda, ninety-six feet in diameter, and ninety-six high, whose circular wall is divided into compartments, ornamented by historical pictures. Four of these have for their subjects prominent events in the revolutionary struggle. They were painted by Colonel Trumbull, himself a member of Washington's staff at the time of their occurrence;[5] from which circumstance they derive a peculiar interest of their own. In this same hall Mr Greenough's large statue[6] of Washington has been lately placed. It has great merits of course, but it struck me as being rather strained and violent for its subject. I could wish, however, to have seen it in a better light than it can ever be viewed in, where it stands.

There is a very pleasant and commodious library in the Capitol; and from a balcony in front, the bird's eye-view, of which I have just spoken, may be had, together with a beautiful prospect of the adjacent country. In one of the ornamented portions of the building, there is a figure of Justice; whereunto the Guide Book says, 'the artist at first contemplated giving more of nudity, but he was warned that the public sentiment in this country would not admit of it, and in his caution he has gone, perhaps, into the opposite extreme.' Poor Justice! she has been made to wear much stranger garments in America than those she pines in, in the Capitol. Let us hope that she has changed her dress-maker since they were fashioned, and that the public sentiment of the country did not cut out the clothes she hides her lovely figure in, just now.

The House of Representatives is a beautiful and spacious hall, of semicircular shape, supported by handsome pillars. One part of the gallery is appropriated to the ladies, and there they sit in front rows, and come in, and go out, as at a play or concert. The chair is canopied, and raised considerably above the floor of the House; and every member has an easy chair and a writing desk to himself: which is denounced by some people out of doors as a most unfortunate and injudicious arrangement, tending to long sittings and prosaic speeches. It is an elegant chamber to look at, but a singularly bad one for all purposes of hearing. The Senate, which is smaller, is free from this objection, and is exceedingly well adapted to the uses for which it is designed. The sittings, I need hardly add, take place in the day; and the parliamentary forms are modelled on those of the old country.

I was sometimes asked, in my progress through other places, whether I had not been very much impressed by the *heads* of the lawmakers at Washington; meaning not their chiefs and leaders, but literally their individual and personal heads, whereon their hair grew, and whereby the phrenological character of each legislator was expressed: [7] and I almost as often struck my questioner dumb with indignant consternation by answering 'No, that I didn't remember being at all overcome.' As I must, at whatever hazard, repeat the avowal here, I will follow it up by relating my impressions on this subject in as few words as possible.

In the first place – it may be from some imperfect development of my organ of veneration – I do not remember having ever fainted away, or having even been moved to tears of joyful pride, at sight of any legislative body. I have borne the House of Commons like a man, and have yielded to no weakness, but slumber, in the House of Lords. I have seen elections for borough and county, and have never been impelled (no matter which party won) to damage my hat by throwing it up into the air in triumph, or to crack my voice by shouting forth any reference to our Glorious Constitution, to the noble purity of our independent voters, or the unimpeachable integrity of our independent members. Having withstood such strong attacks upon my fortitude, it is possible that I may be of a cold and insensible temperament, amounting to iciness, in such matters; and therefore my impressions of the live pillars of the Capitol at Washington must be received with such grains of allowance as this free confession may seem to demand.

Did I see in this public body an assemblage of men, bound to-gether in the sacred names of Liberty and Freedom, and so asserting the chaste dignity of those twin goddesses, in all their discussions, as to exalt at once the Eternal Principles to which their names are given, and their own character and the character of their country-men, in the admiring eyes of the whole world?

It was but a week, since an aged, grey-haired man, a lasting honour to the land that gave him birth, who has done good service to his country, as his forefathers did, and who will be remembered scores upon scores of years after the worms bred in its corruption, are but so many grains of dust – it was but a week, since this old man had stood for days upon his trial before this very body, charged with having dared to assert the infamy of that traffic, which has for its accursed merchandise men and women, and their unborn children.[8] Yes. And publicly exhibited in the same city all the while; gilded, framed and glazed; hung up for general admiration; shown to strangers not with shame, but pride; its face not turned towards the wall, itself not taken down and burned; is the Unanimous Declaration of the Thirteen United States of America, which solemnly declares that All Men are created Equal; and are endowed by their Creator with the Inalienable Rights of Life, Liberty, and the Pursuit of Happiness!

It was not a month, since this same body had sat calmly by, and heard a man, one of themselves, with oaths which beggars in their drink reject, threaten to cut another's throat from ear to ear. There he sat, among them; not crushed by the general feeling of the assembly, but as good a man as any.

There was but a week to come, and another of that body, for doing his duty to those who sent him there; for claiming in a Republic the Liberty and Freedom of expressing their sentiments, and making known their prayer; would be tried, found guilty, and have strong censure passed upon him by the rest. His was a grave offence indeed; for years before, he had risen up and said, 'A gang of male and female slaves for sale, warranted to breed like cattle, linked to each other by iron fetters, are passing now along the open street beneath the windows of your Temple of Equality! Look!' But there are many kinds of hunters engaged in the Pursuit of Happiness, and they go variously armed. It is the Inalienable Right of some among them, to take the field after *their* Happiness, equipped with cat and cartwhip, stocks, and iron collar, and to shout their view halloa! (always in praise of Liberty) to the music of clanking chains and bloody stripes.

Where sat the many legislators of coarse threats; of words and blows such as coalheavers deal upon each other, when they forget their breeding? On every side. Every session had its anecdotes of that kind, and the actors were all there.

Did I recognise in this assembly, a body of men, who, applying themselves in a new world to correct some of the falsehoods and vices of the old, purified the avenues to Public Life, paved the dirty ways to Place and Power, debated and made laws for the Common Good, and had no party but their Country?

I saw in them, the wheels that move the meanest perversion of virtuous Political Machinery that the worst tools ever wrought. Despicable trickery at elections; under-handed tamperings with public officers; cowardly attacks upon opponents, with scurrilous newspapers for shields, and hired pens for daggers; shameful trucklings to mercenary knaves, whose claim to be considered, is, that every day and week they sow new crops of ruin with their venal types, which are the dragon's teeth of yore, in everything but sharpness; aidings and abettings of every bad inclination in the popular mind, and artful suppressions of all its good influences: such things as these, and in a word, Dishonest Faction in its most depraved and most unblushing form, stared out from every corner of the crowded hall.

Did I see among them, the intelligence and refinement: the true, honest, patriotic heart of America? Here and there, were drops of its blood and life, but they scarcely coloured the stream of desperate adventurers which sets that way for profit and for pay. It is the game of these men, and of their profligate organs, to make the strife of politics so fierce and brutal, and so destructive of all self-respect in worthy men, that sensitive and delicate-minded persons shall be kept aloof, and they, and such as they, be left to battle out their selfish views unchecked. And thus this lowest of all scrambling fights goes on, and they who in other countries would, from their intelligence and station, most aspire to make the laws, do here recoil the farthest from that degradation.

That there are, among the representatives of the people in both Houses, and among all parties, some men of high character and great abilities, I need not say. The foremost among those politicians who are known in Europe, have been already described, and I see no reason to depart from the rule I have laid down for my guidance, of abstaining from all mention of individuals. It will be sufficient to add, that to the most favourable accounts that have been written of them, I more than fully and most heartily subscribe; and that personal intercourse and free communication have bred within me, not the result predicted in the very doubtful proverb, but increased admiration and respect. They are striking men to look at, hard to deceive, prompt to act, lions in energy, Crichtons in varied accomplishment,[9] Indians in fire of eye and gesture, Americans in strong and generous impulse; and they as well represent the honour and wisdom of their country at home, as the distinguished gentleman who is now its Minister at the British Court sustains its highest character abroad.

I visited both houses nearly every day, during my stay in Washington. On my initiatory visit to the House of Representatives, they divided against a decision of the chair; but the chair won. The second time I went, the member who was speaking, being interrupted by a laugh, mimicked it, as one child would in quarrelling with another, and added, 'that he would make honourable gentlemen opposite, sing out a little more on the other side of their mouths presently.' But interruptions are rare; the speaker being usually heard in silence. There are more quarrels than with us, and more threatenings than gentlemen are accustomed to exchange in any civilised society of which we have record: but farm-yard imitations have not as yet been imported from the Parliament of the United Kingdom. The feature in oratory which appears to be the most practised, and most relished, is the constant repetition of the same idea or shadow of an idea in fresh words; and the inquiry out of doors is not, 'What did he say?' but, 'How long did he speak?' These, however, are but enlargements of a principle which prevails elsewhere.

The Senate is a dignified and decorous body, and its proceedings are conducted with much gravity and order. Both houses are handsomely carpeted; but the state to which these carpets are reduced by the universal disregard of the spittoon with which every honourable member is accommodated, and the extraordinary improvements on the pattern which are squirted and dabbled upon it in every direction, do not admit of being described. I will merely observe, that I strongly recommend all strangers not to look at the floor; and if they happen to drop anything, though it be their purse, not to pick it up with an ungloved hand on any account.

It is somewhat remarkable too, at first, to say the least, to see so many honourable members with swelled faces; and it is scarcely less remarkable to discover that this appearance is caused by the quantity of tobacco they contrive to stow within the hollow of the cheek. It is strange enough too, to see an honourable gentleman leaning back in his tilted chair with his legs on the desk before him, shaping a convenient 'plug' with his penknife, and when it is quite ready for use, shooting the old one from his mouth, as from a pop-gun, and clapping the new one in its place.

I was surprised to observe that even steady old chewers of great experience, are not always good marksmen, which has rather inclined me to doubt that general proficiency with the rifle, of which we have heard so much in England. Several gentlemen called upon me who, in the course of conversation, frequently missed the spittoon at five paces; and one (but he was certainly short-sighted) mistook the closed sash for the open window, at three. On another occasion, when I dined out, and was sitting with two ladies and some gentlemen round a fire before dinner, one of the company fell short of the fireplace, six distinct times. I am disposed to think, however, that this was occasioned by his not aiming at that object; as there was a white marble hearth before the fender, which was more convenient, and may have suited his purpose better.

The Patent Office at Washington, furnishes an extraordinary

example of American enterprise and ingenuity; for the immense number of models it contains are the accumulated inventions of only five years: the whole of the previous collection having been destroyed by fire. The elegant structure in which they are arranged is one of design rather than execution, for there is but one side erected out of four, though the works are stopped. The Post Office is a very compact and very beautiful building. In one of the departments, among a collection of rare and curious articles, are deposited the presents which have been made from time to time to the American ambassadors at foreign courts by the various potentates to whom they were the accredited agents of the Republic: gifts which by the law they are not permitted to retain. I confess that I looked upon this as a very painful exhibition, and one by no means flattering to the national standard of honesty and honour. That can scarcely be a high state of moral feeling which imagines a gentleman of repute and station, likely to be corrupted, in the discharge of his duty, by the present of a snuff-box, or a richly-mounted sword, or an Eastern shawl; and surely the Nation who reposes confidence in her appointed servants, is likely to be better served, than she who makes them the subject of such very mean and paltry suspicions.

At George Town, in the suburbs, there is a Jesuit College; delightfully situated, and, so far as I had an opportunity of seeing, well managed.[10] Many persons who are not members of the Romish Church, avail themselves, I believe, of these institutions, and of the advantageous opportunities they afford for the education of their children. The heights in this neighbourhood, above the Potomac River, are very picturesque: and are free, I should conceive, from some of the insalubrities of Washington. The air, at that elevation, was quite cool and refreshing, when in the city it was burning hot.

The President's mansion is more like an English club-house, both within and without, than any other kind of establishment with which I can compare it. The ornamental ground about it has been laid out in garden walks; they are pretty, and agreeable to the eye; though they have that uncomfortable air of having been made yesterday, which is far from favourable to the display of such beauties.

My first visit to this house was on the morning after my arrival, when I was carried thither by an official gentleman, who was so kind as to charge himself with my presentation to the President.

We entered a large hall, and having twice or thrice rung a bell which nobody answered, walked without further ceremony through the rooms on the ground floor, as divers other gentlemen (mostly with their hats on, and their hands in their pockets) were doing very leisurely. Some of these had ladies with them, to whom they were showing the premises; others were lounging on the chairs and sofas; others, in a perfect state of exhaustion from listlessness, were yawning drearily. The greater portion of this assemblage were rather asserting their supremacy than doing anything else, as they had no particular business there, that anybody knew of. A few were closely eyeing the movables, as if to make quite sure that the President (who was far from popular) had not made away with any of the furniture, or sold the fixtures for his private benefit.

After glancing at these loungers; who were scattered over a pretty drawing-room, opening upon a terrace which commanded a beautiful prospect of the river and the adjacent country; and who were sauntering, too, about a larger state-room called the Eastern Drawing-room; we went up-stairs into another chamber, where were certain visitors, waiting for audiences. At sight of my conductor, a black in plain clothes and yellow slippers who was gliding noiselessly about, and whispering messages in the ears of the more impatient, made a sign of recognition, and glided off to announce him.

We had previously looked into another chamber fitted all round with a great, bare, wooden desk or counter, whereon lay files of newspapers, to which sundry gentlemen were referring. But there were no such means of beguiling the time in this apartment, which was as unpromising and tiresome as any waiting-room in one of our public establishments, or any physician's dining-room during his hours of consultation at home.

There were some fifteen or twenty persons in the room. One, a tall, wiry, muscular old man, from the west; sunburnt and swarthy; with a brown-white hat on his knees, and a giant umbrella resting between his legs; who sat bolt upright in his chair, frowning steadily at the carpet, and twitching the hard lines about his mouth, as if he had made up his mind 'to fix' the President on what he had to say, and wouldn't bate him a grain. Another, a Kentucky farmer, six-feet-six in height, with his hat on, and his hands under his coat-tails, who leaned against the wall and kicked the floor with his heel, as though he had Time's head under his shoe, and were literally 'killing' him. A third, an oval-faced, bilious-looking man, with sleek black hair cropped close, and whiskers and beard shaved down to blue dots, who sucked the head of a thick stick, and from time to time took it out of his mouth, to see how it was getting on. A fourth did nothing but whistle. A fifth did nothing but spit. And indeed all these gentlemen were so very persevering and energetic in this latter particular, and bestowed their favours so abundantly upon the carpet, that I take it for granted the Presidential house-maids have high wages, or, to speak more genteelly, an ample amount of 'compensation:' which is the American word for salary, in the case of all public servants.

We had not waited in this room many minutes, before the black messenger returned, and conducted us into another of smaller dimensions, where, at a business-like table covered with papers, sat the President himself.[11] He looked somewhat worn and anxious, and well he might; being at war with everybody – but the expression of his face was mild and pleasant, and his manner was remarkably unaffected, gentlemanly, and agreeable. I thought that in his whole carriage and demeanour, he became his station singularly well.

Being advised that the sensible etiquette of the republican court admitted of a traveller, like myself, declining, without any impropriety, an invitation to dinner, which did not reach me until I had concluded my arrangements for leaving Washington some days before that to which it referred, I only returned to this house once. It was on the occasion of one of those general assemblies which are held on certain nights, between the hours of nine and twelve o'clock, and are called, rather oddly, Levees.[12]

I went, with my wife, at about ten. There was a pretty dense crowd of carriages and people in the court-yard, and so far as I could make out, there were no very clear regulations for the taking up or setting down of company. There were certainly no policemen to soothe startled horses, either by sawing at their bridles or flourishing truncheons in their eyes; and I am ready to make oath that no inoffensive persons were knocked violently on the head, or poked acutely in their backs or stomachs; or brought to a stand-still by any such gentle means, and then taken into custody for not moving on. But there was no confusion or disorder. Our carriage reached the porch in its turn, without any blustering, swearing, shouting, backing, or other disturbance: and we dismounted with as much ease and comfort as though we had been escorted by the whole Metropolitan Force from A to Z inclusive.

The suite of rooms on the ground-floor were lighted up; and a military band was playing in the hall. In the smaller drawing-room, the centre of a circle of company, were the President and his daughter-in-law, who acted as the lady of the mansion; and a very interesting, graceful, and accomplished lady too. One gentleman who stood among this group, appeared to take upon himself the functions of a master of the ceremonies. I saw no other officers or attendants, and none were needed.

The great drawing-room, which I have already mentioned, and the other chambers on the ground-floor, were crowded to excess. The company was not, in our sense of the term, select, for it comprehended persons of very many grades and classes; nor was there any great display of costly attire: indeed, some of the costumes may have been, for aught I know, grotesque enough. But the decorum and propriety of behaviour which prevailed, were unbroken by any rude or disagreeable incident; and every man, even among the miscellaneous crowd in the hall who were admitted without any orders or tickets to look on, appeared to feel that he was a part of the Institution, and was responsible for its preserving a becoming character, and appearing to the best advantage.

That these visitors, too, whatever their station, were not without some refinement of taste and appreciation of intellectual gifts, and gratitude to those men who, by the peaceful exercise of great abilities, shed new charms and associations upon the homes of their countrymen, and elevate their character in other lands, was most earnestly testified by their reception of Washington Irving, my dear friend, who had recently been appointed Minister at the court of Spain, and who was among them that night, in his new character, for the first and last time before going abroad.[13] I sincerely believe that in all the madness of American politics, few public men would have been so earnestly, devotedly, and affectionately caressed, as this most charming writer: and I have seldom respected a public assembly more, than I did this eager throng, when I saw them turning with one mind from noisy orators and officers of state, and flocking with a generous and honest impulse round the man of quiet pursuits: proud in his promotion as reflecting back upon their country: and grateful to him with their whole hearts for the store of graceful fancies he had poured out among them. Long may he dispense such treasures with unsparing hand; and long may they remember him as worthily!

The term we had assigned for the duration of our stay in Washington was now at an end, and we were to begin to travel; for the railroad distances we had traversed yet, in journeying among these older towns, are on that great continent looked upon as nothing.

I had at first intended going South – to Charleston.[14] But when I came to consider the length of time which this journey would occupy, and the premature heat of the season, which even at Washington had been often very trying; and weighed moreover, in my own mind, the pain of living in the constant contemplation of slavery, against the more than doubtful chances of my ever seeing it, in the time I had to spare, stripped of the disguises in which it would certainly be dressed, and so adding any item to the host of facts already heaped together on the subject; I began to listen to old whisperings which had often been present to me at home in England, when I little thought of ever being here; and to dream again of cities growing up, like palaces in fairy tales, among the wilds and forests of the west.

The advice I received in most quarters when I began to yield to my desire of travelling towards that point of the compass was, according to custom, sufficiently cheerless: my companion being threatened with more perils, dangers, and discomforts, than I can remember or would catalogue if I could; but of which it will be sufficient to remark that blowings-up in steamboats and breakings-down in coaches were among the least. But, having a western route sketched out for me by the best and kindest authority to which I could have resorted, and putting no great faith in these discouragements, I soon determined on my plan of action.

This was to travel south, only to Richmond in Virginia; and then to turn, and shape our course for the Far West; whither I beseech the reader's company, in a new chapter.

CHAPTER 9

A Night Steamer on the Potomac River. A Virginia Road, and a Black Driver. Richmond. Baltimore. The Harrisburg Mail, and a Glimpse of the City. A Canal Boat

WE were to proceed in the first instance by steamboat: and as it is usual to sleep on board, in consequence of the starting-hour being four o'clock in the morning, we went down to where she lay, at that very uncomfortable time for such expeditions when slippers are most valuable, and a familiar bed, in the perspective of an hour or two, looks uncommonly pleasant.

It is ten o'clock at night: say half-past ten: moonlight, warm, and dull enough. The steamer (not unlike a child's Noah's ark in form, with the machinery on the top of the roof) is riding lazily up and down, and bumping clumsily against the wooden pier, as the ripple of the river trifles with its unwieldy carcase. The wharf is some distance from the city. There is nobody down here; and one or two dull lamps upon the steamer's decks are the only signs of life remaining, when our coach has driven away. As soon as our footsteps are heard upon the planks, a fat negress, particularly favoured by nature in respect of bustle, emerges from some dark stairs, and marshals my wife towards the ladies' cabin, to which retreat she goes, followed by a mighty bale of cloaks and greatcoats. I valiantly resolve not to go to bed at all, but to walk up and down the pier till morning.

I begin my promenade – thinking of all kinds of distant things and persons, and of nothing near – and pace up and down for half-an-hour. Then I go on board again; and getting into the light of one of the lamps, look at my watch and think it must have stopped; and wonder what has become of the faithful secretary whom I brought along with me from Boston.[1] He is supping with our late landlord (a Field Marshal, at least, no doubt[2]) in honour of our departure, and may be two hours longer. I walk again, but it gets duller and duller: the moon goes down: next June seems farther off in the dark, and the echoes of my footsteps make me nervous. It has turned cold too; and walking up and down without any companion in such lonely circumstances, is but poor amusement.

So I break my staunch resolution, and think it may be, perhaps, as well to go to bed.

I go on board again; open the door of the gentlemen's cabin; and walk in. Somehow or other – from its being so quiet, I suppose – I have taken it into my head that there is nobody there. To my horror and amazement it is full of sleepers in every stage, shape, attitude, and variety of slumber: in the berths, upon the chairs, on the floors, on the tables, and particularly round the stove, my detested enemy. I take another step forward, and slip upon the shining face of a black steward, who lies rolled in a blanket on the floor. He jumps up, grins, half in pain and half in hospitality; whispers my own name in my ear; and groping among the sleepers, leads me to my berth. Standing beside it, I count these slumbering passengers, and get past forty. There is no use in going further, so I begin to undress. As the chairs are all occupied, and there is nothing else to put my clothes on, I deposit them upon the ground: not without soiling my hands, for it is in the same condition as the carpets in the Capitol, and from the same cause. Having but partially undressed, I clamber on my shelf, and hold the curtain open for a few minutes while I look round on all my fellow travellers again. That done, I let it fall on them, and on the world: turn round: and go to sleep.

I wake, of course, when we get under weigh, for there is a good deal of noise. The day is then just breaking. Everybody wakes at the same time. Some are self-possessed directly, and some are much perplexed to make out where they are until they have rubbed their eyes, and leaning on one elbow, looked about them. Some yawn, some groan, nearly all spit, and a few get up. I am among the risers: for it is easy to feel, without going into the fresh air, that the atmosphere of the cabin is vile in the last degree. I huddle on my clothes, go down into the fore-cabin, get shaved by the barber, and wash myself. The washing and dressing apparatus for the passengers generally, consists of two jack-towels, three small wooden basins, a keg of water and a ladle to serve it out with, six square inches of looking-glass, two ditto ditto of yellow soap, a comb and brush for the head, and nothing for the teeth. Everybody uses the comb and brush, except myself. Everybody stares to see me using my own; and two or three gentlemen are strongly disposed to banter me on my prejudices, but don't. When I have made my toilet, I go upon the hurricane-deck, and set in for two hours of hard walking up and down. The sun is rising brilliantly; we are passing Mount Vernon, where Washington lies buried; the river is wide and rapid; and its banks are beautiful. All the glory and splendour of the day are coming on, and growing brighter every minute.

At eight o'clock, we breakfast in the cabin where I passed the night, but the windows and doors are all thrown open, and now it is fresh enough. There is no hurry or greediness apparent in the despatch of the meal. It is longer than a travelling breakfast with us; more orderly, and more polite.

Soon after nine o'clock we come to Potomac Creek, where we are to land: and then comes the oddest part of the journey. Seven stage-coaches are preparing to carry us on. Some of them are ready, some of them are not ready. Some of the drivers are blacks, some whites. There are four horses to each coach, and all the horses, harnessed or unharnessed, are there. The passengers are getting out of the steamboat, and into the coaches; the luggage is being transferred in noisy wheelbarrows; the horses are frightened, and impatient to start; the black drivers are chattering to them like so many monkeys; and the white ones whooping like so many drovers: for the main thing to be done in all kinds of hostlering here, is to make as much noise as possible. The coaches are something like the French coaches, but not nearly so good. In lieu of springs, they are hung on bands of the strongest leather. There is very little choice or difference between them; and they may be likened to the car portion of the swings at an English fair, roofed, put upon axle-trees and wheels, and curtained with painted canvas. They are covered with mud from the roof to the wheel-tire, and have never been cleaned since they were first built.

The tickets we have received on board the steamboat are marked No. 1, so we belong to coach No. 1. I throw my coat on the box, and hoist my wife and her maid into the inside. It has only one step, and that being about a yard from the ground, is usually approached by a chair: when there is no chair, ladies trust in Providence. The coach holds nine inside, having a seat across from door to door, where we in England put our legs: so that there is only one feat more difficult in the performance than getting in, and that is, getting out again. There is only one outside passenger, and he sits upon the box. As I am that one, I climb up; and while they are strapping the luggage on the roof, and heaping it into a kind of tray behind, have a good opportunity of looking at the driver.

He is a negro – very black indeed. He is dressed in a coarse pepper-and-salt suit excessively patched and darned (particularly at the knees), grey stockings, enormous unblacked high-low shoes,[3] and very short trousers. He has two odd gloves: one of parti-coloured worsted, and one of leather. He has a very short whip, broken in the middle and bandaged up with string. And yet he wears a low-crowned, broad-brimmed, black hat: faintly shadowing forth a kind of insane imitation of an English coachman! But somebody in authority cries 'Go ahead!' as I am making these observations. The mail takes the lead in a four-horse waggon, and all the coaches follow in procession: headed by No. 1.

By the way, whenever an Englishman would cry 'All right!' an American cries 'Go ahead!' which is somewhat expressive of the national character of the two countries.

The first half-mile of the road is over bridges made of loose planks laid across two parallel poles, which tilt up as the wheels roll over them; and in the river. The river has a clayey bottom and is full of holes, so that half a horse is constantly disappearing unexpectedly, and can't be found again for some time.

But we get past even this, and come to the road itself, which is a series of alternate swamps and gravel-pits. A tremendous place is close before us, the black driver rolls his eyes, screws his mouth up very round, and looks straight between the two leaders, as if he were saying to himself, 'We have done this often before, but *now* I think we shall have a crash.' He takes a rein in each hand; jerks and pulls at both; and dances on the splashboard with both feet (keeping his seat, of course) like the late lamented Ducrow on two of his fiery coursers.[4] We come to the spot, sink down in the mire nearly to the coach windows, tilt on one side at an angle of forty-five degrees, and stick there. The insides scream dismally; the coach stops; the horses flounder; all the other six coaches stop; and their four-and-twenty horses flounder likewise: but merely for company, and in sympathy with ours. Then the following circumstances occur.

BLACK DRIVER (to the horses). 'Hi!'
Nothing happens. Insides scream again.

BLACK DRIVER (to the horses). 'Ho!'

Horses plunge, and splash the black driver.

GENTLEMAN INSIDE (looking out). 'Why, what on airth —'

Gentleman receives a variety of splashes and draws his head in again, without finishing his question or waiting for an answer.

BLACK DRIVER (still to the horses). 'Jiddy! Jiddy!'

Horses pull violently, drag the coach out of the hole, and draw it up a bank; so steep, that the black driver's legs fly up into the air, and he goes back among the luggage on the roof. But he immediately recovers himself, and cries (still to the horses),

'Pill!'

No effect. On the contrary, the coach begins to roll back upon No. 2, which rolls back upon No. 3, which rolls back upon No. 4, and so on, until No. 7 is heard to curse and swear, nearly a quarter of a mile behind.

BLACK DRIVER (louder than before). 'Pill!'

Horses make another struggle to get up the bank, and again the coach rolls backward.

BLACK DRIVER (louder than before). 'Pe-e-e-ill!'

Horses make a desperate struggle.

BLACK DRIVER (recovering spirits). 'Hi, Jiddy, Jiddy, Pill!'

Horses make another effort.

BLACK DRIVER (with great vigour). 'Ally Loo! Hi. Jiddy, Jiddy. Pill. Ally Loo!'

Horses almost do it.

BLACK DRIVER (with his eyes starting out of his head). 'Lee, den. Lee, dere. Hi. Jiddy, Jiddy. Pill. Ally Loo. Lee-e-e-e-e!'

They run up the bank, and go down again on the other side at a fearful pace. It is impossible to stop them, and at the bottom there is a deep hollow, full of water. The coach rolls frightfully. The insides scream. The mud and water fly about us. The black driver dances like a madman. Suddenly we are all right by some extraordinary means, and stop to breathe.

A black friend of the black driver is sitting on a fence. The black driver recognises him by twirling his head round and round like a harlequin, rolling his eyes, shrugging his shoulders, and grinning from ear to ear. He stops short, turns to me, and says:

'We shall get you through sa, like a fiddle, and hope a please you when we get you through sa. Old 'ooman at home sa:'

chuckling very much. 'Outside gentleman sa, he often remember old 'ooman at home sa,' grinning again.

'Ay ay, we'll take care of the old woman. Don't be afraid.'

The black driver grins again, but there is another hole, and beyond that, another bank, close before us. So he stops short: cries (to the horses again) 'Easy. Easy den. Ease. Steady. Hi. Jiddy. Pill. Ally. Loo,' but never 'Lee!' until we are reduced to the very last extremity, and are in the midst of difficulties, extrication from which appears to be all but impossible.

And so we do the ten miles or thereabouts in two hours and a half; breaking no bones, though bruising a great many; and in short getting through the distance, 'like a fiddle.'

This singular kind of coaching terminates at Fredericksburgh, where there is a railway to Richmond. The tract of country through which it takes its course was once productive; but the soil has been exhausted by the system of employing a great amount of slave labour in forcing crops, without strengthening the land: and it is now little better than a sandy desert overgrown with trees. Dreary and uninteresting as its aspect is, I was glad to the heart to find anything on which one of the curses of this horrible institution has fallen; and had greater pleasure in contemplating the withered ground, than the richest and most thriving cultivation in the same place could possibly have afforded me.

In this district, as in all others where slavery sits brooding (I have frequently heard this admitted, even by those who are its warmest advocates:) there is an air of ruin and decay abroad, which is inseparable from the system. The barns and outhouses are mouldering away; the sheds are patched and half roofless; the log cabins (built in Virginia with external chimneys made of clay or wood) are squalid in the last degree. There is no look of decent comfort anywhere. The miserable stations by the railway side; the great wild woodyards, whence the engine is supplied with fuel; the negro children rolling on the ground before the cabin doors, with dogs and pigs; the biped beasts of burden slinking past: gloom and dejection are upon them all.

In the negro car belonging to the train in which we made this journey, were a mother and her children who had just been pur-chased; the husband and father being left behind with their old owner. The children cried the whole way, and the mother was misery's picture. The champion of Life, Liberty, and the Pursuit of Happiness, who had bought them, rode in the same train; and, every time we stopped, got down to see that they were safe. The black in Sinbad's Travels with one eye in the middle of his forehead which shone like a burning coal,[5] was nature's aristocrat compared with this white gentleman.

It was between six and seven o'clock in the evening, when we drove to the hotel: in front of which, and on the top of the broad flight of steps leading to the door, two or three citizens were balancing themselves on rocking-chairs, and smoking cigars. We found it a very large and elegant establishment, and were as well entertained as travellers need desire to be. The climate being a thirsty one, there was never, at any hour of the day, a scarcity of loungers in the spacious bar, or a cessation of the mixing of cool liquors: but they were a merrier people here, and had musical instruments playing to them o' nights, which it was a treat to hear again.

The next day, and the next, we rode and walked about the town, which is delightfully situated on eight hills, overhanging James River; a sparkling stream, studded here and there with bright islands, or brawling over broken rocks. Although it was yet but the middle of March, the weather in this southern temperature was extremely warm; the peach trees and magnolias were in full bloom; and the trees were green. In a low ground among the hills, is a valley known as 'Bloody Run,' from a terrible conflict with the Indians which once occurred there.[6] It is a good place for such a struggle, and, like every other spot I saw associated with any legend of that wild people now so rapidly fading from the earth, interested me very much.

The city is the seat of the local parliament of Virginia; and in its shady legislative halls, some orators were drowsily holding forth to the hot noon day. By dint of constant repetition, however, these constitutional sights had very little more interest for me than so many parochial vestries; and I was glad to exchange this one for a lounge in a well-arranged public library of some ten thousand volumes, and a visit to a tobacco manufactory, where the workmen are all slaves.

I saw in this place the whole process of picking, rolling, pressing, drying, packing in casks, and branding. All the tobacco thus dealt with, was in course of manufacture for chewing; and one would have supposed there was enough in that one storehouse to have filled even the comprehensive jaws of America. In this form, the weed looks like the oilcake on which we fatten cattle; and even without reference to its consequences, is sufficiently uninviting.

Many of the workmen appeared to be strong men, and it is hardly necessary to add that they were all labouring quietly, then. After two o'clock in the day, they are allowed to sing, a certain number at a time. The hour striking while I was there, some twenty sang a hymn in parts, and sang it by no means ill; pursuing their work meanwhile. A bell rang as I was about to leave, and they all poured forth into a building on the opposite side of the street to dinner. I said several times that I should like to see them at their meal; but as the gentleman to whom I mentioned this desire appeared to be suddenly taken rather deaf, I did not pursue the request. Of their appearance I shall have something to say, presently.

On the following day, I visited a plantation or farm, of about twelve hundred acres, on the opposite bank of the river. Here again, although I went down with the owner of the estate, to 'the quarter', as that part of it in which the slaves live is called, I was not invited to enter into any of their huts. All I saw of them, was, that they were very crazy, wretched cabins, near to which groups of half-naked children basked in the sun, or wallowed on the dusty ground. But I believe that this gentleman is a considerate and excellent master, who inherited his fifty slaves, and is neither a buyer nor a seller of human stock; and I am sure, from my own observation and conviction, that he is a kind-hearted, worthy man.

The planter's house was an airy rustic dwelling, that brought Defoe's description of such places strongly to my recollection.[7] The day was very warm, but the blinds being all closed, and the windows and doors set wide open, a shady coolness rustled through the rooms, which was exquisitely refreshing after the glare and heat without. Before the windows was an open piazza, where, in what they call the hot weather – whatever that may be – they sling hammocks, and drink and doze luxuriously. I do not know how their cool refections may taste within the hammocks, but, having experience, I can report that, out of them, the mounds of ices and the bowls of mint-julep and sherry-cobbler[8] they make in these latitudes, are refreshments never to be thought of afterwards, in summer, by those who would preserve contented minds.

There are two bridges across the river: one belongs to the railroad, and the other, which is a very crazy affair, is the private property of some old lady in the neighbourhood, who levies tolls upon the townspeople. Crossing this bridge, on my way back, I saw a notice painted on the gate, cautioning all persons to drive slowly: under a penalty, if the offender were a white man, of five dollars; if a negro, fifteen stripes.

The same decay and gloom that overhang the way by which it is approached, hover above the town of Richmond. There are pretty villas and cheerful houses in its streets, and Nature smiles upon the country round; but jostling its handsome residences, like slavery itself going hand in hand with many lofty virtues, are deplorable tenements, fences unrepaired, walls crumbling into ruinous heaps. Hinting gloomily at things below the surface, these, and many other tokens of the same description, force themselves upon the notice, and are remembered with depressing influence, when livelier features are forgotten.

To those who are happily unaccustomed to them, the countenances in the streets and labouring places, too, are shocking. All men who know that there are laws against instructing slaves, of which the pains and penalties greatly exceed in their amount the fines imposed on those who maim and torture them, must be prepared to find their faces very low in the scale of intellectual expression. But the darkness – not of skin, but mind – which meets the stranger's eye at every turn; the brutalizing and blotting out of all fairer characters traced by Nature's hand; immeasurably outdo his worst belief. That travelled creation of the great satirist's brain, who fresh from living among horses, peered from a high casement down upon his own kind with trembling horror,[9] was scarcely more repelled and daunted by the sight, than those who look upon some of these faces for the first time must surely be.

I left the last of them behind me in the person of a wretched drudge, who, after running to and fro all day till midnight, and moping in his stealthy winks of sleep upon the stairs betweenwhiles, was washing the dark passages at four o'clock in the morning; and went upon my way with a grateful heart that I was not doomed to live where slavery was, and had never had my senses blunted to its wrongs and horrors in a slave-rocked cradle.

It had been my intention to proceed by James River and Chesapeake Bay to Baltimore; but one of the steamboats being absent from her station through some accident, and the means of conveyance being consequently rendered uncertain, we returned to Washington by the way we had come (there were two constables on board the steamboat, in pursuit of runaway slaves), and halting there again for one night, went on to Baltimore next afternoon.

The most comfortable of all the hotels of which I had any experience in the United States, and they were not a few, is Barnum's [10] in that city: where the English traveller will find curtains to his bed, for the first and probably the last time, in America [(this is a disinterested remark, for I never use them)]; and where he will be likely to have enough water for washing himself, which is not at all a common case.

This capital of the state of Maryland is a bustling, busy town, with a great deal of traffic of various kinds, and in particular of water commerce. That portion of the town which it most favours is none of the cleanest, it is true; but the upper part is of a very different character, and has many agreeable streets and public buildings. The Washington Monument, which is a handsome pillar with a statue on its summit; the Medical College; and the Battle Monument in memory of an engagement with the British at North Point; [11] are the most conspicuous among them.

There is a very good prison in this city, and the state Penitentiary is also among its institutions. In this latter establishment there were two curious cases.

One was that of a young man, who had been tried for the murder of his father. The evidence was entirely circumstantial, and was very conflicting and doubtful; nor was it possible to assign any motive which could have tempted him to the commission of so tremendous a crime. He had been tried twice; and on the second occasion the jury felt so much hesitation in convicting him, that they found a verdict of manslaughter, or murder in the second degree; which it could not possibly be, as there had, beyond all doubt, been no quarrel or provocation, and if he were guilty at all, he was unquestionably guilty of murder in its broadest and worst signification.

The remarkable feature in the case was, that if the unfortunate deceased were not really murdered by this own son of his, he must have been murdered by his own brother. The evidence lay in a most remarkable manner, between those two. On all the suspicious points, the dead man's brother was the witness: all the explanations for the prisoner (some of them extremely plausible) went, by construction and inference, to inculpate him as plotting to fix the guilt upon his nephew. It must have been one of them: and the jury had to decide between two sets of suspicions, almost equally unnatural, unaccountable, and strange.

The other case, was that of a man who once went to a certain distiller's and stole a copper measure containing a quantity of liquor. He was pursued and taken with the property in his possession, and was sentenced to two years' imprisonment. On coming out of the jail, at the expiration of that term, he went back to the same distiller's, and stole the same copper measure containing the same quantity of liquor. There was not the slightest reason to suppose that the man wished to return to prison: indeed everything, but the commission of the offence, made directly against that assumption. There are only two ways of accounting for this extraordinary proceeding. One is, that after undergoing so much for this copper measure he conceived he had established a sort of claim and right to it. The other that, by dint of long thinking about, it had become a monomania with him, and had acquired a fascination which he found it impossible to resist; swelling from an Earthly Copper Gallon into an Ethereal Golden Vat.

After remaining here a couple of days I bound myself to a rigid adherence to the plan I had laid down so recently, and resolved to set forward on our western journey without any more delay. Accordingly, having reduced the luggage within the smallest possible compass (by sending back to New York, to be afterwards forwarded to us in Canada, so much of it as was not absolutely wanted); and having procured the necessary credentials to banking-houses on the way; and having moreover looked for two evenings at the setting sun, with as well-defined an idea of the country before us as if we had been going to travel into the very centre of that planet: we left Baltimore by another railway at half-past eight in the morning, and reached the town of York, some sixty miles off, by the early dinner-time of the Hotel which was the starting-place of the four-horse coach, wherein we were to proceed to Harris-burg.

This conveyance, the box of which I was fortunate enough to secure, had come down to meet us at the railroad station, and was as muddy and cumbersome as usual. As more passengers were waiting for us at the inn-door, the coachman observed under his breath, in the usual self-communicative voice, looking the while at his mouldy harness as if it were to that he was addressing himself,

'I expect we shall want *the big* coach.'

I could not help wondering within myself what the size of this big coach might be, and how many persons it might be designed to hold; for the vehicle which was too small for our purpose was something larger than two English heavy night coaches [, and might have been the twin-brother of a French Diligence].[12] My speculations were speedily set at rest, however, for as soon as we had dined, there came rumbling up the street, shaking its sides like a corpulent giant, a kind of barge on wheels. After much blundering and backing, it stopped at the door: rolling heavily from side to side when its other motion had ceased, as if it had taken cold in its damp stable, and between that, and the having been required in its dropsical old age to move at any faster pace than a walk, were distressed by shortness of wind.

'If here ain't the Harrisburg mail at last, and dreadful bright and smart to look at too,' cried an elderly gentleman in some excitement, 'darn my mother!'

I don't know what the sensation of being darned may be, or whether a man's mother has a keener relish or disrelish of the process than anybody else; but if the endurance of this mysterious ceremony by the old lady in question had depended on the accuracy of her son's vision in respect to the abstract brightness and smart-ness of the Harrisburg mail, she would certainly have undergone its infliction. However, they packed twelve people inside; and the luggage (including such trifles as a large rocking-chair, and a good-sized dining-table) being at length made fast upon the roof, we started off in great state.

At the door of another hotel, there was another passenger to be taken up.

'Any room, sir?' cries the new passenger to the coachman.

'Well, there's room enough,' replies the coachman, without getting down or even looking at him.

'There an't no room at all, sir,' bawls a gentleman inside. Which another gentleman (also inside) confirms, by predicting that the attempt to introduce any more passengers 'won't fit nohow.'

The new passenger, without any expression of anxiety, looks into the coach, and then looks up at the coachman: 'Now, how do you mean to fix it?' says he, after a pause: 'for I *must* go.'

The coachman employs himself in twisting the lash of his whip into a knot, and takes no more notice of the question: clearly signifying that it is anybody's business but his, and that the passengers would do well to fix it, among themselves. In this state of things, matters seem to be approximating to a fix of another kind, when another inside passenger in a corner, who is nearly suffocated, cries faintly, 'I'll get out.'

This is no matter of relief or self-congratulation to the driver, for his immovable philosophy is perfectly undisturbed by anything that happens in the coach. Of all things in the world, the coach would seem to be the very last upon his mind. The exchange is made, however, and then the passenger who has given up his seat makes a third upon the box, seating himself in what he calls the middle; that is, with half his person on my legs, and the other half on the driver's.

'Go a-head, cap'en,' cries the colonel, who directs.

'Gŏ-lāng!' cries the cap'en to his company, the horses, and away we go.

We took up at a rural bar-room, after we had gone a few miles, an intoxicated gentleman, who climbed upon the roof among the luggage, and subsequently slipping off without hurting himself, was seen in the distant perspective reeling back to the grog-shop where we had found him. We also parted with more of our freight at different times, so that when we came to change horses, I was again alone outside.

The coachmen always change with the horses, and are usually as dirty as the coach. The first was dressed like a very shabby English baker; the second like a Russian peasant: for he wore a loose purple camlet[13] robe, with a fur collar, tied round his waist with a parti-coloured worsted sash; grey trousers; light blue gloves; and a cap of bearskin. It had by this time come on to rain very heavily, and there was a cold damp mist besides, which penetrated to the skin. I was very glad to take advantage of a stoppage and get down to stretch my legs, shake the water off my great-coat, and swallow the usual anti-temperance recipe for keeping out the cold.

When I mounted to my seat again, I observed a new parcel lying on the coach roof, which I took to be a rather large fiddle in a brown bag. In the course of a few miles, however, I discovered that it had a glazed cap at one end and a pair of muddy shoes at the other; and further observation demonstrated it to be a small boy in a snuff-coloured coat, with his arms quite pinioned to his sides, by deep forcing into his pockets. He was, I presume, a relative or friend of the coachman's, as he lay a-top of the luggage with his face towards the rain; and except when a change of position brought his shoes in contact with my hat, he appeared to be asleep. At last, on some occasion of our stopping, this thing slowly upreared itself to the height of three feet six, and fixing its eyes on me, observed in piping accents, with a complacent yawn, half quenched in an obliging air of friendly patronage, 'Well now, stranger, I guess you find this a'most like an English arternoon, hey?'

The scenery, which had been tame enough at first, was, for the last ten or twelve miles, beautiful. Our road wound through the pleasant valley of the Susquehanna; the river, dotted with innumerable green islands, lay upon our right; and on the left, a steep ascent, craggy with broken rock, and dark with pine trees. The mist, wreathing itself into a hundred fantastic shapes, moved solemnly upon the water; and the gloom of evening gave to all an air of mystery and silence which greatly enhanced its natural interest.

We crossed this river by a wooden bridge, roofed and covered in on all sides, and nearly a mile in length. It was profoundly dark; perplexed, with great beams, crossing and recrossing it at every possible angle; and through the broad chinks and crevices in the floor, the rapid river gleamed, far down below, like a legion of eyes. We had no lamps; and as the horses stumbled and floundered through this place, towards the distant speck of dying light, it seemed interminable. I really could not at first persuade myself as we rumbled heavily on, filling the bridge with hollow noises, and I held down my head to save it from the rafters above, but that I was in a painful dream; for I have often dreamed of toiling through such places, and as often argued, even at the time, 'this cannot be reality.'

At length, however, we emerged upon the streets of Harrisburg, whose feeble lights, reflected dismally from the wet ground, did not shine out upon a very cheerful city. We were soon established in a snug hotel, which, though smaller and far less splendid than many we put up at, is raised above them all in my remembrance, by having for its landlord the most obliging, considerate, and gentlemanly person I ever had to deal with.

As we were not to proceed upon our journey until the afternoon, I walked out, after breakfast the next morning, to look about me: and was duly shown a model prison on the solitary system, just erected, and as yet without an inmate; the trunk of an old tree to which Harris, the first settler here (afterwards buried under it), was tied by hostile Indians, with his funeral pile about him, when he was saved by the timely appearance of a friendly party on the opposite shore of the river; the local legislature (for there was another of those bodies here again, in full debate); and the other curiosities of the town.

I was very much interested in looking over a number of treaties made from time to time with the poor Indians, signed by the different chiefs at the period of their ratification, and preserved in the office of the Secretary to the Commonwealth. These signatures, traced of course by their own hands, are rough drawings of the creatures or weapons they were called after. Thus, the Great Turtle makes a crooked pen-and-ink outline of a great turtle; the Buffalo sketches a buffalo; the War Hatchet sets a rough image of that weapon for his mark. So with the Arrow, the Fish, the Scalp, the Big Canoe, and all of them.

I could not but think – as I looked at these feeble and tremulous productions of hands which could draw the longest arrow to the head in a stout elk-horn bow, or split a bead or feather with a rifle-ball – of Crabbe's musings over the Parish Register, and the irregular scratches made with a pen, by men who would plough a lengthy furrow straight from end to end.[14] Nor could I help bestowing many sorrowful thoughts upon the simple warriors whose hands and hearts were set there, in all truth and honesty; and who only learned in course of time from white men how to break their faith, and quibble out of forms and bonds. I wondered, too, how many times the credulous Big Turtle, or trusting Little Hatchet, had put his mark to treaties which were falsely read to him; and had signed away, he knew not what, until it went and cast him loose upon the new possessors of the land, a savage indeed.

Our host announced, before our early dinner, that some members of the legislative body proposed to do us the honour of calling. He had kindly yielded up to us his wife's own little parlour, and when I begged that he would show them in, I saw him look with painful apprehension at its pretty carpet; though, being otherwise occupied at the time, the cause of his uneasiness did not occur to me.

It certainly would have been more pleasant to all parties concerned, and would not, I think, have compromised their independence in any material degree, if some of these gentlemen had not only yielded to the prejudice in favour of spittoons, but had abandoned themselves, for the moment, even to the conventional absurdity of pocket-handkerchiefs.

It still continued to rain heavily, and when we went down to the Canal Boat (for that was the mode of conveyance by which we were to proceed) after dinner, the weather was as unpromising and obstinately wet as one would desire to see. Nor was the sight of this canal boat, in which we were to spend three or four days, by any means a cheerful one; as it involved some uneasy speculations concerning the disposal of the passengers at night, and opened a wide field of inquiry touching the other domestic arrangements of the establishment, which was sufficiently disconcerting.

However, there it was – a barge with a little house in it, viewed from the outside; and a caravan at a fair, viewed from within: the gentlemen being accommodated, as the spectators usually are, in one of those locomotive museums of penny wonders; and the ladies being partitioned off by a red curtain, after the manner of the dwarfs and giants in the same establishments, whose private lives are passed in rather close exclusiveness.

We sat here, looking silently at the row of little tables, which extended down both sides of the cabin, and listening to the rain as it dripped and pattered on the boat, and plashed with a dismal merriment in the water, until the arrival of the railway train, for whose final contribution to our stock of passengers, our departure was alone deferred. It brought a great many boxes, which were bumped and tossed upon the roof, almost as painfully as if they had been deposited on one's own head, without the intervention of a porter's knot; and several damp gentlemen, whose clothes, on their drawing round the stove, began to steam again. No doubt it would have been a thought more comfortable if the driving rain, which now poured down more soakingly than ever, had admitted of a window being opened, or if our number had been something less than thirty; but there was scarcely time to think as much, when a train of three horses was attached to the tow-rope, the boy upon the leader smacked his whip, the rudder creaked and groaned complainingly, and we had begun our journey.

CHAPTER 10

Some Further Account of the Canal Boat, its Domestic Economy, and its Passengers. Journey to Pittsburg across the Alleghany Mountains. Pittsburg

As it continued to rain most perseveringly, we all remained below: the damp gentlemen round the stove, gradually becoming mildewed by the action of the fire; and the dry gentlemen lying at full length upon the seats, or slumbering uneasily with their faces on the tables, or walking up and down the cabin, which it was barely possible for a man of the middle height to do, without making bald places on his head by scraping it against the roof. At about six o'clock, all the small tables were put together to form one long table, and everybody sat down to tea, coffee, bread, butter, salmon, shad, liver, steak, potatoes, pickles, ham, chops, black-puddings, and sausages.

'Will you try,' said my opposite neighbour, handing me a dish of potatoes, broken up in milk and butter, 'will you try some of these fixings?'

There are few words which perform such various duties as this word 'fix.' It is the Caleb Quotem[1] of the American vocabulary. You call upon a gentleman in a country town, and his help informs you that he is 'fixing himself' just now, but will be down directly: by which you are to understand that he is dressing. You inquire, on board a steamboat, of a fellow passenger, whether breakfast will be ready soon, and he tells you he should think so, for when he was last below, they were 'fixing the tables:' in other words, laying the cloth. You beg a porter to collect your luggage, and he entreats you not to be uneasy, for he'll 'fix it presently:' and if you complain of indisposition, you are advised to have recourse to Doctor So-and-so, who will 'fix you' in no time.

One night, I ordered a bottle of mulled wine at an hotel where I was staying, and waited a long time for it; at length it was put upon the table with an apology from the landlord that he feared it wasn't 'fixed properly.' And I recollect once, at a stage-coach dinner, over-hearing a very stern gentleman demand of a waiter who presented him with a plate of underdone roast beef, 'whether he called *that*, fixing God A'mighty's vittles?'

There is no doubt that the meal, at which the invitation was tendered to me which has occasioned this digression, was disposed of somewhat ravenously; and that the gentlemen thrust the broad-bladed knives and the two-pronged forks further down their throats than I ever saw the same weapons go before, except in the hands of a skilful juggler: but no man sat down until the ladies were seated; or omitted any little act of politeness which could contribute to their comfort. Nor did I ever once, on any occasion, anywhere, during my rambles in America, see a woman exposed to the slightest act of rudeness, incivility, or even inattention.

By the time the meal was over, the rain, which seemed to have worn itself out by coming down so fast, was nearly over too; and it became feasible to go on deck: which was a great relief, notwith-standing its being a very small deck, and being rendered still smaller by the luggage, which was heaped together in the middle under a tarpaulin covering; leaving, on either side, a path so narrow, that it became a science to walk to and fro without tumbling overboard into the canal. It was somewhat embarrassing at first, too, to have to duck nimbly every five minutes whenever the man at the helm cried 'Bridge!' and sometimes, when the cry was 'Low Bridge,' to lie down nearly flat. But custom familiarises one to anything, and there were so many bridges that it took a very short time to get used to this.

As night came on, and we drew in sight of the first range of hills, which are the outposts of the Alleghany mountains, the scenery, which had been uninteresting hitherto, became more bold and striking. The wet ground reeked and smoked, after the heavy fall of rain; and the croaking of the frogs (whose noise in these parts is almost incredible) sounded as though a million of fairy teams with bells were travelling through the air, and keeping pace with us. The night was cloudy yet, but moonlight too: and when we crossed the Susquehanna river – over which there is an extraordinary wooden bridge with two galleries, one above the other, so that even there, two boat teams meeting, may pass without confusion – it was wild and grand.

I have mentioned my having been in some uncertainty and doubt, at first, relative to the sleeping arrangements on board this boat. I remained in the same vague state of mind until ten o'clock or thereabouts, when going below, I found suspended on either side of the cabin, three long tiers of hanging book-shelves, designed apparently for volumes of the small octavo size. Looking with greater attention at these contrivances (wondering to find such literary preparations in such a place), I descried on each shelf a sort of microscopic sheet and blanket; then I began dimly to comprehend that the passengers were the library, and that they were to be arranged, edge-wise, on these shelves, till morning.

I was assisted to this conclusion by seeing some of them gathered round the master of the boat, at one of the tables, drawing lots with all the anxieties and passions of gamesters depicted in their countenances; while others, with small pieces of cardboard in their hands, were groping among the shelves in search of numbers corresponding with those they had drawn. As soon as any gentleman found his number, he took possession of it by immediately undressing himself and crawling into bed. The rapidity with which an agitated gambler subsided into a snoring slumberer, was one of the most singular effects I have ever witnessed. As to the ladies, they were already abed, behind the red curtain, which was carefully drawn and pinned up the centre; though as every cough, or sneeze, or whisper, behind this curtain, was perfectly audible before it, we had still a lively consciousness of their society.

The politeness of the person in authority had secured to me a shelf in a nook near this red curtain, in some degree removed from the great body of sleepers: to which place I retired, with many acknowledgments to him for his attention. I found it, on after-measurement, just the width of an ordinary sheet of Bath post letter-paper; and I was at first in some uncertainty as to the best means of getting into it. But the shelf being a bottom one, I finally determined on lying upon the floor, rolling gently in, stopping immediately I touched the mattress, and remaining for the night with that side uppermost, whatever it might be. Luckily, I came upon my back at exactly the right moment. I was much alarmed on looking upward, to see, by the shape of his half-yard of sacking (which his weight had bent into an exceedingly tight bag), that there was a very heavy gentleman above me, whom the slender cords seemed quite incapable of holding; and I could not help reflecting upon the grief of my wife and family in the event of his coming down in the night. But as I could not have got up again without a severe bodily struggle, which might have alarmed the ladies; and as I had nowhere to go to, even if I had; I shut my eyes upon the danger, and remained there.

One of two remarkable circumstances is indisputably a fact, with reference to that class of society who travel in these boats. Either they carry their restlessness to such a pitch that they never sleep at all; or they expectorate in dreams, which would be a remarkable mingling of the real and ideal. All night long, and every night, on this canal, there was a perfect storm and tempest of spitting; and once my coat, being in the very centre of a hurricane sustained by five gentlemen (which moved vertically, strictly carrying out Reid's Theory of the Law of Storms[2]), I was fain the next morning to lay it on the deck, and rub it down with fair water before it was in a condition to be worn again.

Between five and six o'clock in the morning we got up, and some of us went on deck, to give them an opportunity of taking the shelves down; while others, the morning being very cold, crowded round the rusty stove, cherishing the newly-kindled fire, and filling the grate with those voluntary contributions of which they had been so liberal all night. The washing accommodations were primitive. There was a tin ladle chained to the deck, with which every gentleman who thought it necessary to cleanse himself (some were superior to this weakness), fished the dirty water out of the canal, and poured it into a tin basin, secured in like manner. There was also a jack-towel. And, hanging up before a little looking-glass in the bar, in the immediate vicinity of the bread and cheese and biscuits, were a public comb and hair-brush.

At eight o'clock, the shelves being taken down and put away and the tables joined together, everybody sat down to the tea, coffee, bread, butter, salmon, shad, liver, steak, potatoes, pickles, ham, chops, black-puddings, and sausages, all over again. Some were fond of compounding this variety, and having it all on their plates at once. As each gentleman got through his own personal amount of tea, coffee, bread, butter, salmon, shad, liver, steak, potatoes, pickles, ham, chops, black-puddings, and sausages, he rose up and walked off. When everybody had done with everything, the fragments were cleared away: and one of the waiters appearing anew in the character of a barber, shaved such of the company as desired to be shaved; while the remainder looked on, or yawned over their newspapers. Dinner was breakfast again, without the tea and coffee; and supper and breakfast were identical.

There was a man on board this boat, with a light fresh-coloured face, and a pepper-and-salt suit of clothes, who was the most inquisitive fellow that can possibly be imagined. He never spoke otherwise than interrogatively. He was an embodied inquiry. Sitting down or standing up, still or moving, walking the deck or taking his meals, there he was, with a great note of interrogation in each eye, two in his cocked ears, two more in his turned-up nose and chin, at least half a dozen more about the corners of his mouth, and the largest one of all in his hair, which was brushed pertly off his forehead in a flaxen clump. Every button in his clothes said, 'Eh? What's that? Did you speak? Say that again, will you?' He was always wide awake, like the enchanted bride who drove her husband frantic;[3] always restless; always thirsting for answers; perpetually seeking and never finding. There never was such a curious man.

I wore a fur great-coat at that time, and before we were well clear of the wharf, he questioned me concerning it, and its price, and where I bought it, and when, and what fur it was, and what it weighed, and what it cost. Then he took notice of my watch, and asked me what *that* cost, and whether it was a French watch, and where I got it, and how I got it, and whether I bought it or had it given me, and how it went, and where the keyhole was, and when I wound it, every night or every morning, and whether I ever forgot to wind it at all, and if I did, what then? Where had I been to last, and where was I going next, and where was I going after that, and had I seen the President, and what did he say, and what did I say, and what did he say when I had said that? Eh? Lor now! do tell!

Finding that nothing would satisfy him, I evaded his questions after the first score or two, and in particular pleaded ignorance respecting the name of the fur whereof the coat was made. I am unable to say whether this was the reason, but that coat fascinated him ever afterwards; he usually kept close behind me as I walked, and moved as I moved, that he might look at it the better; and he frequently dived into narrow places after me at the risk of his life, that he might have the satisfaction of passing his hand up the back, and rubbing it the wrong way.

We had another odd specimen on board, of a different kind. This was a thin-faced, spare-figured man of middle age and stature, dressed in a dusty drabbish-coloured suit, such as I never saw before. He was perfectly quiet during the first part of the journey: indeed I don't remember having so much as seen him until he was brought out by circumstances, as great men often are. The conjunction of events which made him famous, happened, briefly, thus.

The canal extends to the foot of the mountain, and there, of course, it stops; the passengers being conveyed across it by land carriage, and taken on afterwards by another canal-boat, the counterpart of the first, which awaits them on the other side. There are two canal lines of passage-boats; one is called The Express, and one (a cheaper one) The Pioneer. The Pioneer gets first to the mountain, and waits for the Express people to come up; both sets of passengers being conveyed across it at the same time. We were the Express company; but when we had crossed the mountain, and had come to the second boat, the proprietors took it into their heads to draft all the Pioneers into it likewise, so that we were five-and-forty at least, and the accession of passengers was not at all of that kind which improved the prospect of sleeping at night. Our people grumbled at this, as people do in such cases; but suffered the boat to be towed off with the whole freight aboard nevertheless; and away we went down the canal. At home, I should have protested lustily, but being a foreigner here, I held my peace. Not so this passenger. He cleft a path among the people on deck (we were nearly all on deck), and without addressing anybody whomsoever, soliloquised as follows:

'This may suit *you*, this may, but it don't suit *me*. This may be all very well with Down Easters,[4] and men of Boston raising, but it won't suit my figure nohow; and no two ways about *that*; and so I tell you. Now! I'm from the brown forests of the Mississippi, *I* am, and when the sun shines on me, it does shine – a little. It don't glimmer where *I* live, the sun don't. No. I'm a brown forester, I am. I an't a Johnny Cake.[5] There are no smooth skins where I live. We're rough men there. Rather. If Down Easters and men of Boston raising like this, I'm glad of it, but I'm none of that raising nor of that breed. No. This company wants a little fixing, *it* does. I'm the wrong sort of man for 'em, *I* am. They won't like me, *they* won't. This is piling of it up, a little too moŭntaĭnoŭs, this is.' At the end of every one of these short sentences he turned upon his heel, and walked the other way; checking himself abruptly when he had finished another short sentence, and turning back again.

It is impossible for me to say what terrific meaning was hidden in the words of this brown forester, but I know that the other passengers looked on in a sort of admiring horror, and that presently the boat was put back to the wharf, and as many of the Pioneers as could be coaxed or bullied into going away, were got rid of.

When we started again, some of the boldest spirits on board, made bold to say to the obvious occasion of this improvement in our prospects, 'Much obliged to you, sir;' whereunto the brown forester (waving his hand, and still walking up and down as before), replied, 'No you an't. You're none o' my raising. You may act for yourselves, *you* may. I have pinted out the way. Down Easters and Johnny Cakes can follow if they please. I an't a Johnny Cake, *I* an't. I am from the brown forests of the Mississippi, *I* am' – and so on, as before. He was unanimously voted one of the tables for his bed at night – there is a great contest for the tables – in consideration of his public services: and he had the warmest corner by the stove throughout the rest of the journey. But I never could find out that he did anything except sit there; nor did I hear him speak again until, in the midst of the bustle and turmoil of getting the luggage ashore in the dark at Pittsburg, I stumbled over him as he sat smoking a cigar on the cabin steps, and heard him muttering to himself, with a short laugh of defiance, 'I an't a Johnny Cake, *I* an't. I'm from the brown forests of the Mississippi, *I* am, damme!' I am inclined to argue from this, that he had never left off saying so; but I could not make [an] affidavit of that part of the story, if required to do so by my Queen and Country.

As we have not reached Pittsburg yet, however, in the order of our narrative, I may go on to remark that breakfast was perhaps the least desirable meal of the day, as in addition to the many savoury odours arising from the eatables already mentioned, there were whiffs of gin, whiskey, brandy, and rum, from the little bar hard by, and a decided seasoning of stale tobacco. Many of the gentlemen passengers were far from particular in respect of their linen, which was in some cases as yellow as the little rivulets that had trickled from the corners of their mouths in chewing, and dried there. Nor was the atmosphere quite free from zephyr whisperings of the thirty beds which had just been cleared away, and of which we were further and more pressingly reminded by the occasional appearance on the table-cloth of a kind of Game, not mentioned in the Bill of Fare.

And yet despite these oddities – and even they had, for me at least, a humour of their own – there was much in this mode of travelling which I heartily enjoyed at the time, and look back upon with great pleasure. Even the running up, bare-necked, at five o'-clock in the morning, from the tainted cabin to the dirty deck; scooping up the icy water, plunging one's head into it, and drawing it out, all fresh and glowing with the cold; was a good thing. The fast, brisk walk upon the towing-path, between that time and break-fast, when every vein and artery seemed to tingle with health; the exquisite beauty of the opening day, when light came gleaming off from everything; the lazy motion of the boat, when one lay idly on the deck, looking through, rather than at, the deep blue sky; the gliding on, at night, so noiselessly, past frowning hills, sullen with dark trees, and sometimes angry in one red, burning spot high up, where unseen men lay crouching round a fire; the shining out of the bright stars, undisturbed by noise of wheels or steam, or any other sound than the liquid rippling of the water as the boat went on: all these were pure delights.

Then there were news settlements and detached log-cabins and frame-houses, full of interest for strangers from an old country: cabins with simple ovens, outside, made of clay; and lodgings for the pigs, nearly as good as many of the human quarters; broken windows, patched with worn-out hats, old clothes, old boards, fragments of blankets and paper; and home-made dressers standing in the open air without the door, whereon was ranged the household store, not hard to count, of earthen jars and pots. The eye was pained to see the stumps of great trees thickly strewn in every field of wheat, and seldom to lose the eternal swamp and dull morass, with hundreds of rotten trunks and twisted branches steeped in its unwholesome water. It was quite sad and oppressive, to come upon great tracts where settlers had been burning down the trees, and where their wounded bodies lay about, like those of murdered creatures, while here and there some charred and blackened giant reared aloft two withered arms, and seemed to call down curses on his foes. Sometimes, at night, the way wound through some lonely gorge, like a mountain pass in Scotland, shining and coldly glittering in the light of the moon, and so closed in by high steep hills all round, that there seemed to be no egress save through the narrower path by which we had come, until one rugged hill-side seemed to open, and shutting out the moonlight as we passed into its gloomy throat, wrapped our new course in shade and darkness.

We had left Harrisburg on Friday. On Sunday morning we arrived at the foot of the mountain, which is crossed by railroad. There are ten inclined planes; five *a*scending, and five *de*scending; the carriages are dragged up the former, and let slowly down the latter, by means of stationary engines; the comparatively level spaces between, being traversed, sometimes by horse, and sometimes by engine power, as the case demands. Occasionally the rails are laid upon the extreme verge of a giddy precipice; and looking from the carriage window, the traveller gazes sheer down, without a stone or scrap of fence between, into the mountain depths below. The journey is very carefully made, however; only two carriages travelling together; and while proper precautions are taken, is not to be dreaded for its dangers.

It was very pretty travelling thus, at a rapid pace along the heights of the mountain in a keen wind, to look down into a valley full of light and softness; catching glimpses, through the tree-tops, of scattered cabins; children running to the doors; dogs bursting out to bark, whom we could see without hearing; terrified pigs scampering homewards; families sitting out in their rude gardens; cows gazing upward with a stupid indifference; men in their shirt-sleeves looking on at their unfinished houses, planning out to-morrow's work; and we riding onward, high above them, like a whirlwind. It was amusing, too, when we had dined, and rattled down a steep pass, having no other moving power than the weight of the carriages themselves, to see the engine released, long after us, come buzzing down alone, like a great insect, its back of green and gold so shining in the sun, that if it had spread a pair of wings and soared away, no one would have had occasion, as I fancied, for the least surprise. But it stopped short of us in a very business-like manner when we reached the canal; and, before we left the wharf, went panting up this hill again, with the passengers who had waited our arrival for the means of traversing the road by which we had come.

On the Monday evening, furnace fires and clanking hammers on the banks of the canal, warned us that we approached the termination of this part of our journey. After going through another dreamy place – a long aqueduct across the Alleghany River, which was stranger than the bridge at Harrisburg, being a vast, low, wooden chamber full of water – we emerged upon that ugly confusion of backs of buildings and crazy galleries and stairs, which always abuts on water, whether it be river, sea, canal, or ditch: and were at Pittsburg.

Pittsburg is like Birmingham in England; at least its townspeople say so. Setting aside the streets, the shops, the houses, waggons, factories, public buildings, and population, perhaps it may be. It certainly has a great quantity of smoke hanging about it, and is famous for its iron-works. Besides the prison to which I have already referred, this town contains a pretty arsenal and other institutions. It is very beautifully situated on the Alleghany River, over which there are two bridges; and the villas of the wealthier citizens sprinkled about the high grounds in the neighbourhood, are pretty enough. We lodged at a most excellent hotel, and were admirably served. As usual it was full of boarders, was very large, and had a broad colonnade to every story of the house.

We tarried here three days. Our next point was Cincinnati: and as this was a steamboat journey, and western steamboats usually blow up one or two a week in the season, it was advisable to collect opinions in reference to the comparative safety of the vessels bound that way, then lying in the river. One called The Messenger was the best recommended. She had been advertised to start positively, every day for a fortnight or so, and had not gone yet, nor did her captain seem to have any very fixed intention on the subject. But this is the custom: for if the law were to bind down a free and independent citizen to keep his word with the public, what would become of the liberty of the subject? Besides, it is in the way of trade. And if passengers be decoyed in the way of trade, and people be inconvenienced in the way of trade, what man, who is a sharp tradesman himself, shall say, 'We must put a stop to this?'

Impressed by the deep solemnity of the public announcement, I (being then ignorant of these usages) was for hurrying on board in a breathless state, immediately; but receiving private and confidential information that the boat would certainly not start until Friday, April the First, we made ourselves very comfortable in the mean while, and went on board at noon that day.

CHAPTER II

From Pittsburg to Cincinnati in a Western Steamboat. Cincinnati

THE Messenger was one among a crowd of high-pressure steamboats, clustered together by a wharf-side, which, looked down upon from the rising ground that forms the landing-place, and backed by the lofty bank on the opposite side of the river, appeared no larger than so many floating models. She had some forty passengers on board, exclusive of the poorer persons on the lower deck; and in half an hour, or less, proceeded on her way.

We had, for ourselves, a tiny state-room with two berths in it, opening out of the ladies' cabin. There was, undoubtedly, something satisfactory in this 'location,' inasmuch as it was in the stern, and we had been a great many times very gravely recommended to keep as far aft as possible, 'because the steamboats generally blew up forward.' Nor was this an unnecessary caution, as the occurrence and circumstances of more than one such fatality during our stay sufficiently testified. Apart from this source of self-congratulation, it was an unspeakable relief to have any place, no matter how confined, where one could be alone: and as the row of little chambers of which this was one, had each a second glass-door besides that in the ladies' cabin, which opened on a narrow gallery outside the vessel, where the other passengers seldom came, and where one could sit in peace and gaze upon the shifting prospect, we took possession of our new quarters with much pleasure.

If the native packets I have already described be unlike anything we are in the habit of seeing on water, these western vessels are still more foreign to all the ideas we are accustomed to entertain of boats. I hardly know what to liken them to, or how to describe them.

In the first place, they have no mast, cordage, tackle, rigging, or other such boat-like gear; nor have they anything in their shape at all calculated to remind one of a boat's head, stern, sides, or keel. Except that they are in the water, and display a couple of paddle-boxes, they might be intended, for anything that appears to the contrary, to perform some unknown service, high and dry, upon a mountain top. There is no visible deck, even: nothing but a long, black, ugly roof, covered with burnt-out feathery sparks; above which tower two iron chimneys, and a hoarse escape-valve, and a glass steerage-house. Then, in order as the eye descends towards the water, are the sides, and doors, and windows of the state-rooms, jumbled as oddly together as though they formed a small street, built by the varying tastes of a dozen men: the whole is supported on beams and pillars resting on a dirty barge, but a few inches above the water's edge: and in the narrow space between this upper structure and this barge's deck, are the furnace fires and machinery, open at the sides to every wind that blows, and every storm of rain it drives along its path.

Passing one of these boats at night, and seeing the great body of fire, exposed as I have just described, that rages and roars beneath the frail pile of painted wood: the machinery, not warded off or guarded in any way, but doing its work in the midst of the crowd of idlers and emigrants and children, who throng the lower deck: under the management, too, of reckless men whose acquaintance with its mysteries may have been of six months' standing: one feels directly that the wonder is, not that there should be so many fatal accidents, but that any journey should be safely made.

Within, there is one long narrow cabin, the whole length of the boat; from which the state-rooms open, on both sides. A small portion of it at the stern is partitioned off for the ladies; and the bar is at the opposite extreme. There is a long table down the centre, and at either end a stove. The washing apparatus is forward, on the deck. It is a little better than on board the canal boat, but not much. In all modes of travelling, the American customs, with reference to the means of personal cleanliness and wholesome ablution, are extremely negligent and filthy; and I strongly incline to the belief that a considerable amount of illness is referable to this cause.

We are to be on board The Messenger three days: arriving at Cincinnati (barring accidents) on Monday morning. There are three meals a day. Breakfast at seven, dinner at half-past twelve, supper about six. At each, there are a great many small dishes and plates upon the table, with very little in them; so that although there is every appearance of a mighty 'spread,' there is seldom really more than a joint: except for those who fancy slices of beet-root, shreds of dried beef, complicated entanglements of yellow pickle; maize, Indian corn, apple-sauce, and pumpkin.

Some people fancy all these little dainties together (and sweet preserves beside), by way of relish to their roast pig. They are generally those dyspeptic ladies and gentlemen who eat unheard-of quantities of hot corn bread (almost as good for the digestion as a kneaded pin-cushion), for breakfast, and for supper. Those who do not observe this custom, and who help themselves several times instead, usually suck their knives and forks meditatively, until they have decided what to take next: then pull them out of their mouths: put them in the dish; help themselves; and fall to work again. At dinner, there is nothing to drink upon the table, but great jugs full of cold water. Nobody says anything, at any meal, to anybody. All the passengers are very dismal, and seem to have tremendous secrets weighing on their minds. There is no conversation, no laughter, no cheerfulness, no sociality, except in spitting; and that is done in silent fellowship round the stove, when the meal is over. Every man sits down, dull and languid; swallows his fare as if breakfasts, dinners, and suppers, were necessities of nature never to be coupled with recreation or enjoyment; and having bolted his food in a gloomy silence, bolts himself in the same state. But for these animal observances, you might suppose the whole male portion of the company to be the melancholy ghosts of departed book-keepers, who had fallen dead at the desk: such is their weary air of business and calculation. Undertakers on duty would be sprightly beside them; and a collation of funeral-baked meats, in comparison with these meals, would be a sparkling festivity.

The people are all alike, too. There is no diversity of character. They travel about on the same errands, say and do the same things in exactly the same manner, and follow in the same dull cheerless round. All down the long table, there is scarcely a man who is in anything different from his neighbour. It is quite a relief to have, sitting opposite, that little girl of fifteen with the loquacious chin: who, to do her justice, acts up to it, and fully identifies nature's handwriting, for of all the small chatterboxes that ever invaded the repose of a drowsy ladies' cabin, she is the first and foremost. The beautiful girl, who sits a little beyond her – further down the table there – married the young man with the dark whiskers, who sits beyond *her*, only last month. They are going to settle in the very Far West, where he has lived four years, but where she has never been. They were both overturned in a stage-coach the other day (a bad omen anywhere else, where overturns are not so common), and his head, which bears the marks of a recent wound, is bound up still. She was hurt too, at the same time, and lay insensible for some days; bright as her eyes are, now.

Further down still, sits a man who is going some miles beyond their place of destination, to 'improve' a newly-discovered copper mine. He carries the village – that is to be – with him: a few frame cottages, and an apparatus for smelting the copper. He carries its people too. They are partly American and partly Irish, and herd together on the lower deck; where they amused themselves last evening till the night was pretty far advanced, by alternately firing off pistols and singing hymns.

They, and the very few who have been left at table twenty minutes, rise, and go away. We do so too; and passing through our little state-room, resume our seats in the quiet gallery without.

A fine broad river always, but in some parts much wider than in others: and then there is usually a green island, covered with trees, dividing it into two streams. Occasionally, we stop for a few minutes, maybe to take in wood, maybe for passengers, at some small town or village (I ought to say city, every place is a city here); but the banks are for the most part deep solitudes, overgrown with trees, which, hereabouts, are already in leaf and very green. For miles, and miles, and miles, these solitudes are unbroken by any sign of human life or trace of human footstep; nor is anything seen to move about them but the blue jay, whose colour is so bright, and yet so delicate, that it looks like a flying flower. At lengthened intervals a log cabin, with its little space of cleared land about it, nestles under a rising ground, and sends its thread of blue smoke curling up into the sky. It stands in the corner of the poor field of wheat, which is full of great unsightly stumps, like earthy butchers'-blocks. Sometimes the ground is only just now cleared: the felled trees lying yet upon the soil: and the log-house only this morning begun. As we pass this clearing, the settler leans upon his axe or hammer, and looks wistfully at the people from the world. The children creep out of the temporary hut, which is like a gipsy tent upon the ground, and clap their hands and shout. The dog only glances round at us, and then looks up into his master's face again, as if he were rendered uneasy by any suspension of the common business, and had nothing more to do with pleasurers. And still there is the same, eternal foreground. The river has washed away its banks, and stately trees have fallen down into the stream. Some have been there so long, that they are mere dry, grizzly skeletons. Some have just toppled over, and having earth yet about their roots, are bathing their green heads in the river, and putting forth new shoots and branches. Some are almost sliding down, as you look at them. And some were drowned so long ago, that their bleached arms start out from the middle of the current, and seem to try to grasp the boat, and drag it under water.

Through such a scene as this, the unwieldy machine takes its hoarse, sullen way: venting, at every revolution of the paddles, a loud high-pressure blast; enough, one would think, to waken up the host of Indians who lie buried in a great mound yonder: so old, that mighty oaks and other forest trees have struck their roots into its earth; and so high, that it is a hill, even among the hills that Nature planted round it. The very river, as though it shared one's feelings of compassion for the extinct tribes who lived so pleasantly here, in their blessed ignorance of white existence, hundreds of years ago, steals out of its way to ripple near this mound: and there are few places where the Ohio sparkles more brightly than in the Big Grave Creek.[1]

All this I see as I sit in the little stern-gallery mentioned just now. Evening slowly steals upon the landscape and changes it before me, when we stop to set some emigrants ashore.

Five men, as many women, and a little girl. All their worldly goods are a bag, a large chest and an old chair: one, old, high-backed, rush-bottomed chair: a solitary settler in itself. They are rowed ashore in the boat, while the vessel stands a little off awaiting its return, the water being shallow. They are landed at the foot of a high bank, on the summit of which are a few log cabins, attainable only by a long winding path. It is growing dusk; but the sun is very red, and shines in the water and on some of the tree-tops, like fire.

The men get out of the boat first; help out the women; take out the bag, the chest, the chair; bid the rowers 'good-bye;' and shove the boat off for them. At the first plash of the oars in the water, the oldest woman of the party sits down in the old chair, close to the water's edge, without speaking a word. None of the others sit down, though the chest is large enough for many seats. They all stand where they landed, as if stricken into stone; and look after the boat. So they remain, quite still and silent: the old woman and her old chair, in the centre; the bag and chest upon the shore, without anybody heeding them: all eyes fixed upon the boat. It comes alongside, is made fast, the men jump on board, the engine is put in motion, and we go hoarsely on again. There they stand yet, without the motion of a hand. I can see them, through my glass, when, in the distance and increasing darkness, they are mere specks to the eye: lingering there still: the old woman in the old chair, and all the rest about her: not stirring in the least degree. And thus I slowly lose them.

The night is dark, and we proceed within the shadow of the wooded bank, which makes it darker. After gliding past the sombre maze of boughs for a long time, we come upon an open space where the tall trees are burning. The shape of every branch and twig is expressed in a deep red glow, and as the light wind stirs and ruffles it, they seem to vegetate in fire. It is such a sight as we read of in legends of enchanted forests: saving that it is sad to see these noble works wasting away so awfully, alone; and to think how many years must come and go before the magic that created them will rear their like upon this ground again. But the time will come; and when, in their changed ashes, the growth of centuries unborn has struck its roots, the restless men of distant ages will repair to these again un-peopled solitudes; and their fellows, in cities far away, that slumber now, perhaps, beneath the rolling sea, will read, in language strange to any ears in being now, but very old to them, of primeval forests where the axe was never heard, and where the jungled ground was never trodden by a human foot.

Midnight and sleep blot out these scenes and thoughts: and when the morning shines again, it gilds the house-tops of a lively city, before whose broad paved wharf the boat is moored; with other boats, and flags, and moving wheels, and hum of men around it; as though there were not a solitary or silent rood of ground within the compass of a thousand miles.

Cincinnati is a beautiful city; cheerful, thriving, and animated. I have not often seen a place that commends itself so favourably and pleasantly to a stranger at the first glance as this does: with its clean houses of red and white, its well-paved roads, and footways of bright tile. Nor does it become less prepossessing on a closer acquaintance. The streets are broad and airy, the shops extremely good, the private residences remarkable for their elegance and neatness. There is something of invention and fancy in the varying styles of these latter erections, which, after the dull company of the steamboat, is perfectly delightful, as conveying an assurance that there are such qualities still in existence. The disposition to ornament these pretty villas and render them attractive, leads to the culture of trees and flowers, and the laying out of well-kept gardens, the sight of which, to those who walk along the streets, is inexpressibly refreshing and agreeable. I was quite charmed with the appearance of the town, and its adjoining suburb of Mount Auburn: from which the city, lying in an amphitheatre of hills, forms a picture of remarkable beauty, and is seen to great advantage.

There happened to be a great Temperance Convention held here on the day after our arrival; and as the order of march brought the procession under the windows of the hotel in which we lodged, when they started in the morning, I had a good opportunity of seeing it. It comprised several thousand men; the members of various 'Washington Auxiliary Temperance Societies;' and was marshalled by officers on horseback, who cantered briskly up and down the line, with scarves and ribbons of bright colours fluttering out behind them gaily. There were bands of music too, and banners out of number: and it was a fresh, holiday-looking concourse altogether.

I was particularly pleased to see the Irishmen, who formed a distinct society among themselves, and mustered very strong with their green scarves; carrying their national Harp and their Portrait of Father Mathew,[2] high above the people's heads. They looked as jolly and good-humoured as ever; and, working [(here)] the hardest for their living and doing any kind of sturdy labour that came in their way, were the most independent fellows there, I thought.

The banners were very well painted, and flaunted down the street famously. There was the smiting of the rock, and the gushing forth of the waters; and there was a temperate man with 'considerable of a hatchet' (as the standard-bearer would probably have said), aiming a deadly blow at a serpent which was apparently about to spring upon him from the top of a barrel of spirits. But the chief feature of this part of the show was a huge allegorical device, borne among the ship-carpenters, on one side whereof the steamboat Alcohol was represented bursting her boiler and exploding with a great crash, while upon the other, the good ship Temperance sailed away with a fair wind, to the heart's content of the captain, crew, and passengers.

After going round the town, the procession repaired to a certain appointed place, where, as the printed programme set forth, it would be received by the children of the different free schools, 'singing Temperance Songs.' I was prevented from getting there, in time to hear these Little Warblers, or to report upon this novel kind of vocal entertainment: novel, at least, to me: but I found in a large open space, each society gathered round its own banners, and listening in silent attention to its own orator. The speeches, judging from the little I could hear of them, were certainly adapted to the occasion, as having that degree of relationship to cold water which wet blankets may claim: but the main thing was the conduct and appearance of the audience throughout the day; and that was admirable and full of promise.

Cincinnati is honourably famous for its free schools, of which it has so many that no person's child among its population can, by possibility, want the means of education, which are extended, upon an average, to four thousand pupils, annually. I was only present in one of these establishments during the hours of instruction. In the boys' department, which was full of little urchins (varying in their ages, I should say, from six years old to ten or twelve), the master offered to institute an extemporary examination of the pupils in algebra; a proposal, which, as I was by no means confident of my ability to detect mistakes in that science, I declined with some alarm.

In the girls' school, reading was proposed; and as I felt tolerably equal to that art, I expressed my willingness to hear a class. Books were distributed accordingly, and some half-dozen girls relieved each other in reading paragraphs from English History. But it seemed to be a dry compilation, infinitely above their powers; and when they had blundered through three or four dreary passages concerning the Treaty of Amiens, and other thrilling topics of the same nature (obviously without comprehending ten words), I expressed myself quite satisfied. It is very possible that they only mounted to this exalted stave in the Ladder of Learning for the astonishment of a visitor; and that at other times they keep upon its lower rounds; but I should have been much better pleased and satisfied if I had heard them exercised in simpler lessons, which they understood.

As in every other place I visited, the Judges here were gentlemen of high character and attainments. I was in one of the courts for a few minutes, and found it like those to which I have already referred. A nuisance cause was trying; there were not many spectators; and the witnesses, counsel, and jury, formed a sort of family circle, sufficiently jocose and snug.

The society with which I mingled, was intelligent, courteous, and agreeable. The inhabitants of Cincinnati are proud of their city as one of the most interesting in America: and with good reason: for beautiful and thriving as it is now, and containing, as it does, a population of fifty thousand souls, but two-and-fifty years have passed away since the ground on which it stands (bought at that time for a few dollars) was a wild wood, and its citizens were but a handful of dwellers in scattered log huts upon the river's shore.

CHAPTER 12

From Cincinnati to Louisville in another Western Steamboat; and from Louisville to St Louis in another. St Louis

LEAVING Cincinnati at eleven o'clock in the forenoon, we embarked for Louisville in the Pike steamboat, which, carrying the mails, was a packet of a much better class than that in which we had come from Pittsburg. As this passage does not occupy more than twelve or thirteen hours, we arranged to go ashore that night: not coveting the distinction of sleeping in a state-room, when it was possible to sleep anywhere else.

There chanced to be on board this boat, in addition to the usual dreary crowd of passengers, one Pitchlynn, a chief of the Choctaw tribe of Indians, who *sent in his card* to me, and with whom I had the pleasure of a long conversation.

He spoke English perfectly well, though he had not begun to learn the language, he told me, until he was a young man grown. He had read many books; and Scott's poetry appeared to have left a strong impression on his mind: especially the opening of The Lady of the Lake, and the great battle scene in Marmion, in which, no doubt from the congeniality of the subjects to his own pursuits and tastes, he had great interest and delight. He appeared to understand correctly all he had read; and whatever fiction had enlisted his sympathy in its belief, had done so keenly and earnestly. I might almost say fiercely. He was dressed in our ordinary every-day costume, which hung about his fine figure loosely, and with indifferent grace. On my telling him that I regretted not to see him in his own attire, he threw up his right arm, for a moment, as though he were brandishing some heavy weapon, and answered, as he let it fall again, that his race were losing many things besides their dress, and would soon be seen upon the earth no more: but he wore it at home, he added proudly.

He told me that he had been away from his home, west of the Mississippi, seventeen months: and was now returning. He had been chiefly at Washington on some negotiations pending between his Tribe and the Government: which were not settled yet (he said in a melancholy way), and he feared never would be: for what could a few poor Indians do, against such well-skilled men of business as the whites? He had no love for Washington; tired of towns and cities very soon; and longed for the Forest and the Prairie.

I asked him what he thought of Congress? He answered, with a smile, that it wanted dignity, in an Indian's eyes.

He would very much like, he said, to see England before he died; and spoke with much interest about the great things to be seen there. When I told him of that chamber in the British Museum wherein are preserved household memorials of a race that ceased to be, thousands of years ago,[1] he was very attentive, and it was not hard to see that he had a reference in his mind to the gradual fading away of his own people.

This led us to speak of Mr Catlin's gallery,[2] which he praised highly: observing that his own portrait was among the collection, and that all the likenesses were 'elegant.' Mr Cooper, he said, had painted the Red Man well;[3] and so would I, he knew, if I would go home with him and hunt buffaloes, which he was quite anxious I should do. When I told him that supposing I went, I should not be very likely to damage the buffaloes much, he took it as a great joke and laughed heartily.

He was a remarkably handsome man; some years past forty, I should judge; with long black hair, an aquiline nose, broad cheek-bones, a sunburnt complexion, and a very bright, keen, dark, and piercing eye. There were but twenty thousand of the Choctaws left, he said, and their number was decreasing every day. A few of his brother chiefs had been obliged to become civilised, and to make themselves acquainted with what the whites knew, for it was their only chance of existence. But they were not many; and the rest were as they always had been. He dwelt on this: and said several times that unless they tried to assimilate themselves to their conquerors, they must be swept away before the strides of civilised society.

When we shook hands at parting, I told him he must come to England, as he longed to see the land so much: that I should hope to see him there, one day: and that I could promise him he would be well received and kindly treated. He was evidently pleased by this assurance, though he rejoined with a good-humoured smile and an arch shake of his head, that the English used to be very fond of the Red Men when they wanted their help, but had not cared much for them, since.

He took his leave; as stately and complete a gentleman of Nature's making, as ever I beheld; and moved among the people in the boat, another kind of being. He sent me a lithographed portrait of himself soon afterwards; very like, though scarcely handsome enough; which I have carefully preserved in memory of our brief acquaintance.

There was nothing very interesting in the scenery of this day's journey, which brought us at midnight to Louisville. We slept at the Galt House; a splendid hotel; and were as handsomely lodged as though we had been in Paris, rather than hundreds of miles beyond the Alleghanies.

The city presenting no objects of sufficient interest to detain us on our way, we resolved to proceed next day by another steamboat, the Fulton, and to join it, about noon, at a suburb called Portland, where it would be delayed some time in passing through a canal.

The interval, after breakfast, we devoted to riding through the town, which is regular and cheerful: the streets being laid out at right angles, and planted with young trees. The buildings are smoky and blackened, from the use of bituminous coal, but an Englishman is well used to that appearance, and indisposed to quarrel with it. There did not appear to be much business stirring; and some unfinished buildings and improvements seemed to intimate that the city had been overbuilt in the ardour of 'going a-head,' and was suffering under the re-action consequent upon such feverish forcing of its powers.

On our way to Portland, we passed a 'Magistrate's office,' which amused me, as looking far more like a dame school than any police establishment: for this awful Institution was nothing but a little lazy, good-for-nothing front parlour, open to the street; wherein two or three figures (I presume the magistrate and his myrmidons) were basking in the sunshine, the very effigies of languor and repose. It was a perfect picture of Justice retired from business for want of customers; her sword and scales sold off; napping comfortably with her legs upon the table.

Here, as elswhere in these parts, the road was perfectly alive with pigs of all ages; lying about in every direction, fast asleep; or grunting along in quest of hidden dainties. I had always a sneaking kindness for these odd animals, and found a constant source of amusement, when all others failed, in watching their proceedings. As we were riding along this morning, I observed a little incident between two youthful pigs, which was so very human as to be inexpressibly comical and grotesque at the time, though I daresay, in telling, it is tame enough.

One young gentleman (a very delicate porker with several straws sticking about his nose, betokening recent investigations in a dunghill) was walking deliberately on, profoundly thinking, when suddenly his brother, who was lying in a miry hole unseen by him, rose up immediately before his startled eyes, ghostly with damp mud. Never was pig's whole mass of blood so turned. He started back at least three feet, gazed for a moment, and then shot off as hard as he could go: his excessively little tail vibrating with speed and terror like a distracted pendulum. But before he had gone very far, he began to reason with himself as to the nature of this frightful appearance; and as he reasoned, he relaxed his speed by gradual degrees; until at last he stopped, and faced about. There was his brother, with the mud upon him glazing in the sun, yet staring out of the very same hole, perfectly amazed at his proceedings! He was no sooner assured of this; and he assured himself so carefully that one may almost say he shaded his eyes with his hand to see the better; than he came back at a round trot, pounced upon him, and summarily took off a piece of his tail; as a caution to him to be careful what he was about for the future, and never to play tricks with his family any more.

We found the steamboat in the canal, waiting for the slow process of getting through the lock, and went on board, where we shortly afterwards had a new kind of visitor in the person of a certain Kentucky Giant whose name is Porter, and who is of the moderate height of seven feet eight inches, in his stockings.[4]

There never was a race of people who so completely gave the lie to history as these giants, or whom all the chroniclers have so cruelly libelled. Instead of roaring and ravaging about the world, constantly catering for their cannibal larders, and perpetually going to market in an unlawful manner, they are the meekest people in any man's acquaintance: rather inclining to milk and vegetable diet, and bearing anything for a quiet life. So decidedly are amiability and mildness their characteristics, that I confess I look upon that youth who distinguished himself by the slaughter of these inoffensive persons, as a false-hearted brigand, who, pretending to philanthropic motives, was secretly influenced only by the wealth stored up within their castles, and the hope of plunder. And I lean the more to this opinion from finding that even the historian of those exploits, with all his partiality for his hero, is fain to admit that the slaughtered monsters in question were of a very innocent and simple turn; extremely guileless and ready of belief; lending a credulous ear to the most improbable tales; suffering themselves to be easily entrapped into pits; and even (as in the case of the Welsh Giant) with an excess of the hospitable politeness of a landlord, ripping themselves open, rather than hint at the possibility of their guests being versed in the vagabond arts of sleight-of-hand and hocus-pocus.[5]

The Kentucky Giant was but another illustration of the truth of this position. He had a weakness in the region of the knees, and a trustfulness in his long face, which appealed even to five-feet nine for encouragement and support. He was only twenty-five years old, he said, and had grown recently, for it had been found necessary to make an addition to the legs of his inexpressibles. At fifteen he was a short boy, and in those days his English father and his Irish mother had rather snubbed him, as being too small of stature to sustain the credit of the family. He added that his health had not been good, though it was better now; but short people are not wanting who whisper that he drinks too hard.

I understand he drives a hackney-coach, though how he does it, unless he stands on the footboard behind, and lies along the roof upon his chest, with his chin in the box, it would be difficult to comprehend. He brought his gun with him, as a curiosity. Christened 'The Little Rifle,' and displayed outside a shop-window, it would make the fortune of any retail business in Holborn. When he had shown himself and talked a little while, he withdrew with this pocket-instrument, and went bobbing down the cabin, among men of six feet high and upwards, like a lighthouse walking among lamp-posts.

Within a few minutes afterwards, we were out of the canal, and in the Ohio river again.

The arrangements of the boat were like those of the Messenger, and the passengers were of the same order of people. We fed at the same times, on the same kind of viands, in the same dull manner, and with the same observances. The company appeared to be oppressed by the same tremendous concealments, and had as little capacity of enjoyment or light-heartedness. I never in my life did see such listless, heavy dulness as brooded over these meals: the very recollection of it weighs me down, and makes me, for the moment, wretched. Reading and writing on my knee, in our little cabin, I really dreaded the coming of the hour that summoned us to table; and was as glad to escape from it again, as if it had been a penance or a punishment. Healthy cheerfulness and good spirits forming a part of the banquet, I could soak my crusts in the fountain with Le Sage's strolling player, and revel in their glad enjoyment:[6] but sitting down with so many fellow-animals to ward off thirst and hunger as a business; to empty, each creature, his

Yahoo's trough[7] as quickly as he can, and then slink sullenly away; to have these social sacraments stripped of everything but the mere greedy satisfaction of the natural cravings; goes so against the grain with me, that I seriously believe the recollection of these funeral feasts will be a waking nightmare to me all my life.

There was some relief in this boat, too, which there had not been in the other, for the captain (a blunt, good-natured fellow) had his handsome wife with him, who was disposed to be lively and agreeable, as were a few other lady-passengers who had their seats about us at the same end of the table. But nothing could have made head against the depressing influence of the general body. There was a magnetism of dulness in them which would have beaten down the most facetious companion that the earth ever knew. A jest would have been a crime, and a smile would have faded into a grinning horror. Such deadly leaden people; such systematic plodding weary insupportable heaviness; such a mass of animated indigestion in respect of all that was genial, jovial, frank, social, or hearty; never, sure, was brought together elsewhere since the world began.

Nor was the scenery, as we approached the junction of the Ohio and Mississippi rivers, at all inspiriting in its influence. The trees were stunted in their growth; the banks were low and flat; the settlements and log cabins fewer in number: their inhabitants more wan and wretched than any we had encountered yet. No songs of birds were in the air, no pleasant scents, no moving lights and shadows from swift passing clouds. Hour after hour, the changeless glare of the hot, unwinking sky, shone upon the same monotonous objects. Hour after hour, the river rolled along, as wearily and slowly as the time itself.

At length, upon the morning of the third day, we arrived at a spot so much more desolate than any we had yet beheld, that the forlornest places we had passed were, in comparison with it, full of interest. At the junction of the two rivers, on ground so flat and low and marshy, that at certain seasons of the year it is inundated to the house-tops, lies a breeding-place of fever, ague, and death; vaunted in England as a mine of Golden Hope, and speculated in, on the faith of monstrous representations, to many people's ruin.[8] A dismal swamp, on which the half-built houses rot away: cleared here and there for the space of a few yards; and teeming, then, with rank unwholesome vegetation, in whose baleful shade the wretched wanderers who are tempted hither, droop, and die, and lay their bones; the hateful Mississippi circling and eddying before it, and turning off upon its southern course a slimy monster hideous to behold; a hotbed of disease, an ugly sepulchre, a grave uncheered by any gleam of promise: a place without one single quality, in earth or air or water, to commend it: such is this dismal Cairo.

But what words shall describe the Mississippi, great father of rivers, who (praise be to Heaven) has no young children like him! An enormous ditch, sometimes two or three miles wide, running liquid mud, six miles an hour: its strong and frothy current choked and obstructed everywhere by huge logs and whole forest trees: now twining themselves together in great rafts, from the interstices of which a sedgy, lazy foam works up, to float upon the water's top; now rolling past like monstrous bodies, their tangled roots showing like matted hair; now glancing singly by like giant leeches; and now writhing round and round in the vortex of some small whirlpool, like wounded snakes. The banks low, the trees dwarfish, the marshes swarming with frogs, the wretched cabins few and far apart, their inmates hollow-cheeked and pale, the weather very hot, mosquitoes penetrating into every crack and crevice of the boat, mud and slime on everything: nothing pleasant in its aspect, but the harmless lightning which flickers every night upon the dark horizon.

For two days we toiled up this foul stream, striking constantly against the floating timber, or stopping to avoid those more dangerous obstacles, the snags, or sawyers, which are the hidden trunks of trees that have their roots below the tide. When the nights are very dark, the look-out stationed in the head of the boat, knows by the ripple of the water if any great impediment be near at hand, and rings a bell beside him, which is the signal for the engine to be stopped: but always in the night this bell has work to do, and after every ring, there comes a blow which renders it no easy matter to remain in bed.

The decline of day here was very gorgeous; tingeing the firmament deeply with red and gold, up to the very keystone of the arch above us. As the sun went down behind the bank, the slightest blades of grass upon it seemed to become as distinctly visible as the arteries in the skeleton of a leaf; and when, as it slowly sank, the red and golden bars upon the water grew dimmer, and dimmer yet, as if they were sinking too; and all the glowing colours of departing day paled, inch by inch, before the sombre night; the scene became a thousand times more lonesome and more dreary than before, and all its influences darkened with the sky.

We drank the muddy water of this river while we were upon it. It is considered wholesome by the natives, and is something more opaque than gruel. I have seen water like it at the Filter-shops, but nowhere else.

On the fourth night after leaving Louisville, we reached St Louis, and here I witnessed the conclusion of an incident, trifling enough in itself, but very pleasant to see, which had interested me during the whole journey.

There was a little woman on board, with a little baby; and both little woman and little child were cheerful, good-looking, bright-eyed, and fair to see. The little woman had been passing a long time with her sick mother in New York, and had left her home in St Louis, in that condition in which ladies who truly love their lords desire to be. The baby was born in her mother's house; and she had not seen her husband (to whom she was now returning), for twelve months: having left him a month or two after their marriage.

Well, to be sure, there never was a little woman so full of hope, and tenderness, and love, and anxiety, as this little woman was: and all day long she wondered whether 'He' would be at the wharf; and whether 'He' had got her letter; and whether, if she sent the baby ashore by somebody else, 'He' would know it, meeting it in the street: which, seeing that he had never set eyes upon it in his life, was not very likely in the abstract, but was probable enough, to the young mother. She was such an artless little creature; and was in such a sunny, beaming, hopeful state; and let out all this matter clinging close about her heart, so freely; that all the other lady passengers entered into the spirit of it as much as she; and the captain (who heard all about it from his wife) was wondrous sly, I promise you: inquiring, every time we met at table, as in forgetfulness, whether she expected anybody to meet her at St Louis, and whether she would want to go ashore the night we reached it (but he supposed she wouldn't), and cutting many other dry jokes of that nature. There was one little weazen, dried-apple-faced old woman, who took occasion to doubt the constancy of husbands in such circumstances of bereavement; and there was another lady (with a lap-dog) old enough to moralize on the lightness of human affections, and yet not so old that she could help nursing the baby, now and then, or laughing with the rest, when the little woman called it by its father's name, and asked it all manner of fantastic questions concerning him in the joy of her heart.

It was something of a blow to the little woman, that when we were within twenty miles of our destination, it became clearly necessary to put this baby to bed. But she got over it with the same good humour; tied a handkerchief round her head; and came out into the little gallery with the rest. Then, such an oracle as she became in reference to the localities! and such facetiousness as was displayed by the married ladies! and such sympathy as was shown by the single ones! and such peals of laughter as the little woman herself (who would just as soon have cried) greeted every jest with!

At last, there were the lights of St Louis, and here was the wharf, and those were the steps: and the little woman covering her face with her hands, and laughing (or seeming to laugh) more than ever, ran into her own cabin, and shut herself up. I have no doubt that in the charming inconsistency of such excitement, she stopped her ears, lest she should hear 'Him' asking for her: but I did not see her do it.

Then, a great crowd of people rushed on board, though the boat was not yet made fast, but was wandering about, among the other boats, to find a landing-place: and everybody looked for the husband: and nobody saw him: when, in the midst of us all – Heaven knows how she ever got there – there was the little woman clinging with both arms tight round the neck of a fine, good-looking, sturdy young fellow! and in a moment afterwards, there she was again, actually clapping her little hands for joy, as she dragged him through the small door of her small cabin, to look at the baby as he lay asleep!

We went to a large hotel, called the Planters' House: built like an English hospital, with long passages and bare walls, and skylights above the room-doors for the free circulation of air. There were a great many boarders in it; and as many lights sparkled and glistened from the windows down into the street below, when we drove up, as if it had been illuminated on some occasion of rejoicing. It is an excellent house, and the proprietors have most bountiful notions of providing the creature comforts. Dining alone with my wife in our own room, one day, I counted fourteen dishes on the table at once.

In the old French portion of the town, the thoroughfares are narrow and crooked, and some of the houses are very quaint and picturesque: being built of wood, with tumbledown galleries before the windows, approachable by stairs or rather ladders from the street. There are queer little barbers' shops and drinking-houses too, in this quarter; and abundance of crazy old tenements with blinking casements, such as may be seen in Flanders. Some of these ancient habitations, with high garret gable-windows perking into the roofs, have a kind of French shrug about them; and being lop-sided with age, appear to hold their heads askew, besides, as if they were grimacing in astonishment at the American Improvements.

It is hardly necessary to say, that these consist of wharfs and warehouses, and new buildings in all directions; and of a great many vast plans which are still 'progressing.' Already, however, some very good houses, broad streets, and marble-fronted shops, have gone so far a-head as to be in a state of completion; and the town bids fair in a few years to improve considerably: though it is not likely ever to vie, in point of elegance or beauty, with Cincinnati.

The Roman Catholic religion, introduced here by the early French settlers, prevails extensively. Among the public institutions are a Jesuit college;[9] a convent for 'the Ladies of the Sacred Heart;' and a large chapel attached to the college, which was in course of erection at the time of my visit, and was intended to be consecrated on the second of December in the present year. The architect of this building, is one of the reverend fathers of the school, and the works proceed under his sole direction. The organ will be sent from Belgium.

In addition to these establishments, there is a Roman Catholic cathedral, dedicated to Saint Francis Xavier;[10] and a hospital, founded by the munificence of a deceased resident, who was a member of that church. It also sends missionaries from hence among the Indian tribes.

The Unitarian church is represented, in this remote place, as in most other parts of America, by a gentleman of great worth and excellence. The poor have good reason to remember and bless it; for it befriends them, and aids the cause of rational education, without any sectarian or selfish views. It is liberal in all its actions; of kind construction; and of wide benevolence.

There are three free-schools already erected, and in full operation in this city. A fourth is building, and will soon be opened.

No man ever admits the unhealthiness of the place he dwells in (unless he is going away from it), and I shall therefore, I have no doubt, be at issue with the inhabitants of St Louis, in questioning the perfect salubrity of its climate, and in hinting that I think it must rather dispose to fever, in the summer and autumnal seasons. Just adding, that it is very hot, lies among great rivers, and has vast tracts of undrained swampy land around it, I leave the reader to form his own opinion.

As I had a great desire to see a Prairie before turning back from the furthest point of my wanderings; and as some gentlemen of the town had, in their hospitable consideration, an equal desire to gratify me; a day was fixed, before my departure, for an expedition to the Looking-Glass Prairie, which is within thirty miles of the town. Deeming it possible that my readers may not object to know what kind of thing such a gipsy party may be at that distance from home, and among what sort of objects it moves, I will describe the jaunt in another chapter.

CHAPTER 13

A Jaunt to the Looking-glass Prairie and Back[1]

I MAY premise that the word Prairie is variously pronounced *paraaer*, *parearer*, and *paroarer*.[2] The latter mode of pronunciation is perhaps the most in favour.

We were fourteen in all, and all young men: indeed it is a singular though very natural feature in the society of these distant settlements, that it is mainly composed of adventurous persons in the prime of life, and has very few grey heads among it. There were no ladies: the trip being a fatiguing one: and we were to start at five o'clock in the morning punctually.

I was called at four, that I might be certain of keeping nobody waiting; and having got some bread and milk for breakfast, threw up the window and looked down into the street, expecting to see the whole party busily astir, and great preparations going on below. But as everything was very quiet, and the street presented that hopeless aspect with which five o'clock in the morning is familiar elsewhere, I deemed it as well to go to bed again, and went accordingly.

I woke again at seven o'clock, and by that time the party had assembled, and were gathered round one light carriage, with a very stout axletree; one something on wheels like an amateur carrier's cart; one double phaeton of great antiquity and unearthly construction; one gig with a great hole in its back and a broken head; and one rider on horseback who was to go on before. I got into the first coach with three companions; the rest bestowed themselves in the other vehicles; two large baskets were made fast to the lightest; two large stone jars in wicker cases, technically known as demijohns, were consigned to the 'least rowdy' of the party for safekeeping; and the procession moved off to the ferry-boat, in which it was to cross the river bodily, men, horses, carriages, and all, as the manner in these parts is.

We got over the river in due course, and mustered again before a little wooden box on wheels, hove down all aslant in a morass, with 'MERCHANT TAILOR' painted in very large letters over the door. Having settled the order of proceeding, and the road to be taken, we started off once more and began to make our way through an ill-favoured Black Hollow, called, less expressively, the American Bottom.

The previous day had been – not to say hot, for the term is weak and lukewarm in its power of conveying an idea of the temperature. The town had been on fire; in a blaze. But at night it had come on to rain in torrents, and all night long it had rained without cessation. We had a pair of very strong horses, but travelled at the rate of little more than a couple of miles an hour, through one unbroken slough of black mud and water. It had no variety but in depth. Now it was only half over the wheels, now it hid the axletree, and now the coach sank down in it almost to the windows. The air resounded in all directions with the loud chirping of the frogs, who, with the pigs (a coarse, ugly breed, as unwholesome-looking as though they were the spontaneous growth of the country), had the whole scene to themselves. Here and there we passed a log hut: but the wretched cabins were wide apart and thinly scattered, for though the soil is very rich in this place, few people can exist in such a deadly atmosphere. On either side of the track, if it deserve the name, was the thick 'bush;' and everywhere was stagnant, slimy, rotten, filthy water.

As it is the custom in these parts to give a horse a gallon or so of cold water whenever he is in a foam with heat, we halted for that purpose, at a log inn in the wood, far removed from any other residence. It consisted of one room, bare-roofed and bare-walled of course, with a loft above. The ministering priest was a swarthy young savage, in a shirt of cotton print like bed-furniture, and a pair of ragged trousers. There were a couple of young boys, too, nearly naked, lying idly by the well; and they, and he, and *the* traveller at the inn, turned out to look at us.

The traveller was an old man with a grey gristly beard two inches long, a shaggy moustache of the same hue, and enormous eyebrows; which almost obscured his lazy, semi-drunken glance, as he stood regarding us with folded arms: poising himself alternately upon his toes and heels. On being addressed by one of the party, he drew nearer, and said, rubbing his chin (which scraped under his horny hand like fresh gravel beneath a nailed shoe), that he was from Delaware, and had lately bought a farm 'down there,' pointing into one of the marshes where the stunted trees were thickest. He was 'going,' he added, to St Louis, to fetch his family, whom he had left behind; but he seemed in no great hurry to bring on these encumbrances, for when we moved away, he loitered back into the cabin, and was plainly bent on stopping there so long as his money lasted. He was a great politician of course, and explained his opinions at some length to one of our company; but I only remember that he concluded with two sentiments, one of which was, Somebody for ever! and the other, Blast everybody else! which is by no means a bad abstract of the general creed in these matters.

When the horses were swollen out to about twice their natural dimensions (there seems to be an idea here, that this kind of inflation improves their going), we went forward again, through mud and mire, and damp, and festering heat, and brake and bush, attended always by the music of the frogs and pigs, until nearly noon, when we halted at a place called Belleville.

Belleville was a small collection of wooden houses, huddled together in the very heart of the bush and swamp. Many of them had singularly bright doors of red and yellow; for the place had been lately visited by a travelling painter, 'who got along,' as I was told, 'by eating his way.' The criminal court was sitting, and was at that moment trying some criminals for horse-stealing: with whom it would most likely go hard: for live stock of all kinds being necessarily very much exposed in the woods, is held by the community in rather higher value than human life; and for this reason, juries generally make a point of finding all men indicted for cattle-stealing, guilty, whether or no.

The horses belonging to the bar, the judge, and witnesses, were tied to temporary racks set up roughly in the road; by which is to be understood, a forest path, nearly knee-deep in mud and slime.

There was an hotel in this place, which, like all hotels in America, had its large dining-room for the public table. It was an odd, shambling, low-roofed out-house, half-cowshed and half-kitchen, with a coarse brown canvas table-cloth, and tin sconces stuck against the walls, to hold candles at supper-time. The horseman had gone forward to have coffee and some eatables prepared, and they were by this time nearly ready. He had ordered 'wheat-bread and chicken fixings,' in preference to 'corn-bread and common doings.' The latter kind of refection includes only pork and bacon. The former comprehends broiled ham, sausages, veal cutlets, steaks, and such other viands of that nature as may be supposed, by a tolerably wide poetical construction, to 'fix' a chicken comfortably in the digestive organs of any lady or gentleman.

On one of the door-posts at this inn, was a tin plate, whereon was inscribed in characters of gold, 'Doctor Crocus;' and on a sheet of paper, pasted up by the side of this plate, was a written announcement that Dr Crocus would that evening deliver a lecture on Phrenology for the benefit of the Belleville public; at a charge, for admission, of so much a head.[3]

Straying up-stairs, during the preparation of the chicken fixings, I happened to pass the Doctor's chamber; and as the door stood wide open, and the room was empty, I made bold to peep in.

It was a bare, unfurnished, comfortless room, with an unframed portrait hanging up at the head of the bed; a likeness, I take it, of the Doctor, for the forehead was fully displayed, and great stress was laid by the artist upon its phrenological developments. The bed itself was covered with an old patchwork counterpane. The room was destitute of carpet or of curtain. There was a damp fireplace without any stove, full of wood ashes; a chair, and a very small table; and on the last-named piece of furniture was displayed, in grand array, the doctor's library, consisting of some half-dozen greasy old books.

Now, it certainly looked about the last apartment on the whole earth out of which any man would be likely to get anything to do him good. But the door, as I have said, stood coaxingly open, and plainly said in conjunction with the chair, the portrait, the table, and the books, 'Walk in, gentlemen, walk in! Don't be ill, gentlemen, when you may be well in no time. Doctor Crocus is here, gentlemen, the celebrated Dr Crocus! Doctor Crocus has come all this way to cure you, gentlemen. If you haven't heard of Dr Crocus, it's your fault, gentlemen, who live a little way out of the world here: not Dr Crocus's. Walk in, gentlemen, walk in!'

In the passage below, when I went down-stairs again, was Dr Crocus himself. A crowd had flocked in from the Court House, and a voice from among them called out to the landlord, 'Colonel! introduce Doctor Crocus.'

'Mr Dickens,' says the colonel, 'Doctor Crocus.'

Upon which Doctor Crocus, who is a tall, fine-looking Scotchman, but rather fierce and warlike in appearance for a professor of the peaceful art of healing, bursts out of the concourse with his right arm extended, and his chest thrown out as far as it will possibly come, and says:

'Your countryman, sir!'

Whereupon Doctor Crocus and I shake hands; and Doctor Crocus looks as if I didn't by any means realise his expectations, which, in a linen blouse, and a great straw hat with a green ribbon, and no gloves, and my face and nose profusely ornamented with the stings of mosquitoes and the bites of bugs, it is very likely I did not.

'Long in these parts, sir?' says I.

'Three or four months, sir,' says the Doctor.

'Do you think of soon returning to the old country, sir?' says I.

Doctor Crocus makes no verbal answer, but gives me an imploring look, which says so plainly 'Will you ask me that again, a little louder, if you please?' that I repeat the question.

'Think of soon returning to the old country, sir!' repeats the Doctor.

'To the old country, sir,' I rejoin.

Doctor Crocus looks round upon the crowd to observe the effect he produces, rubs his hands, and says, in a very loud voice:

'Not yet awhile, sir, not yet. You won't catch me at that just yet, sir. I am a little too fond of freedom for *that*, sir. Ha ha! It's not so easy for a man to tear himself from a free country such as this is, sir. Ha ha! No no! Ha ha! None of that till one's obliged to do it, sir. No, no!'

As Doctor Crocus says these latter words, he shakes his head, knowingly, and laughs again. Many of the bystanders shake their heads in concert with the doctor, and laugh too, and look at each other as much as to say, 'A pretty bright and first-rate sort of chap is Crocus!' and unless I am very much mistaken, a good many people went to the lecture that night, who never thought about phrenology, or about Doctor Crocus either, in all their lives before.

From Belleville, we went on, through the same desolate kind of waste, and constantly attended, without the interval of a moment, by the same music; until, at three o'clock in the afternoon, we halted once more at a village called Lebanon to inflate the horses again, and give them some corn besides: of which they stood much in need. Pending this ceremony, I walked into the village, where I met a full-sized dwelling-house coming down-hill at a round trot, drawn by a score or more of oxen.

The public-house was so very clean and good a one, that the managers of the jaunt resolved to return to it and put up there for the night, if possible. This course decided on, and the horses being well refreshed, we again pushed forward, and came upon the Prairie at sunset.

It would be difficult to say why, or how – though it was possibly from having heard and read so much about it – but the effect on me was disappointment. Looking towards the setting sun, there lay, stretched out before my view, a vast expanse of level ground; unbroken, save by one thin line of trees, which scarcely amounted to a scratch upon the great blank; until it met the glowing sky, wherein it seemed to dip: mingling with its rich colours, and mellowing in its distant blue. There it lay, a tranquil sea or lake without water, if such a simile be admissible, with the day going down upon it: a few birds wheeling here and there: and solitude and silence reigning paramount around. But the grass was not yet high; there were bare black patches on the ground; and the few wild flowers that the eye could see, were poor and scanty. Great as the picture was, its very flatness and extent, which left nothing to the imagination, tamed it down and cramped its interest. I felt little of that sense of freedom and exhilaration which a Scottish heath inspires, or even our English downs awaken. It was lonely and wild, but oppressive in its barren monotony. I felt that in traversing the Prairies, I could never abandon myself to the scene, forgetful of all else; as I should do instinctively, were the heather underneath my feet, or an iron-bound coast beyond; but should often glance towards the distant and frequently-receding line of the horizon, and wish it gained and passed. It is not a scene to be forgotten, but it is scarcely one, I think (at all events, as I saw it), to remember with much pleasure, or to covet the looking-on again, in after life.

We encamped near a solitary log-house, for the sake of its water, and dined upon the plain. The baskets contained roast fowls, buffalo's tongue (an exquisite dainty, by the way), ham, bread, cheese, and butter; biscuits, champagne, sherry; lemons and sugar for punch; and abundance of rough ice. The meal was delicious, and the entertainers were the soul of kindness and good humour. I have often recalled that cheerful party to my pleasant recollection since, and shall not easily forget, in junketings nearer home with friends of older date, my boon companions on the Prairie.

Returning to Lebanon that night, we lay at the little inn at which we had halted in the afternoon. In point of cleanliness and comfort it would have suffered by no comparison with any English alehouse, of a homely kind, in England.

Rising at five o'clock next morning, I took a walk about the village: none of the houses were strolling about to-day, but it was early for them yet, perhaps: and then amused myself by lounging in a kind of farm-yard behind the tavern, of which the leading features were, a strange jumble of rough sheds for stables; a rude colonnade, built as a cool place of summer resort; a deep well; a great earthen mound for keeping vegetables in, in winter time; and a pigeon-house, whose little apertures looked, as they do in all pigeon-houses, very much too small for the admission of the plump and swelling-breasted birds who were strutting about it, though they tried to get in never so hard. That interest exhausted, I took a survey of the inn's two parlours, which were decorated with coloured prints of Washington, and President Madison,[4] and of a white-faced young lady (much speckled by the flies), who held up her gold neck-chain for the admiration of the spectator, and informed all admiring comers that she was 'Just Seventeen:' although I should have thought her older. In the best room were two oil portraits of the kit-cat size,[5] representing the landlord and his infant son; both looking as bold as lions, and staring out of the canvas with an intensity that would have been cheap at any price. They were painted, I think, by the artist who had touched up the Belleville doors with red and gold; for I seemed to recognise his style immediately.

After breakfast, we started to return by a different way from that which we had taken yesterday, and coming up at ten o'clock with an encampment of German emigrants carrying their goods in carts, who had made a rousing fire which they were just quitting, stopped there to refresh. And very pleasant the fire was; for, hot though it had been yesterday, it was quite cold to-day, and the wind blew keenly. Looming in the distance, as we rode along, was another of the ancient Indian burial-places, called The Monks' Mound; in memory of a body of fanatics of the order of La Trappe,[6] who founded a desolate convent there, many years ago, when there were no settlers within a thousand miles, and were all swept off by the pernicious climate: in which lamentable fatality, few rational people will suppose, perhaps, that society experienced any very severe deprivation.

The track of to-day had the same features as the track of yesterday. There was the swamp, the bush, [and] the perpetual chorus of frogs, the rank unseemly growth, the unwholesome steaming earth. Here and there, and frequently too, we encountered a solitary broken-down waggon, full of some new settler's goods. It was a pitiful sight to see one of these vehicles deep in the mire; the axle-tree broken; a wheel lying idly by its side; the man gone miles away, to look for assistance; the woman seated among their wandering household gods with a baby at her breast, a picture of forlorn, dejected patience; the team of oxen crouching down mournfully in the mud, and breathing forth such clouds of vapour from their mouths and nostrils, that all the damp mist and fog around seemed to have come direct from them.

In due time we mustered once again before the merchant tailor's, and having done so, crossed over to the city in the ferry-boat: passing, on the way, a spot called Bloody Island, the duelling-ground of St Louis, and so designated in honour of the last fatal combat fought there, which was with pistols, breast to breast.[7] Both combatants fell dead upon the ground; and possibly some rational people may think of them, as of the gloomy madmen on the Monks' Mound, that they were no great loss to the community.

CHAPTER 14

Return to Cincinnati. A Stage-coach Ride from that City to Columbus, and Thence to Sandusky. So, by Lake Erie, to the Falls of Niagara

As I had a desire to travel through the interior of the state of Ohio, and to 'strike the lakes,' as the phrase is, at a small town called Sandusky, to which that route would conduct us on our way to Niagara, we had to return from St Louis by the way we had come, and to retrace our former track as far as Cincinnati.

The day on which we were to take leave of St Louis being very fine; and the steamboat, which was to have started I don't know how early in the morning, postponing, for the third or fourth time, her departure until the afternoon; we rode forward to an old French village on the river, called properly Carondelet, and nicknamed Vide Poche, and arranged that the packet should call for us there.

The place consisted of a few poor cottages, and two or three public-houses; the state of whose larders certainly seemed to justify the second designation of the village, for there was nothing to eat in any of them. At length, however, by going back some half a mile or so, we found a solitary house where ham and coffee were procurable; and there we tarried to await the advent of the boat, which would come in sight from the green before the door, a long way off.

It was a neat, unpretending village tavern, and we took our repast in a quaint little room with a bed in it, decorated with some old oil paintings, which in their time had probably done duty in a Catholic chapel or monastery. The fare was very good, and served with great cleanliness. The house was kept by a characteristic old couple, with whom we had a long talk, and who were perhaps a very good sample of that kind of people in the West.

The landlord was a dry, tough, hard-faced old fellow (not so very old either, for he was but just turned sixty, I should think), who had been out with the militia in the last war with England, and had seen all kinds of service, – except a battle; and he had been very near seeing that, he added: very near. He had all his life been restless and locomotive, with an irresistible desire for change; and was still the son of his old self: for if he had nothing to keep him at home, he said (slightly jerking his hat and his thumb towards the window of the room in which the old lady sat, as we stood talking in front of the house), he would clean up his musket, and be off to Texas to-morrow morning. He was one of the very many descendants of Cain proper to this continent, who seem destined from their birth to serve as pioneers in the great human army: who gladly go on from year to year extending its outposts, and leaving home after home behind them; and die at last, utterly regardless of their graves being left thousands of miles behind, by the wandering generation who succeed.

His wife was a domesticated, kind-hearted old soul, who had come with him, 'from the queen city of the world,' which, it seemed, was Philadelphia; but had no love for this Western country, and indeed had little reason to bear it any; having seen her children, one by one, die here of fever, in the full prime and beauty of their youth. Her heart was sore, she said, to think of them; and to talk on this theme, even to strangers, in that blighted place, so far from her old home, eased it somewhat, and became a melancholy pleasure.

The boat appearing towards evening, we bade adieu to the poor old lady and her vagrant spouse, and making for the nearest landing-place, were soon on board The Messenger again, in our old cabin, and steaming down the Mississippi.

If the coming up this river, slowly making head against the stream, be an irksome journey, the shooting down it with the turbid current is almost worse; for then the boat, proceeding at the rate of twelve or fifteen miles an hour, has to force its passage through a labyrinth of floating logs, which, in the dark, it is often impossible to see beforehand or avoid. All that night, the bell was never silent for five minutes at a time; and after every ring the vessel reeled again, sometimes beneath a single blow, sometimes beneath a dozen dealt in quick succession, the lightest of which seemed more than enough to beat in her frail keel, as though it had been pie-crust. Looking down upon the filthy river after dark, it seemed to be alive with monsters, as these black masses rolled upon the surface, or came starting up again, head first, when the boat, in ploughing her way among a shoal of such obstructions, drove a few among them for the moment under water. Sometimes the engine stopped during a long interval, and then before her and behind, and gathering close about her on all sides, were so many of these ill-favoured obstacles that she was fairly hemmed in; the centre of a floating island; and was constrained to pause until they parted, somewhere, as dark clouds will do before the wind, and opened by degrees a channel out.

In good time next morning, however, we came again in sight of the detestable morass called Cairo; and stopping there to take in wood, lay alongside a barge, whose starting timbers scarcely held together. It was moored to the bank, and on its side was painted 'Coffee House;' that being, I suppose, the floating paradise to which the people fly for shelter when they lose their houses for a month or two beneath the hideous waters of the Mississippi. But looking southward from this point, we had the satisfaction of seeing that intolerable river dragging its slimy length and ugly freight abruptly off towards New Orleans; and passing a yellow line which stretched across the current, were again upon the clear Ohio, never, I trust, to see the Mississippi more, saving in troubled dreams and nightmares. Leaving it for the company of its sparkling neighbour, was like the transition from pain to ease, or the awakening from a horrible vision to cheerful realities.

We arrived at Louisville on the fourth night, and gladly availed ourselves of its excellent hotel. Next day we went on in the Ben Franklin, a beautiful mail steamboat, and reached Cincinnati shortly after midnight. Being by this time nearly tired of sleeping upon shelves, we had remained awake to go ashore straightway; and groping a passage across the dark decks of other boats, and among labyrinths of engine-machinery and leaking casks of molasses, we reached the streets, knocked up the porter at the hotel where we had staid before, and were, to our great joy, safely housed soon afterwards.

We rested but one day at Cincinnati, and then resumed our journey to Sandusky. As it comprised two varieties of stage-coach travelling, which, with those I have already glanced at, comprehend the main characteristics of this mode of transit in America, I will take the reader as our fellow-passenger, and pledge myself to perform the distance with all possible despatch.

Our place of destination in the first instance is Columbus. It is distant about a hundred and twenty miles from Cincinnati, but there is a macadamised road (rare blessing!) the whole way, and the rate of travelling upon it is six miles an hour.

We start at eight o'clock in the morning, in a great mail-coach, whose huge cheeks are so very ruddy and plethoric, that it appears to be troubled with a tendency of blood to the head. Dropsical it certainly is, for it will hold a dozen passengers inside. But, wonderful to add, it is very clean and bright, being nearly new; and rattles through the streets of Cincinnati gaily.

Our way lies through a beautiful country, richly cultivated, and luxuriant in its promise of an abundant harvest. Sometimes we pass a field where the strong bristling stalks of Indian corn look like a crop of walking-sticks, and sometimes an enclosure where the green wheat is springing up among a labyrinth of stumps; the primitive worm-fence[1] is universal, and an ugly thing it is; but the farms are neatly kept and, save for these differences, one might be travelling just now in Kent.

We often stop to water at a roadside inn, which is always dull and silent. The coachman dismounts and fills his bucket, and holds it to the horses' heads. There is scarcely ever any one to help him; there are seldom any loungers standing round; and never any stable-company with jokes to crack. Sometimes, when we have changed our team, there is a difficulty in starting again, arising out of the prevalent mode of breaking a young horse: which is to catch him, harness him against his will, and put him in a stage-coach without further notice: but we get on somehow or other, after a great many kicks and a violent struggle; and jog on as before again.

Occasionally, when we stop to change, some two or three half-drunken loafers will come loitering out with their hands in their pockets, or will be seen kicking their heels in rocking-chairs, or lounging on the window-sill, or sitting on a rail within the colonnade: they have not often anything to say though, either to us or to each other, but sit there idly staring at the coach and horses. The landlord of the inn is usually among them, and seems, of all the party, to be the least connected with the business of the house. Indeed he is with reference to the tavern, what the driver is in relation to the coach and passengers: whatever happens in his sphere of action, he is quite indifferent, and perfectly easy in his mind.

The frequent change of coachmen works no change or variety in the coachman's character. He is always dirty, sullen, and taciturn. If he be capable of smartness of any kind, moral or physical, he has a faculty of concealing it which is truly marvellous. He never speaks to you as you sit beside him on the box, and if you speak to him, he answers (if at all) in monosyllables. He points out nothing on the road, and seldom looks at anything: being, to all appearance, thoroughly weary of it and of existence generally. As to doing the honours of his coach, his business, as I have said, is with the horses. The coach follows because it is attached to them and goes on wheels: not because you are in it. Sometimes, towards the end of a long stage, he suddenly breaks out into a discordant fragment of an election song, but his face never sings along with him: it is only his voice, and not often that.

He always chews and always spits, and never encumbers himself with a pocket-handkerchief. The consequences to the box passenger, especially when the wind blows towards him, are not agreeable.

Whenever the coach stops, and you can hear the voices of the inside passengers; or whenever any bystander addresses them, or any one among them; or they address each other; you will hear one phrase repeated over and over and over again to the most extraordinary extent. It is an ordinary and unpromising phrase enough, being neither more nor less than 'Yes, sir;' but it is adapted to every variety of circumstance, and fills up every pause in the conversation. Thus: –

The time is one o'clock at noon. The scene, a place where we are to stay to dine, on this journey. The coach drives up to the door of an inn. The day is warm, and there are several idlers lingering about the tavern, and waiting for the public dinner. Among them, is a stout gentleman in a brown hat, swinging himself to and fro in a rocking-chair on the pavement.

As the coach stops, a gentleman in a straw hat looks out of the window:

STRAW HAT. (To the stout gentleman in the rocking-chair.) I reckon that's Judge Jefferson, an't it?

BROWN HAT. (Still swinging; speaking very slowly; and without any emotion whatever.) Yes, sir.

STRAW HAT. Warm weather, Judge.

BROWN HAT. Yes, sir.

STRAW HAT. There was a snap of cold, last week.

BROWN HAT. Yes, sir.

STRAW HAT. Yes, sir.

A pause. They look at each other, very seriously.

STRAW HAT. I calculate you'll have got through that case of the corporation, Judge, by this time, now?

BROWN HAT. Yes, sir.

STRAW HAT. How did the verdict go, sir?

BROWN HAT. For the defendant, sir.

STRAW HAT. (Interrogatively.) Yes, sir?

BROWN HAT. (Affirmatively.) Yes, sir.

BOTH. (Musingly, as each gazes down the street.) Yes, sir.

Another pause. They look at each other again, still more seriously than before.

BROWN HAT. This coach is rather behind its time to-day, I guess.

STRAW HAT. (Doubtingly.) Yes, sir.

BROWN HAT. (Looking at his watch.) Yes, sir; nigh upon two hours.

STRAW HAT. (Raising his eyebrows in very great surprise.) Yes, sir!

BROWN HAT. (Decisively, as he puts up his watch.) Yes, sir.

ALL THE OTHER INSIDE PASSENGERS. (Among themselves.) Yes, sir.

COACHMAN. (In a very surly tone.) No it an't.

STRAW HAT. (To the coachman.) Well, I don't know, sir. We were a pretty tall time coming that last fifteen mile. That's a fact.

The coachman making no reply, and plainly declining to enter into any controversy on a subject so far removed from his sympathies and feelings, another passenger says, 'Yes, sir;' and the gentleman in the straw hat in acknowledgment of his courtesy, says 'Yes, sir,' to him, in return. The straw hat then inquires of the brown hat, whether that coach in which he (the straw hat) then sits is not a new one? To which the brown hat again makes answer, 'Yes, sir.'

STRAW HAT. I thought so. Pretty loud smell of varnish, sir?

BROWN HAT. Yes, sir.

ALL THE OTHER PASSENGERS. Yes, sir.

BROWN HAT. (To the company in general.) Yes, sir.

The conversational powers of the company having been by this time pretty heavily taxed, the straw hat opens the door and gets out; and all the rest alight also. We dine soon afterwards with the boarders in the house, and have nothing to drink but tea and coffee. As they are both very bad and the water is worse, I ask for brandy; but it is a Temperance Hotel, and spirits are not to be had for love or money. This preposterous forcing of unpleasant drinks down the reluctant throats of travellers is not at all uncommon in America, but I never discovered that the scruples of such wincing landlords induced them to preserve any unusually nice balance between the quality of their fare, and their scale of charges: on the contrary, I rather suspected them of diminishing the one and exalting the other, by way of recompense for the loss of their profit on the sale of spirituous liquors. After all, perhaps, the plainest course for persons of such tender consciences, would be, a total abstinence from tavern-keeping.

Dinner over, we get into another vehicle which is ready at the door (for the coach has been changed in the interval), and resume our journey; which continues through the same kind of country until evening, when we come to the town where we are to stop for tea and supper; and having delivered the mail bags at the Post-office, ride through the usual wide street, lined with the usual stores and houses (the drapers always having hung up at their door, by way of sign, a piece of bright red cloth), to the hotel where this meal is prepared. There being many boarders here, we sit down, a large party, and a very melancholy one as usual. But there is a buxom hostess at the head of the table, and opposite, a simple Welsh schoolmaster with his wife and child; who came here, on a specula- tion of greater promise than performance, to teach the classics: and they are sufficient subjects of interest until the meal is over, and another coach is ready. In it we go on once more, lighted by a bright moon, until midnight; when we stop to change the coach again, and remain for half an hour or so in a miserable room, with a blurred lithograph of Washington over the smoky fireplace, and a mighty jug of cold water on the table: to which refreshment the moody passengers do so apply themselves that they would seem to be, one and all, keen patients of Dr Sangrado.[2] Among them is a very little boy, who chews tobacco like a very big one; and a droning gentle-man, who talks arithmetically and statistically on all subjects, from poetry downwards; and who always speaks in the same key, with exactly the same emphasis, and with very grave deliberation. He came outside just now, and told me how that the uncle of a certain young lady who had been spirited away and married by a certain captain, lived in these parts; and how this uncle was so valiant and ferocious that he shouldn't wonder if he were to follow the said captain to England, 'and shoot him down in the street wherever he found him;' in the feasibility of which strong measure I, being for the moment rather prone to contradiction, from feeling half asleep and very tired, declined to acquiesce: assuring him that if the uncle did resort to it, or gratified any other little whim of the like nature, he would find himself one morning prematurely throttled at the Old Bailey: and that he would do well to make his will before he went, as he would certainly want it before he had been in Britain very long.

On we go, all night, and by-and-by the day begins to break, and presently the first cheerful rays of the warm sun come slanting on us brightly. It sheds its light upon a miserable waste of sodden grass, and dull trees, and squalid huts, whose aspect is forlorn and grievous in the last degree. A very desert in the wood, whose growth of green is dank and noxious like that upon the top of standing water: where poisonous fungus grows in the rare footprint on the oozy ground, and sprouts like witches' coral,[3] from the crevices in the cabin wall and floor; it is a hideous thing to lie upon the very threshold of a city. But it was purchased years ago, and as the owner cannot be discovered, the State has been unable to reclaim it. So there it remains, in the midst of cultivation and improvement, like ground accursed, and made obscene and rank by some great crime.

We reached Columbus shortly before seven o'clock, and staid there, to refresh, that day and night: having excellent apartments in a very large unfinished hotel called the Neill House, which were richly fitted with the polished wood of the black walnut, and opened on a handsome portico and stone verandah, like rooms in some Italian mansion. The town is clean and pretty, and of course is 'going to be' much larger. It is the seat of the State legislature of Ohio, and lays claim, in consequence, to some consideration and importance.

There being no stage-coach next day, upon the road we wished to take, I hired 'an extra,' at a reasonable charge, to carry us to Tiffin; a small town from whence there is a railroad to Sandusky. This extra was an ordinary four-horse stage-coach, such as I have described, changing horses and drivers, as the stage-coach would, but was exclusively our own for the journey. To ensure our having horses at the proper stations, and being incommoded by no strangers, the proprietors sent an agent on the box, who was to accompany us the whole way through; and thus attended, and bearing with us, besides, a hamper full of savoury cold meats, and fruit, and wine, we started off again in high spirits, at half-past six o'clock next morning, very much delighted to be by ourselves, and disposed to enjoy even the roughest journey.

It was well for us, that we were in this humour, for the road we went over that day, was certainly enough to have shaken tempers that were not resolutely at Set Fair, down to some inches below Stormy. At one time we were all flung together in a heap at the bottom of the coach, and at another we were crushing our heads against the roof. Now, one side was down deep in the mire, and we were holding on to the other. Now, the coach was lying on the tails of the two wheelers; and now it was rearing up in the air, in a frantic state, with all four horses standing on the top of an insurmountable eminence, looking coolly back at it, as though they would say 'Unharness us. It can't be done.' The drivers on these roads, who certainly get over the ground in a manner which is quite miraculous, so twist and turn the team about in forcing a passage, corkscrew fashion, through the bogs and swamps, that it was quite a common circumstance on looking out of the window, to see the coachman with the ends of a pair of reins in his hands, apparently driving nothing, or playing at horses, and the leaders staring at one unexpectedly from the back of the coach, as if they had some idea of getting up behind. A great portion of the way was over what is called a corduroy road,[4] which is made by throwing trunks of trees into a marsh, and leaving them to settle there. The very slightest of the jolts with which the ponderous carriage fell from log to log, was enough, it seemed, to have dislocated all the bones in the human body. It would be impossible to experience a similar set of sensations, in any other circumstances, unless perhaps in attempting to go up to the top of St Paul's in an omnibus. Never, never once, that day, was the coach in any position, attitude, or kind of motion to which we are accustomed in coaches. Never did it make the smallest approach to one's experience of the proceedings of any sort of vehicle that goes on wheels.

Still, it was a fine day, and the temperature was delicious, and though we had left Summer behind us in the west, and were fast leaving Spring, we were moving towards Niagara, and home. We alighted in a pleasant wood towards the middle of the day, dined on a fallen tree, and leaving our best fragments with a cottager, and our worst with the pigs (who swarm in this part of the country like grains of sand on the sea-shore, to the great comfort of our commissariat in Canada), we went forward again, gaily.

As night came on, the track grew narrower and narrower, until at last it so lost itself among the trees, that the driver seemed to find his way by instinct. We had the comfort of knowing, at least, that there was no danger of his falling asleep, for every now and then a wheel would strike against an unseen stump with such a jerk, that he was fain to hold on pretty tight and pretty quick, to keep himself upon the box. Nor was there any reason to dread the least danger from furious driving, inasmuch as over that broken ground the horses had enough to do to walk; as to shying, there was no room for that; and a herd of wild elephants could not have run away in such a wood, with such a coach at their heels. So we stumbled along, quite satisfied.

These stumps of trees are a curious feature in American travelling. The varying illusions they present to the unaccustomed eye as it grows dark, are quite astonishing in their number and reality. Now, there is a Grecian urn erected in the centre of a lonely field; now there is a woman weeping at a tomb; now a very commonplace old gentleman in a white waistcoat, with a thumb thrust into each arm-hole of his coat; now a student poring on a book; now a crouching negro; now, a horse, a dog, a cannon, an armed man; a hunch-back throwing off his cloak and stepping forth into the light. They were often as entertaining to me as so many glasses in a magic lantern, and never took their shapes at my bidding, but seemed to force themselves upon me, whether I would or no; and strange to say, I sometimes recognised in them counterparts of figures once familiar to me in pictures attached to childish books, forgotten long ago.

It soon became too dark, however, even for this amusement, and the trees were so close together that their dry branches rattled against the coach on either side, and obliged us all to keep our heads within. It lightened too, for three whole hours; each flash being very bright, and blue, and long; and as the vivid streaks came darting in among the crowded branches, and the thunder rolled gloomily above the tree tops, one could scarcely help thinking that there were better neighbourhoods at such a time than thick woods afforded.

At length, between ten and eleven o'clock at night, a few feeble lights appeared in the distance, and Upper Sandusky, an Indian village, where we were to stay till morning, lay before us.

They were gone to bed at the log Inn, which was the only house of entertainment in the place, but soon answered to our knocking, and got some tea for us in a sort of kitchen or common room, tapestried with old newspapers, pasted against the wall. The bed-chamber to which my wife and I were shown, was a large, low, ghostly room; with a quantity of withered branches on the hearth, and two doors without any fastening, opposite to each other, both opening on the black night and wild country, and so contrived, that one of them always blew the other open: a novelty in domestic architecture, which I do not remember to have seen before, and which I was somewhat disconcerted to have forced on my attention after getting into bed, as I had a considerable sum in gold for our travelling expenses, in my dressing-case. Some of the luggage, however, piled against the panels, soon settled this difficulty, and my sleep would not have been very much affected that night, I believe, though it had failed to do so.

My Boston friend[5] climbed up to bed, somewhere in the roof, where another guest was already snoring hugely. But being bitten beyond his power of endurance, he turned out again, and fled for shelter to the coach, which was airing itself in front of the house. This was not a very politic step, as it turned out: for the pigs scenting him, and looking upon the coach as a kind of pie with some manner of meat inside, grunted round it so hideously, that he was afraid to come out again, and lay there shivering, till morning. Nor was it possible to warm him, when he did come out, by means of a glass of brandy: for in Indian villages, the legislature, with a very good and wise intention, forbids the sale of spirits by tavern keepers. The precaution, however, is quite inefficacious, for the Indians never fail to procure liquor of a worse kind, at a dearer price, from travelling pedlars.

It is a settlement of the Wyandot Indians who inhabit this place. Among the company at breakfast was a mild old gentleman, who had been for many years employed by the United States Government in conducting negotiations with the Indians, and who had just concluded a treaty with these people by which they bound themselves, in consideration of a certain annual sum, to remove next year to some land provided for them, west of the Mississippi, and a little way beyond St Louis. He gave me a moving account of their strong attachment to the familiar scenes of their infancy, and in particular to the burial-places of their kindred; and of their great reluctance to leave them. He had witnessed many such removals, and always with pain, though he knew that they departed for their own good. The question whether this tribe should go or stay, had been discussed among them a day or two before, in a hut erected for the purpose, the logs of which still lay upon the ground before the inn. When the speaking was done, the ayes and noes were ranged on opposite sides, and every male adult voted in his turn. The moment the result was known, the minority (a large one) cheerfully yielded to the rest, and withdrew all kind of opposition.

We met some of these poor Indians afterwards, riding on shaggy ponies. They were so like [the meaner sort of] gipsies, that if I could have seen any of them in England, I should have concluded, as a matter of course, that they belonged to that wandering and restless people.

Leaving this town directly after breakfast, we pushed forward again, over a rather worse road than yesterday, if possible, and arrived about noon at Tiffin, where we parted with the extra. At two o'clock we took the railroad; the travelling on which was very slow, its construction being indifferent, and the ground wet and marshy; and arrived at Sandusky in time to dine that evening. We put up at a comfortable little hotel on the brink of Lake Erie, lay there that night, and had no choice but to wait there next day, until a steamboat bound for Buffalo appeared. The town, which was sluggish and uninteresting enough, was something like the back of an English watering-place, out of the season.

Our host, who was very attentive and anxious to make us comfortable, was a handsome middle-aged man, who had come to this town from New England, in which part of the country he was 'raised.' When I say that he constantly walked in and out of the room with his hat on; and stopped to converse in the same free-and-easy state; and lay down on our sofa, and pulled his newspaper out of his pocket, and read it at his ease; I merely mention these traits as characteristic of the country: not at all as being matter of complaint, or as having been disagreeable to me. I should undoubtedly be offended by such proceedings at home, because there they are not the custom, and where they are not, they would be impertinencies; but in America, the only desire of a good-natured fellow of this kind, is to treat his guests hospitably and well; and I had no more right, and I can truly say no more disposition, to measure his conduct by our English rule and standard, than I had to quarrel with him for not being of the exact stature which would qualify him for admission into the Queen's grenadier guards. As little inclination had I to find fault with a funny old lady who was an upper domestic in this establishment, and who, when she came to wait upon us at any meal, sat herself down comfortably in the most convenient chair, and producing a large pin to pick her teeth with, remained performing that ceremony, and steadfastly regarding us meanwhile with much gravity and composure (now and then pressing us to eat a little more), until it was time to clear away. It was enough for us, that whatever we wished done was done with great civility and readiness, and a desire to oblige, not only here, but everywhere else; and that all our wants were, in general, zealously anticipated.

We were taking an early dinner at this house, on the day after our arrival, which was Sunday, when a steamboat came in sight, and presently touched at the wharf. As she proved to be on her way to Buffalo, we hurried on board with all speed, and soon left Sandusky far behind us.

She was a large vessel of five hundred tons, and handsomely fitted up, though with high-pressure engines; which always conveyed that kind of feeling to me, which I should be likely to experience, I think, if I had lodgings on the first-floor of a powder-mill. She was laden with flour, some casks of which commodity were stored upon the deck. The captain coming up to have a little conversation, and to introduce a friend, seated himself astride of one of these barrels, like a Bacchus[6] of private life; and pulling a great clasp-knife out of his pocket, began to 'whittle' it as he talked, by paring thin slices off the edges. And he whittled with such industry and hearty good will, that but for his being called away very soon, it must have disappeared bodily, and left nothing in its place but grist and shavings.

After calling at one or two flat places, with low dams stretching out into the lake, whereon were stumpy lighthouses, like windmills without sails, the whole looking like a Dutch vignette,[7] we came at midnight to Cleveland, where we lay all night, and until nine o'clock next morning.

I entertained quite a curiosity in reference to this place, from having seen at Sandusky a specimen of its literature in the shape of a newspaper, which was very strong indeed upon the subject of Lord Ashburton's recent arrival at Washington, to adjust the points in dispute between the United States Government and Great Britain:[8] informing its readers that as America had 'whipped' England in her infancy, and whipped her again in her youth, so it was clearly necessary that she must whip her once again in her maturity; and pledging its credit to all True Americans, that if Mr Webster did his duty in the approaching negotiations,[9] and sent the English Lord home again in double quick time, they should, within two years, 'sing Yankee Doodle in Hyde Park, and Hail Columbia in the scarlet courts of Westminster!' I found it a pretty town, and had the satisfaction of beholding the outside of the office of the journal from which I have just quoted. I did not enjoy the delight of seeing the wit who indited the paragraphs in question, but I have no doubt he is a prodigious man in his way, and held in high repute by a select circle.

There was a gentleman on board, to whom, as I unintentionally learned through the thin partition which divided our state-room from the cabin in which he and his wife conversed together, I was unwittingly the occasion of very great uneasiness. I don't know why or wherefore, but I appeared to run in his mind perpetually, and to dissatisfy him very much. First of all I heard him say: and the most ludicrous part of the business was, that he said it in my very ear, and could not have communicated more directly with me, if he had leaned upon my shoulder, and whispered me: 'Boz is on board still, my dear.' After a considerable pause, he added, complainingly, 'Boz keeps himself very close;' which was true enough, for I was not very well, and was lying down, with a book. I thought he had done with me after this, but I was deceived; for a long interval having elapsed, during which I imagine him to have been turning restlessly from side to side, and trying to go to sleep; he broke out again, with 'I suppose that Boz will be writing a book by-and-by, and putting all our names in it!' at which imaginary consequence of being on board a boat with Boz, he groaned, and became silent.

We called at the town of Erie, at eight o'clock that night, and lay there an hour. Between five and six next morning, we arrived at Buffalo, where we breakfasted; and being too near the Great Falls to wait patiently anywhere else, we set off by the train, the same morning at nine o'clock, to Niagara.

It was a miserable day; chilly and raw; a damp mist falling; and the trees in that northern region quite bare and wintry. Whenever the train halted, I listened for the roar; and was constantly straining my eyes in the direction where I knew the Falls must be, from seeing the river rolling on towards them; every moment expecting to behold the spray. Within a few minutes of our stopping, not before, I saw two great white clouds rising up slowly and majestically from the depths of the earth. That was all. At length we alighted: and then for the first time, I heard the mighty rush of water, and felt the ground tremble underneath my feet.

The bank is very steep, and was slippery with rain, and half-melted ice. I hardly know how I got down, but I was soon at the bottom, and climbing, with two English officers who were crossing and had joined me, over some broken rocks, deafened by the noise, half-blinded by the spray, and wet to the skin. We were at the foot of the American Fall. I could see an immense torrent of water tearing headlong down from some great height, but had no idea of shape, or situation, or anything but vague immensity.

When we were seated in the little ferry-boat, and were crossing the swoln river immediately before both cataracts, I began to feel what it was: but I was in a manner stunned, and unable to comprehend the vastness of the scene. It was not until I came on Table

Rock, and looked – Great Heaven, on what a fall of bright-green water! – that it came upon me in its full might and majesty.

Then, when I felt how near to my Creator I was standing, the first effect, and the enduring one – instant and lasting – of the tremendous spectacle, was Peace. Peace of Mind, Tranquillity, Calm recollections of the Dead, Great Thoughts of Eternal Rest and Happiness: nothing of Gloom or Terror. Niagara was at once stamped upon my heart, an Image of Beauty; to remain there, changeless and indelible, until its pulses cease to beat, for ever.

Oh, how the strife and trouble of daily life receded from my view, and lessened in the distance, during the ten memorable days we passed on that Enchanted Ground! What voices spoke from out the thundering water; what faces, faded from the earth, looked out upon me from its gleaming depths; what Heavenly promise glistened in those angels' tears, the drops of many hues, that showered around, and twined themselves about the gorgeous arches which the changing rainbows made!

I never stirred in all that time from the Canadian side, whither I had gone at first. I never crossed the river again; for I knew there were people on the other shore, and in such a place it is natural to shun strange company. To wander to and fro all day, and see the cataracts from all points of view; to stand upon the edge of the great Horse-Shoe Fall,[10] marking the hurried water gathering strength as it approached the verge, yet seeming, too, to pause before it shot into the gulf below; to gaze from the river's level up at the torrent as it came streaming down; to climb the neighbouring heights and watch it through the trees, and see the wreathing water in the rapids hurrying on to take its fearful plunge; to linger in the shadow of the solemn rocks three miles below; watching the river as, stirred by no visible cause, it heaved and eddied and awoke the echoes, being troubled yet, far down beneath the surface, by its giant leap; to have Niagara before me, lighted by the sun and by the moon, red in the day's decline, and grey as evening slowly fell upon it; to look upon it every day, and wake up in the night and hear its ceaseless voice: this was enough.

I think in every quiet season now, still do those waters roll and leap, and roar and tumble, all day long; still are the rainbows spanning them, a hundred feet below. Still, when the sun is on them, do they shine and glow like molten gold. Still, when the day is gloomy, do they fall like snow, or seem to crumble away like the front of a great chalk cliff, or roll adown the rock like dense white smoke. But always does the mighty stream appear to die as it comes down, and always from its unfathomable grave arises that tremendous ghost of spray and mist which is never laid: which has haunted this place with the same dread solemnity since Darkness brooded on the deep, and that first flood before the Deluge – Light – came rushing on Creation at the word of God.

CHAPTER 15

In Canada; Toronto; Kingston; Montreal; Quebec; St John's. In the United States again; Lebanon; the Shaker Village; and West Point

I WISH to abstain from instituting any comparison, or drawing any parallel whatever, between the social features of the United States and those of the British Possessions in Canada. For this reason, I shall confine myself to a very brief account of our journeyings in the latter territory.

But before I leave Niagara, I must advert to one disgusting circumstance which can hardly have escaped the observation of any decent traveller who has visited the Falls.

On Table Rock, there is a cottage belonging to a Guide, where little relics of the place are sold, and where visitors register their names in a book kept for the purpose. On the wall of the room in which a great many of these volumes are preserved, the following request is posted: 'Visitors will please not copy nor extract the remarks and poetical effusions from the registers and albums kept here.'

But for this intimation, I should have let them lie upon the tables on which they were strewn with careful negligence, like books in a drawing-room: being quite satisfied with the stupendous silliness of certain stanzas with an anti-climax at the end of each, which were framed and hung up on the wall. Curious, however, after reading this announcement, to see what kind of morsels were so carefully preserved, I turned a few leaves, and found them scrawled all over with the vilest and the filthiest ribaldry that ever human hogs delighted in.

It is humiliating enough to know that there are among men, brutes so obscene and worthless, that they can delight in laying their miserable profanations upon the very steps of Nature's greatest altar. But that these should be hoarded up for the delight of their fellow swine, and kept in a public place where any eyes may see them, is a disgrace to the English language in which they are written (though I hope few of these entries have been made by Englishmen), and a reproach to the English side, on which they are preserved.

The quarters of our soldiers at Niagara, are finely and airily situated. Some of them are large detatched houses on the plain above the Falls, which were originally designed for hotels; and in the evening time, when the women and children were leaning over the balconies watching the men as they played at ball and other games upon the grass before the door, they often presented a little picture of cheerfulness and animation which made it quite a pleasure to pass that way.

At any garrisoned point where the line of demarcation between one country and another is so very narrow as at Niagara, desertion from the ranks can scarcely fail to be of frequent occurrence: and it may be reasonably supposed that when the soldiers entertain the wildest and maddest hopes of the fortune and independence that await them on the other side, the impulse to play traitor, which such a place suggests to dishonest minds, is not weakened. But it very rarely happens that the men who do desert, are happy or contented afterwards; and many instances have been known in which they have confessed their grievous disappointment, and their earnest desire to return to their old service if they could but be assured of pardon, or of lenient treatment. Many of their comrades, notwithstanding, do the like, from time to time; and instances of loss of life in the effort to cross the river with this object, are far from being uncommon. Several men were drowned in the attempt to swim across, not long ago; and one, who had the madness to trust himself upon a table as a raft, was swept down to the whirlpool, where his mangled body eddied round and round some days.

I am inclined to think that the noise of the Falls is very much exaggerated; and this will appear the more probable when the depth of the great basin in which the water is received, is taken into account. At no time during our stay there, was the wind at all high or boisterous, but we never heard them, three miles off, even at the very quiet time of sunset, though we often tried.

Queenston, at which place the steamboats start for Toronto (or I should rather say at which place they call, for their wharf is at Lewiston, on the opposite shore), is situated in a delicious valley, through which the Niagara river, in colour a very deep green, pursues its course. It is approached by a road that takes its winding way among the heights by which the town is sheltered; and seen from this point is extremely beautiful and picturesque. On the most conspicuous of these heights stood a monument erected by the Provincial Legislature in memory of General Brock, who was slain in a battle with the American forces, after having won the victory.[1] Some vagabond, supposed to be a fellow of the name of Lett, who is now, or who lately was, in prison as a felon, blew up this monument two years ago,[2] and it is now a melancholy ruin, with a long fragment of iron railing hanging dejectedly from its top, and waving to and fro like a wild ivy branch or broken vine stem. It is of much higher importance than it may seem, that this statue should be repaired at the public cost, as it ought to have been long ago. Firstly, because it is beneath the dignity of England to allow a memorial raised in honour of one of her defenders, to remain in this condition, on the very spot where he died. Secondly, because the sight of it in its present state, and the recollection of the unpunished outrage which brought it to this pass, is not very likely to soothe down border feelings among English subjects here, or compose their border quarrels and dislikes.

I was standing on the wharf at this place, watching the passengers embarking in a steamboat which preceded that whose coming we awaited, and participating in the anxiety with which a sergeant's wife was collecting her few goods together – keeping one distracted eye hard upon the porters, who were hurrying them on board, and the other on a hoopless washing-tub for which, as being the most utterly worthless of all her movables, she seemed to entertain particular affection – when three or four soldiers with a recruit came up and went on board.

The recruit was a likely young fellow enough, strongly built and well made, but by no means sober: indeed he had all the air of a man who had been more or less drunk for some days. He carried a small bundle over his shoulder, slung at the end of a walking-stick, and had a short pipe in his mouth. He was as dusty and dirty as recruits usually are, and his shoes betokened that he had travelled on foot some distance, but he was in a very jocose state, and shook hands with this soldier, and clapped that one on the back, and talked and laughed continually, like a roaring idle dog as he was.

The soldiers rather laughed at this blade than with him: seeming to say, as they stood straightening their canes in their hands, and looking coolly at him over their glazed stocks, 'Go on, my boy, while you may! you'll know better by-and-by:' when suddenly the novice, who had been backing towards the gangway in his noisy merriment, fell overboard before their eyes, and splashed heavily down into the river between the vessel and the dock.

I never saw such a good thing as the change that came over these soldiers in an instant. Almost before the man was down, their professional manner, their stiffness and constraint, were gone, and they were filled with the most violent energy. In less time than is required to tell it, they had him out again, feet first, with the tails of his coat flapping over his eyes, everything about him hanging the wrong way, and the water streaming off at every thread in his threadbare dress. But the moment they set him upright and found that he was none the worse, they were soldiers again, looking over their glazed stocks more composedly than ever.

The half-sobered recruit glanced round for a moment, as if his first impulse were to express some gratitude for his preservation, but seeing them with this air of total unconcern, and having his wet pipe presented to him with an oath by the soldier who had been by far the most anxious of the party, he stuck it in his mouth, thrust his hands into his moist pockets, and without even shaking the water off his clothes, walked on board whistling; not to say as if nothing had happened, but as if he had meant to do it, and it had been a perfect success.

Our steamboat came up directly this had left the wharf, and soon bore us to the mouth of the Niagara; where the stars and stripes of America flutter on one side and the Union Jack of England on the other: and so narrow is the space between them that the sentinels in either fort can often hear the watchword of the other country given. Thence we emerged on Lake Ontario, an inland sea; and by half-past six o'clock were at Toronto.

The country round this town being very flat, is bare of scenic interest; but the town itself is full of life and motion, bustle, business, and improvement. The streets are well paved, and lighted with gas; the houses are large and good; the shops excellent. Many of them have a display of goods in their windows, such as may be seen in thriving county towns in England; and there are some which would do no discredit to the metropolis itself. There is a good stone prison here; and there are, besides, a handsome church, a courthouse, public offices, many commodious private residences, and a government observatory for noting and recording the magnetic variations. In the College of Upper Canada, which is one of the public establishments of the city, a sound education in every department of polite learning can be had, at a very moderate expense: the annual charge for the instruction of each pupil, not exceeding nine pounds sterling. It has pretty good endowments in the way of land, and is a valuable and useful institution.[3]

The first stone of a new college had been laid but a few days before, by the Governor General.[4] It will be a handsome, spacious edifice, approached by a long avenue, which is already planted and made available as a public walk. The town is well adapted for wholesome exercise at all seasons, for the footways in the thoroughfares which lie beyond the principal street, are planked like floors, and kept in very good and clean repair.

It is a matter of deep regret that political differences should have run high in this place, and led to most discreditable and disgraceful results. It is not long since guns were discharged from a window in this town at the successful candidates in an election, and the coachman of one of them was actually shot in the body, though not dangerously wounded. But one man was killed on the same occasion; and from the very window whence he received his death, the very flag which shielded his murderer (not only in the commission of his crime, but from its consequences), was displayed again on the occasion of the public ceremony performed by the Governor General, to which I have just adverted. Of all the colours in the rainbow, there is but one which could be so employed: I need not say that flag was orange.[5]

The time of leaving Toronto for Kingston is noon. By eight o'clock next morning, the traveller is at the end of his journey, which is performed by steamboat upon Lake Ontario, calling at

Port Hope and Coburg, the latter a cheerful, thriving little town. Vast quantities of flour form the chief item in the freight of these vessels. We had no fewer than one thousand and eighty barrels on board, between Coburg and Kingston.

The latter place, which is now the seat of government in Canada, is a very poor town, rendered still poorer in the appearance of its market-place by the ravages of a recent fire. Indeed, it may be said of Kingston, that one half of it appears to be burnt down, and the other half not to be built up. The Government House is neither elegant nor commodious, yet it is almost the only house of any importance in the neighbourhood.

There is an admirable jail here, well and wisely governed, and excellently regulated, in every respect. The men were employed as shoemakers, ropemakers, blacksmiths, tailors, carpenters, and stonecutters; and in building a new prison, which was pretty far advanced towards completion. The female prisoners were occupied in needlework. Among them was a beautiful girl of twenty, who had been there nearly three years. She acted as bearer of secret despatches for the self-styled Patriots on Navy Island,[6] during the Canadian Insurrection: sometimes dressing as a girl, and carrying them in her stays; sometimes attiring herself as a boy, and secreting them in the lining of her hat. In the latter character she always rode as a boy would, which was nothing to her, for she could govern any horse that any man could ride, and could drive four-in-hand with the best whip in those parts. Setting forth on one of her patriotic missions, she appropriated to herself the first horse she could lay her hands on; and this offence had brought her where I saw her. She had quite a lovely face, though, as the reader may suppose from this sketch of her history, there was a lurking devil in her bright eye, which looked out pretty sharply from between her prison bars.

There is a bomb-proof fort here of great strength, which occupies a bold position, and is capable, doubtless, of doing good service; though the town is much too close upon the frontier to be long held, I should imagine, for its present purpose in troubled times. There is also a small navy-yard, where a couple of Government steamboats were building, and getting on vigorously.

We left Kingston for Montreal on the tenth of May, at half-past nine in the morning, and proceeded in a steamboat down the St

Lawrence river. The beauty of this noble stream at almost any point, but especially in the commencement of this journey when it winds its way among the thousand Islands, can hardly be imagined. The number and constant succession of these islands, all green and richly wooded; their fluctuating sizes, some so large that for half an hour together one among them will appear as the opposite bank of the river, and some so small that they are mere dimples on its broad bosom; their infinite variety of shapes; and the numberless combinations of beautiful forms which the trees growing on them present: all form a picture fraught with uncommon interest and pleasure.

In the afternoon we shot down some rapids where the river boiled and bubbled strangely, and where the force and headlong violence of the current were tremendous. At seven o'clock we reached Dickenson's Landing, whence travellers proceed for two or three hours by stage-coach: the navigation of the river being rendered so dangerous and difficult in the interval, by rapids, that steamboats do not make the passage. The number and length of those *portages*,[7] over which the roads are bad, and the travelling slow, render the way between the towns of Montreal and Kingston, somewhat tedious.

Our course lay over a wide, uninclosed tract of country at a little distance from the river-side, whence the bright warning lights on the dangerous parts of the St Lawrence shone vividly. The night was dark and raw, and the way dreary enough. It was nearly ten o'clock when we reached the wharf where the next steamboat lay; and went on board, and to bed.

She lay there all night, and started as soon as it was day. The morning was ushered in by a violent thunderstorm, and was very wet, but gradually improved and brightened up. Going on deck after breakfast, I was amazed to see floating down with the stream, a most gigantic raft, with some thirty or forty wooden houses upon it, and at least as many flag-masts, so that it looked like a nautical street. I saw many of these rafts afterwards, but never one so large. All the timber, or 'lumber,' as it is called in America, which is brought down the St Lawrence, is floated down in this manner. When the raft reaches its place of destination, it is broken up; the materials are sold; and the boatmen return for more.

At eight we landed again, and travelled by a stage-coach for four hours through a pleasant and well-cultivated country, perfectly

French in every respect: in the appearance of the cottages; the air, language, and dress of the peasantry; the sign-boards on the shops and taverns: and the Virgin's shrines, and crosses, by the wayside. Nearly every common labourer and boy, though he had no shoes to his feet, wore round his waist a sash of some bright colour: generally red: and the women, who were working in the fields and gardens, and doing all kinds of husbandry, wore, one and all, great flat straw hats with most capacious brims. There were Catholic Priests and Sisters of Charity in the village streets; and images of the Saviour at the corners of cross-roads, and in other public places.

At noon we went on board another steamboat, and reached the village of Lachine, nine miles from Montreal, by three o'clock. There, we left the river, and went on by land.

Montreal is pleasantly situated on the margin of the St Lawrence, and is backed by some bold heights, about which there are charming rides and drives. The streets are generally narrow and irregular, as in most French towns of any age; but in the more modern parts of the city, they are wide and airy. They display a great variety of very good shops; and both in the town and suburbs there are many excellent private dwellings. The granite quays are remarkable for their beauty, solidity, and extent.

There is a very large Catholic cathedral here, recently erected; with two tall spires, of which one is yet unfinished. In the open space in front of this edifice, stands a solitary, grim-looking, square brick tower, which has a quaint and remarkable appearance, and which the wiseacres of the place have consequently determined to pull down immediately. The Government House is very superior to that at Kingston, and the town is full of life and bustle. In one of the suburbs is a plank road – not footpath – five or six miles long, and a famous road it is too. All the rides in the vicinity were made doubly interesting by the bursting out of spring, which is here so rapid, that it is but a day's leap from barren winter, to the blooming youth of summer.

The steamboats to Quebec perform the journey in the night; that is to say, they leave Montreal at six in the evening, and arrive at Quebec at six next morning. We made this excursion during our stay in Montreal (which exceeded a fortnight), and were charmed by its interest and beauty.

The impression made upon the visitor by this Gibraltar of

America: its giddy heights; its citadel suspended, as it were, in the air; its picturesque steep streets and frowning gateways; and the splendid views which burst upon the eye at every turn: is at once unique and lasting. It is a place not to be forgotten or mixed up in the mind with other places, or altered for a moment in the crowd of scenes a traveller can recall. Apart from the realities of this most picturesque city, there are associations clustering about it which would make a desert rich in interest. The dangerous precipice along whose rocky front, Wolfe and his brave companions climbed to glory; the Plains of Abraham, where he received his mortal wound;[8] the fortress so chivalrously defended by Montcalm;[9] and his soldier's grave, dug for him while yet alive, by the bursting of a shell; are not the least among them, or among the gallant incidents of history. That is a noble Monument too, and worthy of two great nations, which perpetuates the memory of both brave generals, and on which their names are jointly written.

The city is rich in public institutions and in Catholic churches and charities, but it is mainly in the prospect from the site of the Old Government House, and from the Citadel, that its surpassing beauty lies. The exquisite expanse of country, rich in field and forest, mountain-height and water, which lies stretched out before the view, with miles of Canadian villages, glancing in long white streaks, like veins along the landscape; the motley crowd of gables, roofs, and chimney tops in the old hilly town immediately at hand; the beautiful St Lawrence sparkling and flashing in the sunlight; and the tiny ships below the rock from which you gaze, whose distant rigging looks like spiders' webs against the light, while casks and barrels on their decks dwindle into toys, and busy mariners become so many puppets; all this, framed by a sunken window in the fortress and looked at from the shadowed room within, forms one of the brightest and most enchanting pictures that the eye can rest upon.

In the spring of the year, vast numbers of emigrants who have newly arrived from England or from Ireland, pass between Quebec and Montreal on their way to the backwoods and new settlements of Canada. If it be an entertaining lounge (as I very often found it) to take a morning stroll upon the quay at Montreal, and see them grouped in hundreds on the public wharfs about their chests and boxes, it is matter of deep interest to be their fellow-passenger on

one of these steamboats, and mingling with the concourse, see and
hear them unobserved.

The vessel in which we returned from Quebec to Montreal was
crowded with them, and at night they spread their beds between
decks (those who had beds, at least), and slept so close and thick
about our cabin door, that the passage to and fro was quite blocked
up. They were nearly all English; from Gloucestershire the greater
part; and had had a long winter-passage out; but it was wonderful
to see how clean the children had been kept, and how untiring in
their love and self-denial all the poor parents were.

Cant as we may, and as we shall to the end of all things, it is very
much harder for the poor to be virtuous than it is for the rich; and
the good that is in them, shines the brighter for it. In many a noble
mansion lives a man, the best of husbands and of fathers, whose
private worth in both capacities is justly lauded to the skies. But
bring him here, upon this crowded deck. Strip from his fair young
wife her silken dress and jewels, unbind her braided hair, stamp early
wrinkles on her brow, pinch her pale cheek with care and much
privation, array her faded form in coarsely patched attire, let there
be nothing but his love to set her forth or deck her out, and you
shall put it to the proof indeed. So change his station in the world,
that he shall see in those young things who climb about his knee:
not records of his wealth and name: but little wrestlers with him for
his daily bread; so many poachers on his scanty meal; so many units
to divide his every sum of comfort, and farther to reduce its small
amount. In lieu of the endearments of childhood in its sweetest
aspect, heap upon him all its pains and wants, its sicknesses and ills,
its fretfulness, caprice, and querulous endurance: let its prattle be,
not of engaging infant fancies, but of cold, and thirst, and hunger:
and if his fatherly affection outlive all this, and he be patient, watch-
ful, tender; careful of his children's lives, and mindful always of
their joys and sorrows; then send him back to Parliament, and
Pulpit, and to Quarter Sessions, and when he hears fine talk of
the depravity of those who live from hand to mouth, and labour
hard to do it, let him speak up, as one who knows, and tell those
holders forth that they, by parallel with such a class, should be High
Angels in their daily lives, and lay but humble siege to Heaven at
last.

Which of us shall say what he would be, if such realities, with small relief or change all through his days, were his! Looking round upon these people: far from home, houseless, indigent, wandering, weary with travel and hard living: and seeing how patiently they nursed and tended their young children: how they consulted ever their wants first, then half supplied their own; what gentle ministers of hope and faith the women were; how the men profited by their example; and how very, very seldom even a moment's petulance or harsh complaint broke out among them: I felt a stronger love and honour of my kind come glowing on my heart, and wished to God there had been many Atheists in the better part of human nature there, to read with me this simple lesson in the book of Life.

We left Montreal for New York again, on the thirtieth of May; crossing to La Prairie, on the opposite shore of the St Lawrence, in a steamboat; we then took the railroad to St John's, which is on the brink of Lake Champlain. Our last greeting in Canada was from the English officers in the pleasant barracks at that place (a class of gentlemen who had made every hour of our visit memorable by their hospitality and friendship); and with 'Rule Britannia' sounding in our ears, soon left it far behind.

But Canada has held, and always will retain, a foremost place in my remembrance. Few Englishmen are prepared to find it what it is. Advancing quietly; old differences settling down, and being fast forgotten; public feeling and private enterprise alike in a sound and wholesome state; nothing of flush or fever in its system, but health and vigour throbbing in its steady pulse: it is full of hope and promise. To me – who had been accustomed to think of it as something left behind in the strides of advancing society, as something neglected and forgotten, slumbering and wasting in its sleep – the demand for labour and the rates of wages; the busy quays of Montreal; the vessels taking in their cargoes, and discharging them; the amount of shipping in the different ports; the commerce, roads, and public works, all made *to last*; the respectability and character of the public journals; and the amount of rational comfort and happiness which honest industry may earn: were very great surprises. The steamboats on the lakes, in their conveniences, cleanliness, and safety; in the gentlemanly character and bearing of their captains; and in the politeness and perfect comfort of their social regulations; are unsurpassed even by the famous Scotch vessels, deservedly so much esteemed at home. The inns are usually bad; because the custom of boarding at hotels is not so general here as in the States, and the British officers, who form a large portion of the society of every town, live chiefly at the regimental messes: but in every other respect, the traveller in Canada will find as good provision for his comfort as in any place I know.

There is one American boat – the vessel which carried us on Lake Champlain, from St John's to Whitehall – which I praise very highly, but no more than it deserves, when I say that it is superior even to that in which we went from Queenston to Toronto, or to that in which we travelled from the latter place to Kingston, or I have no doubt I may add to any other in the world. This steamboat, which is called the Burlington, is a perfectly exquisite achievement of neatness, elegance, and order. The decks are drawing-rooms; the cabins are boudoirs, choicely furnished and adorned with prints, pictures, and musical instruments; every nook and corner in the vessel is a perfect curiosity of graceful comfort and beautiful contrivance. Captain Sherman, her commander, to whose ingenuity and excellent taste these results are solely attributable, has bravely and worthily distinguished himself on more than one trying occasion: not least among them, in having the moral courage to carry British troops, at a time (during the Canadian rebellion) when no other conveyance was open to them. He and his vessel are held in universal respect, both by his own countrymen and ours; and no man ever enjoyed the popular esteem, who, in his sphere of action, won and wore it better than this gentleman.

By means of this floating palace we were soon in the United States again, and called that evening at Burlington; a pretty town, where we lay an hour or so. We reached Whitehall, where we were to disembark, at six next morning; and might have done so earlier, but that these steamboats lie by for some hours in the night, in consequence of the lake becoming very narrow at that part of the journey, and difficult of navigation in the dark. Its width is so contracted at one point, indeed, that they are obliged to warp round by means of a rope.

After breakfasting at Whitehall, we took the stage-coach for Albany: a large and busy town, where we arrived between five and six o'clock that afternoon; after a very hot day's journey, for we were now in the height of summer again. At seven we started for

New York on board a great North River steamboat, which was so crowded with passengers that the upper deck was like the box lobby of a theatre between the pieces, and the lower one like Tottenham Court Road on a Saturday night. But we slept soundly, notwithstanding, and soon after five o'clock next morning reached New York.

Tarrying here, only that day and night, to recruit after our late fatigues, we started off once more upon our last journey in America. We had yet five days to spare before embarking for England, and I had a great desire to see 'the Shaker Village,' which is peopled by a religious sect from whom it takes its name.[10]

To this end, we went up the North River again, as far as the town of Hudson, and there hired an extra to carry us to Lebanon, thirty miles distant: and of course another and a different Lebanon from that village where I slept on the night of the Prairie trip.

The country through which the road meandered, was rich and beautiful; the weather very fine; and for many miles the Kaatskill mountains, where Rip Van Winkle and the ghastly Dutchmen played at ninepins one memorable gusty afternoon,[11] towered in the blue distance, like stately clouds. At one point, as we ascended a steep hill, athwart whose base a railroad, yet constructing, took its course, we came upon an Irish colony. With means at hand of building decent cabins, it was wonderful to see how clumsy, rough, and wretched, its hovels were. The best were poor protection from the weather; the worst let in the wind and rain through wide breaches in the roofs of sodden grass, and in the walls of mud; some had neither door nor window; some had nearly fallen down, and were imperfectly propped up by stakes and poles; all were ruinous and filthy. Hideously ugly old women and very buxom young ones, pigs, dogs, men, children, babies, pots, kettles, dunghills, vile refuse, rank straw, and standing water, all wallowing together in an inseparable heap, composed the furniture of every dark and dirty hut.

Between nine and ten o'clock at night, we arrived at Lebanon: which is renowned for its warm baths, and for a great hotel, well adapted, I have no doubt, to the gregarious taste of those seekers after health or pleasure who repair here, but inexpressibly comfortless to me. We were shown into an immense apartment, lighted by two dim candles, called the drawing-room: from which there was a descent by a flight of steps, to another vast desert, called the dining-room: our bed-chambers were among certain long rows of little white-washed cells, which opened from either side of a dreary passage; and were so like rooms in a prison that I half expected to be locked up when I went to bed, and listened involuntarily for the turning of the key on the outside. There need be baths somewhere in the neighbourhood, for the other washing arrangements were on as limited a scale as I ever saw, even in America: indeed, these bed-rooms were so very bare of even such common luxuries as chairs, that I should say they were not provided with enough of anything, but that I bethink myself of our having been most bountifully bitten all night.

The house is very pleasantly situated, however, and we had a good breakfast. That done, we went to visit our place of destination, which was some two miles off, and the way to which was soon indicated by a finger-post, whereon was painted, 'To the Shaker Village.'

As we rode along, we passed a party of Shakers, who were at work upon the road; who wore the broadest of all broad-brimmed hats; and were in all visible respects such very wooden men, that I felt about as much sympathy for them, and as much interest in them, as if they had been so many figure-heads of ships. Presently we came to the beginning of the village, and alighting at the door of a house where the Shaker manufactures are sold, and which is the head-quarters of the elders, requested permission to see the Shaker worship.

Pending the conveyance of this request to some person in authority, we walked into a grim room, where several grim hats were hanging on grim pegs, and the time was grimly told by a grim clock, which uttered every tick with a kind of struggle, as if it broke the grim silence reluctantly, and under protest. Ranged against the wall were six or eight stiff, high-backed chairs, and they partook so strongly of the general grimness that one would much rather have sat on the floor than incurred the smallest obligation to any of them.

Presently, there stalked into this apartment, a grim old Shaker, with eyes as hard, and dull, and cold, as the great round metal buttons on his coat and waistcoat; a sort of calm goblin. Being informed of our desire, he produced a newspaper wherein the body of elders, whereof he was a member, had advertised but a few days before, that in consequence of certain unseemly interruptions which their worship had received from strangers, their chapel was closed to the public for the space of one year.

As nothing was to be urged in opposition to this reasonable arrangement, we requested leave to make some trifling purchases of Shaker goods; which was grimly conceded. We accordingly repaired to a store in the same house and on the opposite side of the passage, where the stock was presided over by something alive in a russet case, which the elder said was a woman; and which I suppose *was* a woman, though I should not have suspected it.

On the opposite side of the road was their place of worship: a cool, clean edifice of wood, with large windows and green blinds: like a spacious summer-house. As there was no getting into this place, and nothing was to be done but walk up and down, and look at it and the other buildings in the village (which were chiefly of wood, painted a dark red like English barns, and composed of many stories like English factories), I have nothing to communicate to the reader, beyond the scanty results I gleaned the while our purchases were making.

These people are called Shakers from their peculiar form of adoration, which consists of a dance, performed by the men and women of all ages, who arrange themselves for that purpose in opposite parties: the men first divesting themselves of their hats and coats, which they gravely hang against the wall before they begin; and tying a ribbon round their shirt-sleeves, as though they were going to be bled. They accompany themselves with a droning, humming noise, and dance until they are quite exhausted, alternately advancing and retiring in a preposterous sort of trot. The effect is said to be unspeakably absurd: and if I may judge from a print of this ceremony which I have in my possession; and which I am informed by those who have visited the chapel, is perfectly accurate; it must be infinitely grotesque.

They are governed by a woman, and her rule is understood to be absolute, though she has the assistance of a council of elders. She lives, it is said, in strict seclusion, in certain rooms above the chapel, and is never shown to profane eyes. If she at all resemble the lady who presided over the store, it is a great charity to keep her as close as possible, and I cannot too strongly express my perfect concurrence in this benevolent proceeding.

All the possessions and revenues of the settlement are thrown into a common stock, which is managed by the elders. As they have made converts among people who were well to do in the world, and are frugal and thrifty, it is understood that this fund prospers: the more especially as they have made large purchases of land. Nor is this at Lebanon the only Shaker settlement: there are, I think, at least, three others.

They are good farmers, and all their produce is eagerly purchased and highly esteemed. 'Shaker seeds,' 'Shaker herbs,' and 'Shaker distilled waters,' are commonly announced for sale in the shops of towns and cities. They are good breeders of cattle, and are kind and merciful to the brute creation. Consequently, Shaker beasts seldom fail to find a ready market.

They eat and drink together, after the Spartan model, at a great public table.[12] There is no union of the sexes, and every Shaker, male and female, is devoted to a life of celibacy. Rumour has been busy upon this theme, but here again I must refer to the lady of the store, and say, that if many of the sister Shakers resemble her, I treat all such slander as bearing on its face the strongest marks of wild improbability. But that they take as proselytes, persons so young that they cannot know their own minds, and cannot possess much strength of resolution in this or any other respect, I can assert from my own observation of the extreme juvenility of certain youthful Shakers whom I saw at work among the party on the road.

They are said to be good drivers of bargains, but to be honest and just in their transactions, and even in horse-dealing to resist those thievish tendencies which would seem, for some undiscovered reason, to be almost inseparable from that branch of traffic. In all matters they hold their own course quietly, live in their gloomy, silent commonwealth, and show little desire to interfere with other people.

This is well enough, but nevertheless I cannot, I confess, incline towards the Shakers; view them with much favour, or extend towards them any very lenient construction. I so abhor, and from my soul detest that bad spirit, no matter by what class or sect it may be entertained, which would strip life of its healthful graces, rob youth of its innocent pleasures, pluck from maturity and age their pleasant ornaments, and make existence but a narrow path towards the grave: that odious spirit which, if it could have had full scope and sway upon the earth, must have blasted and made barren the imaginations of the greatest men, and left them, in their power of raising up enduring images before their fellow-creatures yet unborn, no better than the beasts: that, in these very broad-brimmed hats and very sombre coats – in stiff-necked, solemn-visaged piety, in short, no matter what its garb, whether it have cropped hair as in a Shaker village, or long nails as in a Hindoo temple – I recognise the worst among the enemies of Heaven and Earth, who turn the water at the marriage feasts of this poor world, not into wine, but gall. And if there must be people vowed to crush the harmless fancies and the love of innocent delights and gaieties, which are a part of human nature: as much a part of it as any other love or hope that is our common portion: let them, for me, stand openly revealed among the ribald and licentious; the very idiots know that *they* are not on the Immortal road, and will despise them, and avoid them readily.

Leaving the Shaker village with a hearty dislike of the old Shakers, and a hearty pity of the young ones: tempered by the strong probability of their running away as they grow older and wiser, which they not uncommonly do: we returned to Lebanon, and so to Hudson, by the way we had come upon the previous day. There, we took [the] steamboat down the North River towards New York, but stopped, some four hours' journey short of it, at West Point, where we remained that night, and all next day, and next night too.

In this beautiful place: the fairest among the fair and lovely Highlands of the North River: shut in by deep green heights and ruined forts, and looking down upon the distant town of Newburgh, along a glittering path of sunlit water, with here and there a skiff, whose white sail often bends on some new track as sudden flaws of wind come down upon her from the gullies in the hills: hemmed in, besides, all round with memories of Washington, and events of the revolutionary war: is the Military School of America.

It could not stand on more appropriate ground, and any ground more beautiful can hardly be. The course of education is severe, but well devised, and manly. Through June, July, and August, the young men encamp upon the spacious plain whereon the college stands; and all the year their military exercises are performed there, daily. The term of study at this institution, which the State requires from all cadets, is four years; but, whether it be from the rigid nature of the discipline, or the national impatience of restraint, or both causes combined, not more than half the number who begin their studies here, ever remain to finish them.

The number of cadets being about equal to that of the members of Congress, one is sent here from every Congressional-district: its member influencing the selection. Commissions in the service are distributed on the same principle. The dwellings of the various Professors are beautifully situated; and there is a most excellent hotel for strangers, though it has the two drawbacks of being a total abstinence house (wines and spirits being forbidden to the students), and of serving the public meals at rather uncomfortable hours: to wit, breakfast at seven, dinner at one, and supper at sunset.

The beauty and freshness of this calm retreat, in the very dawn and greenness of summer – it was then the beginning of June – were exquisite indeed. Leaving it upon the sixth, and returning to New York, to embark for England on the succeeding day, I was glad to think that among the last memorable beauties which had glided past us, and softened in the bright perspective, were those whose pictures, traced by no common hand, are fresh in most men's minds; not easily to grow old, or fade beneath the dust of Time: the Kaatskill Mountains, Sleepy Hollow, and the Tappaan Zee.[13]

CHAPTER 16

The Passage Home

I NEVER had so much interest before, and very likely I shall never have so much interest again, in the state of the wind, as on the long looked-for morning of Tuesday the Seventh of June. Some nautical authority had told me a day or two previous, 'anything with west in it, will do;' so when I darted out of bed at daylight, and throwing up the window, was saluted by a lively breeze from the north-west which had sprung up in the night, it came upon me so freshly, rustling with so many happy associations, that I conceived upon the spot a special regard for all airs blowing from that quarter of the compass, which I shall cherish, I dare say, until my own wind has breathed its last frail puff, and withdrawn itself for ever from the mortal calendar.

The pilot had not been slow to take advantage of this favourable weather, and the ship which yesterday had lain in such a crowded dock that she might have retired from trade for good and all, for any chance she seemed to have of going to sea, was now full sixteen miles away. A gallant sight she was, when we, fast gaining on her in a steamboat, saw her in the distance riding at anchor: her tall masts pointing up in graceful lines against the sky, and every rope and spar expressed in delicate and thread-like outline: gallant, too, when, we being all aboard, the anchor came up to the sturdy chorus 'Cheerily men, oh cheerily!' and she followed proudly in the towing steamboat's wake: but bravest and most gallant of all, when the tow-rope being cast adrift, the canvas fluttered from her masts, and spreading her white wings she soared away upon her free and solitary course.

In the after cabin we were only fifteen passengers in all, and the greater part were from Canada, where some of us had known each other. The night was rough and squally, so were the next two days, but they flew by quickly, and we were soon as cheerful and snug a party, with an honest, manly-hearted captain at our head, as ever came to the resolution of being mutually agreeable, on land or water.

We breakfasted at eight, lunched at twelve, dined at three, and took our tea at half-past seven. We had abundance of amusements, and dinner was not the least among them: firstly, for its own sake; secondly, because of its extraordinary length: its duration, inclusive of all the long pauses between the courses, being seldom less than two hours and a half; which was a subject of never-failing entertainment. By way of beguiling the tediousness of these banquets, a select association was formed at the lower end of the table, below the mast, to whose distinguished president modesty forbids me to make any further allusion, which, being a very hilarious and jovial institution, was (prejudice apart) in high favour with the rest of the community, and particularly with a black steward, who lived for three weeks in a broad grin at the marvellous humour of these incorporated worthies.

Then, we had chess for those who played it, whist, cribbage, books, backgammon, and shovelboard. In all weathers, fair or foul, calm or windy, we were every one on deck, walking up and down in pairs, lying in the boats, leaning over the side, or chatting in a lazy group together. We had no lack of music, for one played the accordion, another the violin, and another (who usually began at six o'clock, A.M.) the key-bugle: the combined effect of which instruments, when they all played different tunes in different parts of the ship, at the same time, and within hearing of each other, as they sometimes did (everybody being intensely satisfied with his own performance), was sublimely hideous.

When all these means of entertainment failed, a sail would heave in sight: looming, perhaps, the very spirit of a ship, in the misty distance, or passing us so close that through our glasses we could see the people on her decks, and easily make out her name, and whither she was bound. For hours together we could watch the dolphins and porpoises as they rolled and leaped and dived around the vessel; or those small creatures ever on the wing, the Mother Carey's chickens, which had borne us company from New York bay, and for a whole fortnight fluttered about the vessel's stern. For some days we had a dead calm, or very light winds, during which the crew amused themselves with fishing, and hooked an unlucky dolphin, who expired, in all his rainbow colours, on the deck: an event of such importance in our barren calendar, that afterwards we dated from the dolphin, and made the day on which he died, an era.

Besides all this, when we were five or six days out, there began to be much talk of icebergs, of which wandering islands an unusual number had been seen by the vessels that had come into New York a day or two before we left that port, and of whose dangerous neighbourhood we were warned by the sudden coldness of the weather, and the sinking of the mercury in the barometer. While these tokens lasted, a double look-out was kept, and many dismal tales were whispered, after dark, of ships that had struck upon the ice and gone down in the night; but the wind obliging us to hold a southward course, we saw none of them, and the weather soon grew bright and warm again.

The observation every day at noon, and the subsequent working of the vessel's course, was, as may be supposed, a feature in our lives of paramount importance; nor were there wanting (as there never are) sagacious doubters of the captain's calculations, who, so soon as his back was turned, would, in the absence of compasses, measure the chart with bits of string, and ends of pocket-handkerchiefs, and points of snuffers, and clearly prove him to be wrong by an odd thousand miles or so. It was very edifying to see these un-believers shake their heads and frown, and hear them hold forth strongly upon navigation: not that they knew anything about it, but that they always mistrusted the captain in calm weather, or when the wind was adverse. Indeed, the mercury itself is not so variable as this class of passengers, whom you will see, when the ship is going nobly through the water, quite pale with admiration, swearing that the captain beats all captains ever known, and even hinting at subscriptions for a piece of plate; and who, next morning, when the breeze has lulled, and all the sails hang useless in the idle air, shake their despondent heads again, and say, with screwed-up lips, they hope that captain is a sailor, but they shrewdly doubt him; that they do.

It even became an occupation in the calm, to wonder when the wind *would* spring up in the favourable quarter, where, it was clearly shown by all the rules and precedents, it ought to have sprung up long ago. The first mate, who whistled for it zealously, was much respected for his perseverance, and was regarded even by the unbelievers as a first-rate sailor. Many gloomy looks would be cast upward through the cabin skylights at the flapping sails while dinner was in progress; and some, growing bold in rueful-ness, predicted that we should land about the middle of July. There are always on board ship, a Sanguine One, and a Despondent One. The latter character carried it hollow at this period of the voyage, and triumphed over the Sanguine One at every meal, by inquiring where he supposed the Great Western (which left New York a week after us) was *now*: and where he supposed the 'Cunard' steam-packet was *now*: and what he thought of sailing vessels, as compared with steamships *now*: and so beset his life with pestilent attacks of that kind, that he too was obliged to affect despondency, for very peace and quietude.

These were additions to the list of entertaining incidents, but there was still another source of interest. We carried in the steerage nearly a hundred passengers: a little world of poverty: and as we came to know individuals among them by sight, from looking down upon the deck where they took the air in the daytime, and cooked their food, and very often ate it too, we became curious to know their histories, and with what expectations they had gone out to America, and on what errands they were going home, and what their circumstances were. The information we got on these heads from the carpenter, who had charge of these people, was often of the strangest kind. Some of them had been in America but three days, some but three months, and some had gone out in the last voyage of that very ship in which they were now returning home. Others had sold their clothes to raise the passage-money, and had hardly rags to cover them; others had no food, and lived upon the charity of the rest; and one man, it was discovered nearly at the end of the voyage, not before – for he kept his secret close, and did not court compassion – had had no sustenance whatever but the bones and scraps of fat he took from the plates used in the after-cabin dinner, when they were put out to be washed.

The whole system of shipping and conveying these unfortunate persons, is one that stands in need of thorough revision. If any class deserve to be protected and assisted by the Government, it is that class who are banished from their native land in search of the bare means of subsistence. All that could be done for these poor people by the great compassion and humanity of the captain and officers was done, but they require much more. The law is bound, at least upon the English side, to see that too many of them are not put on board one ship: and that their accommodations are decent: not demoralising and profligate.[1] It is bound, too, in common humanity, to declare that no man shall be taken on board without his stock of provisions being previously inspected by some proper officer, and pronounced moderately sufficient for his support upon the voyage. It is bound to provide, or to require that there be provided, a medical attendant; whereas in these ships there are none, though sickness of adults, and deaths of children, on the passage, are matters of the very commonest occurrence. Above all it is the duty of any Government, be it monarchy or republic, to interpose and put an end to that system by which a firm of traders in emigrants purchase of the owners the whole 'tween-decks of a ship, and send on board as many wretched people as they can lay hold of, on any terms they can get, without the smallest reference to the conveniences of the steerage, the number of berths, the slightest separation of the sexes, or anything but their own immediate profit. Nor is even this the worst of the vicious system: for, certain crimping agents of these houses, who have a percentage on all the passengers they inveigle, are constantly travelling about those districts where poverty and discontent are rife, and tempting the credulous into more misery, by holding out monstrous inducements to emigration which can never be realised.

The history of every family we had on board was pretty much the same. After hoarding up, and borrowing, and begging, and selling everything to pay the passage, they had gone out to New York, expecting to find its streets paved with gold; and had found them paved with very hard and very real stones. Enterprise was dull; labourers were not wanted; jobs of work were to be got, but the payment was not. They were coming back, even poorer than they went. One of them was carrying an open letter from a young English artisan, who had been in New York a fortnight, to a friend near Manchester, whom he strongly urged to follow him. One of the officers brought it to me as a curiosity. 'This is the country, Jem,' said the writer. 'I like America. There is no despotism here; that's the great thing. Employment of all sorts is going a-begging, and wages are capital. You have only to choose a trade, Jem, and be it. I haven't made a choice of one yet, but I shall soon. *At present I haven't quite made up my mind whether to be a carpenter — or a tailor.*'

There was yet another kind of passenger, and but one more, who, in the calm and the light winds, was a constant theme of conversation and observation among us. This was an English sailor, a smart, thorough-built, English man-of-war's-man from his hat to his shoes, who was serving in the American navy, and having got leave of absence was on his way home to see his friends. When he presented himself to take and pay for his passage, it had been suggested to him that being an able seaman he might as well work it and save the money, but this piece of advice he very indignantly rejected: saying, 'He'd be damned but for once he'd go aboard ship, as a gentleman.' Accordingly, they took his money, but he no sooner came aboard, than he stowed his kit in the forecastle, arranged to mess with the crew, and the very first time the hands were turned up, went aloft like a cat, before anybody. And all through the passage there he was, first at the braces, outermost on the yards, perpetually lending a hand everywhere, but always with a sober dignity in his manner, and a sober grin on his face, which plainly said, 'I do it as a gentleman. For my own pleasure, mind you!'

At length and at last, the promised wind came up in right good earnest, and away we went before it, with every stitch of canvas set, slashing through the water nobly. There was a grandeur in the motion of the splendid ship, as overshadowed by her mass of sails, she rode at a furious pace upon the waves, which filled one with an indescribable sense of pride and exultation. As she plunged into a foaming valley, how I loved to see the green waves, bordered deep with white, come rushing on astern, to buoy her upward at their pleasure, and curl about her as she stooped again, but always own her for their haughty mistress still! On, on we flew, with changing lights upon the water, being now in the blessed region of fleecy skies; a bright sun lighting us by day, and a bright moon by night; the vane pointing directly homeward, alike the truthful index to the favouring wind and to our cheerful hearts; until at sunrise, one fair Monday morning – the twenty-seventh of June, I shall not easily forget the day – there lay before us, old Cape Clear, God bless it, showing, in the mist of early morning, like a cloud: the brightest and most welcome cloud, to us, that ever hid the face of Heaven's fallen sister – Home.

Dim speck as it was in the wide prospect, it made the sunrise a more cheerful sight, and gave to it that sort of human interest which it seems to want at sea. There, as elsewhere, the return of day is inseparable from some sense of renewed hope and gladness; but the light shining on the dreary waste of water, and showing it in all its vast extent of loneliness, presents a solemn spectacle, which even night, veiling it in darkness and uncertainty, does not surpass. The rising of the moon is more in keeping with the solitary ocean; and has an air of melancholy grandeur, which in its soft and gentle influence, seems to comfort while it saddens. I recollect when I was a very young child having a fancy that the reflection of the moon in water was a path to Heaven, trodden by the spirits of good people on their way to God; and this old feeling often came over me again, when I watched it on a tranquil night at sea.

The wind was very light on this same Monday morning, but it was still in the right quarter, and so, by slow degrees, we left Cape Clear behind, and sailed along within sight of the coast of Ireland. And how merry we all were, and how loyal to the George Washington, and how full of mutual congratulations, and how venturesome in predicting the exact hour at which we should arrive at Liverpool, may be easily imagined and readily understood. Also, how heartily we drank the captain's health that day at dinner; and how restless we became about packing up: and how two or three of the most sanguine spirits rejected the idea of going to bed at all that night as something it was not worth while to do, so near the shore, but went nevertheless, and slept soundly; and how to be so near our journey's end, was like a pleasant dream, from which one feared to wake.

The friendly breeze freshened again next day, and on we went once more before it gallantly: descrying now and then an English ship going homeward under shortened sail, while we, with every inch of canvas crowded on, dashed gaily past, and left her far behind. Towards evening, the weather turned hazy, with a drizzling rain; and soon became so thick, that we sailed, as it were, in a cloud. Still we swept onward like a phantom ship, and many an eager eye glanced up to where the Look-out on the mast kept watch for Holyhead.

At length his long-expected cry was heard, and at the same moment there shone out from the haze and mist ahead, a gleaming light, which presently was gone, and soon returned, and soon was gone again. Whenever it came back, the eyes of all on board, brightened and sparkled like itself: and there we all stood, watching this revolving light upon the rock at Holyhead, and praising it for its brightness and its friendly warning, and lauding it, in short, above all other signal lights that ever were displayed, until it once more glimmered faintly in the distance, far behind us.

Then, it was time to fire a gun, for a pilot; and almost before its smoke had cleared away, a little boat with a light at her mast-head came bearing down upon us, through the darkness, swiftly. And presently, our sails being backed, she ran alongside; and the hoarse pilot, wrapped and muffled in pea-coats and shawls to the very bridge of his weather-ploughed-up nose, stood bodily among us on the deck. And I think if that pilot had wanted to borrow fifty pounds for an indefinite period on no security, we should have engaged to lend it to him, among us, before his boat had dropped astern, or (which is the same thing) before every scrap of news in the paper he brought with him had become the common property of all on board.

We turned in pretty late that night, and turned out pretty soon next morning. By six o'clock we clustered on the deck, prepared to go ashore; and looked upon the spires, and roofs and smoke, of Liverpool. By eight we all sat down in one of its Hotels, to eat and drink together for the last time. And by nine we had shaken hands all round, and broken up our social company for ever.

The country, by the railroad, seemed, as we rattled through it, like a luxuriant garden. The beauty of the fields (so small they looked!), the hedge-rows, and the trees; the pretty cottages, the beds of flowers, the old churchyards, the antique houses, and every well-known object; the exquisite delights of that one journey, crowding in the short compass of a summer's day, the joy of many years, and winding up with Home and all that makes it dear; no tongue can tell, or pen of mine describe.

CHAPTER 17

Slavery[1]

THE upholders of slavery in America – of the atrocities of which system, I shall not write one word for which I have not [had] ample proof and warrant – may be divided into three great classes.

The first, are those more moderate and rational owners of human cattle, who have come into the possession of them as so many coins in their trading capital, but who admit the frightful nature of the Institution in the abstract, and perceive the dangers to society with which it is fraught: dangers which however distant they may be, or howsoever tardy in their coming on, are as certain to fall upon its guilty head, as is the Day of Judgment.

The second, consists of all those owners, breeders, users, buyers and sellers of slaves, who will, until the bloody chapter has a bloody end, own, breed, use, buy, and sell them at all hazards; who doggedly deny the horrors of the system in the teeth of such a mass of evidence as never was brought to bear on any other subject, and to which the experience of every day contributes its immense amount; who would at this or any other moment, gladly involve America in a war, civil or foreign, provided that it had for its sole end and object the assertion of their right to perpetuate slavery, and to whip and work and torture slaves, unquestioned by any human authority, and unassailed by any human power; who, when they speak of Freedom, mean the Freedom to oppress their kind, and to be savage, merciless, and cruel; and of whom every man on his own ground, in republican America, is a more exacting, and a sterner, and a less responsible despot than the Caliph Haroun Alraschid [2] in his angry robe of scarlet.

The third, and not the least numerous or influential, is composed of all that delicate gentility which cannot bear a superior, and cannot brook an equal; of that class whose Republicanism means, 'I will not tolerate a man above me: and of those below, none must approach too near;' whose pride, in a land where voluntary servitude is shunned as a disgrace, must be ministered to by slaves; and whose inalienable rights can only have their growth in negro wrongs.

It has been sometimes urged that, in the unavailing efforts which have been made to advance the cause of Human Freedom in the republic of America (strange cause for history to treat of!), sufficient regard has not been had to the existence of the first class of persons; and it has been contended that they are hardly used, in being confounded with the second. This is, no doubt, the case; noble instances of pecuniary and personal sacrifice have already had their growth among them; and it is much to be regretted that the gulf between them and the advocates of emancipation should have been widened and deepened by any means: the rather, as there are, beyond dispute, among these slave-owners, many kind masters who are tender in the exercise of their unnatural power. Still, it is to be feared that this injustice is inseparable from the state of things with which humanity and truth are called upon to deal. Slavery is not a whit the more endurable because some hearts are to be found which can partially resist its hardening influences; nor can the indignant tide of honest wrath stand still, because in its onward course it overwhelms a few who are comparatively innocent, among a host of guilty.

The ground most commonly taken by these better men among the advocates of slavery, is this: 'It is a bad system; and for myself I would willingly get rid of it, if I could; most willingly. But it is not so bad, as you in England take it to be. You are deceived by the representations of the emancipationists. The greater part of my slaves are much attached to me. You will say that I do not allow them to be severely treated; but I will put it to you whether you believe that it can be a general practice to treat them inhumanly, when it would impair their value, and would be obviously against the interests of their masters.'

Is it the interest of any man to steal, to game, to waste his health and mental faculties by drunkenness, to lie, forswear himself, indulge hatred, seek desperate revenge, or do murder? No. All these are roads to ruin. And why, then, do men tread them? Because such inclinations are among the vicious qualities of mankind. Blot out, ye friends of slavery, from the catalogue of human passions, brutal lust, cruelty, and the abuse of irresponsible power (of all earthly temptations the most difficult to be resisted), and when ye have done so, and not before, we will inquire whether it be the interest of a master to lash and maim the slaves, over whose lives and limbs he has an absolute control!

But again: this class, together with that last one I have named, the miserable aristocracy spawned of a false republic, lift up their voices and exclaim 'Public opinion is all-sufficient to prevent such cruelty as you denounce.' Public opinion! Why, public opinion in the slave States *is* slavery, is it not? Public opinion, in the slave States, has delivered the slaves over, to the gentle mercies of their masters. Public opinion has made the laws, and denied them legislative protection. Public opinion has knotted the lash, heated the branding-iron, loaded the rifle, and shielded the murderer. Public opinion threatens the abolitionist with death, if he venture to the South; and drags him with a rope about his middle, in broad unblushing noon, through the first city in the East. Public opinion has, within a few years, burned a slave alive at a slow fire in the city of St Louis; and public opinion has to this day maintained upon the bench that estimable Judge who charged the Jury, impanelled there to try his murderers, that their most horrid deed was an act of public opinion, and being so, must not be punished by the laws the public sentiment had made.[3] Public opinion hailed this doctrine with a howl of wild applause, and set the prisoners free, to walk the city, men of mark, and influence, and station, as they had been before.

Public opinion! what class of men have an immense preponderance over the rest of the community, in their power of representing public opinion in the legislature? the slave-owners. They send from their twelve States one hundred members, while the fourteen free States, with a free population nearly double, return but a hundred and forty-two. Before whom do the presidential candidates bow down the most humbly, on whom do they fawn the most fondly, and for whose tastes do they cater the most assiduously in their servile protestations? The slave-owners always.

Public opinion! hear the public opinion of the free South, as expressed by its own members in the House of Representatives at Washington. 'I have a great respect for the chair,' quoth North Carolina, 'I have a great respect for the chair as an officer of the house, and a great respect for him personally; nothing but that respect prevents me from rushing to the table and tearing that petition which has just been presented for the abolition of slavery in the district of Columbia, to pieces.' – 'I warn the abolitionists,' says South Carolina, 'ignorant, infuriated barbarians as they are, that if chance shall throw any of them into our hands, he may expect a felon's death.' – 'Let an abolitionist come within the borders of South Carolina,' cried a third; mild Carolina's colleague; 'and if we can catch him, we will try him, and notwithstanding the interference of all the governments on earth, including the Federal government, we will HANG him.'

Public opinion has made this law. – It has declared that in Washington, in that city which takes its name from the father of American liberty, any justice of the peace may bind with fetters any negro passing down the street and thrust him into jail: no offence on the black man's part is necessary. The justice says, 'I choose to think this man a runaway:' and locks him up. Public opinion impowers the man of law when this is done, to advertise the negro in the newspapers, warning his owner to come and claim him, or he will be sold to pay the jail fees. But supposing he is a free black, and has no owner, it may naturally be presumed that he is set at liberty. No: HE IS SOLD TO RECOMPENSE HIS JAILER. This has been done again, and again, and again. He has no means of proving his freedom; has no adviser, messenger, or assistance of any sort or kind; no investigation into his case is made, or inquiry instituted. He, a free man, who may have served for years, and bought his liberty, is thrown into jail on no process, for no crime, and on no pretence of crime: and is sold to pay the jail fees. This seems incredible, even of America, but it is the law.

Public opinion is deferred to, in such cases as the following: which is headed in the newspapers: –

'Interesting Law-Case

'An interesting case is now on trial in the Supreme Court, arising out of the following facts. A gentleman residing in Maryland had allowed an aged pair of his slaves, substantial though not legal freedom for several years. While thus living, a daughter was born to them, who grew up in the same liberty, until she married, a free negro, and went with him to reside in Pennsylvania. They had several children, and lived unmolested until the original owner died, when his heir attempted to regain them; but the magistrate before whom they were brought, decided that he had no jurisdiction in the case. *The owner seized the woman and her children in the night, and carried them to Maryland.*'

'Cash for negroes,' 'cash for negroes,' 'cash for negroes,' is the heading of advertisements in great capitals down the long columns of the crowded journals. Woodcuts of a runaway negro with manacled hands, crouching beneath a bluff pursuer in top boots, who, having caught him, grasps him by the throat, agreeably diversify the pleasant text. The leading article protests against 'that abominable and hellish doctrine of abolition, which is repugnant alike to every law of God and nature.' The delicate mamma, who smiles her acquiescence in this sprightly writing as she reads the paper in her cool piazza, quiets her youngest child who clings about her skirts, by promising the boy 'a whip to beat the little niggers with.' – But the negroes, little and big, are protected by public opinion.

Let us try this public opinion by another test, which is important in three points of view: first, as showing how desperately timid of the public opinion slave-owners are, in their delicate descriptions of fugitive slaves in widely circulated newspapers; secondly, as showing how perfectly contented the slaves are, and how very seldom they run away; thirdly, as exhibiting their entire freedom from scar, or blemish, or any mark of cruel infliction, as their pictures are drawn, not by lying abolitionists, but by their own truthful masters.

The following are a few specimens of the advertisements in the public papers. It is only four years since the oldest among them appeared; and others of the same nature continue to be published every day, in shoals.

'Ran away, Negress Caroline. Had on a collar with one prong turned down.'

'Ran away, a black woman, Betsy. Had an iron bar on her right leg.'

'Ran away, the negro Manuel. Much marked with irons.'

'Ran away, the negress Fanny. Had on an iron band about her neck.'

'Ran away, a negro boy about twelve years old. Had round his neck a chain dog-collar with "De Lampert" engraved on it.'

'Ran away, the negro Hown. Has a ring of iron on his left foot. Also, Grise, *his wife*, having a ring and chain on the left leg.'

'Ran away, a negro boy named James. Said boy was ironed when he left me.'

'Committed to jail, a man who calls his name John. He has a clog of iron on his right foot which will weigh four or five pounds.'

'Detained at the police jail, the negro wench, Myra. Has several marks of LASHING, and has irons on her feet.'

'Ran away, a negro woman and two children. A few days before she went off, I burnt her with a hot iron, on the left side of her face. I tried to make the letter M.'

'Ran away, a negro man named Henry; his left eye out, some scars from a dirk on and under his left arm, and much scarred with the whip.'

'One hundred dollars reward, for a negro fellow, Pompey, 40 years old. He is branded on the left jaw.'

'Committed to jail, a negro man. Has no toes on the left foot.'

'Ran away, a negro woman named Rachel. Has lost all her toes except the large one.'

'Ran away, Sam. He was shot a short time since through the hand, and has several shots in his left arm and side.'

'Ran away, my negro man Dennis. Said negro has been shot in the left arm between the shoulder and elbow, which has paralysed the left hand.'

'Ran away, my negro man named Simon. He has been shot badly, in his back and right arm.'

'Ran away, a negro named Arthur. Has a considerable scar

across his breast and each arm, made by a knife; loves to talk much of the goodness of God.'

'Twenty-five dollars reward for my man Isaac. He has a scar on his forehead, caused by a blow; and one on his back, made by a shot from a pistol.'

'Ran away, a negro girl called Mary. Has a small scar over her eye, a good many teeth missing, the letter A is branded on her cheek and forehead.'

'Ran away, negro Ben. Has a scar on his right hand; his thumb and forefinger being injured by being shot last fall. A part of the bone came out. He has also one or two large scars on his back and hips.'

'Detained at the jail, a mulatto, named Tom. Has a scar on the right cheek, and appears to have been burned with powder on the face.'

'Ran away, a negro man named Ned. Three of his fingers are drawn into the palm of his hand by a cut. Has a scar on the back of his neck, nearly half round, done by a knife.'

'Was committed to jail, a negro man. Says his name is Josiah. His back very much scarred by the whip; and branded on the thigh and hips in three or four places, thus (J M). The rim of his right ear has been bit or cut off.'

'Fifty dollars reward, for my fellow Edward. He has a scar on the corner of his mouth, two cuts on and under his arm, and the letter E on his arm.'

'Ran away, negro boy Ellie. Has a scar on one of his arms from the bite of a dog.'

'Ran away, from the plantation of James Surgette, the following negroes: Randal, has one ear cropped; Bob, has lost one eye; Kentucky Tom, has one jaw broken.'

'Ran away, Anthony. One of his ears cut off, and his left hand cut with an axe.'

'Fifty dollars reward for the negro Jim Blake. Has a piece cut out of each ear, and the middle finger of the left hand cut off to the second joint.'

'Ran away, a negro woman named Maria. Has a scar on one side of her cheek, by a cut. Some scars on her back.'

'Ran away, the Mulatto wench Mary. Has a cut on the left arm, a scar on the left shoulder, and two upper teeth missing.'

I should say, perhaps, in explanation of this latter piece of description, that among the other blessings which public opinion secures to the negroes, is the common practice of violently punching out their teeth. To make them wear iron collars by day and night, and to worry them with dogs, are practices almost too ordinary to deserve mention.

'Ran away, my man Fountain. Has holes in his ears, a scar on the right side of his forehead, has been shot in the hind parts of his legs, and is marked on the back with the whip.'

'Two hundred and fifty dollars reward for my negro man Jim. He is much marked with shot in his right thigh. The shot entered on the outside, halfway between the hip and knee joints.'

'Brought to jail, John. Left ear cropt.'

'Taken up, a negro man. Is very much scarred about the face and body, and has the left ear bit off.'

'Ran away, a black girl, named Mary. Has a scar on her cheek, and the end of one of her toes cut off.'

'Ran away, my Mulatto woman, Judy. She has had her right arm broke.'

'Ran away, my negro man, Levi. His left hand has been burnt, and I think the end of his forefinger is off.'

'Ran away, a negro man, NAMED WASHINGTON. Has lost a part of his middle finger, and the end of his little finger.'

'Twenty-five dollars reward for my man John. The tip of his nose is bit off.'

'Twenty-five dollars reward for the negro slave, Sally. Walks *as though* crippled in the back.'

'Ran away, Joe Dennis. Has a small notch in one of his ears.'

'Ran away, negro boy, Jack. Has a small crop out of his left ear.'

'Ran away, a negro man, named Ivory. Has a small piece cut out of the top of each ear.'

While upon the subject of ears, I may observe that a distinguished abolitionist in New York once received a negro's ear, which had been cut off close to the head, in a general post letter. It was forwarded by the free and independent gentleman who had caused it to be amputated, with a polite request that he would place the specimen in his 'collection.'

I could enlarge this catalogue with broken arms, and broken legs, and gashed flesh, and missing teeth, and lacerated backs, and bites of dogs, and brands of red-hot irons innumerable: but as my readers will be sufficiently sickened and repelled already, I will turn to another branch of the subject.

These advertisements, of which a similar collection might be made for every year, and month, and week, and day; and which are coolly read in families as things of course, and as a part of the current news and small-talk; will serve to show how very much the slaves profit by public opinion, and how tender it is in their behalf. But it may be worth while to inquire how the slave-owners, and the class of society to which great number of them belong, defer to public opinion in their conduct, not to their slaves but to each other; how they are accustomed to restrain their passions; what their bearing is among themselves; whether they are fierce or gentle; whether their social customs be brutal, sanguinary, and violent, or bear the impress of civilisation and refinement.

That we may have no partial evidence from abolitionists in this inquiry, either, I will once more turn to their own newspapers, and I will confine myself, this time, to a selection from paragraphs which appeared from day to day, during my visit to America, and which refer to occurrences happening while I was there. The italics in these extracts, as in the foregoing, are my own.

These cases did not all occur, it will be seen, in territory actually belonging to legalised Slave States, though most, and those the very worst among them did, as their counterparts constantly do; but the position of the scenes of action in reference to places immediately at hand, where slavery is the law; and the strong resemblance between that class of outrages and the rest; lead to the just presumption that the character of the parties concerned was formed in slave districts, and brutalised by slave customs.

'Horrible Tragedy

'By a slip from *The Southport Telegraph*, Wisconsin, we learn that the Hon. Charles C. P. Arndt, Member of the Council for Brown county, was shot dead *on the floor of the Council chamber*, by James R. Vinyard, Member from Grant county. *The affair* grew out of a nomination for Sheriff of Grant county. Mr E. S. Baker was nominated and supported by Mr Arndt. This nomination was opposed by Vinyard, who wanted the appointment to vest in his own brother. In the course of debate, the deceased made some statements which Vinyard pronounced false, and made use of violent and insulting language, dealing largely in personalities, to which Mr A. made no reply. After the adjournment, Mr A. stepped up to Vinyard, and requested him to retract, which he refused to do, repeating the offensive words. Mr Arndt then made a blow at Vinyard, who stepped back a pace, drew a pistol, and shot him dead.

'The issue appears to have been provoked on the part of Vinyard, who was determined at all hazards to defeat the appointment of Baker, and who, himself defeated, turned his ire and revenge upon the unfortunate Arndt.'

'The Wisconsin Tragedy

'Public indignation runs high in the territory of Wisconsin, in relation to the murder of C. C. P. Arndt, in the Legislative Hall of the Territory. Meetings have been held in different counties of Wisconsin, denouncing *the practice of secretly bearing arms in the Legislative chambers of the country*. We have seen the account of the expulsion of James R. Vinyard, the perpetrator of the bloody deed, and are amazed to hear, that, after this expulsion by those who saw Vinyard kill Mr Arndt in the presence of his aged father, who was on a visit to see his son, little dreaming that he was to witness his murder, *Judge Dunn has discharged Vinyard on bail*. The Miners' Free Press speaks *in terms of merited rebuke* at the outrage upon the feelings of the people of Wisconsin. Vinyard was within arm's length of Mr Arndt, when he took such deadly aim at him, that he never spoke. Vinyard might at pleasure, being so near, have only wounded him, but he chose to kill him.'

'Murder

'By a letter in a St Louis paper of the 14th, we notice a terrible outrage at Burlington, Iowa. A Mr Bridgman having had a difficulty with a citizen of the place, Mr Ross; a brother-in-law of the latter provided himself with one of Colt's revolving pistols, met Mr B. in the street, *and discharged the contents of five of the barrels at him: each shot taking effect*. Mr B., though horribly wounded, and dying, returned the fire, and killed Ross on the spot.'

'Terrible Death of Robert Potter

'From the "Caddo Gazette," of the 12th inst., we learn the frightful death of Colonel Robert Potter. . . . He was beset in his house by an enemy, named Rose. He sprang from his couch, seized his gun, and, in his night-clothes, rushed from the house. For about two hundred yards his speed seemed to defy his pursuers; but, getting entangled in a thicket, he was captured. Rose told him *that he intended to act a generous part*, and give him a chance for his life. He then told Potter he might run, and he should not be interrupted till he reached a certain distance. Potter started at the word of command, and before a gun was fired he had reached the lake. His first impulse was to jump in the water and dive for it, which he did. Rose was close behind him, and formed his men on the bank ready to shoot him as he rose. In a few seconds he came up to breathe; and scarce had his head reached the surface of the water when it was completely riddled with the shot of their guns, and he sunk, to rise no more!'

'Murder in Arkansas

'We understand *that a severe rencontre came off* a few days since in the Seneca Nation, between Mr Loose, the sub-agent of the mixed band of the Senecas, Quapaw, and Shawnees, and Mr James Gillespie, of the mercantile firm of Thomas G. Allison and Co., of Maysville, Benton County, Ark., in which the latter was slain with a bowie-knife. Some difficulty had for some time existed between the parties. It is said that Major Gillespie brought on the attack with a cane. A severe conflict ensued, during which two pistols were fired by Gillespie and one by Loose. Loose then stabbed Gillespie with one of those never-failing weapons, a bowie-knife. The death of Major G. is much regretted, as he was a liberal-minded and energetic man. Since the above was in type, we have learned that Major Allison has stated to some of our citizens in town that Mr Loose gave the first blow. We forbear to give any particulars, as *the matter will be the subject of judicial investigation.*'

'Foul Deed

'The steamer Thames, just from Missouri river, brought us a handbill, offering a reward of 500 dollars, for the person who assassinated Lilburn W. Baggs, late Governor of this State, at Independence, on the night of the 6th inst. Governor Baggs, it is stated in a written memorandum, was not dead, but mortally wounded.

'Since the above was written, we received a note from the clerk of the Thames, giving the following particulars. Gov. Baggs was shot by some villain on Friday, 6th inst., in the evening, while sitting in a room in his own house in Independence. His son, a boy, hearing a report, ran into the room, and found the Governor sitting in his chair, with his jaw fallen down, and his head leaning back; on discovering the injury done [to] his father, he gave the alarm. Foot tracks were found in the garden below the window, and a pistol picked up supposed to have been overloaded, and thrown from the hand of the scoundrel who fired it. Three buck shots, of a heavy load, took effect; one going through his mouth, one into the brain, and another probably in or near the brain; all going into the back part of the neck and head. The Governor was still alive on the morning of the 7th; but no hopes for his recovery by his friends, and but slight hopes from his physicians.

'A man was suspected, and the Sheriff most probably has possession of him by this time.

'The pistol was one of a pair stolen some days previous from a baker in Independence, and the legal authorities have the description of the other.'

'Rencontre

'An unfortunate *affair* took place on Friday evening in Chatres Street, in which one of our most respectable citizens received a dangerous wound, from a poignard, in the abdomen. From the Bee (New Orleans) of yesterday, we learn the following particulars. It appears that an article was published in the French side of the paper on Monday last, containing some strictures on the Artillery Battalion for firing their guns on Sunday morning, in answer to those from the Ontario and Woodbury, and thereby much alarm was caused to the families of those persons who were out all night preserving the peace of the city. Major C. Gally, Commander of the battalion, resenting this, called at the office and demanded the Author's name; that of Mr P. Arpin was given to him, who was absent at the time. Some angry words then passed with one of the proprietors, and a challenge followed; the friends of both parties tried to arrange the affair, but failed to do so. On Friday evening, about seven o'clock, Major Gally met Mr P. Arpin in Chatres Street, and accosted him. "Are you Mr Arpin?"

'"Yes, sir."

'"Then I have to tell you that you are a ———" (applying an appropriate epithet).

'"I shall remind you of your words, sir."

'"But I have said I would break my cane on your shoulders."

'"I know it, but I have not yet received the blow."

'At these words, Major Gally, having a cane in his hands, struck Mr Arpin across the face, and the latter drew a poignard from his pocket and stabbed Major Gally in the abdomen.

'Fears are entertained that the wound will be mortal. *We understand that Mr Arpin has given security for his appearance at the Criminal Court to answer the charge.*'

'Affray in Mississippi

'On the 27th ult., in an affray near Carthage, Leake county, Mississippi, between James Cottingham and John Wilburn, the latter was shot by the former, and so horribly wounded, that there was no hope of his recovery. On the 2nd instant, there was an affray at Carthage between A. C. Sharkey and George Goff, in which the latter was shot, and thought mortally wounded. Sharkey delivered himself up to the authorities, *but changed his mind and escaped!*'

'Personal Encounter

'An encounter took place in Sparta, a few days since, between the barkeeper of an hotel, and a man named Bury. It appears that Bury had become somewhat noisy, *and that the barkeeper, determined to preserve order, had threatened to shoot Bury*, whereupon Bury drew a pistol and shot the barkeeper down. He was not dead at the last accounts, but slight hopes were entertained of his recovery.'

'Duel

'The clerk of the steamboat *Tribune* informs us that another duel was fought on Tuesday last, by Mr Robbins, a bank officer in Vicksburg, and Mr Fall, the editor of the Vicksburg Sentinel. According to the arrangement, the parties had six pistols each, which, after the word 'Fire!' *they were to discharge as fast as they pleased.* Fall fired two pistols without effect. Mr Robbins' first shot took effect in Fall's thigh, who fell, and was unable to continue the combat.'

'Affray in Clarke County

'An *unfortunate affray* occurred in Clarke county (Mo.), near Waterloo, on Tuesday the 19th ult., which originated in settling the partnership concerns of Messrs M'Kane and M'Allister, who had been engaged in the business of distilling, and resulted in the death of the latter, who was shot down by Mr M'Kane, because of his attempting to take possession of seven barrels of whiskey, the property of M'Kane, which had been knocked off to M'Allister at a sheriff's sale at one dollar per barrel. M'Kane immediately fled *and at the latest dates had not been taken.*

'*This unfortunate affray* caused considerable excitement in the neighbourhood, as both the parties were men with large families depending upon them and stood well in the community.'

I will quote but one more paragraph, which, by reason of its monstrous absurdity, may be a relief to these atrocious deeds.

'Affair of Honour

'We have just heard the particulars of a meeting which took place on Six Mile Island, on Tuesday, between two young bloods of our city: Samuel Thurston, *aged fifteen*, and William Hine, *aged thirteen* years. They were attended by young gentlemen of the same age. The weapons used on the occasion, were a couple of Dickson's best rifles; the distance, thirty yards. They took one fire, without any damage being sustained by either party, except the ball of Thurston's gun passing through the crown of Hine's hat. *Through the intercession of the Board of Honour,* the challenge was withdrawn, and the difference amicably adjusted.'

If the reader will picture to himself the kind of Board of Honour which amicably adjusted the difference between these two little boys, who in any other part of the world would have been amicably adjusted on two porters' backs and soundly flogged with birchen rods, he will be possessed, no doubt, with as strong a sense of its ludicrous character, as that which sets me laughing whenever its image rises up before me.

Now, I appeal to every human mind, imbued with the commonest of common sense, and the commonest of common humanity; to all dispassionate, reasoning creatures, of any shade of opinion; and ask, with these revolting evidences of the state of society which exists in and about the slave districts of America before them, can they have a doubt of the real condition of the slave, or can they for a moment make a compromise between the institution or any of its flagrant, fearful features, and their own just consciences? Will they say of any tale of cruelty and horror, however aggravated in degree, that it is improbable, when they can turn to the public prints, and, running, read such signs as these, laid before them by the men who rule the slaves: in their own acts and under their own hands?

Do we not know that the worst deformity and ugliness of slavery are at once the cause and the effect of the reckless license taken by these freeborn outlaws? Do we not know that the man who has been born and bred among its wrongs; who has seen in his childhood husbands obliged at the word of command to flog their wives; women, indecently compelled to hold up their own garments that men might lay the heavier stripes upon their legs, driven and harried by brutal overseers in their time of travail, and becoming mothers on the field of toil, under the very lash itself; who has read in youth, and seen his virgin sisters read, descriptions of runaway men and women, and their disfigured persons, which could not be published elsewhere, of so much stock upon a farm, or at a show of beasts: – do we not know that that man, whenever his wrath is kindled up, will be a brutal savage? Do we not know that as he is a coward in his domestic life, stalking among his shrinking men and women slaves armed with his heavy whip, so he will be a coward out of doors, and carrying cowards' weapons hidden in his breast, will shoot men down and stab them when he quarrels? And if our reason did not teach us this and much beyond; if we were such idiots as to close our eyes to that fine mode of training which rears up such men; should we not know that they who among their equals stab and pistol in the legislative halls, and in the counting-house, and on the market-place, and in all the elsewhere peaceful pursuits of life, must be to their dependants, even though they were free servants, so many merciless and unrelenting tyrants?

What! shall we declaim against the ignorant peasantry of Ireland, and mince the matter when these American taskmasters are in question? Shall we cry shame on the brutality of those who ham-string cattle: and spare the lights of Freedom upon earth who notch the ears of men and women, cut pleasant posies in the shrinking flesh, learn to write with pens of red-hot iron on the human face, rack their poetic fancies for liveries of mutilation which their slaves shall wear for life and carry to the grave, breaking living limbs as did the soldiery who mocked and slew the Saviour of the world, and set defenceless creatures up for targets! Shall we whimper over legends of the tortures practised on each other by the Pagan Indians, and smile upon the cruelties of Christian men! Shall we, so long as these things last, exult above the scattered remnant of that stately race, and triumph in the white enjoyment of their broad possessions? Rather, for me, restore the forest and the Indian village; in lieu of stars and stripes, let some poor feather flutter in the breeze; replace the streets and squares by wigwams; and though the death-song of a hundred haughty warriors fill the air, it will be music to the shriek of one unhappy slave.

On one theme, which is commonly before our eyes, and in respect of which our national character is changing fast, let the plain Truth be spoken, and let us not, like dastards, beat about the bush by hinting at the Spaniard and the fierce Italian. When knives are drawn by Englishmen in conflict let it be said and known: 'We owe this change to Republican Slavery. These are the weapons of Freedom. With sharp points and edges such as these, Liberty in America doth hew and hack her slaves; or, failing that pursuit, her sons devote them to a better use, and turn them on each other.'

CHAPTER 18

Concluding Remarks

THERE are many passages in this book, where I have been at some pains to resist the temptation of troubling my readers with my own deductions and conclusions: preferring that they should judge for themselves, from such premises as I have laid before them. My only object in the outset, was, to carry them with me faithfully wheresoever I went: and that task I have discharged.

But I may be pardoned, if on such a theme as the general character of the American people, and the general character of their social system, as presented to a stranger's eyes, I desire to express my own opinions in a few words, before I bring these volumes to a close.

They are, by nature, frank, brave, cordial, hospitable, and affectionate. Cultivation and refinement seem but to enhance their warmth of heart and ardent enthusiasm; and it is the possession of these latter qualities in a most remarkable degree, which renders an educated American one of the most endearing and most generous of friends. I never was so won upon, as by this class; never yielded up my full confidence and esteem so readily and pleasurably, as to them; never can make again, in half a year, so many friends for whom I seem to entertain the regard of half a life.

These qualities are natural, I implicitly believe, to the whole people. That they are, however, sadly sapped and blighted in their growth among the mass; and that there are influences at work which endanger them still more, and give but little present promise of their healthy restoration; is a truth that ought to be told.

It is an essential part of every national character to pique itself mightily upon its faults, and to deduce tokens of its virtue or its wisdom from their very exaggeration. One great blemish in the popular mind of America, and the prolific parent of an innumerable brood of evils, is Universal Distrust. Yet the American citizen plumes himself upon this spirit, even when he is sufficiently dispassionate to perceive the ruin it works; and will often adduce it, in spite of his own reason, as an instance of the great sagacity and acuteness of the people, and their superior shrewdness and independence.

'You carry,' says the stranger, 'this jealousy and distrust into every transaction of public life. By repelling worthy men from your legislative assemblies, it has bred up a class of candidates for the suffrage, who, in their every act, disgrace your Institutions and your people's choice. It has rendered you so fickle, and so given to change, that your inconstancy has passed into a proverb; for you no sooner set up an idol firmly, than you are sure to pull it down and dash it into fragments: and this, because directly you reward a benefactor, or a public servant, you distrust him, merely because he *is* rewarded; and immediately apply yourselves to find out, either that you have been too bountiful in your acknowledgments, or he remiss in his deserts. Any man who attains a high place among you, from the President downwards, may date his downfall from that moment; for any printed lie that any notorious villain pens, although it militate directly against the character and conduct of a life, appeals at once to your distrust, and is believed. You will strain at a gnat in the way of trustfulness and confidence, however fairly won and well deserved; but you will swallow a whole caravan of camels, if they be laden with unworthy doubts and mean suspicions. Is this well, think you, or likely to elevate the character of the governors or the governed, among you?'

The answer is invariably the same: 'There's freedom of opinion here, you know. Every man thinks for himself, and we are not to be easily overreached. That's how our people come to be suspicious.'

Another prominent feature is the love of 'smart' dealing: which gilds over many a swindle and gross breach of trust; many a defalcation, public and private; and enables many a knave to hold his head up with the best, who well deserves a halter; though it has not been without its retributive operation, for this smartness has done more in a few years to impair the public credit, and to cripple the public resources, than dull honesty, however rash, could have effected in a century. The merits of a broken speculation, or a bankruptcy, or of a successful scoundrel, are not gauged by its or his observance of the golden rule, 'Do as you would be done by,' but are considered with reference to their smartness. I recollect, on both occasions of our passing that ill-fated Cairo on the Mississippi, remarking on the bad effects such gross deceits must have when they exploded, in generating a want of confidence abroad, and discouraging foreign investment: but I was given to understand that this was a very smart scheme by which a deal of money had been made: and that its smartest feature was, that they forgot these things abroad, in a very short time, and speculated again, as freely as ever. The following dialogue I have held a hundred times: 'Is it not a very disgraceful circumstance that such a man as So-and-so should be acquiring a large property by the most infamous and odious means, and notwithstanding all the crimes of which he has been guilty, should be tolerated and abetted by your Citizens? He is a public nuisance, is he not?' 'Yes, sir.' 'A convicted liar?' 'Yes, sir.' 'He has been kicked, and cuffed, and caned?' 'Yes, sir.' 'And he is utterly dishonourable, debased, and profligate?' 'Yes, sir.' 'In the name of wonder, then, what is his merit?' 'Well, sir, he is a smart man.'

In like manner, all kinds of deficient and impolitic usages are referred to the national love of trade; though, oddly enough, it would be a weighty charge against a foreigner that he regarded the Americans as a trading people. The love of trade is assigned as a reason for that comfortless custom, so very prevalent in country towns, of married persons living in hotels, having no fireside of their own, and seldom meeting from early morning until late at night, but at the hasty public meals. The love of trade is a reason why the literature of America is to remain for ever unprotected: 'For we are a trading people, and don't care for poetry:' though we *do*, by the way, profess to be very proud of our poets: while healthful amusements, cheerful means of recreation, and wholesome fancies, must fade before the stern utilitarian joys of trade.

These three characteristics are strongly presented at every turn, full in the stranger's view. But, the foul growth of America has a more tangled root than this; and it strikes its fibres, deep in its licentious Press.

Schools may be erected, East, West, North, and South; pupils be taught, and masters reared, by scores upon scores of thousands; colleges may thrive, churches may be crammed, temperance may be diffused, and advancing knowledge in all other forms walk through the land with giant strides: but while the newspaper press of America is in, or near, its present abject state, high moral improvement in that country is hopeless. Year by year, it must and will go back; year by year, the tone of public feeling must sink lower down; year by year, the Congress and the Senate must become of less account before all decent men; and year by year, the memory of the Great Fathers of the Revolution must be outraged more and more, in the bad life of their degenerate child.

Among the herd of journals which are published in the States, there are some, the reader scarcely need be told, of character and credit. From personal intercourse with accomplished gentlemen connected with publications of this class, I have derived both pleasure and profit. But the name of these is Few, and of the others Legion; and the influence of the good, is powerless to counteract the mortal poison of the bad.

Among the gentry of America; among the well-informed and moderate: in the learned professions; at the bar and on the bench: there is, as there can be, but one opinion, in reference to the vicious character of these infamous journals. It is sometimes contended – I will not say strangely, for it is natural to seek excuses for such a disgrace – that their influence is not so great as a visitor would suppose. I must be pardoned for saying that there is no warrant for this plea, and that every fact and circumstance tends directly to the opposite conclusion.

When any man, of any grade of desert in intellect or character, can climb to any public distinction, no matter what, in America, without first grovelling down upon the earth, and bending the knee before this monster of depravity; when any private excellence is safe from its attacks; when any social confidence is left unbroken by it, or any tie of social decency and honour is held in the least regard; when any man in that Free Country has freedom of opinion, and presumes to think for himself, and speak for himself, without humble reference to a censorship which, for its rampant ignorance and base dishonesty, he utterly loathes and despises in his heart; when those who most acutely feel its infamy and the reproach it casts upon the nation, and who most denounce it to each other, dare to set their heels upon, and crush it openly, in the sight of all men: then, I will believe that its influence is lessening, and men are returning to their manly senses. But while that Press has its evil eye in every house, and its black hand in every appointment in the state, from a president to a postman; while, with ribald slander for its only stock in trade, it is the standard literature of an enormous class, who must find their reading in a newspaper, or they will not read at all; so long must its odium be upon the country's head, and so long must the evil it works, be plainly visible in the Republic.

To those who are accustomed to the leading English Journals, or to the respectable journals of the Continent of Europe; to those who are accustomed to anything else in print and paper; it would be impossible, without an amount of extract for which I have neither space nor inclination, to convey an adequate idea of this frightful engine in America. But if any man desire confirmation of my statement on this head, let him repair to any place in this city of London, where scattered numbers of these publications are to be found; and there, let him form his own opinion.*

It would be well, there can be no doubt, for the American people as a whole, if they loved the Real less, and the Ideal somewhat more. It would be well, if there were greater encouragement to lightness of heart and gaiety, and a wider cultivation of what is beautiful, without being eminently and directly useful. But here, I think the general remonstrance, 'we are a new country,' which is so often advanced as an excuse for defects which are quite unjustifiable, as being, of right, only the slow growth of an old one, may be very reasonably urged: and I yet hope to hear of there being some other national amusement in the United States, besides newspaper politics.

They certainly are not a humorous people, and their temperament always impressed me as being of a dull and gloomy character. In shrewdness of remark, and a certain cast-iron quaintness, the Yankees, or people of New England, unquestionably take the lead; as they do in most other evidences of intelligence. But in travelling about, out of the large cities – as I have remarked in former parts of these volumes – I was quite oppressed by the prevailing seriousness and melancholy air of business: which was so general and unvarying, that at every new town I came to, I seemed to meet the very same people whom I had left behind me, at the last. Such defects as are perceptible in the national manners, seem, to me, to be referable, in a great degree, to this cause: which has generated a dull, sullen persistence in coarse usages, and rejected the graces of life as undeserving of attention. There is no doubt that Washington, who was always most scrupulous and exact on points of ceremony, perceived the tendency towards this mistake, even in his time, and did his utmost to correct it.

I cannot hold with other writers on these subjects that the prevalence of various forms of dissent in America, is in any way attributable to the non-existence there of an established church:

* Or let him refer to an able, and perfectly truthful article, in *The Foreign Quarterly Review*, published in the present month of October; to which my attention has been attracted, since these sheets have been passing through the press. He will find some specimens there, by no means remarkable to any man who has been in America, but sufficiently striking to one who has not.

indeed, I think the temper of the people, if it admitted of such an Institution being founded amongst them, would lead them to desert it, as a matter of course, merely because it *was* established. But, supposing it to exist, I doubt its probable efficacy in summoning the wandering sheep to one great fold, simply because of the immense amount of dissent which prevails at home; and because I do not find in America any one form of religion with which we in Europe, or even in England, are unacquainted. Dissenters resort thither in great numbers, as other people do, simply because it is a land of resort; and great settlements of them are founded, because ground can be purchased, and towns and villages reared, where there were none of the human creation before. But even the Shakers emigrated from England; our country is not unknown to Mr Joseph Smith, the apostle of Mormonism, or to his benighted disciples;[1] I have beheld religious scenes myself in some of our populous towns which can hardly be surpassed by an American camp-meeting; and I am not aware that any instance of superstitious imposture on the one hand, and superstitious credulity on the other, has had its origin in the United States, which we cannot more than parallel by the precedents of Mrs Southcote,[2] Mary Tofts the rabbit-breeder,[3] or even Mr Thom of Canterbury:[4] which latter case arose, some time after the dark ages had passed away.

The Republican Institutions of America undoubtedly lead the people to assert their self-respect and their equality; but a traveller is bound to bear those Institutions in his mind, and not hastily to resent the near approach of a class of strangers, who, at home, would keep aloof. This characteristic, when it was tinctured with no foolish pride, and stopped short of no honest service, never offended me; and I very seldom, if ever, experienced its rude or unbecoming display. Once or twice it was comically developed, as in the following case; but this was an amusing incident, and not the rule, or near it.

I wanted a pair of boots at a certain town, for I had none to travel in, but those with the memorable cork soles, which were much too hot for the fiery decks of a steamboat. I therefore sent a message to an artist in boots, importing, with my compliments, that I should be happy to see him, if he would do me the polite favour to call. He very kindly returned for answer, that he would 'look round' at six o'clock that evening.

I was lying on the sofa, with a book and a wine-glass, at about that time, when the door opened, and a gentleman in a stiff cravat, within a year or two on either side of thirty, entered, in his hat and gloves; walked up to the looking-glass; arranged his hair; took off his gloves; slowly produced a measure from the uttermost depths of his coat-pocket; and requested me, in a languid tone, to 'unfix' my straps. I complied, but looked with some curiosity at his hat, which was still upon his head. It might have been that, or it might have been the heat – but he took it off. Then, he sat himself down on a chair opposite to me; rested an arm on each knee; and, leaning forward very much, took from the ground, by a great effort, the specimen of metropolitan workmanship which I had just pulled off: whistling, pleasantly, as he did so. He turned it over and over; surveyed it with a contempt no language can express; and inquired if I wished him to fix me a boot like *that?* I courteously replied, that provided the boots were large enough, I would leave the rest to him; that if convenient and practicable, I should not object to their bearing some resemblance to the model then before him; but that I would be entirely guided by, and would beg to leave the whole subject to, his judgment and discretion. 'You an't partickler, about this scoop in the heel, I suppose then?' says he: 'we don't foller that, here.' I repeated my last observation. He looked at himself in the glass again; went closer to it to dash a grain or two of dust out of the corner of his eye; and settled his cravat. All this time, my leg and foot were in the air. 'Nearly ready, sir?' I inquired. 'Well, pretty nigh,' he said; 'keep steady.' I kept as steady as I could, both in foot and face; and having by this time got the dust out, and found his pencil-case, he measured me, and made the necessary notes. When he had finished, he fell into his old attitude, and taking up the boot again, mused for some time. 'And this,' he said, at last, 'is an English boot, is it? This is a London boot, eh?' 'That, sir,' I replied, 'is a London boot.' He mused over it again, after the manner of Hamlet with Yorick's skull; nodded his head, as who should say, 'I pity the Institutions that led to the production of this boot!'; rose; put up his pencil, notes, and paper – glancing at himself in the glass, all the time – put on his hat; drew on his gloves very slowly; and finally walked out. When he had been gone about a minute, the door reopened, and his hat and his head re-appeared. He looked round the room, and at the boot again, which was still lying on the floor; appeared thoughtful for a minute; and then said 'Well, good arternoon.' 'Good afternoon, sir,' said I: and that was the end of the interview.

There is but one other head on which I wish to offer a remark; and that has reference to the public health. In so vast a country, where there are thousands of millions of acres of land yet unsettled and uncleared, and on every rood of which, vegetable decomposition is annually taking place; where there are so many great rivers, and such opposite varieties of climate; there cannot fail to be a great amount of sickness at certain seasons. But I may venture to say, after conversing with many members of the medical profession in America, that I am not singular in the opinion that much of the disease which does prevail, might be avoided, if a few common precautions were observed. Greater means of personal cleanliness, are indispensable to this end; the custom of hastily swallowing large quantities of animal food, three times a-day, and rushing back to sedentary pursuits after each meal, must be changed; the gentler sex must go more wisely clad, and take more healthful exercise; and in the latter clause, the males must be included also. Above all, in public institutions, and throughout the whole of every town and city, the system of ventilation, and drainage, and removal of impurities requires to be thoroughly revised. There is no local Legislature in America which may not study Mr Chadwick's excellent Report upon the Sanitary Condition of our Labouring Classes, with immense advantage.[5]

I HAVE now arrived at the close of this book. I have little reason to believe, from certain warnings I have had, since I returned to England, that it will be tenderly or favourably received by the American people; and as I have written the Truth in relation to the mass of those who form their judgments and express their opinions, it will be seen that I have no desire to court, by any adventitious means, the popular applause.

It is enough for me, to know, that what I have set down in these pages, cannot cost me a single friend on the other side of the Atlantic, who is, in anything, deserving of the name. For the rest, I put my trust, implicitly, in the spirit in which they have been conceived and penned; and I can bide my time.

I have made no reference to my reception, nor have I suffered it to influence me in what I have written; for, in either case, I should have offered but a sorry acknowledgment, compared with that I bear within my breast, towards those partial readers of my former books, across the Water, who met me with an open hand, and not with one that closed upon an iron muzzle.

THE END

POSTSCRIPT

At a Public Dinner given to me on Saturday the 18th of April, 1868, in the City of New York, by two hundred representatives of the Press of the United States of America, I made the following observations among others:

'So much of my voice has lately been heard in the land, that I might have been contented with troubling you no further from my present standing-point, were it not a duty with which I henceforth charge myself, not only here but on every suitable occasion, whatsoever and wheresoever, to express my high and grateful sense of my second reception in America, and to bear my honest testimony to the national generosity and magnanimity. Also, to declare how astounded I have been by the amazing changes I have seen around me on every side, — changes moral, changes physical, changes in the amount of land subdued and peopled, changes in the rise of vast new cities, changes in the growth of older cities almost out of recognition, changes in the graces and amenities of life, changes in the Press, without whose advancement no advancement can take place anywhere. Nor am I, believe me, so arrogant as to suppose that in five and twenty years there have been no changes in me, and that I had nothing to learn and no extreme impressions to correct when I was here first. And this brings me to a point on which I have, ever since I landed in the United States last November, observed a strict silence, though sometimes tempted to break it, but in reference to which I will, with your good leave, take you into my confidence now. Even the Press, being human, may be sometimes mistaken or misinformed, and I rather think that I have in one or two rare instances observed its information to be not strictly accurate with reference to myself. Indeed, I have, now and again, been more surprised by printed news that I have read of myself, than by any printed news that I have ever read in my present state of existence. Thus, the vigour and perseverance with which I have for some months past been collecting materials for, and hammering away at, a new book on America has much astonished me; seeing that all that time my declaration has been perfectly well known to my publishers on both sides of the Atlantic, that no consideration on earth would induce me to write one. But what I have intended, what I have resolved upon (and this is the confidence I seek to place in you) is, on my return to England, in my own person, in my own Journal,[1] to bear, for the behoof of my countrymen, such testimony to the gigantic changes in this country as I have hinted at to-night. Also, to record that wherever I have been, in the smallest places equally with the largest, I have been received with unsurpassable politeness, delicacy, sweet temper, hospitality, consideration, and with unsurpassable respect for the privacy daily enforced upon me by the nature of my avocation here and the state of my health. This testimony, so long as I live, and so long as my descendants have any legal right in my books, I shall cause to be republished, as an appendix to every copy of those two books of mine in which I have referred to America. And this I will do and cause to be done, not in mere love and thankfulness, but because I regard it as an act of plain justice and honour.'

I said these words with the greatest earnestness that I could lay upon them, and I repeat them in print here with equal earnestness. So long as this book shall last, I hope that they will form a part of it, and will be fairly read as inseparable from my experiences and impressions of America.

CHARLES DICKENS

May, 1868.

APPENDIX 1

Dickens's Discarded Introduction*

'On the 10th of October I heard from him that the chapter intended to be introductory to the *Notes* was written, and waiting our conference whether or not it should be printed. We decided against it; on his part so reluctantly, that I had to undertake for its publication when a more fitting time should come. This in my judgment has arrived, and the chapter first sees the light on this page. There is no danger at present, as there would have been when it was written, that its proper self-assertion should be mistaken for an apprehension of hostile judgments which he was anxious to deprecate or avoid. He is out of reach of all that now; and reveals to us here, as one whom fear or censure can touch no more, his honest purpose in the use of satire even where his humorous temptations were strongest. What he says will on other grounds also be read with unusual interest, for it will be found to connect itself impressively not with his first experiences only, but with his second visit to America at the close of his life. He held always the same high opinion of what was best in that country, and always the same contempt for what was worst in it.' [Forster.]

INTRODUCTORY, AND NECESSARY TO BE READ

I have placed the foregoing title at the head of this page, because I challenge and deny the right of any person to pass judgment on this book, or to arrive at any reasonable conclusion in reference to it, without first being at the trouble of becoming acquainted with its design and purpose.

It is not statistical. Figures of arithmetic have already been heaped upon America's devoted head, almost as lavishly as figures of speech have been piled above Shakespeare's grave.

It comprehends no small talk concerning individuals, and no

*Text from John Forster, *The Life of Charles Dickens* (London, 1904), vol. 1, 304–307.

violation of the social confidences of private life. The very prevalent practice of kidnapping live ladies and gentlemen, forcing them into cabinets, and labelling and ticketing them whether they will or no, for the gratification of the idle and the curious, is not to my taste. Therefore I have avoided it.

It has not a grain of any political ingredient in its whole composition.

Neither does it contain, nor have I intended that it should contain, any lengthened and minute account of my personal reception in the United States: not because I am, or ever was, insensible to that spontaneous effusion of affection and generosity of heart, in a most affectionate and generous-hearted people; but because I conceive that it would ill become me to flourish matter necessarily involving so much of my own praises, in the eyes of my unhappy readers.

This book is simply what it claims to be – a record of the impressions I received from day to day, during my hasty travels in America, and sometimes (but not always) of the conclusions to which they, and after-reflection on them, have led me; a description of the country I passed through; of the institutions I visited; of the kind of people among whom I journeyed; and of the manners and customs that came within my observation. Very many works having just the same scope and range, have been already published, but I think that these two volumes stand in need of no apology on that account. The interest of such productions, if they have any, lies in the varying impressions made by the same novel things on different minds; and not in new discoveries or extraordinary adventures.

I can scarcely be supposed to be ignorant of the hazard I run in writing of America at all. I know perfectly well that there is, in that country, a numerous class of well-intentioned persons prone to be dissatisfied with all accounts of the Republic whose citizens they are, which are not couched in terms of exalted and extravagant praise. I know perfectly well that there is in America, as in most other places laid down in maps of the great world, a numerous class of persons so tenderly and delicately constituted, that they cannot bear the truth in any form. And I do not need the gift of prophecy to discern afar off, that they who will be aptest to detect malice, ill-will, and all uncharitableness in these pages, and to show, beyond any doubt, that they are perfectly inconsistent with that grateful and enduring recollection which I profess to entertain of the welcome I found awaiting me beyond the Atlantic – will be certain native journalists, veracious and gentlemanly, who were at great pains to prove to me, on all occasions during my stay there, that the aforesaid welcome was utterly worthless.

But, venturing to dissent even from these high authorities, I formed my own opinion of its value in the outset, and retain it to this hour; and in asserting (as I invariably did on all public occasions) my liberty and freedom of speech while I was among the Americans, and in maintaining it at home, I believe that I best show my sense of the high worth of that welcome, and of the honourable singleness of purpose with which it was extended to me. From first to last I saw, in the friends who crowded round me in America, old readers, over-grateful and over-partial perhaps, to whom I had happily been the means of furnishing pleasure and entertainment; not a vulgar herd who would flatter and cajole a stranger into turning with closed eyes from all the blemishes of the nation, and into chaunting its praises with the discrimination of a street ballad-singer. From first to last I saw, in those hospitable hands, a home-made wreath of laurel; and not an iron muzzle disguised beneath a flower or two.

Therefore I take – and hold myself not only justified in taking, but bound to take – the plain course of saying what I think, and noting what I saw; and as it is not my custom to exalt what in my judgment are foibles and abuses at home, so I have no intention of softening down, or glozing over, those that I have observed abroad.

If this book should fall into the hands of any sensitive American who cannot bear to be told that the working of the institutions of his country is far from perfect; that in spite of the advantage she has over all other nations in the elastic freshness and vigour of her youth, she is far from being a model for the earth to copy; and that even in those pictures of the national manners with which he quarrels most, there is still (after the lapse of several years, each of which may be fairly supposed to have had its stride in improvement) much that is just and true at this hour; let him lay it down, now, for I shall not please him. Of the intelligent, reflecting, and educated among his countrymen, I have no fear; for I have ample reason to believe, after many delightful conversations not easily to be forgotten, that there are very few topics (if any) on which their sentiments differ materially from mine.

I may be asked – 'If you have been in any respect disappointed in America, and are assured beforehand that the expression of your disappointment will give offence to any class, why do you write at all?' My answer is, that I went there expecting greater things than I found, and resolved as far as in me lay to do justice to the country, at the expense of any (in my view) mistaken or prejudiced statements that might have been made to its disparagement. Coming home with a corrected and sobered judgment, I consider myself no less bound to do justice to what, according to my best means of judgment, I found to be the truth.

APPENDIX 2
Selected Letters

The following selected letters give details of occurrences and opinions not revealed in *American Notes* and also clearly chart that growing disillusionment with America discussed in the Introduction. Of the topics which Dickens considers in these letters a few require brief elaboration.

Although the first of the selected letters was written in September 1841, Dickens had had serious intentions of visiting America for several years prior to that. As early as 1837, in a letter to the Philadelphia publisher Carey, Dickens suggests his interest in a visit: 'I need scarcely say that it affords me great pleasure to hear of *The Pickwick Papers* in America – a country in which, in common with most Englishmen, I take a high interest and with which I hope one day to become better acquainted'[1] (26 October 1837). Several months later he echoes his sentiments in a letter to the same firm concerning the American publication of *Nicholas Nickleby*: 'I shall be glad to hear that *Nicholas* is in favour with our American friends (whom I long to see)'[2] (18 July 1838).

On 7 September 1841 Dickens signed an agreement with his publishers, Chapman and Hall, whereby he would have a rest from writing for fourteen months, commence a new work in monthly numbers beginning November 1842, and receive, during the lull, £150 a month in advance of royalties. This gave him a breathing space in which to make a journey to America and, naturally, his publishers readily agreed to his collecting material for a book of travels.

The letters show how Dickens became increasingly disenchanted with his lack of privacy in the United States. Though he doubtless suffered much inconvenience in this regard, his attitude may justly be described as unreasonable. He *was* the most famous novelist in the world and his books were read to tatters in the most remote parts of America. Early in 1841 Dickens received a letter from a backwoodsman, John Tomlin, stressing how much the Englishman's novels had meant to him. In his answering letter Dickens referred to this as 'a source of the purest delight and pride to me'[3] (23 February 1841). Bret Harte

1. *The Letters of Charles Dickens*, ed. W. Dexter (London, 1938), vol. 1, p. 132. All selections are from this three-volume edition.
2. Dexter, op. cit., p. 170.
3. Ibid., p. 301.

describes rough prospectors sitting round a camp fire enthralled and moved by the pitiable plight of Little Nell[4] and all Dickensians revel in the fact that, as the ship carrying the final numbers of *The Old Curiosity Shop* sailed into New York, a vast crowd waited on the quay shouting 'Is Little Nell dead ?' In the words of J. B. Simons, 'they stood, haggard with anxiety, a dense mass of five or six thousand people'.[5] In this climate, Dickens ought to have known what was coming. There were some excesses, to be sure. One day, in Boston, as Dickens left the studio of the portrait painter, Francis Alexander, a mob of women descended upon him and began snipping away pieces of his fur coat. However, he *does* seem to have both desired and wished to shun lioniz-ation – a not untypical Dickens reaction. The novelist's feelings about lack of privacy help to explain an inconsistency which several critics have noted in *Martin Chuzzlewit*. How is it that such an insignificant young man as Martin can be given so much attention wherever he goes in the United States? Clearly Dickens is here drawing upon a sharp personal memory which he has not sufficiently suppressed in the texture of the novel.

Mention has already been made of the International Copyright ques-tion and several of these letters make clear Dickens's concern over this matter. Writing to Forster on 24 February 1842, Dickens requests a petition from prominent British authors and makes clear the interest of Senator Clay in such a move. Clay presented an International Copy-right Bill to the Senate five times between 1837 and 1842, always without success. When the petition arrived, Dickens sent it to the editor of the *Evening Post* to show that the 'opinions of the great body of British authors'[6] were in line with his. The petition insisted that the passing of such a law would *not* raise the price of British books in America. Despite the notable support of Washington Irving, Cornelius Matthews and Horace Greeley's *New York Tribune*, the petition was successfully countered in April by a meeting of printers and publishers in Boston. Dickens saw clearly the effect of this failure on American literature. At a dinner in his honour at Papanti's in Boston he pointed out that, 'There must be an international arrangement in this respect . . . It becomes the character of a great country; firstly because it is justice; secondly, because without it you never can have, and keep, a literature of your own.'[7] His remarks in his speeches and letters reveal such a careful consideration of the whole problem that one can only regret its

4. Bret Harte, 'Dickens in Camp', *Works* (New York, 1902), vol. 8, p. 209.

5. J. B. Simons, *The Romance and Humanity of Dickens* (London, 1957), p. 9.

6. *Letters*, vol. 1, pp. 446–7. Letter dated 30 April 1842.

7. *The Speeches of Charles Dickens*, ed. K. J. Fielding (Oxford, 1960), p. 21.

exclusion from *American Notes*. Obviously he realized how provoking such comments would be and it is possible that American friends such as Longfellow and Felton may have counselled him against their inclusion. Perhaps the principal reason for their exclusion was his sense that the situation was hopeless. In 1843 he wrote to Charles Babbage: 'I am as well convinced of its invincible hopelessness as if I saw it written by a celestial penman in the Book of Fate'[8] (27 April 1843). He had earlier remarked in a letter to Longfellow: 'I quite agree with you that we shall never live to see the passing of an international Law' (29 December 1842).[9]

Finally, both *American Notes* and the letters have much to say about slavery. Dickens had very little first-hand experience of the slave-system and, though he continued to abhor it on principle it is useful to note that after 1862 his attitude to the American Civil War, like that of so many Englishmen, favoured the Confederate cause. Subsequently he expressed disgust with the politics of Reconstruction. In America in 1868 the appearance and behaviour of freed Negroes disgusted him: 'The mechanical absurdity of giving these people votes, at any rate at present, would glare out of every roll of their eyes, chuckle in their mouths, and bump in their heads, if one did not see ... that their en-franchisement is a mere party trick to get votes.'[10]

TO WILLIAM HALL

> *Broadstairs*
> *14th September 1841*

It would be a good thing, wouldn't it, if I ran over to America about the end of February, and came back after four or five months with a one volume book – such as a ten and sixpenny touch? ... Washington Irving writes me that if I went, it would be a triumph for me from one end of the States to the other, as was never known in any nation. ...

TO JOHN FORSTER

> *Broadstairs*
> *19th September 1841*

... Now to astonish you. After balancing, considering, and weighing the matter in every point of view, I HAVE MADE UP MY MIND (WITH GOD'S LEAVE) TO GO TO AMERICA – AND TO START AS SOON AFTER CHRISTMAS AS IT WILL BE SAFE TO GO. ...

8. *Letters*, vol. 1, p. 516.

9. Quoted in H. W. L. Dana: 'Longfellow and Dickens: The Story of a Trans-Atlantic Friendship', *Cambridge Historical Society*, vol. 28, 1942, p. 80.

10. *Letters*, vol. 3, p. 611. Letter to John Forster dated 30 January 1868.

TO FRANCIS ALEXANDER

Devonshire Terrace, York
Gate, Regent's Park, London
Friday 2nd December 1841

I leave Liverpool on the Fourth of next month by the Britannia Steam Packet. Your welcome communication and all the letters I have received from America fill me with glad and cheerful anticipation. Trust me that my heart warms towards the land and that for every hearty greeting I have as hearty a response.

TO JOHN FORSTER

Banks of Newfoundland
Monday 17th January 1842

Apropos of rolling, I have forgotten to mention that in playing whist we are obliged to put the tricks in our pockets, to keep them from disappearing altogether; and that five or six times in the course of every rubber we are all flung from our seats, roll out at different doors, and keep on rolling until we are picked up by stewards. This has become such a matter of course, that we go through it with perfect gravity; and when we are bolstered up on our sofas again, resume our conversation or our game at the point where it was interrupted.

21st January

I wish you could have seen the crowds cheering the Inimitable in the streets. I wish you could have seen judges, law-officers, bishops, and law-makers welcoming the Inimitable. I wish you could have seen the Inimitable shown to a great elbow-chair by the Speaker's throne, and sitting alone in the middle of the floor of the House of Commons, the observed of all observers, listening with exemplary gravity to the queerest speaking possible, and breaking in spite of himself into a smile as he thought of this commencement to the Thousand and One stories in reserve for home and Lincoln's-inn-fields and Jack Straw's-castle. – Ah, Forster! when I *do* come back again! –

TO JOHN FORSTER

Tremont-House, Boston
Saturday 29th January (1842)

... As the Cunard boats have a wharf of their own at the custom-house, and that a narrow one, we were a long time (an hour at least) working in. I was standing in full fig on the paddle-box beside the captain, staring about me, when suddenly, long before we were moored to the wharf, a dozen men came leaping on board at the peril of their lives, with great bundles of newspapers under their arms; worsted comforters (very much the worse for wear) round their necks; and so forth.

'Aha!' says I, 'this is like our London-bridge': believing of course that these visitors were news-boys. But what do you think of their being EDITORS? And what do you think of their tearing violently up to me and beginning to shake hands like madmen? Oh! If you could have seen how I wrung their wrists! And if you could but know how I hated one man in very dirty gaiters, and with very protruding upper teeth, who said to all comers after him, 'So you've been introduced to our friend Dickens – eh?'

How can I tell you what has happened since that first day? How can I give you the faintest notion of my reception here; of the crowds that pour in and out the whole day; of the people that line the streets when I go out; of the cheering when I went to the theatre; of the copies of verses, letters of congratulation, welcomes of all kinds, balls, dinners, assemblies without end? There is to be a public dinner to me here in Boston, next Tuesday, and great dissatisfaction has been given to the many by the high price (three pounds sterling each) of the tickets. There is to be a ball next Monday week at New York, and 150 names appear on the list of the committee. There is to be a dinner in the same place, in the same week, to which I have had an invitation with every known name in America appended to it. But what can I tell you about any of these things which will give you the slightest notion of the enthusiastic greeting they give me, or the cry that runs through the whole country! I have had deputations from the Far West, who have come from more than two thousand miles distance: from the lakes, the rivers, the back-woods, the log-houses, the cities, factories, villages, and towns. Authorities from nearly all the States have written to me. I have heard from the universities, congress, senate, and bodies, public and private, of every sort and kind. 'It is no nonsense, and no common feeling,' wrote Dr Channing to me yesterday. 'It is all heart. There never was, and never will be, such a triumph.' And it is a good thing, is it not . . . to find those fancies it has given me and you the greatest satisfaction to think of, at the core of it all? It makes my heart quieter, and me a more retiring, sober, tranquil man to watch the effect of those thoughts in all this noise and hurry, even than if I sat, pen in hand, to put them down for the first time. I feel, in the best aspects of this welcome, something of the presence and influence of that spirit which directs my life, and through a heavy sorrow has pointed upward with unchanging finger for more than four years past. And if I know my heart, not twenty times this praise would move me to an act of folly. . . .

'Well,' I can fancy you saying, 'but about his impressions of Boston and the Americans?' – Of the latter, I will not say a word until I have seen more of them, and have gone into the interior. I will only say, now, that we have never yet been required to dine at a table d'hote; that, thus far, our rooms are as much our own here, as they would be at the Clarendon; that but for an odd phrase now and then – such as *Snap of cold weather*; a *tongue-y man* for a talkative fellow; *Possible?* as a solitary interrogation: and *Yes?* for indeed – I should have marked, so far, no difference whatever between the parties here and those I have left behind. The women are very beautiful, but they soon fade; the general breeding is neither stiff nor forward; the good nature, universal. If you ask the way to a place – of some common waterside man, who don't know you from Adam – he turns and goes with you. Universal deference is paid to ladies; and they walk about at all seasons, wholly unprotected. . . . This hotel is a trifle smaller than Finsbury-square; and is made so infernally hot (I use the expression advisedly) by means of a furnace with pipes running through the passages, that we can hardly bear it. There are no curtains to the beds, or to the bedroom windows. I am told there never are, hardly, all through America. The bedrooms are indeed very bare of furniture. Ours is nearly as large as your great room, and has a wardrobe in it of painted wood not larger (I appeal to K) than an English watch box. I slept in this room for two nights, quite satisfied with the belief that it was a shower bath.

29th January

On looking back through these sheets, I am astonished to find how little I have told you, and how much I have, even now, in store which shall be yours by word of mouth. The American poor, the American factories, the institutions of all kinds – I have a book, already. There is no man in this town, or in this State of New England, who has not a blazing fire and a meat dinner every day of his life. A flaming sword in the air would not attract so much attention as a beggar in the streets. There are no charity uniforms, no wearisome repetition of the same dull ugly dress, in that blind school. All are attired after their own tastes, and every boy and girl has his or her individuality as distinct and un-impaired as you would find it in their own homes. At the theatres, all the ladies sit in the fronts of the boxes. The gallery are as quiet as the dress circle at dear Drury-lane. A man with seven heads would be no sight at all, compared with one who couldn't read and write.

Twenty-fourth February

I proceed to my third head: the international copyright question.

I believe there is no country, on the face of the earth, where there is less freedom of opinion on any subject in reference to which there is a broad difference of opinion than in this. . . . There! – I write the words with reluctance, disappointment, and sorrow; but I believe it from the bottom of my soul. I spoke, as you know, of international copyright, at Boston; and I spoke of it again at Hartford. My friends were paralysed with wonder at such audacious daring. The notion that I, a man alone by himself, in America, should venture to suggest to the Americans that there was one point on which they were neither just to their own countrymen nor to us, actually struck the boldest dumb! Washington Irving, Prescott, Hoffman, Bryant, Halleck, Dana, Washington Allston – every man who writes in this country is devoted to the question, and not one of them *dares* to raise his voice and complain of the atrocious state of the law. It is nothing that of all men living I am the greatest loser by it. It is nothing that I have a claim to speak and be heard. The wonder is that a breathing man can be found with temerity enough to suggest to the Americans the possibility of their having done wrong. I wish you could have seen the faces that I saw, down both sides of the table at Hartford, when I began to talk about Scott. I wish you could have heard how I gave it out. My blood so boiled as I thought of the monstrous injustice that I felt as if I were twelve feet high when I thrust it down their throats.

I had no sooner made that second speech than such an outcry began (for the purpose of deterring me from doing the like in this city) as an Englishman can form no notion of. Anonymous letters; verbal dissuasions; newspaper attacks making Colt (a murderer who is attracting great attention here) an angel by comparison with me; assertions that I was no gentleman, but a mere mercenary scoundrel; coupled with the most monstrous mis-representations relative to my design and purpose in visiting the United States; came pouring in upon me every day. The dinner committee here (composed of the first gentlemen in America, remember that) were so dismayed, that they besought me not to pursue the subject *although they every one agreed with me*. I answered that I would. That nothing should deter me. . . . That the shame was theirs, not mine; and that as I would not spare them when I got home, I would not be silenced here. Accordingly, when the night came, I asserted my right, with all the means I could command to give it dignity, in face, manner, or words; and I believe that if you could have seen and heard me, you would have loved me better for it than ever you did in your life.

The New York Herald, which you will receive with this, is the Satirist of America; but having a great circulation (on account of its commercial intelligence and early news) it can afford to secure the best reporters. . . . My speech is done, upon the whole, with remarkable accuracy. There are a great many typographical errors in it; and by the omission of one or two words, or the substitution of one word for another, it is often materially weakened. Thus I did not say that I 'claimed' my right, but that I 'asserted' it; and I did not say that I had 'some claim', but that I had 'a most righteous claim', to speak. But altogether it is very correct.

The effect of all this copyright agitation at least has been to awaken a great sensation on both sides of the subject; the respectable newspapers and reviews taking up the cudgels as strongly in my favour, as the others have done against me. Some of the vagabonds take great credit to themselves (grant us patience!) for having made me popular by publishing my books in newspapers: as if there were no England ,no Scotland, no Germany, no place but America in the whole world. . . .

I will tell you what *I* should like, my dear friend, always supposing that your judgment concurs with mine; and that you would take the trouble to get such a document. I should like to have a short letter addressed to me, by the principal English authors who signed the international copyright petition, expressive of their sense that I have done my duty to the cause. I am sure I deserve it, but I don't wish it on that ground. It is because its publication in the best journals here would unquestionably do great good. As the gauntlet is down, let us go on. Clay has already sent a gentleman to me express from Washington (where I shall be on the 6th or 7th of next month) to declare his strong interest in the matter, his cordial approval of the 'manly' course I have held in reference to it, and his desire to stir in it if possible. I have lighted up such a blaze that a meeting of the foremost people on the other side (very respectfully and properly conducted in reference to me, personally, I am bound to say) was held in this town t'other night. And it would be a thousand pities if we did not strike as hard as we can, now that the iron is so hot.

I have come at last, and it is time I did, to my life here, and intentions for the future. I can do nothing that I want to do, go nowhere where I want to go, and see nothing that I want to see. If I turn into the street, I am followed by a multitude. If I stay at home, the house becomes, with callers, like a fair. If I visit a public institution, with only one friend, the directors come down incontinently, waylay me in the yard, and address me in a long speech. I go to a party in the evening, and am so inclosed and hemmed about by people, stand where I will, that I am exhausted for want of air. I dine out, and have to talk about everything, to everybody. I go to church for quiet, and there is a violent rush to the neighbourhood of the pew I sit in, and the clergyman preaches *at* me. I take my seat in a railroad car, and the very conductor won't leave me alone. I get out at a station, and can't drink a glass of water, without having a hundred people looking down my throat when I open my mouth to swallow. Conceive what all this is! Then by every post, letters on letters arrive, all about nothing, and all demanding an immediate answer. This man is offended because I won't live in his house; and that man is thoroughly disgusted because I won't go out more than four times in one evening. I have no rest or peace, and am in a perpetual worry.

When we reach Baltimore, we are in the regions of slavery. It exists there, in its least shocking and most mitigated form; but there it is. They whisper, here (they dare only whisper, you know, and that below their breaths), that on that place, and all through the South, there is a dull gloomy cloud on which the very word seems written. I shall be able to say, one of these days, that I accepted no public mark of respect in any place where slavery was; – and that's something.

The ladies of America are decidedly and unquestionably beautiful. Their complexions are not so good as those of Englishwomen; their beauty does not last so long; and their figures are very inferior. But they are most beautiful. I still reserve my opinion of the national character – just whispering that I tremble for a radical coming here, unless he is a radical on principle, by reason and reflection, and from the sense of right. I fear that if he were anything else, he would return home a tory. . . . I say no more on that head for two months from this time, save that I do fear that the heaviest blow ever dealt at liberty will be dealt by this country, in the failure of its example to the earth. The scenes that are passing in Congress now, all tending to the separation of the States, fill one with such a deep disgust that I dislike the very name of Washington (meaning the place, not the man), and am repelled by the mere thought of approaching it.

TO JONATHAN CHAPMAN

Carlton House, New York
Twenty-Second February, 1842

My Dear Friend, – Here's my hand, our alliance is complete. Let the sea never rise so high between us, we will rise higher, and when you come to England, we will have such walks and talks together as shall indemnify us for years of separation.

I am sick to death of the life I have been living here – worn out in mind and body – and quite weary and distressed. I have declined all future invitations of a public nature, and mean to be resolute from this time forth. I am a splendid illustration of the wisdom of the fable concerning the old man and his ass. Half the population take it ill if I go where I am asked, and the other half take it ill if I don't, so I mean in future to consult my own wishes and those of no other person in this hemisphere.

I have never in my life been so shocked and disgusted or made so sick and sore at heart as I have been by the treatment I have received here (in America, I mean) in reference to the International Copyright question. I, the greatest cock of the existing law alive, say in perfect good humour and disinterestedness (for God knows that I have little hope of its ever being changed in my time) that I hope the day will come when writers will be justly treated, and straightway there fell upon me scores of your newspapers imputing notices to me the very suggestion of which turns my blood to gall; and attacking me in such terms of vagabond scurrility as they would denounce no murderer with. I vow to Heaven that the scorn and indignation I have felt under this unmanly and ungenerous treatment have been to me an amount of agony such as I have never experienced since my birth. But it has had the one good effect of making me iron upon this theme, and iron I will be here and at home, by word of mouth and in writing as long as I can articulate a syllable or hold a pen.

P.S. – Washington Irving is a *great* fellow. We have laughed most heartily together. He is just the man he ought to be. So is Doctor Channing, with whom I have had an interesting correspondence since I saw him last at Boston. Halleck is a merry little man. Bryant a sad one, and very reserved. Washington Allston the painter (who wrote Monaldi) is a fine specimen of a glorious old genius. Longfellow, whose volume of poems I have got for you, is a frank accomplished man as well as a fine writer, and will be in town 'next fall:' Tell Macready that I suspect prices here must have rather altered since his time. I paid our fortnight's bill here, last night. We have dined out every day (except when I was laid up with a sore throat), and only had in all four bottles of wine. The bill was £70 English!!!

TO JOHN FORSTER

United States Hotel, Philadelphia
Sunday Sixth March 1842

I have often asked Americans in London which were the better railroads – ours or theirs? They have taken time for reflection, and generally replied on mature consideration that they rather thought we excelled; in respect of the punctuality with which we arrived at our stations, and the smoothness of our travelling. I wish you could see what an American railroad is, in some parts where I now have seen them. I won't say I wish you could feel what it is, because that would be an unchristian and savage aspiration. It is never inclosed, or warded off. You walk down the main street of a large town: and, slap-dash, headlong, pell-mell, down the middle of the street; with pigs burrowing and boys flying kites and playing marbles, and men smoking, and women talking, and children crawling, close to the very rails; there comes tearing along a mad locomotive with its train of cars, scattering a red-hot shower of sparks (from its *wood* fire) in all directions; screeching, hissing, yelling, and panting; and nobody one atom more concerned than if it were a hundred miles away. You cross a turnpike-road; and there is no gate, no policeman, no signal – nothing to keep the wayfarer or quiet traveller out of the way, but a wooden arch on which is written in great letters 'Look out for the locomotive.' And if any man, woman, or child, don't look out, why it's his or her fault, and there's an end of it.

The cars are like very shabby omnibuses – only larger; holding sixty or seventy people. The seats, instead of being placed long ways, are put cross-wise, back to front. Each holds two. There is a long row of these on each side of the caravan, and a narrow passage up the centre. The windows are usually all closed, and there is very often, in addition, a hot, close, most intolerable charcoal stove in a red-hot glow. The heat and closeness are quite insupportable. But this is the characteristic of all American houses, of all the public institutions, chapels, theatres, and prisons. From the constant use of the hard anthracite coal in these beastly furnaces, a perfectly new class of diseases is springing up in the country. Their effect upon an Englishman is briefly told. He is always very sick and very faint; and has an intolerable headache, morning, noon, and night.

In the ladies' car, there is no smoking of tobacco allowed. All gentlemen who have ladies with them, sit in this car; and it is usually very full. Before it, is the gentleman's car; which is something narrower. As I had a window close to me yesterday which commanded this gentlemen's car, I looked at it pretty often, perforce. The flashes of saliva flew so perpetually and incessantly out of the windows all the way, that it looked as though they were ripping open feather-beds inside, and letting the wind dispose of the feathers. But this spitting is universal. In the courts of law, the judge has his spittoon on the bench, the counsel have theirs, the witness has his, the prisoner his, and t he crier his. The jury are accommodated at the rate of three men to a spittoon (or spit-box as they call it here); and the spectators in the gallery are provided for, as so many men who in the course of nature expectorate without cessation. There are spit-boxes in every steam-boat, bar-room, public dining-room, house or office, and place of general resort, no matter what it be. In the hospitals, the students are requested, by placard, to use the boxes provided for them, and not to spit upon the stairs. I have twice seen gentlemen, at evening parties in New York, turn aside when they were not engaged in conversation, and spit upon the drawing-room carpet. And in every bar-room and hotel passage the stone floor looks as if it were paved with open oysters – from the quantity of this kind of deposit which tesselates it all over. . . .

The institutions at Boston, and at Hartford, are most admirable. It would be very difficult indeed to improve upon them. But this is not so at New York; where there is an ill-managed lunatic asylum, a bad jail, a dismal work-house, and a perfectly intolerable place of police-imprisonment. A man is found drunk in the streets, and is thrown into a cell below the surface of the earth; profoundly dark; so full of noisome vapours that when you enter it with a candle you see a ring about the light, like that which surrounds the moon in wet and cloudy weather; and so offensive and disgusting in its filthy odours, that you *cannot bear* its stench. He is shut up within an iron door, in a series of vaulted passages where no one stays; has no drop of water, or ray of light, or visitor, or help of any kind; and there he remains until the magistrate's arrival. If he die (as one man did not long ago) he is half eaten by the rats in an hour's time (as this man was). I expressed, on seeing these places the other night, the disgust I felt, and which it would be impossible to repress. 'Well; I don't know,' said the night constable – that's a national answer by the bye – 'Well; I don't know. I've had six and twenty young women locked up here together, and beautiful ones too, and that's a fact.' The cell was certainly no larger than the wine-cellar in Devonshire-terrace; at least three feet lower; and stunk like a common sewer. There was one woman in it then. The magistrate begins his examinations at five o'clock in the morning; the watch is set at seven at night; if the prisoners have been given in charge by an officer, they are not taken out before nine or ten; and in the interval they remain in these places, where they could no more be heard to cry for help, in case of a fit or swoon among them, than a man's voice could be heard after he was coffined up in his grave.

15th March

I said I wouldn't write anything more concerning the American people, for two months. Second thoughts are best. I shall not change, and may as well speak out – to *you*. They are friendly, earnest, hospitable, kind, frank, very often accomplished, far less prejudiced than you would suppose, warm-hearted, fervent, and enthusiastic. They are chivalrous in their universal politeness to women, courteous, obliging, disinterested; and, when they conceive a perfect affection for a man (as I may venture to say of myself), entirely devoted to him. I have received thousands of people of all ranks and grades, and have never once been asked an offensive or unpolite question – except by Englishmen, who, when they have been 'located' here for some years, are worse than the devil in his blackest painting. The State is a parent to its people; has a parental care and watch over all poor children, women labouring of child, sick persons, and captives. The common men render you assistance in the streets, and would revolt from the offer of a piece of money. The desire to oblige is universal; and I have never once travelled in a public conveyance, without making some generous acquaintance whom I have been sorry to part from, and who has in many cases come on miles, to see us again. But I don't like the country. I would not live here, on any consideration. It goes against the grain with me. It would with you. I think it impossible, utterly impossible, for any Englishman to live here, and be happy. I have a confidence that I might be right, because I have everything, God knows, to lead me to the opposite conclusion: and yet I cannot resist coming to this one. As to the causes, they are too many to enter upon here. . . .

TO DAVID C. COLDEN

Fuller's Hotel, Washington
March 10th 1842

We were very comfortably lodged at Philadelphia – and indeed we deserved to be; for the landlord not only charged us half rent for the rooms during the time he had expected us (which was quite right) but charged us also – when I say us, I mean Kate, her maid, and I – for board during the whole of the same period. As I could not help regarding the statement that he had paid for our food while we were paying for it at New York, in the light of a pleasant fiction or ingenious jest, I *did* suggest through my factotum the slightest possible insinuation to that effect. It appeared, however, that it was 'the custom'; and as strangers in Rome do as they do in Rome, I bowed to the custom, and paid.

I passed a whole day in the Penitentiary – where, as you know, the principle of solitary confinement is observed, in the strictest manner, in every case. It is inexpressibly painful to see so many of the prisoners as I did, and to converse with them; but I fear that to a certain extent the system is a good one. I used the expression 'I fear,' because it is dreadful to believe that it is ever necessary to impose such a torture of the mind upon our fellow creatures. But it seems, from all one can learn, to do good: and now and then to effect that reclamation which gives joy in Heaven. In the case of a very long term of imprisonment, however, I cannot but think it cruel, though I know it is mercifully and well intended. One man had been shut up by himself in the same cell, for nearly twelve years. His time is just expiring. I asked him how he felt at the prospect of release – and he answered – plucking in a strange way at his fingers, and looking restlessly about the walls and floor – that he didn't care: that it was all the same to him now: that he had looked forward to it once, but that was so long ago, that he had come to have no regard for anything. And so, with a heavy sigh, he went about his work, and would say no more. We are accustomed to hear it said sometimes that such a person must have felt in a minute, a year of suffering. But if ever twelve years of the most intense mental anguish were written in the small compass of one face, I saw it in this prisoner's. Indeed the men, however unlike naturally, become alike, and strikingly alike, in this place. There is the same bright eye, and haggard look, in them all; and an indescribable something – distantly resembling the attentive and sorrowful expression you see in the blind – which is never to be forgotten. The women bear it better, and acquire a patient and subdued look that makes you very sad, but not distressingly so. Each of them seems a better creature than one feels one's self to be, and that's a comfort. The prison is beautifully – exquisitely – kept, and thoroughly well managed: but I never in my life was more affected by anything which was not strictly my own grief, than I was by this sight. It will live in my recollection always. When I come to tell you something of my brief experience there, you will often think of it too.

We have been to both Houses of the Legislature to-day, and have seen many of the Lions, both living and stuffed. I think of going every day while I remain here.

I went to the President's, too, this morning, in company with a namesake who is Secretary to the Senate. He has a good face (I mean the President) and his manners are very mild and gentlemanly. He expressed great surprise at my being so young. I would have returned the compliment, but he looked so jaded, that it stuck in my throat like Macbeth's amen.

TO CORNELIUS FELTON

March 14th 1842

What do you think of this incendiary card being left at my door last night? 'General G. sends compliments to Mr Dickens, and called with two literary ladies. As the two L. L's are ambitious of the honour of a personal introduction to Mr D., General G. requests the honour of an appointment for to-morrow.' I draw a veil over my sufferings. They are sacred.

TO JOHN FORSTER

Washington
March 21st, 1842, Monday

Richmond is a prettily situated town; but, like other towns in slave districts (as the planters themselves admit), has an aspect of decay and gloom which to an unaccustomed eye is *most* distressing. In the black car (for they don't let them sit with the whites), on the railroad as we went there, were a mother and family whom the steamer was conveying away, to sell; retaining the man (the husband and father I mean) on his plantation. The children cried the whole way. Yesterday, on board the boat, a slave owner and two constables were our fellow-passengers. They were coming here in search of two negroes who had run away on the previous day. On the bridge at Richmond there is a notice against fast driving over it, as it is rotten and crazy: penalty – for whites, five dollars; for slaves, fifteen stripes. My heart is lightened as if a great load had been taken from it, when I think that we are turning our backs on this accursed and detested system. I really don't think I could have borne it any longer. It is all very well to say 'be silent on the subject:' They won't let you be silent. They *will* ask you what you think of it; and *will* expatiate on slavery as if it were one of the greatest blessings of mankind. 'It's not,' said a hard, bad-looking fellow to me the other day, 'it's not the interest of a man to use his slaves ill. It's damned nonsense that you hear in England.' – I told him quietly that it was not a man's interest to get drunk, or to steal, or to game, or to indulge in any other vice, but he *did* indulge in it for all that. That cruelty, and the abuse of irresponsible power, were two of the bad passions of human nature, with the gratification of which, considerations of interest or of ruin had nothing whatever to do; and that, while every candid man must admit that even a slave might be happy enough with a good master, all human beings knew that bad masters, cruel masters who disgraced the form they bore, were matters of experience and history, whose existence was as undisputed as that of slaves themselves. He was a little taken aback by this, and asked me if I believed in the Bible. Yes, I said, but if any man could prove to me that it sanctioned slavery, I would place no further credence in it. 'Well, then,' he said, 'by God, sir, the niggers must be kept down, and the whites have put down the coloured people wherever they have found them.' 'That's the whole question,' said I. 'Yes, and by God,' says he, 'the British had better not stand out on that point when Lord Ashburton comes over, for I never felt so warlike as I do now, – and that's a fact.' I was obliged to accept a public supper in this Richmond, and I saw plainly enough, there, that the hatred which these Southern States bear to us as a nation has been fanned up and revived again by this Creole business, and can scarcely be exaggerated .... We were desperately tired at Richmond, as we went to a great many places, and received a very great number of visitors. We appoint usually two hours in every day for this latter purpose, and have our room so full at that period that it is difficult to move or breathe. Before we left Richmond, a gentleman told me, when I really was so exhausted that I could hardly stand, that 'three people of great fashion' were much offended by having been told, when they called last evening, that I was tired and not visible, then, but would be 'at home' from twelve to two next day! Another gentleman (no doubt of great fashion also) sent a letter to me two hours after I had gone to bed preparatory to rising at four next morning, with instructions to the slave who brought it to knock me up and wait for an answer!

TO MISS COUTTS

Baltimore, United States
March 22nd, 1842

And yet I have not forgotten the book you asked me to bring home for you – nor the pebble I am to gather for Lady Burdett at Niagara – nor the something unstipulated which I am to put in my portmanteau for Miss Meredith. The truth is that they give me everything here, but Time. That they never will leave me alone. That I shake hands every day when I am not travelling, with five or six hundred people. That Mrs Dickens and I hold a formal Levee in every town we come to, and usually faint away (from fatigue) every day while dressing for dinner – In a word, that we devoutly long for Home, and look forward to the seventh of next June when we sail, please God, from New York – most ardently.

TO W. C. MACREADY

Baltimore
Twenty-Second March 1842

Are you quite sure, Mr Macready – and I address myself to you with the sternness of a man in the pit – are you quite sure, sir, that you do not view America through the pleasant mirage which often surrounds a thing that has been, but not a thing that is? Are you quite sure that when you were here you relished it as well as you do now when you look back upon it. The early spring birds, Mr Macready, *do* sing in the groves that you were, very often, not over well pleased with many of the new country's social aspects. Are the birds to be trusted? Again I pause for a reply.

My dear Macready, I desire to be so honest and just to those who have so enthusiastically and earnestly welcomed me, that I burned that last letter I wrote to you – even to you to whom I would speak as to myself – rather than let it come with anything that might seem like an ill-considered word of disappointment. I preferred that you should think me neglectful (if you could imagine anything so wild) rather than I should do wrong in this respect. Still it is of no use. I *am* disappointed. This is not the republic I came to see; this is not the republic of my imagination. I infinitely prefer a liberal monarchy – even with its sickening accompaniments of court circulars – to such a government as this. The more I think of its use and strength, the poorer and more trifling in a thousand aspects it appears in my eyes. In everything of which it has made a boast – excepting its education of the people and its care for poor children – it sinks immeasurably below the level I had placed it upon; and England, even England, bad and faulty as the old land is, and miserable as millions of her people are, rises in the comparison.

You live here, Macready, as I have sometimes heard you imagining! *You!* Loving you with all my heart and soul, and knowing what your disposition really is, I would not condemn you to a year's residence on this side of the Atlantic for any money. Freedom of opinion! Where is it? I see a press more mean, and paltry, and silly, and disgraceful than any country I ever knew. If that is its standard, here it is. But I speak of Bancroft, and am advised to be silent on that subject, for he is 'a black sheep – a Democrat.' I speak of Bryant, and am entreated to be more careful, for the same reason. I speak of international copyright, and am implored not to ruin myself outright. I speak of Miss Martineau, and all parties – Slave Upholders and Abolitionists, Whigs, Tyler Whigs, and Democrats, shower down upon me a perfect cataract of abuse. 'But what has she done? Surely she praised America enough!' 'Yes, but she told us of some of our faults, and Americans can't bear to be told of their faults. Don't split on that rock, Mr Dickens, don't write about America; we are so very suspicious.'

Freedom of opinion! Macready, if I had been born here and had written my books in this country, producing them with no stamp of approval from any other land, it is my solemn belief that I should have lived and died poor, unnoticed, and a 'black sheep' to boot. I never was more convinced of anything than I am of that.

The people are affectionate, generous, open-hearted, hospitable, enthusiastic, good-humoured, polite to women, frank and candid to all strangers, anxious to oblige, far less prejudiced than they have been described to be, frequently polished and refined, very seldom rude or disagreeable. I have made a great many friends here, even in public conveyances, whom I have been truly sorry to part from. In the towns I have formed perfect attachments. I have seen none of that greediness and indecorousness on which travellers have laid so much emphasis. I have returned frankness with frankness; met questions not intended to be rude, with answers meant to be satisfactory; and have not spoken to one man, woman, or child of any degree who has not grown positively affectionate before we parted. In the respects of not being left alone, and of being horribly disgusted by tobacco chewing and tobacco spittle, I have suffered considerably. The sight of slavery in Virginia, the hatred of British feeling upon the subject, and miserable hints of the impotent indignation of the South, have pained me very much! on the last head, of course, I have felt nothing but a mingled pity and amusement; on the other, sheer distress. But however much I like the ingredients of this great dish, I cannot but come back to the point upon which I started, and say that the dish itself goes against the grain with me, and that I don't like it.

You know that I am truly a Liberal. I believe I have as little pride as most men, and I am conscious of not the smallest annoyance from being 'hail fellow well met' with everybody. I have not had greater pleasure in the company of any set of men among the thousands I have received than in that of the carmen of Hartford, who presented themselves in a body in their blue frocks, among a crowd of well-dressed ladies and gentlemen, and bade me welcome through their spokesman. They had all read my books, and all perfectly understood them. It is not these things I have in my mind when I say that the man who comes to this country a Radical and goes home again with his opinions unchanged, must be a Radical on reason, sympathy, and reflection, and one who has so well considered the subject that he has no chance of wavering.

TO JOHN FORSTER

> On Board the Canal Boat, Going to Pittsburgh
> Monday, March Twenty-Eighth, 1842

And now I come to the Canal Boat. Bless your heart and soul, my dear fellow, – if you could only see us on board the canal boat! Let me think, for a moment, at what time of the day or night I should best like you to see us. In the morning? Between five and six in the morning, shall I say? Well! you *would* like to see me, standing on the deck, fishing the dirty water out of the canal with a tin ladle chained to the boat by a long chain; pouring the same into a tin-basin (also chained up in like manner); and scrubbing my face with the jack towel. At night, shall I say? I don't know that you *would* like to look into the cabin at night, only to see me lying on a temporary shelf exactly the width of this sheet of paper when it's open (*I measured it this morning*), with one man above me, and another below; and, in all, eight and twenty in a low cabin, which you can't stand upright in with your hat on. I don't think you would like to look in at breakfast time either, for then these shelves have only just been taken down and put away, and the atmosphere of the place is, as you may suppose, by no means fresh; though there *are* upon the table tea and coffee, and bread and butter, and salmon, and shad, and liver, and steak, and potatoes, and pickles, and ham, and pudding, and sausages; and three and thirty people sitting round it, eating and drinking; and savoury bottles of gin, and whiskey, and brandy, and rum, in the bar hard by; and seven and twenty out of the eight and twenty men, in foul linen, with yellow streams from half-chewed tobacco trickling down their chins. Perhaps the best time for you to take a peep would be the present: eleven o'clock in the fore-noon: when the barber is at his shaving, and the gentlemen are lounging about the stove waiting for their turns, and not more than seventeen are spitting in concert, and two or three are walking overhead (lying down on the luggage every time the man at the helm calls 'Bridge!'), and I am writing this in the ladies'-cabin, which is a part of the gentle-men's, and only screened off by a red curtain. Indeed it exactly resembles the dwarf's private apartment in a caravan at a fair; and the gentlemen, generally, represent the spectators at a penny-a-head. The place is just as clean and just as large as that caravan you and I were in at Greenwich-fair last past. Outside, it is exactly like any canal-boat you have seen near the Regent's-park, or elsewhere.

You never can conceive what the hawking and spitting is, the whole night through. Last night was the worst. *Upon my honor and word* I was obliged, this morning, to lay my fur-coat on the deck, and wipe the half dried flakes of spittle from it with my handkerchief: and the only surprise seemed to be, that I should consider it necessary to do so. When I turned in last night, I put it on a stool beside me, and there it lay, under a cross fire from five men – three opposite; one above; and one below. I make no complaints, and shew no disgust. I am looked upon as highly facetious at night, for I crack jokes with everybody near me until we fall asleep. I am considered very hardy in the morning, for I run up, bare-necked, and plunge my head into the half-frozen water, by half-past five o' clock. I am respected for my activity, inas-much as I jump from the boat to the towing-path, and walk five or six miles before breakfast; keeping up with the horses all the time. In a word, they are quite astonished to find a sedentary Englishman rough-ing it so well, and taking so much exercise; and question me very much on that head. The greater part of the men will sit and shiver round the stove all day; rather than put one foot before the other. As to having a window open, that's not to be thought of.

The scenery, before you reach the mountains, and when you are on them, and after you have left them, is very fine and grand; and the canal winds its way through some deep, sullen gorges, which, seen by moon-light, are very impressive: though immeasurably inferior to Glencoe, to whose terrors I have not seen the smallest *approach*. We have passed, both in the mountains and elsewhere, a great number of new settle-ments, and detached log-houses. Their utterly forlorn and miserable appearance baffles all description. I have not seen six cabins out of six hundred, where the windows have been whole. Old hats, old clothes, old boards, old fragments of blanket and paper, are stuffed into the broken glass; and their air is misery and desolation. It pains the eye to see the stumps of great trees thickly strewed in every field of wheat; and never to lose the eternal swamp and dull morass, with hundreds of rotten trunks, of elm and pine and sycamore and logwood, steeped in its unwholesome water; where the frogs so croak at night that after dark there is an incessant sound as if millions of phantom teams, with bells, were travelling through the upper air, at an enormous distance off. It is quite an oppressive circumstance, too, to *come* upon great tracks, where settlers have been burning down the trees; and where their wounded bodies lie about, like those of murdered creatures; while here and there some charred and blackened giant rears two bare arms aloft, and seems to curse his enemies.

15th April

The last 200 miles of the voyage from Cincinnati to St Louis are upon the Mississippi, for you come down the Ohio to its mouth. It is well for society that this Mississippi, the renowned Father of Waters, had no children who take after him. It is the beastliest river in the world. . . .

Conceive the pleasure of rushing down this stream by night (as we did last night) at the rate of fifteen miles an hour; striking against floating blocks of timber every instant; and dreading some infernal blow at every bump. The helmsman in these boats is in a little glasshouse upon the roof. In the Mississippi, another man stands in the very head of the vessel, listening and watching intently; listening, because they can tell in dark nights by the noise when any great obstruction is at hand. This man holds the rope of a large bell which hangs close to the wheel-house, and whenever he pulls it, the engine is to stop directly, and not to stir until he rings again. Last night, this bell rang at least once in every five minutes; and at each alarm there was a concussion which nearly flung one out of bed. . . . While I have been writing this account, we have shot out of that hideous river, thanks be to God; never to see it again, I hope, but in a nightmare. We are now on the smooth Ohio, and the change is like the transition from pain to perfect ease.

We had a very crowded levee in St Louis. Of course the paper had an account of it. If I were to drop a letter in the street, it would be in the newspaper next day, and nobody would think its publication an outrage. The editor objected to my hair, as not curling sufficiently. He admitted an eye; but objected again to dress, as being somewhat foppish, 'and indeed perhaps rather flash. – But such,' he benevolently adds, 'are the differences between American and English taste – rendered more apparent, perhaps, by all the other gentlemen present being dressed in black.' Oh, that you could have seen the other gentlemen! ...

A St Louis lady complimented Kate upon her voice and manner of speaking, assuring her that she should never have suspected her of being Scotch, or even English. She was so obliging as to add that she would have taken her for an American, anywhere: which she (Kate) was no doubt aware was a very great compliment, as the Americans were admitted on all hands to have greatly refined upon the English language! I need not tell you that out of Boston and New York a nasal drawl is universal, but I may as well hint that the prevailing grammar is also more than doubtful; that the oddest vulgarisms are received idioms; that all the women who have been bred in slave-states speak more or less like negroes, from having been constantly in their childhood with black nurses; and that the most fashionable and aristocratic (these are two words in great use), instead of asking you in what place you were born, enquire where you 'hail from!!'

Lord Ashburton arrived at Annapolis t'other day, after a voyage of forty odd days in heavy weather. Straightway the newspapers state, on the authority of a correspondent who 'rowed round the ship' (I leave you to fancy her condition), that America need fear no superiority from England, in respect of her wooden walls. The same correspondent is 'quite pleased' with the frank manner of the English officers; and patronizes them as being, for John Bulls, quite refined. My face, like Haji Baba's, turns upside down, and my liver is changed to water, when I come upon such things, and think who writes and who reads them. ...

They won't let me alone about slavery. A certain Judge in St Louis went so far yesterday, that I fell upon him (to the indescribable horror of the man who brought him) and told him a piece of my mind. I said that I was very averse to speaking on the subject here, and always forbore, if possible: but when he pitied our national ignorance of the truths of slavery, I must remind him that we went upon indisputable records, obtained after many years of careful investigation, and at all sorts of self-sacrifice; and that I believed we were much more competent to judge of its atrocity and horror, than he who had been brought up in the midst of it. I told him that I could sympathise with men who admitted it to be a dreadful evil, but frankly confessed their inability to devise a means of getting rid of it: but that men who spoke of it as a blessing, as a matter of course, as a state of things to be desired, were out of the pale of reason; and that for them to speak of ignorance or prejudice was an absurdity too ridiculous to be combated. ...

It is not six years ago, since a slave in this very same St Louis, being arrested (I forget for what), and knowing he had no chance of a fair trial be his offence what it might, drew his bowie knife and ripped the constable across the body. A scuffle ensuing, the desperate negro stabbed two others with the same weapon. The mob who gathered round (among whom were men of mark, wealth, and influence in the place) overpowered him by numbers; carried him away to a piece of open ground beyond the city; *and burned him alive*. This, I say, was done within six years in broad day; in a city with its courts, lawyers, tip-staffs, judges, jails, and hangman; and not a hair on the head of one of those men has been hurt to this day. And it is, believe me, it is the miserable, wretched independence in small things; the paltry republic-anism which recoils from honest service to an honest man, but does not shrink from every trick, artifice, and knavery in business; that makes these slaves necessary, and will render them so, until the indigna-tion of other countries sets them free.

They say the slaves are fond of their masters. Look at this pretty vignette (part of the stock-in-trade of a newspaper), and judge how you would feel, when men, looking in your face, told you such tales with the newspaper lying on the table. In all the slave districts, adver-tisements for runaways are as much matters of course as the announce-ment of the play for the evening with us. The poor creatures themselves fairly worship English people: they would do anything for them. They are perfectly acquainted with all that takes place in reference to emanci-pation; and *of course* their attachment to us grows out of their deep devotion to their owners. I cut this illustration out of a newspaper which had a leader in reference to *the abominable and hellish doctrine of Abolition – repugnant alike to every law of God and Nature*. 'I know something,' said a Dr Bartlett (a very accomplished man), late a fellow-passenger of ours: 'I know something of their fondness for their masters. I live in Kentucky; and I can assert upon my honour, that, in my neighbourhood, it is as common for a runaway slave, retaken, to draw his bowie knife and rip his owner's bowels open, as it is for you to see a drunken fight in London.'

Same Boat
Saturday, Sixteenth April, 1842

Now, a prairie is undoubtedly worth seeing – but more that one may say one has seen it, than for any sublimity it possesses in itself. Like most things, great or small, in this country, you hear of it with considerable exaggerations. Basil Hall was really quite right in depre-ciating the general character of the scenery. The widely-famed Far West is not to be compared with even the tamest portions of Scotland or Wales. You stand upon the prairie, and see the unbroken horizon all round you. You are on a great plain, which is like a sea without water. I am exceedingly fond of wild and lonely scenery, and believe that I have the faculty of being as much impressed by it as any man living. But the prairie fell, by far, short of my preconceived idea. I felt no such emotions as I do in crossing Salisbury Plain. The excessive flatness of the scene makes it dreary, but tame. Grandeur is certainly not its characteristic. I retired from the rest of the party, to understand my own feelings the better; and looked all round, again and again. It was fine. It was worth the ride. The sun was going down, very red and bright; and the prospect looked like that ruddy sketch of Catlin's, which attracted our attention (you remember?); except that there was not so much ground as he represents, between the spectator and the horizon. But to say (as the fashion is, here) that the sight is a landmark in one's existence, and awakens a new set of sensations, is sheer gammon. I would say to every man who can't see a prairie – go to Salisbury plain, Marlborough downs, or any of the broad, high, open lands near the sea. Many of them are fully as impressive; and Salisbury plain is *decidedly* more so.

26th April 1842

We lay all Sunday night, at a town (and a beautiful town too) called Cleveland; on Lake Erie. The people poured on board, in crowds, by six on Monday morning, to see me; and a party of 'gentlemen' actually .planted themselves before our little cabin, and stared in at the door and windows *while I was washing, and Kate lay in bed.* I was so incensed at this, and at a certain newspaper published in that town which I had accidentally seen in Sandusky (advocating war with England to the death, saying that Britain must be 'whipped again,' and promising all true Americans that within two years they should sing Yankee-doodle in Hyde-park and Hail Columbia in the courts of Westminster), that when the major came on board to present himself to me, according to custom, I refused to see him, and bade Mr Q tell him why and where-fore. His honour took it very coolly, and retired to the top of the wharf, with a big stick and a whittling knife, with which he worked so lustily (staring at the closed door of our cabin all the time) that long before the boat left the big stick was no bigger than a cribbage peg!

I do perceive a perplexingly divided and subdivided duty, in the matter of the book of travels. Oh! the sublimated essence of comicality that I *could* distil, from the materials I have! . . .

TO JOHN FORSTER

Niagara Falls
Tuesday, Third May, 1842

... I'll tell you what the two obstacles to the passing of an international copyright law with England, are: firstly, the national love of
'doing' a man in any bargain or matter of business; secondly, the
national vanity. Both these characteristics prevail to an extent which no
stranger can possibly estimate.

With regard to the first, I seriously believe that it is an essential part
of the pleasure derived from the perusal of a popular English book,
that the author gets nothing for it. It is so dar-nation 'cute – so knowing
in Jonathan to get his reading on those terms. He has the Englishman
so regularly on the hip that his eye twinkles with slyness, cunning, and
delight; and he chuckles over the humour of the page with an appreciation of it, quite inconsistent with, and apart from, its honest
purchase. The raven hasn't more joy in eating a stolen piece of meat,
than the American has in reading the English book which he gets for
nothing.

With regard to the second, it reconciles that better and more elevated
class who are above this sort of satisfaction, with surprising ease. The
man's read in America! The Americans like him! They are glad to see
him when he comes here! They flock about him, and tell him that they
are grateful to him for spirits in sickness; for many hours of delight in
health; for a hundred fanciful associations which are constantly interchanged between themselves and their wives and children at home! It
is nothing that all this takes place in countries where he is *paid*: it is
nothing that he has won fame for himself elsewhere, and profit too. The
Americans read him; the free, enlightened, independent Americans;
and what more *would* he have? Here's reward enough for any man.
The national vanity swallows up all other countries on the face of the
earth, and leaves but this above the ocean. Now, mark what the real
value of this American reading is. Find me in the whole range of literature one single solitary English book which becomes popular with them,
before it has forced itself on their attention by going through the ordeal
at home and becoming popular there – and I am content that the law
should remain as it is, for ever and a day. I must make one exception.
There *are* some mawkish tales of fashionable life before which crowds
fall down as if they were gilded calves, which at home have been snugly
enshrined in circulating libraries from the date of their publication.

As to telling them they will have no literature of their own, the universal answer (out of Boston) is, 'We don't want one. Why should we
pay for one when we can get it for nothing? Our people don't think of
poetry, sir. Dollars, banks, and cotton are *our* books, sir.' And they

certainly are in one sense; for a lower average of general information than exists in this country on all other topics, it would be very hard to find.

TO JOHN FORSTER

Rasco's Hotel, Montreal, Canada
Twenty-Sixth of May 1842

I have hardly spoken of our letters, which reached us yesterday, shortly before the play began. A hundred thousand thanks for your delightful mainsail of that gallant little packet. I read it again and again; and had it all over again at breakfast time this morning. I heard also, by the same ship, from Talfourd, Miss Coutts, Brougham, Rogers, and others. A delicious letter from Mac too, as good as his painting I swear. Give my hearty love to him. . . . God bless you, my dear friend. As the time draws nearer, we get FEVERED with anxiety for home. . . . Kiss our darlings for us. We shall soon meet, please God, and be happier and merrier than ever we were, in all our lives. . . . Oh home-home-home-home-home-home-home-HOME!!!!!!!!!!! . . .

TO H. P. SMITH

Devonshire Terrace
Thursday, Fourteenth July, 1842

Next time I come into the City I will show you my introductory chapter to the American book. It may seem to prepare the reader for a much greater amount of slaughter than he will meet with; but it is honest and true.

TO JOHN FORSTER

Broadstairs
14th September 1842

. . . I have pleased myself very much to-day in the matter of Niagara. I have made the description very brief (as it should be), but I fancy it is good. I am beginning to think over the introductory chapter, and it has meanwhile occurred to me that I should like, at the beginning of the volumes, to put what follows on a blank page. *I dedicate this Book to those friends of mine in America, who, loving their country, can bear the truth, when it is written good humouredly and in a kind spirit.* What do you think? Do you see any objection? . . .

TO PHILIP HONE

Broadstairs, Kent, England
Sixteen September 1842

The letter to which you refer is, from beginning to end, in every word and syllable, the cross of every *t* and dot of every *i*, a most wicked and nefarious forgery. I have never published one word or line in reference to America in any quarter, except the copyright circular, and the unhung scoundrel who invented that astounding lie knew this as well as I do. It has caused me more pain, and more of a vague desire to take somebody by the throat, than such an event should perhaps have awakened in an honourable man. But I have not contradicted it publicly, deeming that it would not become my character or elevate me in my own self-respect to do so.

TO MRS HENRY BURNETT

October 1842

I don't think it probable that I shall have a copy of my American book until Tuesday. On Tuesday night, I shall send you, by the mail train, a parcel containing its two volumes, and Barnaby. The orders for it from the Trade already, are much larger than have ever been known since Scott's time – taking off 3000 copies in two days, a week before its publication.

TO JONATHAN CHAPMAN

Devonshire Terrace
October Fifteenth, 1842

In lieu of the American people (or the most among them) as a mass, consider them for a moment, as a man. If you could only retain the friendship of an individual by the sacrifice of everything which elevates you in your own respect – by fearing to speak the truth – by keeping a timid silence – by debating within yourself at every turn, as though he were a sick relation, 'Will he take this? Will he be angry if I say that? Will he find out that I am not a toy for his amusement, if I do the other?' Would you seek to hold it for a day? If I know you, no. Neither would I. And because I claim to have been kindly received in America by reason of something I had done to amuse its people and prepossess them in my favour; and not with reference to something I was not to do; therefore I write about its people, and write freely. And as I have never been deterred by hopes of approbation or visions of greatness, from pointing out abuses at home, so no amount of popular breath shall blow me from my purpose, if I see fit to point out what, in my judgment, are abuses abroad, and if my being an honest man bring down caprice and weather-cock fickleness and the falsest kind of insult on my head, what matters it to me – or to you – or to any man who is worth the name and being right, can look down on the crowd, and whistle while they hiss?

What is to prevent my writing, the certainty of not pleasing them?

How does the certainty appear? By every claim I have upon them being disregarded and cast ruthlessly aside, at the printed bidding of some abandoned fellow; and aspersions being freely believed which make me out a lying adventurer.

My dear Chapman, if we yielded to such reasons or such men as these, in five years' time there would be no such thing as truth in the world: and from that hour downward, her cause would be a hopeless, desperate venture.

I am well convinced that in your heart of hearts you think and feel with me. I am well convinced that there is not in my book one solitary line in which you and such as you will not most thoroughly concur.

I dispassionately believe that in the slow fulness of time, what I have written will have some effect of purging your community of evils which threaten its very existence, and I know that it is written kindly and good humouredly: and that I have never for an instant suffered myself to be betrayed with a false or unfair expression, or one I shall at any time regret.

Believe me, my dear friend, the fact is literally so, and that you will find it so to your entire contentment, and when you meet with evidences of a change in the popular opinion towards me, it is not enough to say within yourself. 'If he had not brought about that change himself, he would not be the man who was my friend, but would be some other fellow whom I could hear dispraised with supreme indifference!'

TO LEA AND BLANCHARD

1 Devonshire Terrace, York Gate
Regent's Park
Twenty-Eighth December, 1842

Dear Sirs, – Rest assured that if any personal or private feeling were intermixed with the resolution at which I arrived when I came home in reference to American republications of my books, it would have great weight in your favour. I formed it on principle. Disgusted with the infamous state of the Law in respect of copyright, and confirmed in the opinion I have always held that there is no reasonable ray of hope of its being changed for many years to come, I determined that, so far as I was concerned, the American people should have the full pride, honour, glory and profit of it, that I would be no party to its invasion, and that I would have nothing blown to me by a side wind, which the dishonest breath of the popular legislature withheld.

I hope that the more you see of this plunder and the dirty hands into which it goes, the more you will feel and advocate the necessity of a change. –

TO C. C. FELTON

> *1 Devonshire Terrace, York Gate*
> *Regent's Park, London*
> *Thirty-first December, 1842*

The American book (to begin with that) has been a most complete
and thorough-going success. Four large editions have now been sold
and paid for, and it has won golden opinions from all sorts of men,
except our friend in F—, who is a miserable creature; a disappointed
man in great poverty, to whom I have ever been most kind and considerate (I need scarcely say that); and another friend in B—, no less a
person than an illustrious gentleman named —, who wrote a story
called —. They have done no harm, and have fallen short of their
mark, which, of course, was to annoy me. Now I am perfectly free
from any diseased curiosity in such respects, and whenever I hear of a
notice of this kind, I never read it; whereby I always conceive (don't
you?) that I get the victory. With regard to your slave-owners, they
may cry, till they are as black in the face as their own slaves, that
Dickens lies. Dickens does not write for their satisfaction, and Dickens
will not explain for their comfort. Dickens has the name and date of
every newspaper in which every one of those advertisements appeared,
as they know perfectly well; but Dickens does not choose to give
them, and will not at any time between this and the day of judgment. . . .

APPENDIX 3

A Note on the Reception of American Notes

JAMES GORDON BENNETT, editor of the *New York Herald*, upon reading *American Notes*, immediately nominated Dickens as the most warped of all British visitors: 'the most trashy ... the most contemptible ... the essence of balderdash, reduced to the last drop of silliness and inanity.'[1]

This quotation gives a clear, if extreme, example of the vituperative comment which greeted the book in America. A notable exception was an article in the *North American Review* for January, 1843: '... the favourite of two hemispheres can neither be benefited nor harmed by anything the literary journals can say of him.'[2] The reviewer eulogises to a surprising degree upon Dickens's merits and takes other journalists to task for their sniping. On the whole he supports the novelist's attacks on the state of the American press. The book occasioned little adverse comment among Dickens's friends in the United States. Emerson did not like it, but Felton assured Dickens that 'we agree pretty well here, in thinking it a capital book; lively, spirited, true and good-humored,'[3] and Longfellow was greatly moved by the comments on the barbarities of the slave-system.

If he might have expected the American reaction, Dickens was certainly upset by that in his own country. The comparative commercial success of the book was a relief but many of his closest friends gave it, at best, a lukewarm reception. Macready, who thought Dickens erroneous in some of his judgments of America, wrote in his diary: '... called on Dickens, who gave me his introductory chapter to his book on America. I do not like it.'[4]

1. Quoted in Edgar Johnson, *Charles Dickens: His Tragedy and Triumph* (London, 1953), vol. 1, p. 442.
2. *North American Review*, January 1843, p. 215.
3. Johnson, op. cit., p. 441.
4. W. C. Macready, *Diaries*, ed. W. Toynbee (London, 1912), vol. 2, p. 181.

Rogers and Lever disliked the book, Maclise was uneasy and
Forster's brief dismissal of it in his *Life*, though giving it all praise,
is sufficient to arouse suspicion.[5] Macauley, asked to review the
book for the *Edinburgh Review*, refused: '. . . I pronounce the book,
in spite of some gleams of genius, at once frivolous and dull:'[6]
and Dr Howe wrote to Charles Sumner: 'Dickens has lost ground
here I think, very much, not with regard to Americans only (they
are all very mad) but I think with the English.'[7]

The periodicals, particularly those with a Tory bias, damned it.
The *Monthly Review* was of the opinion that it contained 'absolutely
nothing that can be called the result of mature reflection and of
deep penetration';[8] the *Athenaeum* felt it to be '. . . more offensive
to our Transatlantic cousins than any previous charge brought
against their institutions or social habits, by traveller gentle or
simple:'[9] and the *Quarterly Review* wondered bitterly whether
'Mr Dickens' book might not counterbalance all the good that
had been done by Lord Ashburton's mission.'[10] The last-named
journal characterized the work as being insipid precisely because
Dickens did not wish to offend any of his American friends;
attributed much of what the author had said to 'arrogant selfish-
ness'[11] and rated the book as totally inferior to the books of Hall,
Hamilton and Mrs Trollope.

Spedding, in the *Edinburgh Review*, explained that: 'Even his
habits as a writer of fiction must have been against him; for such a
man will always be tempted to study society, with a view to gathering suggestions and materials for his creative faculty to work upon,
rather than simply to consider and understand it:' and made the
further important point that Dickens was mostly on the move and
so could only have obtained his impressions from the American

5. J. Forster, *The Life of Charles Dickens* (London, 1904), vol. 1, pp. 307–8.
Forster merely agrees with Jeffrey's judgement of the book as a 'faithful,
graphic, amusing, kind-hearted narrative.'

6. Quoted in Ada B. Nisbet, 'The Mystery of *Martin Chuzzlewit*', *Essays
Critical and Historical Dedicated to Lily B. Campbell* (Berkeley and Los
Angles, 1950), p. 209.

7. ibid., pp. 212–13.

8. ibid., p. 211.

9. *Athenaeum*, 1842, p. 929.

10. *Quarterly Review*, vol. 71, March 1843, p. 505.

11. ibid.

people with whom he travelled, 'a class of persons whose manners must, in all countries, be far below the average.'[12]

This wholesale adverse comment hurt Dickens. He could huffily write to the Reverend Edward Taylor that he was determined not to read any American paper or periodical containing allusions to himself,[13] but this was much nearer home, something he could not ignore, and it was a sickening blow to his morale.[14]

12. *Edinburgh Review*, vol. 76, January 1843, pp. 500–507.

13. *The Letters of Charles Dickens*, ed. W. Dexter (London, 1938), vol. 1, p. 597. This letter is dated 29 March 1844.

14. For further information on this, see George H. Ford, *Dickens and his Readers* (Princeton, 1955).

NOTES

TITLE: Dickens anticipated the pirating of *American Notes for General Circulation* by American publishers. His title alludes to this ironic expectation by punning on the current practice of forging paper currency. To make the point even more clear he intended to use a quotation from a recent trial as an epigraph, or 'motto', for the book:

> In reply to a question from the Bench, the Solicitor for the Bank observed, that this kind of notes circulated the most extensively, in those parts of the world where they were stolen and forged. – *Old Bailey Report*.

John Forster, Dickens's friend and biographer, adds, 'The motto was omitted, objection being made to it' (John Forster, *The Life of Charles Dickens* [London, 1904], vol. I, 303).

CHAPTER I

1. (p. 54) *Mr Robins:* George Henry Robins (1778–1847) was an auctioneer famous for writing his own high-flown advertisements for property. In 1842 he was commissioned to dispose of the contents of Strawberry Hill.

2. (p. 54) *one of our friends:* presumably Forster, who helped Dickens to work out details of the trip and who accompanied the novelist and his wife to Liverpool in order to see them off.

3. (p. 57) *the Adelphi Hotel:* in Ranelagh Street, opened by Mr Radley in 1826. It occupied the northern house of a terrace which it gradually took over. J. A. Picton (*Memories of Liverpool*, 1875) says of Mr Radley:

> Polite and easy in his manners, gifted with a nice tact which enabled him to adapt himself to every situation, and endowed with a rare talent for organisation, he soon rendered his house the most popular hotel in Liverpool, and extended its fame far and wide.

4. (p. 59) *Lord Burleigh in his nod:* William Cecil, Lord Burleigh (1520–98), chief minister of Elizabeth I, appears in Sheridan's play, *The Critic*, where, in Puff's tragedy, preoccupied by affairs of the state, he enters, shakes his head and exits. Puff gives a long explanation of the meaning of this shake which has given rise to the expression 'Burleigh's nod'.

5. (p. 59) *the poor President went down:* The steamship *President* sank with all hands in mid-Atlantic in 1840.

6. (p.60) *the very man he ought to be:* On January 29, one week after arriving in Boston, a committee of passengers, with Lord Mulgrave

as chairman and Dickens as treasurer, presented Captain Hewett of the *Britannia* with a piece of inscribed plate as a token of their appreciation of his cool and brave actions during a terrible crossing.

CHAPTER 2

1. (p.63) *summerset:* A now archaic form of 'somersault'.
2. (p. 64) *Mr Willet ... Chigwell:* In Dickens's novel, *Barnaby Rudge* (1841), John Willet, father of one of the novel's heroes, Joe, is landlord of the 'Maypole' at Chigwell. During the Gordon Riots a mob, led by Hugh and Dennis, breaks into his inn, wrecks it, considers hanging old John and finally leaves him tied up. This renders him partially mad.
3. (p. 70) *Vingt-et-un:* a card game, now known as Pontoon or Blackjack.
4. (p. 70) *all the cabins are leaky:* Without doubt Dickens and his wife had the bad luck to participate in one of the worst Atlantic crossings for many years. Years later Thackeray, who could not believe the descriptions in *American Notes*, was assured by a former officer of the *Britannia* that it was the worst crossing he had known; and Captain Hewett admitted to Forster that only a really strong ship could have survived such conditions.
5. (p. 71) *some error ... the cause:* The 'sudden fog' presumably accounts for the navigational error. A large ship should take the main passage into Halifax Harbour, that lying westward of Macnab Island. The eastern passage, a narrow channel between Lawlor and Macnab Islands, westward, and the mainland eastward, has a depth, on the bar, of only 10 feet and thus is suitable only for small vessels.
6. (p. 72) *Elysium:* in Greek mythology, a place where the souls of the virtuous enjoy complete happiness.
7. (p. 72) *The governor:* Lord Falkland (1803–84) was governor of Nova Scotia from 1840 to 1846.
8. (p. 73) *a melodrama at Astley's:* Philip Astley (1742–1814), a great horseman, founded nineteen equestrian theatres, including Astley's Royal Amphitheatre in London, which is referred to here. Dickens loved this circus. One of the more affectionate of the *Sketches by Boz* (1833–6) describes the scene there and in *The Old Curiosity Shop* (1840–41) Kit Nubbles and his family enjoy its magic:

> ... the vague smell of horses suggestive of coming wonders; the curtain that hid such gorgeous mysteries; the clean white sawdust down in the circus; the company coming in and taking their places; the fiddlers looking carelessly up at them while they tuned their instruments, as if they didn't want the play to begin, and knew it all beforehand! [Ch. 39]

9. (p. 73) *telegraphed at Boston:* i.e., news of the *Britannia*'s imminent arrival was sent to Boston by telegraph.

10. (p. 74) *newsmen:* newspaper-sellers.

11. (p. 74) *they were Editors:* Editors were, for Dickens, emblems of the appalling immaturity of the American Press. They are castigated in *Martin Chuzzlewit* (1843–4) in the characters of Colonel Diver and Jefferson Brick. As a matter of fact, the men who boarded the *Britannia* were reporters, not editors.

12. (p. 74) *Mr T. P. Cooke:* Thomas Potter Cooke (1786–1864) joined the Navy at the age of ten and saw action in the defeat of the Spanish fleet off Cape St Vincent in 1797. He left the Navy in 1802 and became an actor, making his name in broadly melodramatic parts. Two of his most famous parts were those of sailors: Long Tom Coffin in Fitzball's version of James Fenimore Cooper's *The Pilot*, which he played 562 times, and William in Douglas Jerrold's *Black-Eyed Susan*, which he played 785 times. According to Clement Scott (*The Drama of Yesterday and Today* [1899]) he was 'the best representative of the British sailor ever seen on the stage'.

13. (p. 74) *Right away:* this phrase may have originally come from an English dialect. The British traveller, Henry Fearon, recorded it in the United States in 1818 and by the late nineteenth century it had become a colloquial term in England, too.

14. (p. 74) *the Tremont House:* This four-storey hotel, built in 1828 with a Grecian portico, did not impress Dickens as much as this account would suggest. In a letter to Forster (see p. 303) he complained of the heat in the hotel and of the lack of curtains. The Tremont House was considered by Americans as one of the best hotels in the country at this time.

CHAPTER 3

1. (p. 75) *Dr Channing:* William Ellery Channing (1780–1842) was pastor of the Federal Street Church in Boston (1803–42). His *The Moral Argument against Calvinism* (1820) made him a leading spokesman for the Unitarians and his detestation of dogma and belief in man's perfectibility paved the way for Transcendentalism. He wrote a number of anti-slavery pamphlets. His nephews, William Henry Channing (1810–84) and William Ellery Channing (1818–1901) were famous Transcendentalists (see below notes 14 and 16) and men of letters.

2. (p. 76) *Harlequin and Columbine:* Characters from Italian comedy who were transferred to English pantomime. In the Italian plays Harlequin (*arlecchino*) was a mixture of ignorance and grace who

was always in trouble. In the English versions he was frequently a mute figure, invisible to the clown and the pantaloon (the foolish old man). In either case he was usually in love with the pantaloon's daughter, Columbine.

3. (p. 77) *University of Cambridge:* Harvard University, Cambridge, Massachusetts: the oldest institution of higher learning in the United States. Founded in 1636, it opened in 1638 and its first class graduated in 1642.

4. (p. 78) *Doctors' Commons:* a name originally given to the table and dining-hall of the College of Doctors of Civil Law in London (near St Paul's). The society was formed in 1509, dissolved in 1858 and its buildings demolished in 1867. In one of the *Sketches by Boz*, Dickens described it with reasonable accuracy as: 'the place where they grant marriage licences to love-sick couples, and divorces to unfaithful ones; register the wills of people who have any property to leave, and punish hasty gentlemen who call ladies by unpleasant names. . . .' ['Doctors' Commons'].

For a period of about three years, from the end of 1828, Dickens was a free-lance reporter in the Consistory Court of Doctors' Commons and this experience is used to good comic effect in his autobiographical novel, *David Copperfield* (1849–50), when David works for the law firm of Spenlow and Jorkins.

5. (p. 79) *The Perkins Institution . . . corporation:* Thomas Handasyd Perkins (1764–1854), merchant and philanthropist, gave his house and grounds as a home for the blind in 1833.

6. (p. 81) *the sense of touch:* Laura Bridgman (1829–89) became so expert at sewing that she remained at Perkins as a teacher of needlework throughout her life. She was the first blind deaf-mute to be successfully educated.

7. (p. 82) *that one man:* Dr Samuel Gridley Howe (1801–76) graduated from Brown University (1821) and Harvard Medical School (1824). In 1829 he became director of the Perkins Institute (then called the New England Asylum for the Blind) and retained that post till 1873. He was also interested in progressive education and the treatment of the mentally retarded. He was chairman of the Massachusetts Board of Charities (1865–74) and both he and his wealthy wife, Julia Ward Howe (1819–1910), were noted philanthropists.

As the account in *American Notes* makes clear, Dickens was a great admirer of Dr Howe's work. See Maud Howe and Florence Howe Hall, *Laura Bridgman, Dr Howe's Famous Pupil and What He Taught Her* (London, 1904), which notes (p. 107) that Dickens quoted Dr Howe's reports. The Annual Reports of the Perkins Institution include Dr Howe's *Education of Laura Bridgman*.

8. (p. 95) *Hanwell:* Kelly's Directory in 1845 commented that Hanwell had 'of late become more known and visited through the number of inmates in the lunatic asylum'. The asylum (now St Bernard's Hospital) was in fact just outside the parish of Hanwell in Norwood, Middlesex, and was built in 1831.

9. (p. 95) *Madge Wildfire:* a mad character in Sir Walter Scott's novel *The Heart of Midlothian* (1818).

10. (p. 97) *a very Chesterfield:* Philip Dormer Stanhope, 4th Earl of Chesterfield (1694–1773), who gave his name to both a kind of overcoat and a kind of couch, was ambassador at The Hague (1728–32), and is principally famous for his *Letters* to his natural son, Philip Stanhope, written almost daily from 1737 onwards and first published in 1774. These were designed for the education of a young man and are particularly concerned with instruction in matters of good breeding: 'In matters of religion and matrimony I never give any advice; because I will not have anybody's torments in this world or the next laid to my charge.'

11. (p. 98) *Poor Law Commissioners:* In 1832 a commission was appointed to study the question of revising the Poor Law. The result was the Poor Law Amendment Act of 1834, whereby able-bodied labourers were to have no outdoor relief and workhouses were to be made as unattractive as possible (including complete segregation of the sexes). To administer the Act, parishes were grouped into unions and placed under elected boards of guardians, and the guardians were put under a central board in London, the Poor Law Commissioners, who met at Somerset House. They were not popular.

12. (p. 99) *demon of a stove ... Heaven:* Dickens, like most British travellers to America at this time, was much upset by the heat from anthracite stoves in American hotels (see pp. 303, 308).

13. (p. 106) *Blue ladies:* 'Blue' here means 'learned' or 'pedantic', and is normally only applied to women, as in the term 'bluestocking'. The Blue Stocking Society (i.e. 'not in full evening dress') was the name given to meetings (c. 1750) at the houses of Mrs Montague. Rather than play cards, ladies at these meetings preferred to discuss literature and art.

14. (p. 106) *Transcendentalists:* Transcendentalism was a nineteenth-century philosophical movement which produced two major American writers, Ralph Waldo Emerson and Henry David Thoreau (1817–62), as well as a host of secondary writers, including Bronson Alcott (1799–1888), Margaret Fuller (1810–50) and Orestes Brownson (1803–76) (see also above, note 1). The Transcendental Club, an informal group, met chiefly at Emerson's

house in Concord and was largely responsible for publication of *The Dial* (1840–44). In reaction against eighteenth-century rational-ism, the Transcendentalists turned to Kant who, in *The Critique of Pure Reason* (1781), declared that the 'transcendental' knowledge in the mind of man was innate. This was translated as meaning that intuition surpassed reason as a guide to the truth. The immanence of God coexisted in the universe and the individual, whose mind was a microcosm of the Oversoul of the universe. From this followed the Transcendental belief in self-reliance and optimistic individ-ualism.

15. (p. 107) *Mr Carlyle:* Thomas Carlyle (1795–1881), Scottish essay-ist and historian, author of *Signs of the Times* (1829), *Sartor Resortus* (1833–4), *The French Revolution* (1837), and other works.

16. (p. 107) *Ralph Waldo Emerson* (1803–82) trained as a Unitarian minister, resigned his pastorate in 1832 and then toured Europe, visiting Carlyle, Wordsworth and Coleridge. On his return to the United States, he became famous as a lecturer, giving addresses which furnished the bases for his essays on such topics as 'Nature', 'Self-Reliance', 'The Oversoul' and 'The American Scholar'. Without developing a complete philosophical system, Emerson discussed most of the Transcendental ideas of his time (see above, note 14). *Essays, First Series* was published in 1841.

17. (p. 107) *Mr Taylor:* Edward Thompson Taylor (1793 -1871) was a seaman who became a Methodist minister. In 1829 he became the minister of the new Seamen's Bethel at Boston and was very popular with sailors because his sermons were full of the language of the sea. Father Mapple in Herman Melville's novel *Moby-Dick* (1851) is based on him.

18. (p. 108) *Collingwood:* Lord Collingwood (1750–1810): British admiral whose ship, the *Royal Sovereign*, led the fleet at the Battle of Trafalgar and who assumed command of the fleet on Nelson's death.

19. (p. 108) *Balfour of Burley:* John Balfour of Burley, a character in Sir Walter Scott's novel, *Old Mortality* (1816).

20. (p. 109) *Duke of Clarence ... smothered easily:* George, Duke of Clarence (1449–78), third son of Richard, Duke of York, and brother of King Edward IV, is supposed, in a popular version of his death, to have been drowned in a butt of malmsey wine.

21. (p. 110) *two theatres in Boston:* The Tremont Theatre (1827–43) and the Warren (later National) Theatre (1832–63).

22. (p. 110) *Gin-sling ... Timber Doodle: Gin-sling:* A jigger of gin added to half a glass of sweetened boiling water. A little lemon peel and nutmeg may be added. 'Sling' in English slang originally meant

any kind of drink. *Cocktail:* It has been suggested that this name came from Americans slurring the French word *coquetier,* meaning 'eggcup'. Cocktails are composed of spirits, bitters, sugar and water. *Sangaree:* Named from the French *sang* meaning 'blood', sangaree frequently contains sliced fruit and has a base of red Bordeaux wine, lemon juice, sugar and cinnamon. *Mint Julep:* Sugar is dissolved into chilled glasses, finely crushed ice is added and covered with bourbon. The mixture is then stirred and topped with sugar syrup and sprigs of fresh mint. *Sherry-cobbler:* Sherry and dissolved sugar are added to shaved ice and served with orange slices. *Timber Doodle:* The ingredients of this drink are not known to the editors.

CHAPTER 4

1. (p. 111) *Lowell:* Francis Cabot Lowell (1775–1817), Boston textile manufacturer and inventor, had the town of Lowell in Massachusetts named after him. Nowhere in America at this time were factory workers treated so paternally as here.

2. (p. 111) *chest . . . Brobdingnag:* In Book Two of *Gulliver's Travels* Gulliver is placed by the giant Brobdingnagians in a large box which is then stolen by an eagle and dropped into the sea.

3. (p. 114) *one-and-twenty years . . . place:* The Lowell mills were built by Patrick Tracy Jackson in 1822.

4. (p. 117) THE LOWELL OFFERING . . . *beginning to end:* The *Operative's Magazine* merged with *The Lowell Offering* in 1842 to become *The Lowell Offering and Magazine* (1842–5), subsequently *The New England Offering* (1847–50).

5. (p. 118) *Bevelinas:* Many British travellers, such as Mrs Trollope, commented on the appetite of American ladies for British novels at this time. Perhaps Dickens had this in mind when choosing 'Bevelina', a name generally evocative of the sentimental novel.

6. (p. 118) *General Jackson:* Andrew Jackson (1767–1845), seventh President of the United States (1829–37), was a distinguished soldier who decisively defeated the British at New Orleans (1815).

7. (p. 118) *General Harrison:* William Henry Harrison (1773–1841), ninth President of the United States, died within a month of his inauguration in 1841. As a general he won a number of victories in the War of 1812.

8. (p. 119) *wood fire . . . storm of fiery snow:* See Introduction, pp. 21–2.

CHAPTER 5

1. (p. 121) *Mr Paap, the celebrated Dwarf:* Mr Simon Paap, a Dutch dwarf, was born in 1789 at Zandvoort. He stopped growing at the end of his third year and at 29 he did not exceed 28 inches in height and weighed only 27 lbs. He spoke Dutch, French and English, was introduced to the English Royal Family in 1815, appeared twice at the Covent Garden Theatre and died in 1828. (See Arthur Vizetelly, 'Some Notable Dwarfs,' *English Illustrated Magazine,* February 1900).

2. (p. 122) *Blue Laws:* restrictive laws designed to support certain standards of morality. In American history they have become connected particularly with New England, but every state had some. In 1781 Samuel Peters, a clergyman, published his *General History of Connecticut* which included a study of that state's 'blue laws' such as that forbidding mothers to kiss their children on Sundays. Many of these laws were not enforced.

3. (p. 122) *oak . . . charter of King Charles:* (Charles = Charles II) According to tradition this tree was a hiding place for the Connecticut Charter of 1662, when in 1686 Governor Andros demanded it in the name of James II. When William of Orange succeeded to the English throne in 1688, the government of Connecticut was restored under its original charter. Charter Oak fell in 1856.

4. (p. 124) *Mormonist:* See Ch. 18, note 1.

5. (p. 126) *Burlington Arcade:* More than 200 yards long, Burlington Arcade was built as a bazaar in 1819 by Lord George Cavendish (afterwards Earl of Burlington) on the west side of Burlington House, the home of the Royal Society.

6. (p. 126) *Hell Gate . . . Diedrich Knickerbocker's History:* Diedrich Knickerbocker is the fictitious narrator of Washington Irving's humorous *History of New York* (1809). Hell Gate is a narrow channel of the East River in New York City. It is a dangerous stretch of water because of rocks, shelves and whirlpools which are known by various names, including Hog's Back and Frying Pan.

CHAPTER 6

1. (p. 128) *Five Points:* in a low valley between Broadway and the Bowery it was named from the convergence of these streets, one block ending in a sharp point. No respectable person could pass through without a police escort. The Rev. J. F. Richmond in hi *New York and its Institutions, 1609–1872* (1872) stated that: 'A

quarter of a century ago the Five Points in New York presented the
most appalling state of society on the American Continent.'

2. (p. 128) *Seven Dials:* an open space in the parish of St Giles-in-
the-Fields, London, from which seven streets radiated. It is, in
present-day London, close to the theatre area of Shaftesbury Avenue.
Designed in the seventeenth century by Thomas Neale, Master of
the Royal Mint, there was in the centre a column with seven sun-
dials, one facing each street, which was taken down in 1773.

The account of this neighbourhood in *Sketches by Boz* shows
that, for Dickens, it was an emblem of the city both in its maze-like
structure – 'But what involutions can compare with those of Seven
Dials' – and in its squalor – 'streets of dirty, struggling houses,
with now and then an unexpected court composed of buildings as
ill-proportioned and deformed as the half-naked children that
wallow in the kennels.' ['Seven Dials'].

3. (p. 128) *gig:* a light, two-wheeled vehicle drawn by one horse.

4. (p. 128) *phaeton:* a light, four-wheeled vehicle, open at the sides,
and sometimes having a top.

5. (p. 128) *tilbury:* a form of gig seating two persons.

6. (p. 128) *drab:* a thick, woollen, yellowish-brown cloth.

7. (p. 128) *nankeen:* a buff-coloured Chinese cotton fabric.

8. (p. 130) *Lombard Street:* Financial centre of London, called after
Lombardy merchants who came to England in the thirteenth
century to help collect dues payable to the pope.

9. (p. 130) *Arabian Nights' Entertainments* or *The Thousand and One
Nights* is a collection of stories written in Arabic and made known
in Europe in the eighteenth century in the French translation of
Antoine Galland. They were translated into English, with omissions,
by Edward William Lane in 1840. An unexpurgated translation, by
Sir Richard Burton, appeared only in 1885–8.

10. (p. 130) *Packet Service:* Packet ships carried dispatches, mails,
passengers and freight at fixed sailing days. The first transatlantic
packet lines were established by New York merchants in 1818. By
1852 the average time for the journey from New York to
Liverpool was thirty-three days. Steamboats finally took over and
the last ocean packet sailing was made in 1881.

11. (p. 131) *The Tombs,* situated at Centre, Elm, Leonard and Franklin
streets, was erected in 1838, and was the city prison. Rebuilt in
1941, it is properly called the Manhattan House of Detention for
Men.

12. (p. 134) *Gil Blas:* In Le Sage's novel *Gil Blas* (1715–35), Gil Blas
goes to Madrid and finds work as valet to a strange old gentleman.
He has little to do but dust his master's clothes every morning,

then return in the evening and wait at the door. Gil thinks the man is a thief, others believe him to be a spy, but it turns out that he is a Castilian nobleman who professes a 'philosophical indolence' and simply walks about all day, doing nothing.

13. (p. 135) *Ten-Pins ... Nine-Pins:* The Dutch settlers brought a bowling game using nine wooden pins to America in the seventeenth century. In the early nineteenth century the sport became so popular that widespread betting took place. As a result it was outlawed in Connecticut in 1841 and shortly afterwards in New York and other States. The law was then circumvented by using ten pins.

14. (p. 135) *heartiest of Greek Professors:* Cornelius Conway Felton (1807–62), who was Professor of Greek at Harvard 1832–60 and president of the university 1860–61. He became a great friend of Dickens on this trip and visited the novelist in England in 1853.

15. (p. 135) *Fantoccinis:* marionettes.

16. (p. 135) *Orchestrinas:* instruments somewhat similar to barrel organs.

17. (p. 135) *of the Utilitarian school:* The Utilitarians, followers of Jeremy Bentham (1772–1832), aimed to test all institutions in the light of human reason and common sense to determine whether they were useful – that is, whether they contributed to the greatest happiness of the greatest number of men. They were bitterly opposed by Carlyle, Newman and Dickens, whose novel *Hard Times* (1854) is a searing attack upon their excesses.

18. (p. 136) *the Halting Devil ... in Spain:* In Le Sage's novel *Le Diable Boiteux* (1707), the devil Asmodée, a monstrous dwarf with the legs of a goat, hobbles around on crutches. He amuses his master by lifting the roofs off the houses in Madrid, giving rise to various satiric views of society.

19. (p. 136) *the Great Desert:* the Sahara.

20. (p. 136) *Black-Eyed Susan:* 'Sweet William's Farewell to Black-Ey'd Susan: A Ballad', by John Gay (1685–1732). Douglas Jerrold's play 'Black-Eyed Susan', first performed in 1829, was based on this ballad and starred T. P. Cooke (see Ch. 2, note 12).

21. (p. 137) *the Bold Smuggler:* 'Will Watch The Smuggler' is a ballad by John Davy (1763–1824):

> One morn when the wind from the northward blew keenly
> While sullenly roared the big waves of the main,
> A famed smuggler, Will Watch, kissed his Sue, then serenely
> Took helm and to sea boldly steered out again.

22. (p. 137) *Paul Jones the Pirate:* John Paul Jones (1747–92), Scottish-born adventurer, entered the American navy in 1775 and harassed British ships. In 1779, his ship the *Bonhomme Richard*, engaged the British warship *Serapis*, off the north-east coast of England. Later he served for a time in the Russian navy and then lived in Paris. He is perhaps the only American ever to attack the English mainland, having spiked the guns at Whitehaven in 1777. He appears as a character in James Fenimore Cooper's *The Pilot* (1823) and Herman Melville's *Israel Potter* (1855).

23. (p. 138) '*Almack's*,' ... *descent:* Almack's, named after Almack's Assembly Room in King Street, St James's, London, was subsequently, in honour of Dickens's visit, called 'Dickens' Place'. 'Peter Williams, its owner, was an amateur actor and a drama enthusiast, who occasionally presented shows for his patrons. For the most part the performances were staged by the waitresses, who doubled as singers and dancers ...' (Eileen Southern, *The Music of Black Americans: A History*).

24. (p. 138) *the greatest dancer known:* 'Juba' (William Henry Lane, *c.* 1825–53) was often called 'the greatest of all dancers' of the time. He toured with minstrel shows in both the U.S. and Europe, one of the few Negroes to appear on the same bill with white men. Reviewing his performance in 1848, the *Illustrated London News* noted that Dickens had 'immortalized him; and he deserved the glory thus conferred'. The Five Points dance halls were the forerunners of the Harlem cabarets of the 1920s. (See Southern, *op. cit.*)

25. (p. 139) *Jim Crow:* a slang term applied to Negroes, derived from the title of a minstrel song.

26. (p. 141) *Simoom:* a hot, dry wind of the desert in Northern Africa.

27. (p. 141) *passage in the Litany ... young children:* 'That it may please thee to preserve all that travel by land or by water, all women labouring of child, all sick persons, and young children; and to show thy pity upon all prisoners and captives.'

28. (p. 142) *Sing Sing:* Sing-Sing Prison was built at Ossining in south-eastern New York State in 1824.

29. (p. 142) *Auburn:* The state prison at Auburn was opened in 1819. The 'silent system' meant that prisoners were sent to separate cells at night and silence was kept at all times.

30. (p. 143) *Mr Mitchell:* William Mitchell (1798–1856) was born in England and went to the United States in 1836, taking over the Olympic Theatre in 1839. He was famous as an impresario and actor and one of his most famous parts was Vincent Crummles in a stage adaptation of *Nicholas Nickleby*.

31. (p. 143) *Niblo's:* Niblo's Garden was originally a summer resort

opened by William Niblo at the corner of Broadway and Prince Street. The Sans Souci theatre was built there in 1828 and housed both circuses and legitimate drama until it burnt down in 1846. The theatre was rebuilt in 1849 and finally demolished in 1895.

CHAPTER 7

1. (p. 145) *Don Guzman ... gloomy walls:* The First Bank of the United States was designed by Samuel Blodget (1757–1814) and first occupied in 1794. It was the first important building in America to be executed in marble.

    The 'statue of Don Guzman' appears to refer to the statue of the Commendatore which takes Don Juan to Hell. Guzman, a very common Spanish name, is not, however, that usually given to the Commendatore. The one occasion on which the name is used appears to be in a burlesque by Thomas John Dibdin (1771–1841) entitled *Don Giovanni, or Spectre on Horseback* (London, 1817). There Guzman is the Father of Donna Anna and the *dramatis personae* includes a reference to 'Don Guzman and the ghost of himself' as performed by 'Mr Smith'.

2. (p. 145) *Mark Lane:* the volume *Philadelphia in 1824* (Philadelphia, 1824) places Mark's Lane just south-east of the junction of Market Street and Broad Street. The lane may have been a part of the Broad Street Market founded in 1814; at any rate it is located close to the central commercial area and hence would be an obvious place of lodging for Quaker businessmen.

3. (p. 146) *Franklin:* The leading American spokesman of eighteenth century rationalism, Benjamin Franklin (1706–90) was a printer, author, philanthropist, scientist, inventor and politician. He served as Postmaster-General, helped to draft the Declaration of Independence and during the War of Revolution was American plenipotentiary to the French court. His most famous works are *Poor Richard's Almanack* (1733–58), a collection of aphorisms, and his unfinished *Autobiography* (1771–4).

4. (p. 146) *a picture by West:* Benjamin West (1738–1820) was born near Philadelphia. After studying painting in Italy, he settled permanently in London in 1763. He was elected President of the Royal Academy in 1792. He is best-known as a teacher and as a painter of historical and biblical scenes.

5. (p. 146) *Mr Sully*: Thomas Sully (1783–1872), English-born, went to the United States in 1792. A pupil of Benjamin West, he became established in Philadelphia as a very successful portrait-painter. His models included Jefferson and Madison, and Queen Victoria.

6. (p. 146) *Shakspeare . . . Vicar of Wakefield:* In Chapter 9 of Oliver Goldsmith's *The Vicar of Wakefield* (1766) the daughters of Dr Primrose are put in the shade by the conversation of the Misses Flamborough:

> for they would talk of nothing but high life, and high-lived company; with other fashionable topics, such as pictures, taste, Shakespeare, and the musical glasses.

7. (p. 146) *Girard College . . . than doing now:* Girard College was eventually completed. An educational institution for white orphan boys, it was founded by philanthropist Stephen Girard (1750–1831).

8. (p. 148) *torturing anxieties and horrible despair:* Edmund Wilson, in *The Wound and the Bow* (1941) describes this section as

> almost the only passage in *American Notes* which shows any real readiness on Dickens' part to enter into the minds and feelings of the people among whom he is travelling. . . .

It is hardly fanciful to suggest that Dickens remembered this chapter of *American Notes* when he came to describe, in *A Tale of Two Cities* (1859), the eighteen-year incarceration of Dr Manette in the Bastille in its effect on his voice:

> Its deplorable peculiarity was, that it was the faintness of solitude and disuse. It was like the last feeble echo of a sound made long and long ago. [Ch. 6]

9. (p. 149) *'The Lady of the Lake':* Sir Walter Scott (1771–1832) published his long poem *The Lady of the Lake* in 1810. As Dickens's encounter with the Choctaw Indian chief (pp. 210–11) suggests, Scott was immensely popular in the United States at this time. James Flint found Scott's novels to be a literary sensation in the Ohio River towns (1818–20), and steamboats were frequently named after his novels and characters. Because of the lack of an international copyright agreement Scott never made any money from his United States sales and in a speech at Hartford Dickens imagined Scott dying, neglected by his American readers:

> 'No, nor brought him from that land in which his own language was spoken, and in every house and hut at which his own books were read in his own tongue, one grateful dollar-piece to buy a garland for his grave.'

CHAPTER 8

1. (p. 161) *canvas-backed ducks:* an American waterfowl famous for its tasty flesh. It is named from the colour of its back feathers. Augustus Foster, writing in the first decade of the nineteenth century, observed:

> They are most delicious eating and . . . are said to owe their excellent flavour to a particular kind of grass seed, wild celery, found only in the Rivers Potomac and Susquehannah. (*Jeffersonian America,* ed. R. B. Davis, 1954.)

2. (p. 162) *Corinthian order:* an order of Greek architecture characterized by ornate, bell-shaped capitols decorated with simulated acanthus leaves.

3. (p. 164) *projector . . . Frenchman:* Major Pierre C. L'Enfant (1754–1825). He had volunteered (at his own expense) to fight against England in the American Revolution. His plan for Washington, D.C., was greatly influenced by Versailles. Major Andrew Ellicott (1754–1820) was responsible for survey and site layout. Expenses ran so high that L'Enfant was allowed to resign his commission, work virtually ceased and it was decades before the original design saw completion.

4. (p. 164) *Barmecide Feast:* In the *Arabian Nights,* Barmecide is a prince of Baghdad who serves an imaginary feast in empty dishes to a beggar. A Barmecide feast is thus any illusory abundance.

5. (p. 164) *Colonel Trumbull . . . occurrence:* Colonel John Trumbull (1756–1843) served in the Continental army as an aide to Washington. He studied painting with Benjamin West in London and in 1784 began his famous series in the 'grand historical style' of West. They included *The Battle of Bunker's Hill.* Four of his large historical canvases are in the National Capitol, including *The Signing of the Declaration of Independence.* He served as President of the American Academy (1816–25).

6. (p. 164) *Mr Greenough's large statue:* Horatio Greenough (1805–52) was probably the first professional American sculptor. He studied under Thorvaldsen in Italy and lived chiefly in Florence from 1829–51. He created *Washington* (1833) for the National Capitol. His ideas on architecture, stressing functionality and integrity of overall conception over decorativeness, have earned him a more lasting fame than his grandiose 'Roman' sculpture.

7. (p. 165) *phrenological character . . . was expressed:* Phrenology is the study of the structure of the cranium as an index to the development and position of organs supposedly related to the various

mental faculties. This pseudo-science, by which a man's character could be detected in the shape of his head, was much in vogue at this time.

8. (p. 166) *that traffic ... unborn children:* T. A. Jackson, in *Charles Dickens: the Progress of a Radical* (1937), cites this as a prominent instance of Dickens's failure to understand what he was observing. The 'aged, grey-haired man' is former President John Quincy Adams (1767–1848), standing in the House of Representatives, fighting for the right to present petitions against slavery. The House had refused to accept them since 1836. Dickens failed to realize (or state) that Adams was not so much an abolitionist as an opponent of the 'gag rule'. He was fighting a winning battle and encouraging abuse as useful propaganda in his struggle. The overthrow of the 'gag rule' came in 1844.

9. (p. 168) *Crichtons in varied accomplishment:* James Crichton (1560–82?), Scottish scholar and soldier, called 'The Admirable Crichton' in Sir Thomas Urquhart's narrative of his career (1652). *The General Biographical Dictionary* (Vol. 11, 1813, p. 9) has this to say about Crichton: 'he appears to have had a fine person, to have been adroit in his bodily exercises, to have possessed a peculiar facility in learning languages, to have enjoyed a remarkably quick and retentive memory, and to have excelled in a power of declamation, a fluency of speech and a readiness of reply.' J. M. Barrie in his charming comedy *The Admirable Crichton* (1914) allows his butler-hero to emulate his namesake in being a paragon.

10. (p. 170) *a Jesuit College; ... well managed:* Georgetown University, founded as Georgetown College in 1789.

11. (p. 172) *the President himself:* John Tyler (1790–1862), tenth President of the United States (1841–5), succeeded to the office on the death of William Henry Harrison a month after his inauguration.

12. (p. 172) *Levees:* Dickens probably thought the term odd because it had originally indicated an official audience held by a person of high rank before or upon rising from bed. It may also be that, like Mrs Trollope, he was puzzled by the pronunciation of this word. She found it droll:

the last syllable is pronounced by every one as long as possible, being exactly the reverse of the French and English manner of pronouncing the same word.

13. (p. 173) *Washington Irving ... going abroad:* Washington Irving (1783–1859), author, historian, diplomat. Famous for the burlesque *History of New York* (1809) and *Sketch Book* (1819–20). Dickens

had been an admirer of Irving since his youth. In 1841 he wrote, 'There is no living writer, and there are few among the dead, whose approbation I should feel so proud to earn.' He saw Irving several times on his trip and their friendship prospered. The publication of *American Notes* and *Martin Chuzzlewit* turned Irving against Dickens, however, and he later refused to meet the Englishman in London. Dickens seems to have remained true to the memory of their friendship throughout his life. (See W. C. D. Pacey, 'Charles Dickens and Washington Irving', *American Literature*, vol. 16, January 1945, p. 337.)

14. (p. 174) *Charleston:* Jane Mesick, in *The English Traveller in America 1785–1835* (1923), says that 'Charleston seems to have been the most agreeable and the most admired of the Southern towns' (p. 123), but Senator Henry Clay warned Dickens against going there.

CHAPTER 9

1. (p. 175) *faithful secretary . . . from Boston:* George W. Putnam was hired as Dickens's secretary soon after the novelist arrived in Boston and stayed with him throughout his American trip. Kate did not take to him but Dickens found him reliable and often unintentionally funny. Putnam published 'Four Months with Charles Dickens' in *The Atlantic Monthly*, October and November, 1870.

2. (p. 175) *a Field Marshal . . . no doubt:* Many British travellers commented on the American delight in military titles. H. Wansey, in *Excursion to the United States in 1794* (1798) commented: 'A man with the title of Major sometimes holds your horse, and Captains are digging by the roadside; it is a vestige of the Revolution.'

3. (p. 178) *high-low shoes:* boots reaching over the ankles.

4. (p. 178) *Ducrow on . . . his fiery coursers:* Andrew Ducrow (1793–1842) was a celebrated circus horseman. He was principal equestrian performer and subsequently a co-proprietor of Astley's circus, London.

5. (p. 181) *shone like a burning coal:* The voyages of Es-Sindiba'd of the Sea form several of the stories in the *Arabian Nights*. On his third voyage he meets a black giant who eats several of the sailor's companions and who is, in turn, blinded by Sinbad and the others. In some versions he had one eye, in others, two. In the Lane translation he is described thus: 'he had two eyes like two blazes of fire, and tusks like the tusks of swine, and a mouth of prodigious size, like the mouth of a well . . .'

6. (p. 181) *'Bloody Run' . . . occurred there:* According to Samuel Mordecai, *Richmond in By-Gone Days* (2nd edition, 1860), 'Bloody

Run' by tradition obtained its name from a batttle betweeen the Indians and Nathaniel Bacon's army. Bacon (1647–76) carried out what is known as 'Bacon's Rebellion' when he attacked the Indians without a commission from Governor Berkeley and thus split Virginia into warring factions. Presumably, 'Bloody Run' is related to his fight against the Susquehannock Indians in 1676.

7. (p. 182) *Defoe's description . . . to my recollection:* Daniel Defoe (1660–1731) wrote two novels involving episodes in Virginia, *Moll Flanders* (1722) and *Colonel Jack* (1722). Dickens is referring to the latter where the narrator becomes a pickpocket, a soldier and finally, after many troubles, a planter in Virginia. His first house as a planter had 'three rooms, a kitchen, an outhouse, and two large sheds at a distance from the house, for storehouses, almost like barns, with stables at the end of them'.

8. (p. 183) *mint-julep and sherry-cobbler:* see Ch. 3, note 22.

9. (p. 183) *living among horses . . . trembling horror:* In Book Four of *Gulliver's Travels* Gulliver, having lived for some time with those ultra-rational horse-creatures, the Houyhnhnms, returns to England and is appalled by the uncouthness of humankind.

10. (p. 184) *Barnum's:* Barnum's Hotel, on the corner of Calvert and Fayette streets, was built about 1819. *The Stranger in Baltimore* (1866) describes it as 'a very ornamental building in the heart of business'.

11. (p. 184) *North Point:* The Battle of North Point occurred on September 12, 1814, when the British attempted to take Fort McHenry and overrun Baltimore. They were repulsed and General Ross was killed.

12. (p. 186) *Diligence:* a large stage-coach.

13. (p. 187) *Camlet:* light cloth of various materials.

14. (p. 189) *Crabbe's musings . . . from end to end:*

> Behold these marks uncouth! how strange that men,
> Who guide the plough, should fail to guide the pen:
> For half a mile, the furrows even lie;
> For half an inch the letters stand awry . . . .

The Rev. George Crabbe (1754–1832) published 'The Parish Register' in 1807.

CHAPTER 10

1. (p. 191) *Caleb Quotem:* character in *The Review* by the younger George Colman, originally taken from a comic opera by Henry Lee. Quotem was an abnormally loquacious jack-of-all-trades.

2. (p. 194) *Reid's Theory . . . of Storms:* Sir William Reid (1791–1858) published *An attempt to develop the law of storms by means of facts, arranged according to place and time, and hence to point out a cause for the variable winds; with the view to practical use in navigation* (London, 1838). This work developed the view that hurricanes have a rotatory movement (hence the fancied central vertical movement of the spit in Dickens's reference) and also observed that storms in southern latitudes revolve in precisely the contrary direction to those in the northern hemisphere.

3. (p. 195) *who drove her husband frantic:* It is difficult to know precisely which story Dickens had in mind. Andrew Lang, in a note to his Gadshill Edition of *American Notes* (London, n.d., p. 520), suggests the ghoul Amina in the *Arabian Nights*, or the girl who keeps her lover awake in *The Black Bull o' Norroway* or some story in the *Cabinet des Fées*. One might add the medieval tale from which comes Anatole France's *La Comédie de Celui qui Épousa une Femme Muette* (1912) or even Ben Jonson's *Epicœne* (1609).

4. (p. 196) *Down Easters:* This term came to be used of men from the New England coast, especially Maine. Reputed to be masters of a sardonic, 'Yankee' wit, they gave rise to such famous humorous characters as Seba Smith's Jack Downing and James Russell Lowell's Hosea Biglow.

5. (p. 197) *I an't a Johnny Cake:* A johnny-cake is a cake made of maize-meal, toasted or baked in a pan. It came to be used as a slang term to describe New Englanders. In Richard Henry Dana's novel, *Two Years Before the Mast* (1840), Captain Thompson, in order to impress his men, describes himself as 'a regular-built down-east johnny-cake, when it's hot, damned good; but when it's cold, damned sour and indigestible. . . .'

CHAPTER 11

1. (p. 205) *Big Grave Creek:* Grave Creek joins the Ohio River at Moundsville in West Virginia, so called because the Grave Creek Mound (320 feet in diameter at base and 70 feet high) is located in the centre of the city. The area of southern Ohio, northern Kentucky and north-western West Virginia is famous for the Adena Indian culture – clusters of burial mounds from a civilization which flourished from 2,000 to 1,200 years ago. This culture gave way to the Hopewell culture which centered in southern Ohio but spread as far as Florida and Louisiana and lasted to about A.D. 500. The area is covered by clusters of burial mounds in which have been found exotic burial offerings. (See Peter Farb, *Man's Rise to*

Civilization, 1968.) An early account of a visit to the mounds can be found in *Journal of a Tour in Unsettled Parts of North America in 1796 and 1797* (1856) by an Englishman, Francis Baily (1774–1844).

2. (pp. 207–8) *Portrait of Father Mathew:* Theobald Matthew (1790–1856), Irish Capuchin priest and temperance leader, went to the United States in the 1840s and gained huge followings in the popular temperance crusades of that time.

CHAPTER 12

1. (p. 210) *that chamber ... thousands of years ago:* Dickens's reference is probably to the collection of Etruscan remains.

2. (p. 211) *Mr Catlin's gallery:* George Catlin (1796–1872) practised law before becoming a painter. In 1830 he began an eight-year journey, covering thousands of miles, sketching landscapes and Indians of forty-eight different tribes. After his death most of his paintings were given to the Smithsonian Institution in Washington. They provide important source material for the study of American Indians.

3. (p. 211) *Mr Cooper ... had painted the Red Man well:* James Fenimore Cooper (1789–1851) was the most famous American author of his time. He wrote some thirty novels, many involving Indians. His most important works were the five 'Leather-stocking' novels, *The Pioneers* (1823), *The Last of the Mohicans* (1826), *The Prairie* (1827), *The Pathfinder* (1840) and *The Deerslayer* (1841), which followed the life of a backwoodsman, Natty Bumppo, and often described the enmity between the Delaware and Huron Indians in the Great Lakes regions.

4. (p. 213) *Kentucky Giant ... in his stockings:* An article entitled 'Giants and Dwarfs II' in the *Strand Magazine*, October 1894 stated that:

Kentucky is said to be a great place for tall people, and is considered to be the native state of the famous American gentleman who had to go up a ladder to shave himself.

Martin Van Buren Bates (1847–?), a Kentucky giant (just short of eight feet) who fought in the Civil War, was famous in the later nineteenth century, and the *Chicago Tribune* in 1888 recorded details of one of the world's fattest women, Sallie McAllister, of Springfield, Kentucky, who weighed 632 lbs. (See Wade Clinton, *Brobdingnagians and Lilliputians*, a hand-written compilation [1906?] currently in the Brighton Reference Library.)

5. (p. 213) *sleight-of-hand and hocus-pocus:* A version of *Jack the Giant-Killer* where Jack begs lodging at a giant's house and then overhears the giant planning to kill him. Putting a billet of wood in his bed, Jack allows the giant to belabour it under the impression that he is killing the youth and, then, in the morning, mystifies the giant by complaining that a rat had slightly disturbed his rest. Jack hides a hasty pudding under his coat, then slits it open and fools the giant into believing that his insides are spilling out with no ill effect. The giant tries it on himself and dies.

6. (p. 214) *Le Sage's strolling player . . . glad enjoyment:* In Book Two of *Gil Blas*, the hero and his companion, Signor Diego de la Fluenta, meet a strolling player, Melchior Zapata, dipping crusts of bread in a spring. They share their breakfast with him and he expounds on the player's life.

7. (p. 215) *his Yahoo's trough:* In the fourth book of *Gulliver's Travels* the Yahoos are filthy, unreasoning creatures who represent Swift's view of man's potential for bestiality.

8. (p. 215) *speculated in . . . to many people's ruin:* Dr J. F. Snyder and some later critics believed that Dickens was one of the victims of the Cairo City and Canal Company, a bubble company established by Darius B. Holbrook in 1837. Holbrook sold bonds through the London Banking House of John Wright and Co. It is an attractive theory, but there is no evidence to support it. Cairo, Illinois, becomes the Eden of *Martin Chuzzlewit.* See W. G. Wilkins, *Charles Dickens in America* (New York, 1911), p. 2.

9. (p. 219) *a Jesuit college:* St Louis University, established as St Louis Academy in 1818.

10. (p. 219) *Saint Francis Xavier* (1506–52) was a Spanish Jesuit missionary who helped Loyola establish the Society of Jesus (1534). He worked in Japan and China and was canonized in 1622.

CHAPTER 13

1. (p. 220) *the Looking-Glass Prairie and back:* Edmund Flagg, the novelist, touring this region in 1836–7, wrote that: 'rosy sunbeams were playing lightly over the pleasant country seats and neat farmhouses . . . imbowered in their young orchards and waving maize fields,' but Dorothy Ann Dondore, in *The Prairie and the Making of Middle America: Four Centuries of Description* (1926) suggests that foreign writers in the nineteenth century had great difficulty in romanticizing the frontier when faced with its brutal loneliness (and sometimes ugliness). Dickens was no exception. See p. 320.

2. (p. 220) *paraaer, parearer, and paroarer:* As Professor G. L. Brook points out in *The Language of Dickens* (1970), the choice of letters to be italicized here seems rather arbitrary and it is difficult to know exactly what pronunciation the spellings are meant to represent. Professor Brook's book, Tadio Yamamoto's *Growth and System of the Language of Dickens* (1952) and Louise Pound's 'The American Dialect of Charles Dickens', *American Speech*, xxii (1927), all contain important comments on Dickens's reproductions of American speech, but it is unwise to rely too heavily on his accuracy.

3. (p. 223) *Dr Crocus . . . a head:* Dr J. F. Snyder (Wilkins, op. cit., p. 220) who, as a boy, saw the arrival of Dickens and his party in Belleville, identified 'Dr Crocus' as a Dr Angus Melrose:

Dr Melrose was over six feet in height, and robust in proportion, with florid face and long nose. Of friendly, social disposition, he was a fluent talker, speaking correct English with broad Scotch accent.

4. (p. 227) *President Madison:* James Madison (1751–1836) was fourth President of the United States (1809–17). Known as the 'Father of the Constitution' he was a chief proponent of the Bill of Rights and, with Alexander Hamilton (1757–1804) and John Jay (1745–1829), contributed to the *Federalist Papers* (1787–8).

5. (p. 227) *kit-cat size:* portraits of less than half-length, but including the hands.

6. (p. 227) *the order of La Trappe:* The Trappists are monks of the Cistercian order observing the reformed rule established in 1664 by De Ronce, Abbot of La Trappe in Normandy. The rule is very austere, observing almost constant silence.

7. (p. 228) *Bloody Island . . . breast to breast:* 'Bloody Island' was a sand-bar in the Mississippi River, opposite St Louis, which became densely wooded and hence a rendezvous for duellists. It first appeared above the water in 1798 and its continued growth menaced St Louis Harbour. In 1837 Captain Robert E. Lee of the USA Engineers established a system of dykes and dams which ultimately joined the island to the Illinois shore.

CHAPTER 14

1. (p. 231) *worm-fence:* a zig-zag fence of rails crossed at their ends.

2. (p. 235) *Dr Sangrado:* A quack physician in *Gil Blas* whose knowledge of medicine was limited to prescribing bleeding and intakes of water. Gil Blas becomes his assistant in Book Two, where the doctor's advice is stated to be: 'Drink water by pails full, it is a universal dissolvent; water liquefies all the salts.'

3. (p. 235) *witches' coral:* also a kind of fungus.

4. (p. 236) *a corduroy road:* Corduroy roads had their uses, as Civil War campaigns later demonstrated, but they appalled British travellers. Henry Tudor, in *Narrative of a Tour in North America* (1834) remarked with asperity:

> I think the unhappy wight who has once travelled over them would never be inclined to wear a garment made of the stuff whence the name is borrowed. . . .

5. (p. 238) *My Boston friend:* See Ch. 9, note 1.

6. (p. 241) *Bacchus:* Greek god of wine.

7. (p. 241) *vignette:* Originally used to indicate a form of manuscript illumination, 'vignette' also came to mean an engraving of indefinite boundary, the marginal areas shading off into the surrounding page.

8. (p. 241) *Lord Ashburton . . . Great Britain:* Alexander Baring, first Baron Ashburton (1774–1848), President of the Board of Trade (1834–5) and Special Commissioner to the United States. He negotiated the Webster-Ashburton Treaty of 1842, which settled several outstanding disagreements concerning rights on the United States–Canadian border.

9. (p. 241) *Mr Webster . . . the approaching negotiations:* Daniel Webster (1782–1852), famous American lawyer and statesman who negotiated the Webster-Ashburton treaty (see previous note).

10. (p. 243) *Horse-Shoe Fall:* Goat Island extends to the brow of the precipice and divides Niagara Falls into two parts: the American Falls and the Canadian, or Horseshoe Falls. The Canadian side is 162 feet high, the American 167 feet.

CHAPTER 15

1. (p. 246) *General Brock . . . the victory:* Sir Isaac Brock (1769–1812) assumed command of British troops in Upper Canada in 1810, and in 1811 was appointed Lieutenant-Governor of the province. In the war of 1812 he made a brilliant attack on Detroit and defeated the Americans at Queenston Heights on the Niagara frontier. He died of wounds received there and a monument was erected to his memory at the spot.

2. (p. 246) *Lett . . . two years ago:* Benjamin Lett (c. 1814–58), joined 'the self-styled Patriots on Navy Island' (see p. 249 and below, note 6) in 1837 and participated in many U.S.–Canadian border incidents (1838–41). He was reported to have been involved in the destruction of the Brock monument in 1840. Arrested in 1841, he spent four years in prison.

3. (p. 248) *a valuable and useful institution:* The University of King's College in Upper Canada, founded in 1827 and destined to become the University of Toronto.

4. (p. 248) *the Governor General:* Sir Charles Bagot (1781–1843) was Governor of Canada 1842–3.

5. (p. 248) *that flag was orange:* The flag of the Orangemen, a political party formed in 1795 to ensure Protestant ascendancy in Ireland and named after William of Orange, who succeeded to the English throne in 1688 on the deposition of the Catholic James II.

6. (p. 249) *Patriots on Navy Island:* Owing to the lack of power of the elected Legislative Assembly and the real power of the Anglican minority in Upper Canada, William Lyon Mackenzie of the Reform Party had gathered a rebel force and attacked Toronto in December, 1837. Though easily defeated, he escaped to Navy Island in the Niagara River and set up a provisional government. He was compelled to retire to the United States where he was imprisoned for breach of the neutrality laws.

7. (p. 250) portages: places where it is necessary to transport boats to avoid rapids or waterfalls or to get from one lake or river to another.

8. (p. 252) *Wolfe ... his mortal wound:* James Wolfe (1727–59) became Second-in-Command of the British forces in the French and Indian War at the age of 32. A great tactician, he and his troops scaled a reputedly impossible cliff before defeating the French forces on the Plains of Abraham (1759). He died of wounds received during the battle.

9. (p. 252) *Montcalm:* Louis-Joseph de Montcalm-Gozon, Marquis de Saint Véran (1712–59) was a veteran commander before being sent to defend Canada in the French and Indian War. He had brilliant successes at Fort Ontario and Fort William Henry before losing an empire on the Plains of Abraham. Like Wolfe, he died of wounds received in that battle.

10. (p. 256) *'the Shaker Village ... takes its name:* The Shakers, a millenarian group who called themselves 'The United Society of Believers in Christ's Second Appearing', originated in England in the eighteenth century and first arrived in the United States in 1774. Excellent farmers and craftsmen, the order has virtually died out because of a commitment to celibacy.

11. (p. 256) *Kaatskill ... gusty afternoon:* The Catskill Mountains are a range of the Appalachian system in south-eastern New York State just west of the Hudson River. A watershed of the Hudson and Delaware rivers, they inspired the 'Hudson River School' of artists and writers. 'Rip Van Winkle' is a tale in Washington

Irving's *Sketch Book* (1819–20). An indolent, good-natured man with a nagging wife, Rip lives on the Hudson River before the Revolution. On a walk in the Catskills, he meets a party of strange, silent men dressed in old-fashioned Dutch costume. After playing ninepins with them he falls asleep for twenty years and then returns, having missed the American Revolution, to his village, where he lives cheerfully with his daughter and her family.

12. (p. 259) *at a great public table:* Every citizen of ancient Sparta had to belong to one of the *philitia* (dining messes or clubs).

13. (p. 261) *Sleepy Hollow . . . Tappaan Zee:* 'The Legend of Sleepy Hollow' is a tale in Washington Irving's *Sketch Book. Tappaan Zee:* The Tappan Sea is an expansion of the Hudson River, in south-eastern New York State, in the vicinity of Tarrytown and Ossining.

CHAPTER 16

1. (p. 265) *not demoralising and profligate:* Dickens's descriptions of steerage travel in *Martin Chuzzlewit* are not all that exaggerated. Henry Fearon in *Sketches of America* (1818), described similar conditions:

> The deck was filthy. The cooking, washing and necessary departments were close together. Such is the mercenary barbarity of the Americans who are engaged in this trade, that they crammed into one of these vessels 500 passengers, 80 of whom died on the passage.

Later the use of special emigrant ships eased these appalling conditions somewhat.

CHAPTER 17

1. (p. 269) *Slavery:* Louise H. Johnson has shown that Dickens took most of the instances in this chapter from a contemporary pamphlet, *American Slavery As It Is* (listed by Stonehouse in his *Catalogue* of Dickens's library), and that some of his criticisms were merely paraphrases of comments by the author. Although not stated on the title page, the author was Theodore D. Weld, who compiled the pamphlet for the American Anti-Slavery Society in 1839. Harriet Beecher Stowe later drew on it for situations in *Uncle Tom's Cabin* (1852). (See Louise H. Johnson, 'The Source of the Chapter on Slavery in Dickens' *American Notes*,' *American Literature*, vol. 14, January 1943, pp. 427–30.)

2. (p. 270) *the Caliph Haroun Alraschid:* Haroun al-Rashid (A.D. 763 or 766–809), Caliph of Baghdad from 786 to 809, best known through the *Arabian Nights*.

3. (p. 271) *burned a slave . . . had made:* In May 1836, a Negro was removed from jail in St Louis and burned at the stake. The grand jury called to investigate the incident was instructed by Judge Luke E. Lawless to bring indictments only if a few individuals were found to be involved. He further blamed the mob's action on the abolitionist editorials of Elija P. Lovejoy, agent of the American Home Missionary Society and editor of the St Louis *Observer.* Lovejoy, in turn, castigated Lawless for giving *carte blanche* to mob action (Dickens's 'public opinion'). See p. 319.

CHAPTER 18

1. (p. 290) *Mr Joseph Smith . . . disciples:* Joseph Smith (1805–44), born of poor farmers in Vermont, published the Book of Mormon in 1830, a book he claimed was given to him by an angel in a vision. On the basis of this book the Church of Latter-Day Saints was organized. When he claimed, in 1843, to have received a revelation authorizing polygamy many of his followers turned against him. He was later arrested and shot to death by a mob at Carthage, Illinois. Led by Brigham Young to Utah, the Mormons prospered.
2. (p. 290) *Mrs Southcote:* Joanna Southcott (1750–1814), an English religious fanatic who claimed to be the woman mentioned in the Apocalypse.
3. (p. 290) *Mary Tofts the rabbit-breeder:* Mary Toft or Tofts (1701?–63), poor and illiterate, created a sensation in 1726 when she claimed to have given birth to 15 rabbits. She was later shown to be an impostor.
4. (p. 290) *Mr Thom of Canterbury:* John Nichols Tom or Thom (1799–1838), a religious maniac who made many claims, including one of being the Messiah. He was shot to death with several of his rioting followers near Canterbury.
5. (p. 292) *Mr Chadwick's excellent Report . . . advantage:* Sir Edwin Chadwick (1800–90) was a major figure in Victorian reform movements. A disciple of Bentham, he joined the Poor Law Commission in 1832, and became its head in 1833. He wrote reports on the conditions of child labour in factories, on the police force, and in 1839 on sanitation.

POSTSCRIPT

1. (p. 296) *Journal:* Dickens's 'Postscript' was printed in *All the Year Round* on Saturday, 6 June 1868.

TEXTUAL NOTES

p. 53, l. 5   burden] *Altered to* burthen *in 1850*

p. 56, l. 24   danced] *Altered to* dancing *in 1868*

p. 57, l. 6   plashing] *Altered to* splashing *in 1868*

p. 67, l. 35   a very pale individual] *Altered to* an individual very pale from sea-sickness *in 1850*

p. 74, lls. 34–5   ; and is some trifle smaller than Bedford Square] *Deleted in 1850*

p. 87, l. 27   and a twining] and *deleted in 1868*

p. 89, l. 22   she shows her Saxon blood] she *deleted in 1868*

p. 93, l. 2   twined] *Altered to* twining *in 1868*

p. 94, l. 9   the affection that] that *altered to* which *in 1868*

p. 96, l. 16   to be highly amused] to *deleted in 1868*

p. 96, l. 19   by these means] these *altered to* those *in 1868*

p. 96, l. 20   the] *Added in 1868*

p. 100, l. 28   among the prisoners] among *altered to* amongst *in 1868*

p. 101, l. 33   *Footnote deleted in 1868*

p. 107, l. 30   Song] *First edition only reads* Songs

p. 107, l. 34   this text] this *altered to* his *in 1850*

p. 109, l. 34   that a guest] that *altered to* and *in 1868*

p. 124, l. 33   'To be sure she has.'] *First edition only reads* he *for* she

p. 126, l. 33   awoke] *Altered to* woke *in 1868*

p. 131, l. 35   are under remand] are *deleted in 1868*

p. 131, l. 37   trial] *Altered to* trials *in 1868*

p. 134, l. 38   been much worried] much *deleted in 1868*

p. 135, l. 21   Fantoccinis] *Altered to* Fantoccini *in 1850*

p. 140, lls. 19–20   , or Rhode Island: I forget which] *Added in 1850*

p. 141, l. 22   on Long Island] *Deleted in 1850*

p. 141, l. 35   Long] *Deleted in 1850*

p. 142, l. 26   Mount] *Deleted in 1850*

p. 142, l. 26   , I believe,] *Added in 1850*

p. 145, l. 27   quakerly] *Altered to* quakery *in 1868*

p. 148, l. 14   wife or children] or *altered to* and *in 1868*

p. 148, l. 24   index to] to *altered to* of *in 1868*

p. 149, l. 7   this long imprisonment] this *altered to* his *in 1868*

p. 152, l. 30   and good fortune] and *deleted in 1868*

p. 154, l. 15   its back] its *altered to* his *in 1850*

p. 161, l. 39   the various impressions] the *altered to* and *in 1868*

p. 162, lls. 22–3 or the straggling outskirts of Paris, where the houses
are smallest,] *Added in 1850*

p. 162, l. 25 occupied there] there *altered to* in Pentonville *in 1850*

p. 168, l. 23 accomplishment] *Altered to* accomplishments in *1868*

p. 170, l. 27 in this neighborhood] in *altered to* of *in 1868*

p. 174, l. 38 chapter] *Two-volume editions read* volume

p. 175, l. 31 without any companion] any *altered to* my *in 1868*

p. 176, l. 9 on the shining face] on *altered to* upon *in 1868*

p. 184, l. 14 (this is a disinterested remark, for I never use them)]
Added in 1850

p. 186, lls. 14–5 , and might have been the twin-brother of a French
Diligence] *Added in 1850*

p. 186, l. 33 packed] *Altered to* booked *in 1850*

p. 188, l. 2 very glad] very *deleted in 1868*

p. 188, l. 37 complacent] *Altered to* complaisant *in 1850*

p. 194, l. 21 the hurricane] the *altered to* a *in 1868*

p. 194, l. 33 some were superior] some *altered to* many *in 1850*

p. 196, l. 7 ever afterward] ever *deleted in 1868*

p. 197, l. 29 consideration of] of *altered to* for *in 1868*

p. 197, l. 38 an] *Added in 1850*

p. 198, l. 31 liquid] *Altered to* limpid *in 1868*

p. 204, l. 9 a drowsy ladies' cabin] a *deleted in 1850*

p. 204, l. 10 further] *Altered to* farther *in 1850*

p. 208, l. 2 (here)] *Added in 1850*

p. 214, l. 18 with this pocket instrument] this *altered to* his *in 1850*

p. 219, l. 27 in the present year] present *altered to* next *in 1850*

p. 224, l. 34 to the old country, sir?',] sir *deleted in 1868*

p. 227, l. 28 and] *Added in 1868*

p. 227, l. 33 a wheel] a *altered to* the *in 1850*

p. 232, l. 33 stay to dine] to *altered to* and *in 1868*

p. 239, l. 28 the meaner sort of] *Added in 1850*

p. 244, l. 3 adown] *Altered to* down *in 1850*

p. 245, l. 30 of lenient treatment] of *deleted in 1868*

p. 254, l. 11 read with me] with me *deleted in 1850*

p. 260, l. 21 the] *Added in 1868*

p. 262, l. 2 had lain] lain *altered to* been *in 1850*

p. 264, l. 13 ; that they do] *Deleted in 1850*

p. 264, l. 20 be cast upward] *First and second editions read* he *for* be

p. 266, l. 18 a choice] a *deleted in 1850*

p. 268, l. 39 pretty soon] soon *altered to* early *in 1850*

p. 269, l. 12 and winding up] and *altered to* with the *in 1868*

p. 269, l. 15 had] *Added in 1868*

p. 271, l. 22 denied them] them *altered to* the slaves *in 1850*

p. 277, l. 22 all] *Altered to* ALL *in 1850*
p. 280, l. 7   to] *Added in 1868*
p. 284, l. 14 that stately race] stately *deleted in 1868*
p. 284, l. 14 their broad possessions] broad *deleted in 1868*
p. 284, l. 27 doth hew and hack] *Altered to* hews and hacks *in 1850*
p. 288, l. 3   the mortal poison] mortal *altered to* moral *in 1868*

Note: All changes made in *1850* were carried over into *1868*.

The manuscript of *American Notes for General Circulation* is in the Forster Collection of the Victoria and Albert Museum Library, London (F. MS. 156, vols. A and B).

READ MORE IN PENGUIN

In every corner of the world, on every subject under the sun, Penguin represents quality and variety – the very best in publishing today.

For complete information about books available from Penguin – including Puffins, Penguin Classics and Arkana – and how to order them, write to us at the appropriate address below. Please note that for copyright reasons the selection of books varies from country to country.

In the United Kingdom: Please write to *Dept. JC, Penguin Books Ltd, FREEPOST, West Drayton, Middlesex UB7 0BR.*

If you have any difficulty in obtaining a title, please send your order with the correct money, plus ten per cent for postage and packaging, to *PO Box No. 11, West Drayton, Middlesex UB7 0BR*

In the United States: Please write to *Consumer Sales, Penguin USA, P.O. Box 999, Dept. 17109, Bergenfield, New Jersey 07621-0120.* VISA and MasterCard holders call 1-800-253-6476 to order all Penguin titles

In Canada: Please write to *Penguin Books Canada Ltd, 10 Alcorn Avenue, Suite 300, Toronto, Ontario M4V 3B2*

In Australia: Please write to *Penguin Books Australia Ltd, P.O. Box 257, Ringwood, Victoria 3134*

In New Zealand: Please write to *Penguin Books (NZ) Ltd, Private Bag 102902, North Shore Mail Centre, Auckland 10*

In India: Please write to *Penguin Books India Pvt Ltd, 706 Eros Apartments, 56 Nehru Place, New Delhi 110 019*

In the Netherlands: Please write to *Penguin Books Netherlands bv, Postbus 3507, NL-1001 AH Amsterdam*

In Germany: Please write to *Penguin Books Deutschland GmbH, Metzlerstrasse 26, 60594 Frankfurt am Main*

In Spain: Please write to *Penguin Books S. A., Bravo Murillo 19, 1° B, 28015 Madrid*

In Italy: Please write to *Penguin Italia s.r.l., Via Felice Casati 20, I–20124 Milano*

In France: Please write to *Penguin France S. A., 17 rue Lejeune, F–31000 Toulouse*

In Japan: Please write to *Penguin Books Japan, Ishikiribashi Building, 2–5–4, Suido, Bunkyo-ku, Tokyo 112*

In Greece: Please write to *Penguin Hellas Ltd, Dimocritou 3, GR–106 71 Athens*

In South Africa: Please write to *Longman Penguin Southern Africa (Pty) Ltd, Private Bag X08, Bertsham 2013*

READ MORE IN PENGUIN

A CHOICE OF CLASSICS

Matthew Arnold	**Selected Prose**
Jane Austen	**Emma**
	Lady Susan/ The Watsons/ Sanditon
	Mansfield Park
	Northanger Abbey
	Persuasion
	Pride and Prejudice
	Sense and Sensibility
Anne Brontë	**Agnes Grey**
	The Tenant of Wildfell Hall
Charlotte Brontë	**Jane Eyre**
	Shirley
	Villette
Emily Brontë	**Wuthering Heights**
Samuel Butler	**Erewhon**
	The Way of All Flesh
Thomas Carlyle	**Selected Writings**
Arthur Hugh Clough	**Selected Poems**
Wilkie Collins	**The Moonstone**
	The Woman in White
Charles Darwin	**The Origin of Species**
	The Voyage of the Beagle
Benjamin Disraeli	**Sybil**
George Eliot	**Adam Bede**
	Daniel Deronda
	Felix Holt
	Middlemarch
	The Mill on the Floss
	Romola
	Scenes of Clerical Life
	Silas Marner
Elizabeth Gaskell	**Cranford** and **Cousin Phillis**
	The Life of Charlotte Brontë
	Mary Barton
	North and South
	Wives and Daughters

READ MORE IN PENGUIN

A CHOICE OF CLASSICS

Charles Dickens	**American Notes for General Circulation**
	Barnaby Rudge
	Bleak House
	The Christmas Books (in two volumes)
	David Copperfield
	Dombey and Son
	Great Expectations
	Hard Times
	Little Dorrit
	Martin Chuzzlewit
	The Mystery of Edwin Drood
	Nicholas Nickleby
	The Old Curiosity Shop
	Oliver Twist
	Our Mutual Friend
	The Pickwick Papers
	Selected Short Fiction
	A Tale of Two Cities
Edward Gibbon	**The Decline and Fall of the Roman Empire**
George Gissing	**New Grub Street**
William Godwin	**Caleb Williams**
Thomas Hardy	**The Distracted Preacher and Other Tales**
	Far from the Madding Crowd
	Jude the Obscure
	The Mayor of Casterbridge
	A Pair of Blue Eyes
	The Return of the Native
	Tess of the d'Urbervilles
	The Trumpet-Major
	Under the Greenwood Tree
	The Woodlanders

READ MORE IN PENGUIN

A CHOICE OF CLASSICS

READ MORE IN PENGUIN

CHARLES DICKENS

'A popular and fecund, but yet profound, serious and wonderfully resourceful practising novelist, a master of it' – Q. D. Leavis

'He was successful beyond any English novelist, probably beyond any novelist that has ever lived, in exactly hitting off the precise tone of thought and feeling' – Leslie Stephen

'All the political futility which has forced men of the calibre of Mussolini, Kemal and Hitler to assume dictatorship might have been saved if people had only believed what Dickens told them in *Little Dorrit*' – Bernard Shaw

'Heaven for the just: for the wicked, Hell. Herein Dickens is true to the opinion of his countrymen and of his time' – André Gide

'Language and morality add dimensions to his cartoons and turn them into literature' – Anthony Burgess

Barnaby Rudge
The Christmas Books
Dombey and Son
Hard Times
Martin Chuzzlewit
Nicholas Nickleby
Oliver Twist
The Pickwick Papers
American Notes for General
  Circulation

Bleak House
David Copperfield
Great Expectations
Little Dorrit
The Mystery of Edwin
  Drood
The Old Curiosity Shop
Out Mutual Friend
A Tale of Two Cities
Selected Short Fiction